SEX ED

KRISTEN BAILEY

Storm

To request permissions, contact the publisher at rights@stormpublishing.co

Ebook ISBN: 978-1-80508-015-2
Paperback ISBN: 978-1-80508-016-9

Cover design: Emma Rogers
Cover images: Shutterstock

Published by Storm Publishing.
For further information, visit:
www.stormpublishing.co

ALSO BY KRISTEN BAILEY

This book is for all the men who came before Nick.
Quite literally.
Including one called Ed.

PROLOGUE

8th April 2011, MIA

I think it might be happening today. Laura said it would happen, but I don't trust Laura because she's a massive fan of Justin Bieber (she has a Justin Bieber duvet set) and there was one time she told everyone at school that his tour bus broke down outside her house and he stopped at hers to use the downstairs toilet. Anyway, she sits next to Toby in English, and she reckons when he opened his bag to take out his copy of *Pride & Prejudice*, she saw that he had a pack of ribbed Durex in there which can only mean one thing.

I'm going to have sex today after school.

It's no big deal. It's Toby. I've been Toby's official girlfriend for a year, ever since we got together at that party in the community centre, the one where we all smuggled in alcohol in water bottles and someone's mum threw a fit and wrote a really angry Facebook post. It's just sex. With Toby. I know Toby. I think I love Toby. I've let him touch my boobs.

Anyway, he might not even want sex *today*. Maybe he bought the condoms as a joke. And it will also depend if he's on the bus. I climb the stairs to the top level of our double decker and scan the heads. I cross my fingers. Crap, he's here. Be cool.

'You alright?' Toby says, turning to look at me. He looks different. Has he had a haircut? He's definitely wearing product. I didn't wash my hair today. I wish I had now.

'You alright?' I reply, nodding, trying to act chill by tossing my rucksack on the double seat opposite him. Across the way, an older lady watches me, and I can see she's judging the length of my skirt and the thickness of my foundation. She can swivel.

Toby shifts uncomfortably in his seat then looks at me. Is he going to ask me on the bus? *Hey, let's have sex this afternoon?* If he does, that judgy old lady will die. 'My mum and dad are both on shift, working till late, if you want to come round?' he asks, casually.

Shit. 'Yeah...' I say.

'We can watch a film or something,' he suggests. The two boys behind him giggle, elbowing each other. One of them is Leon Mount who once caught his hair alight on a Bunsen burner. I don't appreciate being the butt of their jokes, so I scowl at them. All I feel is panic. Am I wearing the right pants? Is this how I want to lose my virginity? Since that first kiss at the party, we've hung out in our bedrooms, kissing and touching each other, but we've never gone the whole way. Mainly because our mums were always downstairs cooking the dinner. I've felt his penis. He's learnt how to squeeze my boobs, because at first he'd just place his hands on them like a human hand bra. I think I love him though. I do love him. I've signed my name with his and I've picked the canapés at our wedding (crispy prawns). I've thought about how our kids would have his swishy hair and my blue eyes. He bought me that giant bear on Valentine's Day and I had to drag it around all day. We named him Bob. He's kind and funny and he holds my hand in public and buys me bottles of Cherry Coke. I should just do it with him and get it out of the way, right? It's just my virginity. I can think of worse people to lose it to. It's no big deal.

'We can stop at the Tesco Metro and get some snacks and that...' I mention. Yeah, we can just eat Skittles and have some sex, you know?

'Oh no, I've got stuff in. It's cool,' he says, like he's prepared a meal to go with the sex.

I am hungry though. Can you have sex on an empty stomach? I only had a doughnut for lunch because the queue at the canteen was so long. And just like that, a million sex questions go through my head. What if I get my period? Can you get pregnant from your first time? Will it hurt?

Toby presses the bell and the bus lurches to a standstill at his stop. It's time to get off. Those boys are still sniggering, so I stick my middle finger up at them. You can do this, Mia.

I have an overwhelming need to call my sister. She's at university and she's definitely had sex because she came back that first Christmas and told us about this boy who had a piercing through his pickle, and she screamed when she saw it. I shouldn't call it a pickle, should I? Is that just a my-family thing? Pickles and noo-noos, right?

'You had a good day?' Toby asks me as we stroll past the parade of shops at the top of his road.

'I had Geography,' I say, pulling a face and sighing.

'Hate Geography,' he replies.

Then we're silent. It's not normally like this. We normally chat shit about people at school and all the beef we've witnessed that day. We share headphones, listen to Frank Ocean, dance down the street and throw sweets at each other. But today is different. He can't even hold my hand. We know what's going to happen. We get to his house and he finds his keys and puts them in the door.

'MUM! ARE YOU IN?' he bellows through the house as we go in, double checking to see if she's about. There's an eerie silence. All I can hear is the low hum of his fridge, the creak of his blue front door.

'Are we going to have sex?' I blurt out in the hallway.

He looks absolutely petrified. 'I don't know. I knew we were going to have the house to ourselves, so I thought... We don't have to do it if you don't want to. If you're not ready...'

I'm sixteen. I don't think I'll ever be ready. But then what happens? You can't just stay a virgin for a lifetime because you're scared, because you have questions, because you don't know when's the right time. I stand there for what feels like forever, watching him wait to hear what I'll decide, grateful he's giving me the option to back out.

'Laura said you bought a pack of ribbed condoms...'

'I did. Just because if it did happen then I wanted to be prepared. That's all.'

'What's the difference between ribbed and normal?' I ask him, my only frame of reference being tights and vests when it comes to ribbed.

'I dunno. They were on offer.'

'OK. Just when we're done, make sure you don't flush it down the toilet because they float back up. That happened to Olly Horne and his mum went ballistic.'

'But I can't put it in the bin. What if my mum sees?'

'Your mum goes through the rubbish? I guess we can put it in the outside bin?'

'Could you take it with you and dump it in the bin by the bus stop?'

I nod. I like that we have a plan. I hope he gives me something to put the condom in though because I don't just want to put it in my pocket – that's gross.

'How many condoms do you think we'll need?' he asks me.

'How many penises do you have?' I try and joke.

I laugh. I'm not sure why. I hope it's not more than one. But he smiles in reply, and I immediately see his panic melt away.

That's the Toby I know. I take him by the hand and lead him up
to his room and the top of the stairs.

When we get in his room, he kicks away Reeboks and piles
of clothes dotted around the room, and I stand there and look at
his A3 poster of Lewis Hamilton. Lewis is going to watch me
have sex for the first time. As soon as Toby finishes tidying, he
stands in front of me. He starts to take off his tie. I start with my
shoes and tights. He gets caught in his jumper and I help him
remove it. I've never taken my clothes off more slowly. Do I fold
my clothes? When I take off my bra, I think I hear him gulp.
Boobs. I have my boobs out. Maybe I should have left my bra on
for him to take off? Once he's down to his pants, he pulls the
duvet back from his bed and we both scurry over to it as quickly
as possible, taking cover.

'Are we doing this then?' I ask him. I realise this is not
particularly sexy talk. I reach over to kiss him until I feel his
penis prodding my thigh. He arches his hips into the air and
takes off his underwear. I feel I should see his penis before I let
it in me, so I peek under the covers. Hello. Nice to meet you.
You're a real-life willy. Toby reaches into his school bag beside
the bed and tears open the pack of condoms. He rips at the foil
wrapper and then fumbles under the duvet, trying to put it on
himself without looking. I think he should maybe have eyes on
the situation, paranoid he may be doing it wrong, but I don't tell
him that. I watch as his face goes more and more pink trying to
put it on. Then he just lies there. Oh. He's ready.

I peel my knickers down and use my heel to kick them off
the end of the bed. Let's do this then.

'I love you, Mia,' he tells me before adjusting his body over
mine, his penis brushing against my thigh. I should say it back,
but I can't. I close my eyes and take a deep breath.

'Could you just hold my peeny for a minute? Before we...'

I stop. His what now?

'Oh yeah...' I say, reaching down to hold it, almost like I

need to firmly shake its hand before this agreement is made. I see Toby's expression change, a sound like he's straining, his eyes bulging, the sound of the condom rustling as I move my hand up and down.

'My peeny loves that...' he mumbles.

Oh god, he said the word again. I think that's worse than pickle. I try and pull him close to me, biting my lip. Don't laugh, Mia. This isn't funny. This is sex. It's serious.

'Can I...?' But before he has a chance to say peeny again, I lead him towards my vagina. Is that it? No. I think that's my leg. Hold up.

Oh.

I think that's sex. That's new. He pushes his body up to look me in the eye. Please don't say peeny again, I beg you.

'How does that feel in your va-gee-na?' he asks me.

'Toby...'

I can't correct him, can I? It's vagina, Toby. I can't tell if he's being funny or deathly serious. How does he not know this? We've got our biology exam in three months. We've got a girl called Gina in our French class. But it's not the time to say anything, is it? Not when he's in me. He's in me. In my noo-noo. I'm not a virgin anymore. He moves his hips over me, looking nervous, worried. I don't want him to feel like that. I grab his cheeks and kiss him on the lips.

'It feels... cool...' I reply. 'I love you, too...'

I pull him into a hug before he can spoil this with more words and try to focus on the feeling of him inside me as he starts to move. We're actually doing it. I think I like this. But before I can even tell him that much, Toby thrusts a few more times and his body stiffens and shudders, a grunting noise like he's finished running a race. Whoa. Is that it? He collapses on me and rests his head near my collarbone.

I'm not sure what to say but I look up, right into the big

gleaming face of Lewis Hamilton. You saw all of that, didn't you? Don't tell anyone, OK?

21st June 2015, ED

Hi, Sarah. Why don't you come in and take off your coat and make yourself comfortable? Would you like a beverage? A beverage? Who calls it a beverage? I'm not a vending machine. Sarah's just texted to say she's on her way and now I'm sweating. It's not very attractive at all. Why am I sweating so much? Is this normal? Maybe something is wrong with one of my glands. Could this be related to my penis? Can penises sweat?

I take off my shirt and stand by the pedestal fan in my university bedroom to air out my armpits. If I just roll deodorant all over me then I can't fail in this endeavour. How much deodorant will I need though? That's a lot of chemicals. Why do these rooms get so hot? I know it's the summer, but the ventilation is awful. That's the problem when you're trying to pack as many university students in a building as possible. Sarah has been in here to study before, but I wonder if I needed to do anything more to make this place look nice. Maybe a houseplant? A poster? Should I play some music? I catch a look at myself in my mirror wearing the underwear that I bought especially for the occasion. It almost looks too new, too box fresh. I should have worn it a few times or ironed the folds out of it. I'd have thought the heat radiating off my body would have got the creases out. I need to put on clothes. I pull out a T-shirt from my cupboard with a giant panda on it, a gift from a Chinese exchange student. I try it on. Pandas are not sexy. I can't just answer the door in my pants. Maybe just shorts and a T-shirt. Collar or no collar? A collar gives the occasion a sense of formality which is fitting if I'm losing my virginity.

Fuck. I'm losing my virginity.

Sarah's on my course and for the last few months we've been lab partners and have struck up a lovely rapport. We both like biology, we understand the importance of precision and safety goggles. We seem to have similar experiences of university life: we drink in moderation, we eat a shedload of pasta and favour film clubs and societies over nightclubs and recreational drugs. Sarah is not a virgin. She had a boyfriend at college. Did I tell her I was a virgin when we started dating? Of course I bloody didn't. I'm twenty. It's weird and she'd have run away from me, so I pretended I had an ex called Monica. This was a half lie. Monica does exist. She was in the same sixth form college as me and stuck her tongue down my throat at our end-of-year dance. It was like being attacked by an eel. We did not take the moment further because she was so drunk that after accosting me, she tried to jump off the bars in the school gym and broke her collarbone. Dating Sarah has been a dreamy haze of shared lunches, kissing and waving at her from across the library but now it's time to take this relationship to the next level. It's time to have the sex. Or just sex. We know what's going to happen. This is why I put fresh sheets on and have chilled some bottles of Becks in my room sink. I'm keeping it classy.

There's a light knock on my door. Oh dear, I might be ill. I rest my head against the wall. You can do this, Ed Rogers.

'Hey...'

'Hello, stranger,' she says. 'It's bloody hot, isn't it?' She fans herself. She's wearing a lilac sundress with trainers and kisses me on the cheek. She smells good. Should I tell her she smells good? She's not bread.

'Boiling,' I reply. 'Please enter.' I give a swish of my arm.

Enter? I am lucky she finds this funny. I close the door but as my hand comes off the handle, she backs me against it and kisses me passionately. Oh. This is quick. It looks like we're not having drinks. It's fine. We can just go straight into it. The kissing is nice, it's always been nice, but there's an urgency now in how hard she presses against me, how close her body is to mine.

'I'm not wearing any knickers...' she whispers into my ear.

'Yay...' I reply. I might cry. I don't know what to do. Does she want me to check for the knickers just in case I thought she was lying?

She smiles. I'm glad she still finds me mildly amusing. This is a Sarah I've not seen before. As awful as it sounds, she reminds me of my mum's cat when she's on heat.

'I've been waiting for this... You're such a tease...'

Not really, Sarah. I just kept putting it off because I was petrified and have thus spent the last month watching so much porn I almost went cross-eyed trying to give myself some sort of crash course in sex education. I'm not sure it helped.

'I can't wait to...' I whisper. Have you? Fuck you? Make the sex with you?

She takes off my shirt and runs her hands all over my chest. 'Look at what you've been hiding from me.' She then proceeds to lick me. I don't know if I like this but I think I should, so I make noises that suggest I do.

Then, in one movement, she pulls down my shorts and underwear and I'm standing there essentially naked, the sense of vulnerability slightly overwhelming as she still has her shoes and dress on. But no knickers. I am naked in front of an attractive woman. This could go one of two ways. I brace myself for laughter or Sarah making a swift exit, but instead she takes my penis in her hand, a little aggressively, truth be told. She doesn't stimulate it, just grabs and squeezes it. She then looks me up and down and backs on to my bed, sitting down and parting her legs slightly. It's an extremely sexy move bar the fact I can't see what I'm working with down there, the view obscured by her dress.

What do I do? I go over, right? This is easy. Get erect, stride over, kiss her, push that dress up, maybe take it off, see if she's wearing a bra, look at her boobs and then have sex. Easy, Ed.

I grab my penis in my hand and try to summon up an erection. That worked. It should work because it's been aching to do this for a while, but how do I stride over now? Just walk casually like it's not there? I kick off my pants and shorts from around my ankles, then walk awkwardly towards her. Possibly like a cowboy.

'Have you got a condom?' she asks sweetly.

I chuckle. Do I have condoms? I have a box of thirty-two. I am dependable like that. I open the drawer of my desk and hold one up in the air. I tear at the wrapper and place the condom over my erect penis. I may have practised doing this with a cucumber in preparation. Oh my. It's going to happen. I am prepared. There is a willing, pretty girl on my bed without any knickers.

'Could you just move the fan, Ed? It's a bit strong,' she tells me.

'Oh god, sure.' I walk over to it. 'Maybe if I put it on oscillate? Or tilt the fan head?' Don't talk about your fan to her. That is not sexy. I turn the speed down to a solid three and set it to oscillate. This will create a nice mood and improve air circulation through the room. I won't sweat to death. I feel the breeze pass through my nether regions. That is very pleasant. You can do this, Ed. I close my eyes and move to turn around.

Except I don't.

I'm not sure how it happens but the tip of the condom gets caught in the wiring netting of the fan. It's pulled instantly off my penis and sucked through the wire so that it is spinning on the fan blades. What is happening? What circulates now is air but also the slight whiff of lubricant and rubber through the room. In a panic, I try to turn the fan off but increase the speed instead. No. Shut down. Off. Off. I get too close and vibrations of the metal in the fan skim my still erect penis. I shriek and try to turn it into a manly howl of pain, while falling back, trying to work out if my penis is still on me, whether I need medical help, whether I can save this.

'Oh my... Shit... Ed...What have you done? And what is...' But before Sarah can finish her sentence, the condom which was spinning around catapults off the fan blade and through the wire like some kind of rubber projectile and smacks Sarah on the face. She screams and puts her hand to her cheek. The blood drains from my face, every part of me, in fact, and I stand there, paralysed, watching in horror as she glares at me.

This is not how sex should happen, is it? I'm on the brink of finding my voice to say I'm sorry but the door to my room creaks open and three people peer inside, slowly. I cover my penis with my hands.

'Oh my god, are you OK?' one of them shouts, seeing Sarah lying there, holding her face.

The door. We didn't lock the door. I recognise one of the boys who lives opposite me. He's a biochemist. He uses my mugs. I wave at him, keeping the other hand firmly in situ.

'The johnny hit me...' Sarah squeaks.

'Are you Johnny?' One of them turns to me angrily. I am naked, so naked. I step behind the fan for cover, even though it is, in essence, see-through.

'God, no.... I'm Ed. There was an accident. The condom, my knob, her eye... I'm so sorry, Sarah...'

I find I'm waving my hands around in the air trying to explain, as their faces turn from incredulity to laughter. And as the fan head pivots away, I reveal myself to the room. Not just myself. My very lonely penis, just dangling there, alone.

I look down. I'm sorry. I don't think it's happening today.

ONE

PRESENT DAY

MIA

'I love you. Do you know how much I love you? You're my favouritest.'

I go over and plant a massive smacker on Ed's forehead because I know the physical proximity will make him blush and I love nothing more than making Ed Rogers the centre of attention and firing up his cute rosy cheeks. He looks around this big, open-plan staffroom hoping no one saw that. They all did, Ed.

'Yes, yes, yes... Stop that now. It's because I was getting sick of you stealing my crisps and cereal bars. That's not lunch, Mia. That's not good for you.'

I steal Ed's crisps and his cereal bars because he doesn't scrimp on these things. I'd steal Henry from Geography's lunch, but he buys all the budget lines of snack goods and strange things like fruit. Beth, on the sofa opposite, only deals in suspect leftovers.

'But you made me a sandwich, that's adorable!' I exclaim.

'Don't get too excited. It's cheese.'

'It's veggie, too? Why are there bits in the mayo?' I ask, examining the contents.

'It is veggie because I've known you for five years so know better than to give you meat. I run a bit of pesto through the mayo. I didn't know if you like salad, but I also reckoned you needed the vitamins.'

'I do,' I say, pouting. I go and sit next to him and rest my head on his shoulder. 'I don't deserve you, Eddie.'

'This is true,' he says, as I unwrap the package carefully, and then take advantage of the proximity and slip my hand into his packet of crisps.

He laughs and shakes his head. 'Share,' he commands.

'Always,' I say, taking a bite out of my sandwich. 'The pesto works. Well done, you.'

He shrugs his shoulders and tucks into his own. He's a careful eater, Eddie. He never relaxes in this staffroom, just sits knees together, back poker straight. I watch him as he takes a finger and dots it around his trousers, picking up all the crumbs. I don't know anyone who does that. I am a stand up and dust it all off on the floor kind of gal. Is Ed hot? To someone out there. Like me, he's twenty-eight, but maybe five years older than me in maturity. I know this because he talks a lot at me about mort-gages and flossing. He's cute and well-built in a preppy, safe, sitcom kinda way – bright hazel eyes, clean shaven and his brown short-back-and-sides styled in a way that I fear hasn't changed since his teens. Maybe I just prefer my men to be a little more HBO-18+ rating-special.

We started at this school in the same year, fresh out of teacher training, clinging to each other for safety. Our orienta-tions were the same day. I had to borrow a pen. He had many pens. His look has not changed since then: freshly ironed chinos, light blue shirt, an outdoor jacket with proper down ratings. He's so careful in life that he doesn't even wear a rucksack on one shoulder, always two. Does he remind me of anyone? He reminds me of someone's dad, in waiting.

'Thank you, by the way, for coming in during period three and sorting out my Year 9s,' he whispers.

Such is the nature of our working relationship that whilst he always lets me borrow his pens, he leans on me to sort out the parts of his job that he struggles with. He's an organised, methodical teacher who knows how to work the photocopier. I still have no clue about the photocopier, but if you have that class who are loud and unruly and who should know better, then you know that I'm your girl to come in, scream and dole out empty threats about detentions.

'Did they simmer down?' I ask.

'Sort of?' He shrugs, not seeming sure of himself.

'Did you reverse psychology them like I told you?' I ask him.

'They see right through that. I'm not a good liar. My right eye twitches and I can't get the words out. I look like I'm having a stroke when I'm trying to be authoritative.'

I don't disagree with him. For his faults, he's a gentle soul and you can't force people like that into personalities that they're not. I take another crisp. He eyeballs me to tell me I've had enough of his snacks. I turn to Beth, sitting opposite us, who's on her phone looking like she's scrolling through Instagram.

'Beth, what do you do with the rowdy ones? I've seen you, you're like a snake charmer with the kids.'

We like Beth. Like me, she's one of a gaggle of sisters, so we hard relate to each other in many ways. She's been teaching in my department for a lifetime but she's one of the cool teachers who rejects promotion beyond the department because she doesn't want the added responsibility. Outside of work, she has kids, she goes to music festivals, she gets that nice level of drunk at the Christmas party where she's a laugh. I also admire how sometimes her lunch is a sharing pack of Doritos and a whole tub of guacamole.

She looks up. 'Talk to them like they're humans, set the tone. Is it all of them, or just one or two rocking the boat?'

'Charlie Coxhead,' Ed tells her.

Beth pulls a face. 'Attention-seeker, I taught his sister. They weren't hugged enough as kids. Basically, find the ones who follow him like disciples. Praise them, overmark their work and lure them away so they like you more. Then he has no audience for his bullshit.'

We both stare at Beth in complete awe.

'Sometimes those kids can't be saved, though. They're too far gone, just get them over the line. Now, can you tell me if I look a complete state? I slept face down on Lego last night as my youngest is teething, and I'm about to walk into a meeting.'

'You look fine,' Ed tells her, his eye twitching to let us know he thinks differently.

'You are shit at lying, Ed,' she says, laughing. 'If you're making sandwiches for everyone, I like ham,' she says, laughing and grabbing her belongings. 'Stay cool, kids – wish me luck.'

You can see Ed's brain working overtime; he'll have to buy more pesto. As Beth leaves the staffroom, she holds the door open for the P.E. lads. My nostrils flare instantly, and Ed recognises this look so offers me another of his sacred crisps. The P.E. department have their own staffroom, which admittedly is a shoe cupboard that smells like crotch, but they like to come here of a lunchtime and just linger, and when I say linger, they perch on desks, manspread and ask the foreign languages department what they did at the weekend. Tommy is the main culprit for this. I've never known a man to adjust his balls as many times as Tommy does when he's talking to the very blonde, very petite and very married Sylvie who teaches French. If I sound judgemental, it's also my bitterness shining through, as I possibly fell for all his P.E. teacher charms last parents' evening, and we had a quickie in the shoe cupboard office that smells like crotch.

Tommy waves at me from across the room when he clocks me and even though I love this sandwich that I'm holding, it takes all my will not to throw it at him. He never called me after we slept together. He did the teenage boy thing of ghosting me by text and then avoiding me in the corridors. The worst thing is that he's very good looking, very charming. He hangs around with the similarly handsome Steve and they charm all the older female teachers who feed them biscuits and puff their hair out when they're in the room.

'If looks could kill...' says Ed, grinning.

'My eyes would laser off his penis.'

'Ouch. That would be a sight. Would it fall to the floor, or would it evaporate into thin air? The latter would be less messy, I guess, and it would cauterise the veins, so essentially help with any corrective surgery.'

'Spoken like a true biology teacher.' I cackle and it captures Tommy and Steve's attention for one second. Yes, I'm talking about you and the ways I would remove your penises. I move closer to Ed and try to look interested in him to see if I can evoke some sort of reaction from Tommy. The only reaction it invokes is from Ed. He raises an eyebrow and shuffles away from me along the sofa.

'That'll work. Don't drag me into your drama and use me like a pawn. I have feelings,' he says, sarcastically.

'But you love me. You made me a sandwich.'

'Because I worry about your health, Mia Johnson. You're mostly made out of biscuits and carbonated drinks. You are better than him in many, many ways.'

I nudge him cheekily with my elbow. 'Ta, Eddie. I still can't believe how relentlessly he pursues Sylvie. She literally got married last summer. Have you seen her husband? He looks like Henry Cavill. I like how Tommy thinks he's even comparable.

Do you know who Henry Cavill is?' I ask him, knowing he doesn't always get my pop culture references.

Ed looks offended. 'He's *Superman* and *The Witcher*. I'm a geek, Mia. I know some things. Word is that they have bets about how many they can bed within these walls,' Ed says, nonchalantly tearing at a piece of flapjack.

'Hold up there, sparky. You're telling me I was part of a bet?'

Again, Ed's eye starts to twitch. 'Possibly. I don't know. I'm not party to their games. He's a knobhead. He calls me Steady Eddie,' he says, looking hurt.

'Because of your steady hand?'

'Because I had to car share with him once at a conference and he mocked my driving.'

'Because you respect the law of the road.'

'I can't tell if you're taking the mick out of me now. You've been in my car many times; I don't feel the need to use my driving skills as an indicator of my machismo.'

'Which is why I love you.'

'Now you're taking the piss. Eat your sandwich.'

'Umm... hello? Hello.' Our conversation is interrupted by a shrill voice from the middle of the room and a slow clap which can only mean it's our headteacher, Alicia. She likes the slow clap to control a room like we're all eight years old in a singalong music session. Everyone comes to a standstill, people put down their mugs and devices, a bird stops chirping outside, even the kettle stops boiling. Only Henry, newest recruit to the Geography department, who still doesn't know what it means, starts clapping, trying to join in.

'So, some of you will have heard that Monica in Maths fell down the A-Block stairs the other day. She wants to thank you for all the cards and hampers and the person who sent her the soaps. Anyway, we are very lucky that as a temporary replacement, St Quentin's have sent us Caitlin Bell to help. I am sure you will all make her feel very welcome.'

I visually sift through the crowd of people by the door until Caitlin comes into view. Please be nice, please be normal, please be a pub-at-lunchtime kind of girl. Well, she looks like she's about our age, light brown hair, pinafore dress, Alice band. Very straight down the line, which is fitting given she teaches Maths. She will not like my swearing, will she? Is it strange that when I meet other women for the first time, I always check out the footwear? Are we the same size? May I potentially be able to borrow shoes from her? I peer at her feet. Patent leather moccasins. Maybe not. She clutches a satchel and lunchbox close to her as the Maths department regulars come over to introduce themselves. Naturally, my eyes fall to Tommy and Steve, already talking in whispers. Fresh meat. Bastards.

'You can already tell they're plotting. It's so unbelievably predictable. Poor girl. Maybe we should go over and warn her,' I mumble, finishing the last of my sandwich and looking over at Ed. 'Eddie? You alright?'

But his eyes are fixed in one direction. It's a perfect time to steal a couple more crisps.

ED

I made Mia a sandwich because a month ago she got stomach flu after eating a bad kebab and she's not looked right since. She looks gaunt and in certain lights, when her eyes shine a certain blue and her messy brown bob falls right, she can look a bit vampiric. Her self-care regimen is the worst I know. She washes her face with shampoo, sleeps on a mattress she found on the street (I know, I helped her carry it and made her steam clean it first), she'll call me at eleven at night when I'm listening to my happy sleep podcast and she's frantically marking, fuelled by energy drinks and bad pizza. She tells me all pizza is good pizza but I'm not sure that's the case if you have to smell it three times before you put it in your mouth to check it's still good.

Mia and I bonded in this place because even though she's one of the cool kids, she's a nice cool kid who took me under her wing and has never dropped me. She has a wonderful sense of inclusivity, knowing how to make everyone laugh and feel part of the conversation. Do I wish she'd order her life, make better choices and not steal all my pens? Yes. Is she one of my best friends? Also, yes. But don't tell her that. She'll call me sad and do something weird like kiss me and announce that she loves me to a whole busload of people who don't need to know that information.

She also has the worst taste in men. If I take my Psychology A-Level and analyse why, it's because beneath the loud and confident exterior is a girl who just wants to be loved and validated. You see it in how she dates. She finds a man on Tinder, she has and enjoys sex with him, and she revels in telling me about the sex (in far too much detail). But then she'll get drunk after school on Fridays, I'll walk her home from the pub, and she will cry over her cheesy chips and philosophise about why this sex she's having never blossoms into relationships, how maybe she'll be alone forever. I tell her she'll always have me, but she usually laughs in response to that.

It was obvious she was going to shag Tommy from P.E. because he's that sort of man. He has what the young people call rizz. I don't know if he walks like that because his appendage is bigger than average or because of the amount of sex he is having. I hear the stories because I used to go along to the 'lads' sessions in the pub where the men mainly talk about football and women. Neither are my strong suit, but I can tell you now that I've learnt a lot about Pep Guardiola's management style, and to stay away from Sandy the lab technician who apparently is quite the wild one in bed and had a short-lived affair with Andrew from Business Studies who had to have a tetanus shot because she bit him. But the last time I went, they talked about Mia like she was some sort of currency and that upset me, so I stopped going. I've never repeated to Mia what they said because she's my friend but also because I fear what she would do in response. English teachers come with a certain level of passion. It's all that literature; it gives her a way with words which often involves inventive swearing and talking about the painful ways in which she'd end people.

'Eddie! Earth to Ed? What's up?' Mia asks me again.

'I'm good,' I tell Mia as she steals a few more of my crisps, like I'm not physically there. I mean, I am but a woman has just entered the room. Caitlin. Teaches Maths. Crikey. She's pretty. She looks like a young Cate Blanchett. That is some awesome bone structure. I watch as she stands behind Alicia, scanning the room with those piercing green eyes. I take a long deep breath.

'Oh me, oh my, Eddie, are you crushing on the new girl?' Mia asks me, cheekily observing my gaze.

'No. Stop that...'

'You're blushing...'

'My face is red from anger at you stealing my food,' I tell her. It's warm in here. Too warm. I thought we were supposed to be cutting costs in this school; they should turn down the heating. I put a finger underneath my collar, watching her with one eye as she moves around the staffroom meeting people. Not that meeting me will mean anything once she sees the P.E. guys, but maybe we could have a chat and I could introduce myself. *Hi, I'm Ed. I teach Biology and I have a cat.* She looks like she'd be an ally, someone with pens.

'Do you know her?' Mia asks, still intrigued. 'She's not an ex-girlfriend, is she?'

'No... never seen her before,' I reply, trying to act relaxed.

Mia smiles back at me. 'Oh, she has a lunchbox.'

'She looks like the sort of person who understands the need for good nutrition.'

'You're so funny... You're staring at her.'

'I am not...' Is it obvious? If she's going to sit at Monica's desk, then that's perpendicular to mine. That would be nice. Not in a strange stalker, 'I'm-going-to-stare-at-you-a-lot' kind of way, but I'm currently next to Lyle from History who loves mackerel for lunch and Heidi from Art who makes things with her own hair.

'Ed, Mia...' our head's voice booms over us. We stand to attention. 'This is Caitlin.'

'Biology and English,' Mia intervenes. 'Nice to meet you. Welcome to the madhouse.'

Alicia's eyebrows are raised at this comment. She's not half wrong though. Caitlin laughs and something inside me sighs.

'Interesting choice of footwear, Miss Johnson,' Alicia says, scanning Mia's leopard print Converse. I keep telling Mia there is a dress code in our contracts, but she still comes into school daring to subvert the rules and upset the higher school management. If it's not the shoes, it's the many bracelets stacked up her forearm, the literary T-shirts with questionable quotes. I'm not Mia so my pulse quickens on her behalf to hear her being reproached.

'I'm sorry. I was in a rush. I keep forgetting about the rules.' She pauses, unfazed and I will her silently to stop there. But then she bites her lip, a cheeky glint in her eye and I know she's going to challenge the status quo. 'We do let the P.E. department wear trainers though?' And there it is.

'Because they teach P.E.,' she says plainly. 'It's hard enough getting these kids to part with their Air Forces.'

Mia nods, none of it going in though. All she owns is trainers. She has a wall of them in her flat piled like shoe Jenga. The conversation goes painfully quiet for a moment. This is where I need to say something and not sound like a complete and utter idiot.

'You teach Maths,' I say to Caitlin, failing miserably in my goal.

'I do,' she replies. 'For my sins. I like numbers.'

'So do I,' I say, smiling broadly, knowing I look too happy about this fact and need to play it cool. If I knew how to do that.

'Well, who doesn't like numbers? They essentially make the world go round.'

'That and gravity...' I add. God, I'm smooth with my science talk. So smooth. Mia knows this and puts an arm around me, almost in condolence.

'I also like your lunchbox,' I fumble.

Mia turns her head to me, her eyebrows raised, trying to stop herself from giggling through this bin fire of a first meet.

Caitlin smirks. 'Why, thank you. I'm hoping I get a minute to eat before my first lessons.'

'Anything nice in there?' Shoot me, someone. Just physically stop me.

'Umm... pesto chicken salad.'

'I love pesto!' I say, a little too enthusiastically. And loudly because I hear someone across the room laugh.

'Who doesn't? Don't mind him. He's obsessed with lunch,' Mia intervenes, trying to save me.

Caitlin scans us both. Oh dear, instant fail. 'Well, it's good to meet you both. The teacher over there... Tommy?'

I glance at Mia and see her clench her teeth at the very mention of his name.

'He's mentioned a welcome drink at The Otter's Pocket after school if you're free. Would be great to have you there,' she says, sweetly.

'Yeah, we can go. Right, Mia?' I say, perhaps a little too quickly, elbowing her.

'I don't turn down pub invitations so yes, we will be there,' Mia replies.

She moves on to the next people in the room as I stare into space, wondering how and when I became such a buffoon when it came to the opposite sex. Is it genetic? Is it a product of too many teen years spent in my bedroom and not engaging with the world? Is it just not in my nature?

'Did you just say you liked her box?' Mia whispers as she's out of earshot.

'I did. I also asked if there was anything nice in her box.'

'Classy, Eddie. Super classy.'

TWO

MIA

I dance everywhere I go. It's a bad habit but also something I attribute to the natural rhythm and joy that just flows through me. Ed doesn't agree. He thinks my dancing looks like I'm swatting away swarms of imaginary insects. Naturally, the kitchen sees the best of my moves but if we're in a pub and I've had just the right amount of alcohol in my system then we are set to launch. Plus, I bloody LOVE this song.

'Really?' Ed says, watching me do my moves as he stands there waiting for our drinks to be served, his card hovering, waiting to tap the card machine. He's so bloody efficient. I'm the sort who has to rummage through all four compartments of her handbag and both coat pockets to check it's about my person, and even then I'll try to pay with a library card.

'This song was all over TikTok... Come on, I'll teach you the moves,' I say, dragging his arm towards an open space.

'That would be a firm no,' he replies, arms crossed stubbornly.

'But it's The Weeknd.'

'No, technically it's still Friday.'

'No, the dude singing the song, that's his name.'

'That's not a name.'

'I actually despair of you.'

I break into a move and plant an elbow into a man next to me.

'Control your girlfriend, mate,' he mutters.

'Not my girlfriend,' Ed replies. 'Thank God...'

I narrow my eyes at him. Oh, you would be so lucky to have this rhythm in your life, Eduardo. I don't know why you fight it. I laugh and hug him and feel his body relent. It is my life's mission to break this man's barriers down.

'You never told me about that bloke you're seeing? That bloke you met on Plenty of Fish,' he asks me.

I like that I can talk about my dating antics with Ed. He listens and offers counsel, but I think even he'll admit my stories are a good source of entertainment too.

'Oh, that's not happening anymore,' I explain.

'Why not?' he asks, disappointed. 'You had sex with him, and you told me how much you enjoyed the event...'

I grin to hear him talk about it so politely. My actual words were that I orgasmed so hard, I yodelled.

'So, it turns out he was a bit of a dick...'

'Yeah, you mentioned that,' Ed says, smirking.

'No, the personality. We went on a date, and he showed up drunk, spent five hours telling me football anecdotes while getting more drunk, so I put him in an Uber which he threw up in. This meant I had to pay the fouling charge AND the bar bill.'

Ed looks supremely appalled. 'I'm sorry. That is grim. Did he at least try to repay you?'

'No.'

'And I guess no sex is worth that, right?'

'You are correct. I just don't know what's happening with men and me at the moment. There's always something; either the sex is good and they're dicks or they're nice but don't know what to do with their dicks. I think I'm just better off with my vibrator.' Ed flinches to hear me talk like this in public. He just about tolerates my ridiculous dancing but sometimes when I talk frankly and loudly about sex I see his body recoil with embarrassment, telling me how far we've travelled out of his comfort zone.

'Or just go on dates. Get to know people and build a relationship first,' he advises me like a grown-up adult.

'But if I was that sensible, Eddie, I would have no stories for you and that would be dull. I wouldn't be able to tell you about the bloke who brought me back to his for sex and his mum came in the room and made us tea.'

'Or the time that man farted in Pizza Express and blamed it on you,' Ed reminds me, bent over in hysterics. The reason he can laugh and I won't get insulted is that there is enough space there now for these to be pub stories. In the moment, it always feels like I'm just some sort of bad man magnet.

'I just need a break from you men. You're the exception though. Our platonic love affair will and must continue. If only for the free sandwiches.'

His expression brightens to hear me change the subject, and he looks reasonably happy with that suggestion. And, like making him blush, I do love to make Ed happy, to hear those laughs, even if they are usually at my expense. It does nice things to his face. If only I could make him dance though, just a little. I try and bop my hips into his. Yep, that's definitely not happening.

'Who do I have to thank for this?' Beth asks us as she comes over and half downs a beer. Ed puts his hand in the air. She slaps him on the back to say thank you. 'Needed today. From the sounds of it, it's been a hard week for all...'

'That's because it's April,' I say.

We all toast in agreement with that. April is the three-quarter point in the school calendar where the finish line still feels far away, exams are looming, and the kids are starting to turn on each other.

'Well, here's to willing the month away without event. Keep those drinks coming, kids,' she tells us.

Ed salutes her and we watch our colleagues across the pub, all of whom are trading their weekly horror stories, security lanyards removed so no one can identify us when we start calling the kids bad names. I spy Henry from Geography who always starts the week looking relatively normal and finishes like he's lost a fight with some feral cats. These pub visits are common practice with us – birthdays, promotions, leaving drinks, the completion of building works in the Art department – and the arrival of Caitlin today is as good an excuse as any to convene, despair and get steaming pissed this Friday.

'You're still staring at her,' I tell Ed as he faces away from the bar to glance outside at the beer garden, where Caitlin sits with some of the Maths department, most likely chatting calculators and set squares. The light starts to fade, fairy lights hang off the ivy trellises, a mist from vapes and cigarettes fogging the air.

'I'm looking. Looking is different to staring. Staring is like...' He bulges his eyes at me to demonstrate.

I grab a bottle of beer from the bar and take a large sip to stop it overflowing. I turn to look at her too. 'Is that your type then?' I ask. 'She's quite...'

'Pretty?'

'Plain. She'd be the sort who pulls the covers up to her neck, lights off. The sort who wears a nightie.'

'You don't wear a nightie?' Ed asks me, his nose wrinkled up to imagine the alternative.

'Ed, I usually sleep in just knickers, tits out so they can get an airing.'

'Too much information.'

'You did ask. How do you sleep?'

'Clothed. What if there's a fire and you have to make a quick escape from your house?' he tells me.

'Then I'd make a fireman very happy,' I joke, confused about how someone has contingencies for sleep-related emergencies. He doesn't notice the joke because he's still looking over at Caitlin.

'I bet she uses hand cream too,' I say, nibbling at a nail that has scraps of nail polish on it. 'You're quite taken with the young maiden, aren't you?' I add in Austen tones but still burping slightly under my breath.

He takes a deep resigned sigh. 'Maybe, but I don't want to overstep at work.'

'How professional of you, Rogers,' I say, half laughing, knowing that I've slept with at least two people in this faculty. Yes, unprofessional but not as bad as the I.T. department who Ed and I suspect are into a bit of wife swapping. I reckon their USB sticks are filthy. I turn to Ed, and he downs his drink quite quickly for him. He is usually a sipper, a sensible sipper of real ales.

'Hold up there, kiddo. Is this how we're drinking this evening? I'll have to get chips...'

'I think I'm just nervous. Is that weird? I don't even really know her.'

I smile. Mainly because I've never seen Ed like this before. The Ed I know usually tells me about how he revived a banana plant or how he's adding barley to his stews now. We buddy watch *The Walking Dead* and I steal his lunch. If we are ever talking of romantic endeavours, then it's usually me telling him about my sex and dating adventures and him looking at me with the same horror he generally reserves for flesh-eating zombies. So to see him crushing is ridiculously cute. We never talk about him finding love.

'Just go and chat to her. Maybe don't bring up pesto again though... or her lunchbox.'

'You see, I'm not like you. I'll say everything I'm not supposed to. I have absolutely zero conversational prowess.'

'Bullshit, you talk to me every day. I've heard you chatting away to your mum on the phone. You talk to the ladies in the school office.'

'That's because she's my mum. And the ladies in the office do good work and appreciate my baking. Shall I talk about cookies?'

'No, Ed. Just be normal.'

He gives me a look like we've only just met. 'Shall I buy her a drink? Or maybe I should ask her first. It feels presumptuous to just buy her one. Maybe she's not thirsty and then it'll be a waste.'

'Or maybe you're overthinking this.' I scrunch my face up trying to hold in my laughter. But then a brilliant idea occurs to me. 'Actually, given what Beth just told us, do you know what everyone out there will thank you for?'

Ed looks at me and shrugs.

I turn to the bar. 'Hi, can I get twelve tequila shots? Salt and lemon, too?'

The barman looks back at me with an expression that clearly says, *Love, it's 6.45p.m.* Tequila is not a drink for this time of the evening. It's a drink for the last hour of the evening so you don't remember the finer messier details of those closing moments. He waits, giving me a moment to re-think that order.

Ed puts a hand on my arm. 'Seriously? I don't really do tequila.'

I roll my eyes at him, groaning. 'That's like telling me you don't do fun.'

'Not when I'm wearing light colours,' he jokes.

'Turn around, Ed.' We both turn in the direction of the garden where Caitlin sits flanked by Tommy and Steve from P.E. They're all sharing in some sort of joke that involves Tommy looking like he's mimicking riding a horse. Caitlin is in hysterics. 'That's what you're competing with. I pray to God that poor sweet girl doesn't succumb to those dickish charms. But carry a tray of tequila out there and you're suddenly cool. You're bringing the party to the masses.'

'This feels like a weapon you've used in your arsenal on many an occasion, Mia,' replies Ed.

'Slippery Nipples,' I inform him.

'Pardon me...?'

'I worked nightclub bars at university. They're Baileys and Schnapps. I was known for my Slippery Nipples.'

'I don't want to know.'

'Trust me.' I turn to the barman to give him the nod, his eyes still reading faint horror at what may unfold. 'We walk out with those, and those poor tired teachers will thank you for bringing a sliver of joy and fun to their Friday nights.'

ED

Mia Johnson may indeed be one of the most evil and foolish people I know. I lie on her bathroom floor in a state of complete delirium but also slightly unsure whether this surface is sanitary. I roll over and am faced with a box of light flow Tampax so I roll the other way. There's a light knocking on the door.

'Ed, are you OK? Are you alive?' I can hear Mia laughing. We are no longer friends. Yes, we bought tequila, tequila for everyone, and she walked into that beer garden, the tray perched on her fingers, hand on her hip and announced her arrival. And the crowd moaned as they relived memories of their past experiences with tequila, recoiling with pained grimaces –but did that deter them? No. Their eyes also lit up to see the saltshakers, the lemon wedges, pulling up their sleeves and clenching their fists to relive it all over again.

Naturally, the P.E. boys grabbed the shots and may as well have beat their chests before they downed them. I saw Caitlin look up at Tommy in wild admiration, her head thrown back in laughter, so I reached for a glass and I did the same.

Except I did not look like Tommy after I downed mine. Tommy roared to the skies. I gurned so hard, I thought my face may never recover. One stiff breeze and I'd have looked like I was having a stroke for the rest of my living days. Mia, who was also post-shot, saw that face and snorted something through her nose, possibly a bit of lemon zest. In short, it was possibly my most unattractive moment on this planet, so I hope Caitlin didn't see any of it. However, the problem was that Mia didn't stop there. Sure, the shots relaxed the tone of the place. The ladies from the office used that tequila to get a few decibels louder and take two hundred filtered selfies. Henry from Geography used the moment to indulge in a bit of Cossack dancing. So this encouraged Mia to unleash bedlam. She may as well have been wearing devil horns. She bought more shots. I felt compelled to keep up with the room. I drank the shots.

'Do you want some water?' I hear her voice whisper through the door.

'I think I may need a drip. Do you have anything intravenous in the house?'

'Unfortunately, no. Do I need to get an exorcist? I've not heard sounds like that before.'

I crawl across the bathroom tiles to the door and reach up to undo the latch, falling to the floor dramatically once it's done. I turn over and see Mia's face looking down at me, chomping on a toasted bagel. She holds it over me.

'It's peanut butter? You want?' she asks me, licking her lips, crumbs falling onto my face. 'It's smooth, I know you don't do crunchy.'

'Noooooo. I think I'm dying,' I moan, putting my cold face to the tiles. 'Why did you do that?'

'I did nothing,' she says innocently, eyes wide like a drunk kitten. How is she still standing? She also seems to have changed into what appear to be tiny zebra print boxer shorts and a cropped T-shirt, her belly button and a flash of her knickers on display.

'You enabled the situation. Harriet from the office won't be allowed in the pub ever again. They may need to re-decorate.'

'That's because Harriet still drinks those alcopop drinks from the nineties. They don't mix well with anything. They are nasty.'

'I think I may have thrown up a lung.'

'As long as it doesn't block my toilet,' she murmurs through a mouthful of bagel.

She crouches down beside me, putting her back to the wall of the corridor and pats my head like one would a pet. All I see is animal print and for a small moment I hallucinate that an actual jungle beast is coming to eat me.

'Did you get a chance to chat to her then? Caitlin?' she asks me.

At present, Caitlin is the last thing on my mind. I think I may have possibly wet myself.

'No. I've killed that.' I can't quite tell if I'm floating or if I'm on the floor. The tile patterns are making me poorly.

'Not necessarily. Those shots finished Tommy off. When we left, he was asleep on a bench in the pub garden. You at least outdid him in that respect. Lightweight.'

'Yes, but do you think she saw me throwing up outside the chicken shop opposite though? That's not a good look...'

'She was long gone by then.'

I cringe at the memory of thinking fried chicken was a good idea. 'I may never eat again. Did Caitlin leave with anyone?' I enquire.

'Not that I saw. She told me she needed to be up bright and early for a Park Run. She's a runner like you, see? Something in common. We had a nice chat, seems like a sound girl.'

I can't feel my face. I think it might actually be stuck to these tiles. There is also a fair bit of hair down here, collected in tumbleweed style balls. I hope it's hair from a head. The thought that I may be inhaling errant pubes makes my stomach turn again. I want to ask questions. What did you talk about? Did you at least mention my name so I'm in her sphere of consciousness?

'I'm cold,' I mutter. Mia reaches up and throws a towelling dressing gown over me. 'Is this what death feels like?'

'That is what tequila feels like.' She finishes her bagel and takes an unusually noisy sip of tea.

'So loud... How does someone drink tea so loud?' I moan, her big slurps moving me to tears.

'I don't think you've ruined your chances there, you know? I think we've given her a glimpse into the fact you go down the pub, you're one of the cool kids.'

'Except I'm not.'

'You are. Know your worth, Ed Rogers. You're cool to me.' Mia sits there next to me, puts down her mug of tea and begins scrolling through her phone, pausing only to push a pint glass of water in my direction. I raise my head and attempt to take a small sip, through puckered aching lips. My stomach lurches again, feeling raw, like I've turned it inside out. I can feel everything and nothing in my body. I want to apologise to it so badly. Please forgive this abuse. 'I think I've found her on social media too.'

She holds a phone to my eyes, and I squint to adjust my vision. CB_Teaches_Maths. Oh, the joy of a teacher username so the kids can never find us. My heart aches to see squares of perfectly curated pictures of her, nothing off-putting like skewed political opinions or an over-reliance on filters and hashtags. She just seems really, really nice. And she runs. And brings her own lunch to school. And likes pesto.

'It's OK. It'll never happen. Just forget it,' I say, pushing the phone away drunkenly. The room swirls for a moment like we're at sea. I see glimpses of things in that moment, Mia's look of pity, a cobweb on the underside of her sink, three empty toilet roll tubes lying sadly on the floor.

'It might happen,' Mia says.

'Things like that don't happen for me...' I start to drone on, and then laugh under my breath at how the roles have reversed today. It's usually Mia lying here, drunk, tearfully murmuring about how she's done nothing meaningful with her life, me making sure she doesn't choke on her own vomit. 'I just think it's never going to happen. I've left it too late.'

'Stop being dramatic, you tool. You've known her for twelve hours,' she says, her face illuminated by her phone light. Is she sat there on Twitter while I'm dying?

'I'm twenty-eight. How has it not happened yet?'

'You're losing me. Like you keep telling me, we're still young for all of that... We have time,' she mumbles, trying to placate me.

'But how have I not had sex yet?' I splutter. Shit.

'With her?' Mia asks me, confused.

But my defences are gone, they are down. They got washed away in a wave of tequila and now I'm lying here shipwrecked on this bathroom floor, vulnerable, exposed. Quite literally. Where did my trousers go?

'No, like ever.'

And with that there's a loud thump to my forehead as Mia drops her phone and it lands on my temple, potentially crushing any sense of self-esteem I had left. I just said that out loud, didn't I? I told her. Shit, shit, shit.

'ED, ARE YOU A VIRGIN?' she shrieks.

And with that, a door opens on the other side of the corridor, and a figure emerges in avocado print pyjamas. 'Mia, how many times do I have to tell you... If you're bringing visitors back, then keep the noise down! It's past midnight! And why the fuck is he covering his balls with my dressing gown?'

THREE

MIA

Ed is a virgin. I didn't know those existed. Not at our age anyway. Maybe he was so drunk that he forgot all the times he's had sex. I wish I could get that drunk.

I'd definitely erase the memory of that man I brought back from a nightclub at uni once who literally hurled while he was on top of me. Not on me, he thrusted and then leant over the side of the bed, but, as you can imagine, mood killer. That said, for all the times I've wanted to forget the sex I've had, I've also had some pretty awesome sex. I don't think it defines my being but it's something I enjoy, something I gain a lot of happiness from, something I can't quite imagine not having in my life. Ed doesn't have sex in his life and that makes me strangely sad.

After Ed told me, he closed his eyes, possibly because my phone knocked him out, or because of the shame? But it was followed by some light snoring, so I did the good friend thing of putting him on his side and leaving him to sleep it off. There was no way I was going to move him or ask my housemates to help me shift him. I then went into the kitchen, finished off the chips Ed abandoned there with some mayo from the fridge that's been there since last summer, and fell asleep on my sofa watching some Netflix programme about bad cake. When I woke up, he was gone.

Since then, I've not heard from him, which is mildly strange as normally he drops me a text on Sunday reminding me to set an alarm or flagging up important departmental meetings and charity dress-up days. I hope he's still alive. Maybe all that tequila made him spontaneously combust. I did send a text on Saturday morning. It was a tequila meme. He read it but didn't reply.

Now I'm sat on the number sixty-five bus on the way to school trying to figure out how I broach this. Do I pretend the tequila gave me temporary amnesia and forget he ever told me? Do I do what I normally do with Ed and just laugh it out, go super acerbic? Will that make him feel bad? I don't want to make him feel bad. There are a lot of men out there who are virgins. Religious peeps who want to wait until they're married. Men who live in lighthouses and never see women. Steve Carrell made a very good film about the whole subject. To be a good friend, I even googled it to see if it was a thing. Three percent of adults over twenty-five in this country are virgins. I don't know how they got people to admit to that statistic, but I read their stories and their experiences. They live among us.

The bus slows down on the high street at Ed's stop. I arch my head over the crowd of people to see if he's there but he's not. This is disappointing mainly because sometimes on a Monday he will buy me a coffee. I bite my lip. I hope he's OK. Ed never misses the bus. I miss the bus and then he calls me to tell me I've missed the bus. In his place, a group of kids from our school get on which is going to give me all the joy this Monday morning. Our kids at Griffin Road are a motley crew, which is often the way of a British comprehensive on the outskirts of London. It's phones in hand, AirPods in ears, short skirts, puffer jackets and black school bags sponsored by Nike, Adidas and Vans.

'Miss Johnson!' one of them squeals at me as they all herd in my direction.

'Lola Kissey, good morning... I never see you on this bus, kids?' I announce to them as they decide to sit around me, marvelling in the novelty of seeing one of their teachers on the bus.

'Oh, we're going in for the GCSE booster sessions... we were told we'd get breakfast if we go,' says one of the lads.

'I wouldn't get too excited about that, just in case you're holding out for a McMuffin,' I joke.

'Don't you drive, Miss?'

'I do but the car parking situation sucks at school and this way I'm saving the planet,' I say, yawning. I miss Ed. I miss Ed's coffee.

Lola scans my look from my feet up to my hair. I was never going to be the sort of teacher who comes in wearing a tailored suit and a mid-heel. I'm the Converse and leather jacket teacher, the one who had to try on three pairs of tights this morning before finding a pair that didn't have holes, who carries her belongings in a big fluffy tote. I can't quite tell if this impresses her.

'So, what booster subject today?'

'Biology with Mr Rogers,' says a voice.

I smile for a moment, realising why Ed is not on this bus. He'd have been first in with the caretakers, knowing Ed.

'Then knowing Mr Rogers, he will give you breakfast and likely, he will have baked it himself. He's good like that. If he hasn't made them for you this morning, then apple cinnamon crumble muffins. They will change your life. I keep telling him he should be on Bake Off.'

A few of the kids laugh, snapping their fingers. 'I'm gonna tell him. Mr Rogers on the television would be mad.'

'You guys like him then?' I say.

'He don't shout, that's always a good start, but he tries hard,' Lola explains.

I smile in return. Ed's not a big character teacher but that describes him to a tee. I look at Lola's well-foundationed face, wondering how someone so young managed to get up so early to apply that eyeliner. How the hell is it so straight? I'm twenty-eight and still can't manage that. Next to her, a lad has his hand on her knee, and it brings me back to when I was that age. Sitting on a bus, going to school, an aisle separating the girls from the boys as we flirted with each other, the banter strong, the skirts still as short as they are now. Talk of parties, fake IDs and stealing our sisters' clothes, gateway moments to losing one's virginity at that age.

'Is he married?' one girl asks, laughing.

'That's not for you to know, young lady.'

'Is he gay?'

'Also, none of your business.' Christ, was Ed telling me he was a gay virgin? There's a lot to unravel from his revelation.

'Are you married, Miss?' a voice says from the throng of kids.

'I will answer, purely to avoid speculation; yes, I'm married to Harry Styles. We haven't told many people because we want to keep it low-key, you know? I don't even wear a ring.'

They all laugh a little too loudly at this, so loudly I see the bus driver's eyes in the rear-view mirror looking at the source of the volume. I shush them. The last thing I want is to get thrown off the 65 with a bunch of kids.

'You wouldn't be a teacher if you were married to Harry Styles,' one of them jokes.

'Excuse me, just because I'm married to a global millionaire superstar, doesn't mean I would leave you guys and my vocation in life. I am all about the education and the young people,' I say in earnest tones.

They all howl merrily in response like groups of teens do and to have won over this small crowd on a Monday morning already feels like a victory.

I seize the moment. 'Speaking of which, we've been doing English boosters at lunch. Miss Callaghan and I never see any of you there?'

'You don't provide food,' one boy says.

'Would that make a difference?'

'Yes,' the boys all shout in harmony. I hadn't realised it was that easy to win them over.

'Well, now I know, I expect to see all of you there tomorrow. We're covering *Macbeth*.'

'He the one with the crazy bitch wife?' a voice says.

'Yes, but I will teach you different ways to write that for your GCSEs,' I say, trying to sound teacher-like.

The bus pulls to a stop outside the large sprawling school building, and we all disembark, the bus driver still glaring at us. Griffin Road is one of those schools undergoing expansion so it's a mix of redbrick buildings with primary coloured windows, next to crumbling seventies buildings that are eighty percent concrete and leaking roofs. It is early so not all the lights are on. I see Zoe from Maths getting out of her car, a sensible raincoat over her floral dress, weighed down with plastic bags full of exercise books. Fun weekend for her then. I follow the kids over to the Biology block to see the classroom already lit and boxes of muffins and juice boxes waiting.

'Well done for getting in everyone. Take a seat... Help yourself to food,' I hear a familiar voice say.

I stand there by the doorway, waiting to catch Ed's eye. How does he look so fresh and orderly this Monday morning? I'm messy bun and half-arsed make up whereas he looks like he's showered, the chinos are ironed, not a hair is out of place. He's lined up everything so nicely. There's also milk for anyone who wants tea and I know for a fact he'll have gone out of his way to buy that from the big supermarket because he gets angry about how the smaller shops charge him 40p more.

As soon as he sees me, he responds strangely by waving. 'Hello, Miss Johnson!' he says in unnatural tones, rolling up the sleeves of his green jumper.

'Mr Rogers!' I say, entering the classroom. 'Good morning.'

'What are you doing here?' he mutters as the kids organise themselves and take off their coats. Please don't be weird with me, Ed.

'I was told you do a breakfast service,' I say, nicking a muffin.

He stops for a moment as I grab at one, smiling with clenched teeth and I see his shoulders relax as he exhales softly. Look at him with all his treats for his kids. He's an excellent human, a good teacher.

'Food thief,' he mutters.

'You know it.'

I then look to his whiteboard where he's projected his topic of the day. *Reproduction.* Oh.

ED

You never quite know what you're going to get with Mia. The girl can't keep a secret. We know this because I ran a marathon once and got awful chafing with my nipples, so she announced this to the staffroom and Beth lent me some of her breastfeeding cream to relieve them.

After I woke up on Mia's bathroom floor, having used a bathmat as a makeshift blanket, it was all I could think about. Not Caitlin, not the fact it felt like a cat had defecated inside my mouth, but the fact that I'd drunkenly told Mia – Mia with the big mouth – that I was a virgin. Why? I'd managed to keep it a secret to myself for that long, so why tell someone now? I left pretty swiftly. Did I bleach her toilet beforehand? I'm not an animal.

I never intended to be a virgin at twenty-eight. Who does? I don't know how I got to this point having never had sex. I nearly had it. Once. After the story of that spread around my halls of residence, I had the nickname of Fan Boy for the rest of my university days, so I stopped trying. I studied. I got involved in all those endeavours where one doesn't really meet women. I stayed in and drank with my housemates who were all physicists and chemical engineers. I joined the board games society. I can tell you all the squares on a Monopoly board but have never seen a real-life woman's clitoris. After my degree, it was on to teacher training and as the years passed, it became an embarrassment, a source of shame, the reverse of a scarlet letter. I thought of ways to non-virginise myself, the obvious being paying a lady to have sex with me, but I wanted someone to want me. I also just never had the balls to go through with it. I mean, I had the balls. My balls actually ached with how much I wanted to have sex, but I sorted that out with my own hand, my longest-running relationship thus far. That is so very sad.

So now, I worry that this secret is like a ticking time bomb. Who will Mia tell? Has she told anyone already? Her housemate may have heard. How will I walk into that staffroom ever again? Maybe I can blag it – tell her that it's a religious thing. Or maybe I have a mechanical issue with my male parts? It's medical, people. But folk will still laugh and point and ask questions. Maybe I need to quit, move, leave the country. Mia just came in here now. She didn't say anything. She smiled, but for her that can mean a number of things, usually that she's up to no good. But at least she didn't shun me or avoid me. That's something, I guess.

'Mr Rogers, you baked these? These are better than them ones you can buy in Starbucks,' a voice says from the back of the classroom.

'Thank you. I did... they are banana and maple syrup with cream cheese frosting. No one in here has allergies, right?' I ask again. I did do a form that their parents all signed. 'All good vitamins, kids.'

'Miss Johnson was just telling us she thinks you could go on Bake Off. Why don't you apply, Sir?' I hear another voice say.

My body stiffens for a moment. They spoke to Miss Johnson? I don't know if that's a good thing. When? Where? Miss Johnson knows too much.

'She did, did she? What else did she say?' I say, my voice quivering slightly.

'She wouldn't tell us if you were married!'

'Well, I am not married.'

'Are you single? Are you dating anyone?' a girl asks.

I feel my cheeks redden at the question. This is not professional talk.

'You should go on Tinder, Sir. Girls love a man who can bake,' another girl says.

I can see it now. *Ed, 28, bakes well. Virgin. Like the olive oil.*

'Maybe. Where did you bump into Miss Johnson then?' I enquire.

'On the 65 bus.'

I stop to look at all of them. Surely if Mia had said, 'He's not married, he's not even knocked boots with anyone' then they would be looking at me strangely, with pity, with laughter. Not even my muffins could have calmed down that chatter. But that's not Mia. That would have been cruel and that's not her. Mia is eccentric, brash, really annoying at times, but never cruel.

'She also told us she's married to Harry Styles, is that right?' a boy pipes up.

'This is true. I went to their wedding. I made the cake.'

They all laugh, and the sound is a relief. They are a good bunch, this lot. Normally you do get the year groups and the odd class that act as the best contraceptive known to man, but this group seem keen on at least scraping through their exams and trying to have something at the end to show for it.

'Right, enough of Miss Johnson's wedding... Biology. I know half of you are here for the muffins, the other half are here to heckle whilst we talk about sex.' There is sniggering across the boys in the back row which is not uncommon. 'So, I marked the practice exam questions you did the other day. We need to talk through some things. I've not attached names to any of these, but here are some of the answers you gave me.'

I click a slide through on my board presentation.

'What is E in this diagram? It is not a "plant wang." It is a stamen, and it doesn't "jizz pollen everywhere."'

I knew what I was doing when I made these slides – I had to get them on side with some big humour because it's 8 a.m. on a Monday morning.

'And another, what is the function of the testes? Someone put to make "man milk" and "make sure the penis isn't lonely hanging there on his own."'

Someone high fives someone else at the back of the room. I raise my eyebrows at them.

'And my favourite... I asked you all to label this pregnant woman's uterus and someone labelled the foetus "Dave."'

'But he looks like a Dave, Sir.'

I smile back at the kids as the room simmers with giggles.

'All, I applaud the humour and creativity in your answers. You are right, sex is hilarious but, in all seriousness, you put those answers in a proper exam paper and you leave here with nothing. I would hate that to happen to you. You're good kids. I'm also worried about how many of you are unaware of basic anatomy.'

'How so, Sir?'

'Well, what was quite telling was that the boys knew nothing about the female body and the girls knew nothing about the male body. You, hopefully, will leave here and find boyfriends, girlfriends and have children of your own. P.S.H.E. have a whole curriculum on this for you, but at least let me teach you where things are...'

I say this but as I stand here knowing all the parts of all the plants, all the human anatomy, I also know full well at least thirty percent of the room here are not virgins. They're fifteen, sixteen and they go to parties and drink and get all the life experience that I've not had. The sheer irony that I have to teach them the basic mechanics of sex is not lost on me. I put up a picture of a man's penis. Not an actual picture, of course. One of my textbook labelled versions. He hangs straight down the middle, average sized, well-balanced balls. Not what any penis in real life looks like, but hey. The room snickers, which is expected.

'So, can anyone else tell me what testes are for? Apart from producing semen?' I ask the room.

'Is that where wee is stored?' a voice asks.

Everyone stops laughing. Please tell me they don't actually think this. Please.

'No, hormones. They create hormones. We have some work to do, eh? Open up your textbooks to page 92, please.'

They all do as they're told.

FOUR

MIA

I remember having such high hopes for being a teacher – I was going to change the world, one kid at a time. At university, I absorbed all that training like a sponge, dedicating myself to beautifully structured lesson plans, learning about ways of assessing student development and modelling strategies designed to start debate and generate these kids' amazing ideas. Then they added the kids to the equation. These teenage wonders, all amazing in their own ways but all different, all trying to exist and work out who they are. And all raging for reasons they don't quite understand. This is when I found out my training meant jack shit.

'YOU ARE A FUCKING SLAG! GET OUT OF MY FACE!' Today it's all about breaking up the fights as two girls face off. I don't remember a degree module in this sort of conflict resolution. It's a sudden snap of hair pulling, bag tossing and them trying to wrestle each other without ruining the other's make up. I run across the courtyard as some of the younger members of our school, fresh-faced and unaware, look on in horror. This is a reason to wear trainers, I'd have got to this melee ten seconds later if I'd been in proper shoes. I put my body between both the girls.

'LESS OF THIS, PLEASE! And can everyone put away their phones? We don't need this on Snapchat, kids.'

I won't lie. I like this sort of power. It makes me feel like a bouncer in a nightclub. I'd wear a headset if I could.

'But Miss, she's been sending nudes to my boyfriend. You are such a nasty bitch...'

'Language!' Another teacher, Caitlin, intervenes, holding the other girl back, and helps put her belongings back in her bag. 'I don't care what she's done. We don't do this here.'

'Then I'll do it at the gate after school,' she tells me.

'No, you won't, because Miss Bell and I are going to walk both of you to the deputy head's office.'

'But she attacked me!' cries the other girl, waving a finger in the air. 'Not my fault your boyfriend's been flirting with every girl in this year.'

'Enough! Both of you. We're walking...'

Caitlin widens her eyes at me as we walk them through the courtyard and corridors of this place, making sure we have our bodies in between them. The deputy head is Phil and as I knock at the door, he's just about to bite into a sandwich. I love my timing here.

'Mr Bush. Two young ladies who started a physical fight in the courtyard,' I tell him. He rolls his eyes to see me and the two sullen sorts by my side, sighing that I've interrupted his chicken salad on wholewheat.

'Come in. Oh, Morgan and Hayley. Always a pleasure. How have you pissed each other off this time?' he says, backing into his chair and folding his arms to hear their stories of injustice. Caitlin and I back away as we hear both girls start to squawk in protest.

'Expertly done,' Caitlin tells me.

'Oh, I'm the youngest of three sisters. Those sorts of fights featured highly in my teen years. Do the kids kick off like this at your other school?'

'Yeah, but I just volunteer in the library, so I don't have to do the lunch rounds and hang out with the little cretins.'

It's a strange comment to make for a person who hangs out with young people all day, every day, and I feel a surprising urge to defend the kids. 'They're not all bad. It's just like anywhere. You can't squeeze one thousand people into one place and expect them all to get along.'

'True,' she replies but I can only suppose she occasionally gets intimidated by it all, like someone else I know. She has library mouse written all over her. Organised, hair behind the ear, reading the classics. God, she's perfect for my Ed.

'Actually, I wanted to say thank you for coming along on Friday. It was fun. Is it always like that?' she asks me, as we move out of the school past the Art department.

'Oh, the shots *and* the dancing? We usually reserve that for Christmas and end of year. But it's a good faculty.'

'The P.E. guys seem nice?' she asks me.

'Yes and no.' I don't know how to tell her not to touch Tommy without incriminating myself as some sort of faculty bike. She'll work it out for herself, I hope.

'So, tell me more about you. You run, you're twenty-five and you like a gin and tonic...'

'That's a good memory,' she tells me. I open the door to the playground, and we re-enter the madness like prison guards on patrol looking for fights and contraband, i.e., people with nuts and vapes. I expertly catch a football before it hits me in the face.

'Lads? We spent a lot of money on a 3G pitch so you could kick a ball over there,' I suggest. The group of boys are in Year 8, so younger, and still respect me as an authority figure.

'Yes, Miss. Good skills, Miss. Like Courtois.'

I nod. They are correct even though I don't know who Courtois is.

'What do you want to know?' Caitlin asks me, as the boys dribble away.

'Married, single, kids?'

'Oh, very single. I was dating someone at my old school but no one serious since.'

'Then snap,' I tell her, smiling. 'Not the boyfriend thing. I haven't really had one of those for a while. But this is good. Us single ladies need to stick together for all the social events. It also helps to have an ally when they need volunteers. The marrieds and the parents always have instant excuses so the responsibility always falls to us.'

'Right? Same at my other school,' she responds. 'So what's the deal with the vending machines? They have fruit in them.'

'Oh, that's a new thing we're trying. They buy the fruit to throw at each other but it means the corner shops near us run an excellent trade in junk food, so I feel it feeds back into the local economy.'

She laughs and I notice she has very symmetrical teeth, the sort that show me she's into her flossing and, unlike me, she never went over the handlebars on a bike in Copenhagen and chipped her front tooth on a cobble.

'And how's it been today? You learning the lay of the land?' I ask her.

She sighs with relief to be able to offload to someone. 'Good, I think. I've got some easy groups, caught up with where I need to be with the syllabus. I don't get the photocopier room though.'

'Oh, you need a card for that... It's because someone last year printed a shitload of flyers for their am-dram group and we had an end of year prank where a kid photocopied their arse for all of us.'

'That's awful.'

'Yeah, I'd always recommend hand sanitiser after use.'

A small flicker of an idea suddenly comes into view. 'Actually, come with me. I know someone who's an ace with the photocopier. He knows what all the buttons mean, too.'

I walk her up a staircase to the staffroom and I head to the sofa areas, where Ed and I usually set up camp, to find him tucking into one of his good sandwiches.

'Eduardo... how goes it?' I greet him, sitting down beside him.

'Good,' he replies curiously, his eyes shifting between me and Caitlin. He's probably wondering what mischief I've been up to now. He narrows his eyes at me, I mimic his expression. I haven't told your crush you're a virgin if that's what you're worried about. In fact, I haven't uttered a word to a soul about what he told me on that cold bathroom floor but if he was looking to solve a problem then this might be the solution? He glares back at me, looking utterly baffled.

'I was just chatting to Caitlin about how you are a dab hand at...'

He coughs and a bit of lettuce flies to the carpet. I pat him sharply on the back.

'...the photocopier.'

It takes him a moment to work out that I'm not talking in innuendo.

'Oh... yeah? You had questions about the photocopier?' he asks.

'Well, you know me, Ed. I've lost my photocopier card more times than any other member of staff. I've set records,' I tell him. This makes Caitlin giggle. 'Ed can enlarge things and photocopy on both sides of the paper. He's an actual wizard.'

'Ignore her, but yeah, I can talk you through it if you want? We could do it now?'

As Caitlin looks away, I give a thumbs up to Ed who frowns at me in return. I don't get his problem. He likes the girl and wanted an introduction. This is perfect – plus he really loves that photocopier and understands it like no other person I know.

'You can eat first if you want, I don't want to interrupt your lunch,' Caitlin interjects.

'Oh, no, I'm good. I can eat later,' he says, standing up, though he looks flummoxed at having to alter his lunch plans.

'Perfect, I'll leave you two to it,' I say, a little too jovially, winking at Ed. He doesn't look impressed. For that, I steal his sandwich which he has stupidly left unattended on the sofa. I love tuna.

ED

I've been at this school too long today. I left my house at 6.30 a.m. to go to the big supermarket to buy milk, and then arrived super early to lay out muffins and juice boxes and revision booklets that no one will look at. I even used graphics and stapled them together, but I can see those booklets now left in lockers, at the bottom of schoolbags, abandoned for trendier subjects like Photography and Psychology. As I leave, a certain conversation from earlier lingers in my head too.

'So, this enlarges, and you just press this for a few seconds and then...' I explained.

'That's pretty big. I don't think I'll ever need anything that big,' she replied.

'Size is good. You can never be too big.' Silence followed. 'I mean, for wall displays – I have a student who has an unfortunate squint, so I copy everything big for him.'

Did I squint to illustrate my point? Yes, I did.

'Well, I think I get it now. Swipe the card, paper in here and keypad there.'

'Pretty much.'

It was a tutorial that took all of three minutes in our little photocopy room that's basically shelves and reams of paper and passive-aggressive signs from the office about saving the planet and only making as many copies as you need. All in Comic Sans with smiley faces, all designed to hurt my eyes. All the while, I noticed little things about her. Neatly polished nails, a small daisy bracelet, the fact she smelt like vanilla, not that I was totally weird and inhaled her. But I don't think I made an impression, not even the smallest of dents. I will be lucky if she remembers my name.

'BOO!' a voice comes at me, as I leave the school building and head to my car. Bloody Mia. She likes to jump out at me a lot and thinks it's funny. I spill a lot of tea as a result.

'Fuck! Don't do that!' I moan at her, pushing her playfully.

She pouts and makes sad puppy eyes at me. 'Sorry! You swore! You never swear!'

'I'm very tired and on edge. You could have been a mugger or a wild... animal...'

'Like a fox?' she asks.

'Yes, an urban rabid fox...'

Normally, she'd laugh hysterically at this but instead she is still, a great big grin on her face, trying to work out what to say to me. I've not really seen Mia all day and yes, I have been avoiding her. Is she going to ambush me again with the virgin thing? Here? Now? Outside our place of work?

'Are you mad at me?' she asks, still pouting.

'Sort of. What was that photocopier thing? That was so embarrassing,' I tell her.

'It was a perfect moment for you two to have a conversation. I'm crap with the photocopier.'

'I ballsed it up.'

'How?'

'By talking... Once I finished explaining the photocopier to her, I randomly told her I liked running. I sounded like Forrest

Gump,' I confess. 'I like running, you like running?' I demonstrate in a deep Southern drawl.

'Oh dear,' she says, giggling, sympathy in her eyes for once. 'Not in that accent, right?'

'No. I just thought it was something we had in common and then I said we could have the runs together. Using those exact words because I didn't know what I was saying so now it sounds like I want to give her diarrhoea.'

'Oh, Ed,' she says, linking an arm into mine, a look on her face like I might just be beyond her help. 'Do you know what might make you feel better?'

'Light sedation?'

'If you gave your friend a lift home?'

'Is that why you were waiting for me?'

'Yeah. We can get food? Falafel will make it all better.'

'Is this because you stole my tuna salad roll?' I ask her.

'Well, that too...'

I could make a very long list about the different things Mia does which grate a little but at the top of the list is the way she eats. It's very hands on and I question how sanitary it is to be picking up slices of tomato, dangling them in your mouth and then making nom-nom-nom sounds like a three-year-old. I also feel like I want to tuck a napkin in her before she starts because she's getting yoghurt dressing all down her front. I watch as she scrapes it off her T-shirt and then licks it off the same fingers, laughing at what a mess she is. Errant pieces of lettuce sprout out of her mouth like she's a small pony, one falling onto my car seat.

'Tasty...?'

'Falafel is a reason to be alive, Edward,' she tells me.

The weather has turned on us, April showers meant she ran into the deli, pulling her coat over her head and we're now eating our falafel parked on the high street, watching as shoppers and commuters run up and down, the reflection of shop signs painting the streets. I don't want to be seen to agree with Mia, but falafel was an excellent idea.

'You didn't tell me you weren't going to be on the bus today?' Mia says, a little indignant. 'I always get a message from you.'

'I drove. I had to get in early. Are you upset you didn't get a lift?' I tell her.

'No, I'd never have got up in time and then you'd have been grumpy at me for making you late.'

'I'm always grumpy with you.'

'I thrive off making you grumpy...' she says, smiling. There is a small moment of silence. I say silence, but I can still hear Mia chewing. 'You know, Ed, I've been thinking. I share a lot with you. Maybe too much because I am an over-sharer and I think that my life is vaguely amusing and entertaining for those who may not be a part of it...' she continues. 'But over the weekend, I realised, you don't do the same with me. You never have...'

I take quite a large mouthful of falafel at that point as I can see where the conversation is going, and I don't know if I know what to say next. Please let deep fried chickpeas be the answer here.

She turns to me, wiping her mouth with the back of her hand, leaning forward and catching my eye. 'You shared something with me that was quite important, and I want to be a good friend here. I know you were drunk. If you want me to forget it then I will pretend I never heard it and we can carry on as we were, but if that was some sort of cry for help or you want to chat more then you know that I'm here, right?'

I am quiet because this was not the reaction I was expecting. That was sincere, warm. And this is Mia. Half our conversations end with a punchline or innuendo or making me the butt of her jokes but there is a moment here that feels caring, authentic. So much so that I'm waiting for the joke. Surely, there is a joke here? The joke is me. The sound of rain thunders heavy on my car roof.

'You're either quiet because the falafel is too damn tasty, or you're embarrassed. If it's option two, then blink twice.'

I turn to her, quietly. I blink twice. I really don't know what to say to her, to follow up that revelation, because to do so would mean telling her my whole back story of how we've got to this point. Maybe it all was some subconscious cry for help in a way.

'Ed, remember when I went out with that bloke from Tinder and he asked me to pee on him and I did and then I farted on him as well? I told you that story.' I like how she can recount that story and still continue to gobble down her falafel.

'You did,' I whisper. I actually thought I'd wiped that from memory.

'You can tell me anything. You think I've got a big gob, but I also know when to keep it shut...' she mutters quietly.

'You do have a big mouth. I've just seen you fit a whole pitta in there...'

She laughs and sprays more lettuce around my car.

'You didn't tell Caitlin I was a virgin then?' I ask.

'No. I did not.' She looks affronted.

'You've told no one else?'

She puts a hand to her chest. 'I swear on all my nieces' and nephews' lives. I have been very good.'

'Then yes, Mia Johnson. I am a virgin.'

She doesn't laugh. She looks strangely thoughtful, raindrops still caught in her hairline.

'Define virgin,' she enquires. 'Like if we go with the American baseball analogy. You've gone to first base and kissed a girl, yeah?'

'Yes.'

'Touched boob?'

'Over bra.'

'So that means you've never touched a nipple so certainly not a lady's vajajay?'

'No. Someone has touched my penis though…'

'As in jerked you off?'

'Not quite.'

'So no blow jobs either?'

'Definitely not.'

She sits there with a serious look to her brow, like she's conducting a job interview. *So you've created an Excel spreadsheet before? Yes but no. I would need further experience and a brief tutorial, but I've seen it done. I think I could do it.*

'Ed. Dude, you're missing out.'

'I know this already.'

'Do you watch porn?'

'Yes.'

'Like, are you into strange sex things? Is it a religious thing?'

'I don't think so. I'm an atheist, a man of science. Why all the questions?' I ask her, watching as she's trying to compute the situation.

'I'm just working out if you told me because you'd like me to have sex with you?' she says, plainly.

I spit out a bit of pitta which lands on my dashboard, herbs and beetroot spraying all over my chinos. Beside my car, a bus pulls up just as I have a massive coughing fit, and a couple of passengers look through my window to see Mia sharply patting my back.

'God, don't die, you pillock!' she shrieks at me.

'That's not why I told you!' I yell back. She starts laughing and it instantly alleviates the tension. 'I was drunk. *In vino veritas* and it's very much my reality and my truth, my biggest secret.'

'You could have kept far worse secrets from me,' she adds.

'Like?'

'You have questionable politics, you've extorted money out of pensioners, you have a dead body under your porch?' she lists, counting each one off on her fingers.

'I live in a flat. I don't have a porch.'

'But it's just one thing. One thing you've never done. I've never watched a *Star Wars* film.'

'That's different.'

'Kind of, but I do feel I am judged quite unfairly for it. My nieces and nephews are mean to me about it.'

I laugh under my breath, but I am judging her for it. How has she managed this? How? I have zero popular cultural reference touchstones; those films may be my only one.

'So, Caitlin... That could be the solution?' she says, with hope in her eyes.

I shake my head firmly. 'But no. I don't think you realise that when you push me into a sexy photocopier situation with a really pretty girl, it's like flinging someone who's never swum before into a swimming pool and telling them to do laps. I feel behind on everything. I've not got years of experience to draw on. I'd be naked in a bed with this woman and would have zero idea what to do,' I confess quietly.

'What you need is a practical classroom sesh,' Mia jokes.

I laugh a little too hard, clinging to my falafel.

'Ed... dear Ed. Then maybe that's what we do...' she says, looking thoughtful while still chewing exceptionally loudly given we're in an enclosed space together.

'I don't get you.'

'I know you almost choked to think of the idea of having sex with me just now. But let's just do it. Have sex. I'm not in a relationship at the moment, I'm a free agent and, to be frank, I do have hard-earned years of experience that you don't. I may as well put them to good use,' she says, almost a little too matter-of-factly. In a way that almost says, you have a hole in your garden, I have a spade. Let me help you fill it in.

'Mia...'

'Ed, this is an actual thing. I did some reading on the subject. People who want more sex experience sometimes pay therapists and surrogates to walk them through it. I could do that for you. Let's face it, even though we're friends I don't think we're meant to be in a relationship. I don't really feel any attraction here,' she tells me, waiting for me to gesture that she is right. She is right. I'm not even going to argue with her on that one. 'This would purely be a way for you to be a non-virgin. I'll walk you through it. If this is a cause of stress in your life then let me take that away from you and give you a safe, consensual space to have sex for the first time. Let me be helpful for once in my life and repay you for all those times I've stolen your lunch...'

'You could just repay me in falafel,' I suggest.

'But you'd still be a virgin.'

I have no choice but to laugh under my breath at her reply. 'You'd actually do that?' I say, half in shock, half worried.

'Yeah?' she says, like it's no big deal.

'What's in this for you?'

'I'd need to see you naked first before I answer that,' she says, pointing at me.

'NOW?'

'Obviously no. Send me a pic...'

'Really?'

'Ed. No,' she laughs. This is not funny. How can she be so calm? I watch her fill her face with chips and think about what she's just suggested. Surely sex should be about being attracted to one another, about a shared intimacy, passion, raw animal instinct. Offering sex in the way she has feels strange, almost a little too official, not romantic in any way, shape or form. I know I'm twenty-eight, but I have fantasised over what my first time would look like. It didn't involve discussing the mechanics of the situation sitting in my Skoda, eating steaming hot falafel and fries.

'Mia, I don't want to take advantage of you, or for it to feel weird... Wouldn't this get in the way of our friendship? I like you as a friend. I don't think it'll be the same once you've seen my thing...'

She smiles. 'Your thing? You describe it like it's something out of a horror film. It is a penis, a cock, a wang...' A thought strikes her, and her eyes shift to me, panicked. 'Is there something wrong with your penis? Is that why you're a virgin?'

'No! I think it's normal.'

'Then this wouldn't get in the way. I wouldn't want to lose you as a friend either,' she says, coming close to me and trying to rest her head on my shoulder. 'Come on, Ed, let me help you.'

I take a deep, deep breath. 'Only if you promise one thing?'

'Condoms? Well, yeah.'

'Can you watch a *Star Wars* film please?'

'Whilst we're doing it?'

'If that's what it takes.'

FIVE

MIA

So it turns out that I've agreed to have sex with Ed Rogers. I'm not sure what I was thinking in that car. Part of me is strangely curious, and I feel my love for falafel may have affected my judgement, but I did think about all the times I've been judged and sex-shamed as a woman, and I didn't want him to feel the same for being a virgin. That said, I also have an affection for Ed. He's mildly awkward and super serious but, by that same measure, he is kind and generous, not laddy, he's the best sort of work husband. And he deserves to have sex. He should be able to feel physical pleasure with another person and discover how awesome it can be. And maybe I'm the perfect person to do this with. I've been around the block when it comes to sex (not too many times, I'll have you know) and I will look after him and not expect the world. I won't shame his lack of experience, I will make this as light and painless as possible.

However, I do feel we need to chat more about when and where this will happen. Maybe we need a solid plan at least, because I've come round for our Wednesday takeaway night and Ed is in a suit. I'm thinking he may have taken the idea of hump day quite literally.

'Hello!' I say with gusto as the door opens. To his credit, it's a well-fitting suit but I've realised that since Monday we've not really ironed out the finer details of our arrangement. 'You're wearing a suit.'

'You're wearing a tracksuit. It's very bright. You look like a children's TV presenter,' he says, as I step over the threshold and give him a peck on the cheek.

'You smell nice, too.'

'Thank you,' he says awkwardly.

'Have you come from somewhere? A job interview perhaps? A court appearance?' I ask, leading him into the kitchen.

'No,' he says, grabbing the takeaway from me, trying to hide the fact he's gone formal this evening.

'Ed, are you wearing date clothes?' I ask him, eyebrows raised.

'I didn't know what this was... I just thought...'

'You'd go formal. For takeaway Wednesday. I guess I should be glad you didn't answer the door naked at least, with a flower in between your cheeks.'

He blushes. Takeaway Wednesday has been our thing since we started at this school, a type of check-in moment where we can decompress from the week's madness and, more often than not, he can help me fill in some of my difficult teacher paperwork.

'You do look very smart though. A for effort.'

He pouts in return. 'Remember to take off your shoes.'

I nod. Ed likes his hygiene, so I scrappily use my back heel to kick my trainers off without undoing the laces. He stares at me while I do it and I wait for him to tell me I'm going to spoil my shoes, but he's strangely quiet. Pensive. As he leads me

through the house, I realise I'm taking in details of this place
that I never have before. Ed isn't me. I waste away my well-
earned wages in a house share with other young professionals
where I assumed we'd all hang around a lot and drink coffee,
like *Friends* but not. Instead, we fight over cheese and the
whereabouts of all the teaspoons. Ed lives alone in a newbuild
flat where he personally hoovers the communal staircases. It's
tidy, grown-up and everything has a place, from the thriving
houseplants to the books and Kandinsky prints hanging on the
wall. I hang bras off my radiators.

Ed does have one very lovely housemate though, who makes
his way towards me now.

'Nigel!' I say, picking him up as he nestles his feline face
next to mine. 'How you doing, kitty cat?'

Naturally, Nigel doesn't reply but I will admit that I've
always rated Ed in how much he loves this cat and invests in
quality toys and premium treats for him. I put him down and he
slinks off to Ed who carries him and rubs his belly, making him
purr.

'See? You are good with pussy!' I say.

'You're funny,' he says flatly, trying to hide the fact he finds
me completely hilarious.

He's mopped, hasn't he? Bless him. I get an even bigger
surprise when I turn the corner to his open-plan kitchen and see
the table laid with glassware, a candle in the middle of the table.
I try to hold back my smile. He puts the bag on the countertop,
getting out all the containers and noisily sifting through his
cutlery drawer, swearing a little at not being able to find his
chopsticks. I eye him curiously.

'You seem extremely nervous. Did you think we were
having sex tonight?'

'Maybe? I don't know! I just wanted to be ready... just in
case...'

'...I jumped you?' He laughs but I still see his hand shaking as he removes the covers from the takeaway lids. 'I'm not a jungle cat, I'm not going to just pounce on you and de-sex you. You watch too much Planet Earth,' I joke.

I look at him; his body is tense, his eyes are scanning the room, as if he doesn't really know what he's doing. I go over to the counter, removing his gripped hands from the side and wrap my arms around his tense, arrow-straight body. It's how I'd imagine people at Greenpeace feel when they're hugging trees.

'Eduardo. Relax, hug me back.'

He puts his arms around me and pats my back, like one would an old aunt. Warm citrus tones let me know he's showered thoroughly and spritzed with some aftershave, too. This man is really all about the prep.

'Thank you for making an effort. I don't think anyone's lit a candle for me before,' I say, as his body softens and relents against mine.

'It's an LED tealight...'

'I like that you're trying to create ambience.'

'I bought incense, too. Shall I light incense?'

'No. I also don't want to sit across a table from you like we're in a restaurant.'

'If this was going to happen, I just wanted to make it special.'

'For you?' I realise that maybe I haven't thought this through properly. Maybe I was being a little remiss in thinking he wanted to take away more from this given it's his first time. It's a memory to preserve for the ages. He might want to add some romance to the situation.

'For you,' he adds. 'I wanted to be respectful. I don't want you to think I'm just using you.'

I laugh and melt at the same time. This is also Ed, thoughtful with deep kind layers. It's having a terrible day at work and him leaving a Snickers on your desk or coming to pick you up in his car because it's raining, and he knows you're trying to cart home five classes of exercise books.

'Thank you, but seriously, I don't need this. Do you also have Bruno Mars lined up on Alexa?'

He freezes for a moment.

'YOU DO!'

'Marvin Gaye.'

'ED!' He leans against the counter with his head in his hands. 'Ed, I will tell you now, it's very unlikely we'll be having sex tonight.'

'Because of the suit? The LED candle?' he questions, slightly disappointed.

'I know I agreed to all of this, but I thought we were just going to eat Singapore noodles and watch some *Star Wars* tonight. I didn't think we were going to multitask. In any case, I haven't prepared.'

'Prepared?' he asks me, eyes wide.

'For a lady, there is shaving to do and hair to wash. Even I have my standards. I don't need to scare you off for the first time when you see the state of my...'

'Wookiee?' he asks.

'That's a *Star Wars* reference! See? We're both learning!' I put my hand up and he high-fives it reluctantly.

'Ed. When this happens, I don't need to be dated. I don't need you feeling nervous and weird around me either,' I say, placing a hand on his shoulder to reassure him.

'I don't. This is just different. You usually come round here for beer and pizza.'

'I'll be doing different things with the pepperoni this time, that's all,' I joke, making an action with my hands that makes him take pause.

'Stop talking like that, it's scaring me,' he says, half-crying, half-laughing.

'Yes, I come here for pizza, and we put on a film, and I usually drink one too many beers and fall asleep on your sofa, drool into the cushions and you leave me there, sometimes throw a blanket over me and pop a bin next to me in case I need to throw up.'

'This is a romantic image,' he jests, starting to dish out the rice from the takeaway containers.

'Ed...' I tell him, standing close beside him, resting my head on his shoulder. 'It's still me. Mia. You don't have to prove anything to me today. You've seen it all when it comes to me.'

'Well, not everything,' Ed corrects me.

This is true and perhaps a barrier that is making Ed nervous, so, to prove a point, I stand there in Ed's kitchen and take off my hoodie and t-shirt in one fell swoop. I then reach around to unclasp my bra. This way he'll see that beneath it all, I'm literally skin, bones, organs and a touch of cellulite. Ed immediately averts his eyes as I whip them out. I sense Nigel the cat in the corner of the kitchen, confused as fuck, thinking this isn't what you usually do when you come round on a Wednesday.

'It's not the sun, Ed. Look at my boobs.'

He does. I thought I'd seen Ed blush before now. I was wrong. If the whites of his eyes could blush now, they would.

'You have your breasts out in my kitchen,' he states plainly, his palms upturned.

'Is this a hygiene issue? Like the shoes?'

'No, but... my curtains are open.' He points towards the window and a flat across the way where an Asian family seem to be enjoying a quiz show on the television. And the sight of my bare breasts.

ED

I've seen breasts before. Naturally, in films and porn and in art museums where you can't turn a corner without some Titian nipples in your face, but Mia's are the first I've seen in the flesh. It's not that I hadn't noticed Mia's boobs before (she sometimes goes a little too low-cut in the summer), but I hadn't really anticipated seeing them in my kitchen or her to be so comfortable with whipping them out whilst our takeaway sat there getting cold. Pretty sure my neighbours hadn't anticipated seeing them either.

Had I planned the night? In my head, yes. I thought sex would be an add-on to our regular takeaway evening given that there was time and opportunity and space. I anticipated that she would have turned up in a dress perhaps, with trainers as I know she can't walk in heels, and we'd have had a lovely candlelit takeaway and then made a quiet sojourn hand-in-hand to the bedroom where we would have had the opportunity to indulge in some quiet yet sensitive first-time lovemaking.

'WATCH ME FLIP THIS PRAWN CRACKER IN MY MOUTH!'

I forgot, though, that this is Mia.

As soon as I saw the aghast faces of my neighbours through the window, I tried to cover her up with an oven glove and I realised that everything I'd planned in terms of creating a mood and wooing her was a bad idea. So, I changed out of my suit into jeans, I didn't burn anything with a fragrance, we migrated the takeaway to the sofa.

'That's very good, you're like a seal,' I say, clapping.

This is not romance. I'm not sure what this is or, indeed, where it is going.

'You really should try this tofu,' she tells me. 'It's very good.'

I watch as she piles her Szechuan tofu high, raking through her rice with her fork. Whereas having sex with Mia is all I can think about, she seems unbelievably chilled around me. Nothing fazes her, does it? I just want to get to the point where I'm not preoccupied by the thought, where it no longer becomes the elephant in the room. All I know is that it won't be tonight.

'So, I just want to be sure. If not tonight, shall we maybe put a date in the calendar for our...'

'Grand de-virgining?' Mia jokes, laughing so hard at her own joke that she chokes a little. 'Are we seriously diarising this? Well, the weekend is a no-go – I'm out with Beth and then a birthday lunch with my family.'

I look at her curiously, knowing my social life mainly involves running on my own and then meeting Henry from Geography online so we can play *Call of Duty*.

'Next Wednesday, after work?' she suggests like a doctor's receptionist. 'Gives us both time to prepare.'

I nod blankly though in the back of my mind wonder what sort of state her pubic hair is in that it will take one week to tame. A week's time it is. I don't know if that's a good or bad thing. In a week's time, I won't be a virgin. I don't know how to process that. My mind races with a million and one questions.

'Well, we've sorted that much. Can I ask you something?' I say, picking up some noodles with my chopsticks.

'Shoot.'

'When did you lose your virginity? I'm sorry if that's a personal question,' I spurt out.

'Ed, you've seen my boobs. We have no secrets now. I was sixteen. I was dating a lad called Toby at school and we did it after school one day when his parents were both still at work.'

'Do you still keep in touch with Toby?'

She laughs under her breath. 'That would be a no. I don't think we were destined to be together. He still lives locally and last time I stalked him on Facebook, he was an electrician.'

'You stalk him?'

She wobbles her head from side to side. 'It's a turn of

phrase. I can't speak for all women but sometimes I do get drunk and search for people to check in on them.'

'That's...'

'Sad and desperate, I know. It wasn't hugely special. He had a massive poster of Lewis Hamilton on his wall and all the sex we had afterwards, he kept making "vroom vroom" noises, every time he thrust into me.' She relates this detail so casually, shovelling food into her face at the same time. I'm not sure how it's possible to be able to see her back teeth while she does this.

'Really?' I reply, cackling.

'Ed, the first thing you need to know is beyond the mechanics of sex, people are into their things. I don't sex shame, but I feel I've met a number of them in my lifetime.'

'When you say number...?' I ask, an eyebrow slightly raised.

'I've slept with about twenty people, Ed.' Again, this is a fact she relays to me quite coolly, not bragging in any way but just stating the facts like her height or weight. 'It's just sex. When I was younger, it was certainly something I did to keep up with my peers but once you work out your pleasure, what gets you off, it can be... fun...'

I feel like I'm miles away from the fun stage of sex yet. 'Twenty is a respectable number,' I tell her.

'Did you think it was higher?' she asks, her eyes reading cheeky as opposed to insulted.

'You talk a lot about sex and relationships to me, so I didn't know what to think,' I reply diplomatically.

'I get tested regularly, too, in case you were wondering.'

'I wasn't.'

She widens her eyes at me because she knows that's a small white lie. I am conscious about my health and she eats very messily so I worry. She doesn't even use a napkin. I watch her settle into my sofa, curling her feet up so that they're wedged against me, remnants of satsuma nail polish on her toenails.

'So, my turn to ask some questions. When you say you haven't had sex...' she enquires. 'Have you ever seen a vagina?'

I inhale sharply. 'You mean a vulva?'

'OK, Mr Biology,' she replies, giggling. 'Seriously, have you ever seen a snatch?'

'In real life, no. Please don't whip yours out now while we're eating,' I say, putting a hand in the air.

She grins, spring onion caught in her teeth. 'Have you used a fleshlight or a sex toy?'

My blank looks tell her everything she needs to know, so she gets her phone out and goes to a sex toy website 'The Love Shack' to show me. 'You can buy objects that resemble vulvic parts and you can stick your dong in them and get yourself off.'

'But they're not attached to anything. Do you hold them, or what?' I say, confused, also wondering about the cleaning involved.

'They have suction cups.'

'Well, that's only useful if you have a hard floor. What if you have carpets?' I ask practically.

'Then you attach it to the wall? You don't have carpet on your wall.'

I frown, trying to work out those angles, and scroll through the website, gulping physically at the paraphernalia on sale. This is a bookmarked website. There will be extras? I didn't even think those would be necessary. If this evening had escalated to sex, all I have in my room are fresh sheets and a box of Durex.

Mia glances at my face and looks concerned. 'Ed, you've gone pale. Don't look at that website in too much detail. Your eyes will pop out of their sockets. You really haven't got much experience, eh?'

'I just never really hung out with girls at school and then at university, I didn't really put myself out there.'

'Obviously. Do you wank?'

Crikey, Mia. I wind an extraordinarily large amount of noodles on to my fork, more than the fork can handle.

'Yes.'

'Why are you nervous telling me about wanking?'

'It feels a little sad that it's the length and breadth of my experience.'

'Ed, I wank nearly every night or I can't get to sleep. How do you get off? Tell me.'

I stare back at her, part of me wishing we could go back in time when she would just ask me questions about the school photocopier and take my crisps.

'Because having sex is also about pleasure,' she says. 'It's not a dirty word and it's something you should enjoy. You keep blushing. Tell me how you get off. Now!'

'I use lotion!' I snap back at her.

'Good. I get off by stimulating my clitoris.'

'I have questions about that,' I say with trepidation.

'About where it is?'

'About how you operate it.'

Mia smiles. I shrug in apology. I've referred to her clitoris like a kitchen appliance. She puts her plate down. 'Ed, do you have a mouse?'

'For the cat?' I ask, alarmed at the direction this conversation is going.

'No, a computer mouse.' She seems slightly worried that I misconstrued that completely.

I nod and head over to my desk in the corner of the room to retrieve one, handing it over to her.

'This little button bit in the middle. The lightest of touches, small circles,' she says, showing me. 'Don't press too hard. Here, try.' She presents the mouse to me on the palm of her hand.

I do as I'm told as she watches me. 'But it's easy on a mouse, how will I know if I'm pressing too hard?'

'I'll tell you. That's good. How's your kissing? How many girls have you kissed?' she asks.

'Three.'

'Details?'

'A girl at school, we were on a trip to the Isle of Wight, and I think she just wanted to see what it was like. A girl in sixth form who was drunk, and I nearly lost my virginity at university but that never happened in the end.'

'Because...?'

'It just didn't...' I say, my voice trailing off to bring that trauma into full view. 'We got naked and then I got the johnny stuck in a fan and then...'

Mia's eyes widen. 'For the love of fuck, is that why you're a virgin? Did a fan take off your tip?' she says, recoiling in shock.

'No. I still have a penis. It was just a... comedy of errors. But three girls. I've kissed three. Why are you looking at me like that? You look like you're pitying me.'

'I am not. I just... You've just been slow off the blocks. Let's bring you back up to speed.' She takes my plate of noodles from my lap and puts them down on my coffee table. She then tucks her hair behind her ear, taking a deep breath, then leans into me, putting a hand to my cheek, slowly drawing my face in to hers until our lips touch. I close my eyes, mainly because that's what I think the accepted protocol is in that situation, but her lips feel soft, her breath warm – although that could be because she's eating Szechuan tofu. Her lips move against mine and I feel something released inside of me like a breath, exhaled. I put a hand to her face as she moves away from me.

'Now you've kissed four,' she whispers. 'Your eyes are still closed.'

I open them, my mouth suddenly dry. My hand is still gently against her face. I pull it back and reach for a swig of beer.

'You could have warned me,' I mutter. 'I could have had a spring roll in my mouth, I could have choked.'

'Where's the fun in that?' She smiles.

I smile back. She reaches over me to grab at the remote control.

'Less kissing, more noodles. Once the film is over, I'll let you feel a boob. Let's ease you in gently.'

'You've obviously seen the size of me,' I joke in a deadpan voice.

'ED! You made a sex joke!' she says proudly, eyeballing me. 'We'll get there.'

SIX

Spotify Playlist: Ed's Music

Oh, my deary me. I scroll through the playlist that Ed has sent me and scrunch up my face at the choices on there. What on earth? It feels like the playlist of a fifty-year-old man who listens to Magic and likes a trip to the supermarket to see what's new in cheese. There are some soul classics in there, I would never query the presence of Fleetwood Mac, but otherwise, it is not sexy. I'm on the Tube and actually hide my phone from Beth, next to me, and her sister Lucy, who's standing beside us and has a dangerously good vantage point. I can't have her think this is mine.

What is this? What have you just sent me?

It's my work and car compilation.

It's like you want my ears to bleed. You like Taylor Swift?

She's a quality songwriter. She's won Grammys.

Are you a twenty-year-old woman in a floaty dress holding an oat milk latte?

No, I am not, and you know this.

Ed sends me a GIF of Taylor Swift that I hope he doesn't have saved to his phone. Whilst I don't want to change who he is, I am trying to research the man behind the virgin. What is he into? Why is he possibly still a virgin? His music choices give me some insight into this.

Like what do you dance to? This is all very pedestrian.

I don't dance.

Everyone dances. When you're in the kitchen on your own or when you're happy, you must dance.

I don't dance. When I am happy, I smile, like most humans. You use any opportunity to dance.

Because it's a form of emotional release and expression. I am going to send you one of my playlists and I want you to dance. To reconnect to your body, to let go. Dancing is pretty much sex standing up.

Well, that's a biological impossibility for a start. You can't get pregnant from dancing.

You've obviously never watched videos of Prince. I want you to try and dance.

Or not. People don't need to see that.

Or come out with me now. I'm with Beth, we're going dancing.

No. But say hello to Beth for me.

You're not a very good student, are you? Sharing my playlist now, you boring sod. That's your homework before next Wednesday.

He doesn't reply. Before next Wednesday, when, to set his mind at ease, we've agreed to have sex. I say agree, Ed's put it in his calendar and linked it to mine just in case I forget. He originally named the event 'Dinner with Mia' but then gets angry when I keep editing it to a line of cherry emojis.

'New boyfriend?' Beth asks me, trying to see my conversation as the Tube pulls to a stop at Covent Garden. I pull my phone away. I like outside-of-work-Beth. She likes a big earring and a bright trainer, and she also has some contact in the music business so always has concert/event tickets and, because she sees me most days, I'm the one that gets asked to come along.

'Nosy... No, just Ed. He says hello. I asked him to come along tonight.'

Beth laughs so hard, a man opposite crumples up his newspaper. She puts a hand to her mouth. 'I'm so sorry, I shouldn't laugh.'

'What are we laughing about?' asks Lucy, hanging onto the handrails. I've never met Lucy before tonight but there's an audacity there in the length of her skirt and the size of her bucket hat. Beth comes from some long line of sisters that have been introduced to me via staffroom anecdotes. I don't think this one is the divorced heart surgeon or the widowed accountant so she must be the one who does children's parties dressed as Elsa from *Frozen*.

'This teacher we both know. Mia was going to invite him along. Let's just say he'd stick out like a sore thumb.'

He would but I do feel compelled to defend my well-ironed, Taylor Swift-loving Ed. 'He's a nice bloke, he just... He's very buttoned up, right to the top, you know?' I add.

Lucy looks intrigued. 'He doesn't have an alter ego? He might have a serious work face but could be into different shit when he's at home. I once did night shifts in a supermarket and there was a bloke who liked a spreadsheet but turns out he would go home and let his wife walk him round the front room on a leash...'

The man with the newspaper opposite looks up. No article will now compare with our conversation. I smile, knowing that Ed wouldn't know what to do with a leash. He'd be calling out for the dog he thought it belonged to.

'No, just a bit vanilla. Not even vanilla. What's one level below vanilla?'

'Natural yoghurt?' Beth says.

Lucy laughs so hard I worry it might stop the train.

'But how do you teach someone like that to let go?' I ask these girls, curious for their input.

'Baby steps?' Beth tells me. 'We're about to go to a club classics night with about two thousand people, he'd drown. Maybe take him to a bar, few drinks... Are you worried about him?' she asks.

'No. Just... I don't think he has a lot of fun in his life.'

Don't tell these girls, one of whom you've only just met, that he's a virgin. He just doesn't have fun in general. He takes his life and work so seriously, too seriously, and before it was something to rib him about. Now, I fear he doesn't enjoy his life, that he's never really let go and it feels like my life's mission to at least help him achieve that, whether that be sexually or not. Maybe it starts with a dance. Or a date with Lucy here who I feel is all about the fun. Maybe I should introduce her to Ed. That could be a thing, though would possibly be like two planets colliding.

'But Ed does have you,' Beth tells me. 'And I think you're fun.' This is so very true. The Tube rolls into our station and we disembark from the train, Lucy going through her purse to pass me a mini bottle of vodka. Maybe not the legal or done thing to be doing in public but I'm past caring. And I like a girl who carries travel alcohol. I watch her walk ahead of me, linking an arm through Beth's, and feel a sudden twinge of sadness at how the dynamic is very different to the one I have with my sisters who I'm lunching with tomorrow. These two share raucous family in-jokes, they're ride-or-dies. It actually seems that they like each other. I don't think my sisters even know my middle name.

'So, ladies, I managed to get VIP passes for all of us,' Beth explains, turning to me, as we traverse ourselves around quite the crowded platform, everyone I assume to be headed in the same direction from the buzz and the clubbing outfits. 'Just behave yourself,' she says, pointing to her sister. I raise an eyebrow and Lucy laughs and winks back. We come to a stop as the sheer volume of people causes a bottleneck at the bottom of the escalators. It's then we hear it. Music. Usually in Tube stations, the music comes from buskers, but the beat is heavy with this one. Lucy and I turn around to see a man stood by the wall with a wearable mixing desk. He's dressed in a vintage shell suit, with a visor, clashing trainers, a whistle in his mouth, there are lights and sweat bands and despite the probably very heavy load, this man is ready to take on this Underground station, on his own until the place throbs with his beats. He feels like the human opposite of Ed.

'ARE WE READY, LONDON?!' he shouts.

'FUCK, YEAH!' Lucy screams at him, abandoning the escalator, and I see Beth's eyes close for a second given that there are also children in the vicinity.

'LET'S GOOOOO!' And with that the beat drops. It's Lucy who starts jumping and for a moment, everyone who was planning to get out of here starts joining in; it's the pre-party and it's free. Fuelled by my mini vodka, I may very well get down. Hell, it's a Saturday night in my favourite city and I've danced in worse places. It's not a practised dance style that I have but by God, I love that my shoulders always find that beat first before my feet, until the song reverbs to my neck and hips. I'm wearing my favourite dance outfit, too; a gold skirt that makes me look a little like a Quality Street, but I pair it with a vintage T-shirt and matching Gold Converse. They're my happy clothes and as I put two arms into the air something makes me lose control of my limbs on those tiles. I think it might be joy. I glance over at Lucy who has one arm around her sister's neck, the other pointing in the air as she sings along.

'EVERYBODY DANCE NOW!' It's the most classic of club classics and she looks at me, pointing her fingers, and sings along.

'I'm so sorry,' a man beside me says as his arm flies into me but I don't think I care. I look him up and down and smile, watching him dance along with his mates.

'What's your name?' he asks me.

'Mia.'

'Howard.'

'Ouch, sorry about that...'

He laughs, for which I'm thankful. Is he good looking? Good hair. It's a bit scruffy, and I like the smattering of facial hair, the polo shirt I could do without but he's dancing and that's excellent. I see Lucy stick her tongue out at me to see I may have already pulled before we've even got to the concert.

'Are you headed to the Club Classics gig?' he asks me.

'Yeah,' I say, trying to play it coy.

'Well, that is good,' he says, grinning.

'Really?' I reply, laughing.

ED

People are not kind about Taylor Swift, but I think people forget that sometimes simple melodies with happy undertones are all that's needed. I am a fan. Not that I have her poster on my wall, but I'll happily listen to her songs in my car and sometimes I may also sing along. She's also very pretty but if we ended up together, she'd probably write a song about me. I can imagine the lyrics now. She could rhyme virgin with urging. I think about what Mia said to me yesterday. She set me actual homework ahead of our sex date next week. Our sex date. I need a better way to describe this but as you can imagine, I am a mixture of anxiety, nausea and paranoia. What should I wear? Should I eat more protein in the days leading up to it? Is there something I should read? Maybe I should do the homework she set me then, shouldn't I? I should prepare myself within an inch of my being so nothing can go wrong, and I can't humiliate myself in front of Mia.

So, as I prepare my vegetables for Sunday lunch, I do the unthinkable.

'Alexa, bring up Mia's Music playlist on Spotify.'

Playing Mia's Music on Spotify.

She's sending me noise, isn't she? I feel that her taste is noise with no lyrics and a healthy beat, but I'm strangely surprised that the first song that comes up is *Sir Duke* by Stevie Wonder. This is clever because this song is hugely recognisable, and you have to be some sort of evil entity to not be a fan of Stevie Wonder. Even I know this song. I top and tail some French beans. She asked me if I danced in my kitchen. I've never really felt the need but maybe this is where it starts. I need to do the prep. Will she know if I haven't danced? Do I need to film myself as proof? My hands otherwise occupied, I side step. I feel like I'm in the middle of a dancefloor at a wedding. Hips. Maybe if I sway them. Front to back or side to side? Side to side feels the safer option. I put my knife down and start clicking my fingers. I'm reminded of a scene from *Footloose*. I need to channel Kevin Bacon. The clicking feels wrong. I feel like someone's dad. I don't think this is how you should dance, and this is confirmed by the fact Nigel leaves the room to not have to witness it anymore. This is why Taylor Swift is the right choice for someone like me.

The doorbell goes, like some divine intervention, and I go to answer it.

'EDDIE!'

'Mum...?' I smile. It could be my mum, but her face is covered by a lot of foliage. She peers around it and brushes leaves out of her mouth. 'You brought me a...'

'Fern. It's been looking sad in my house, I think I'm overwatering it. I was hoping you might bring it back to life. His name is Leonard.'

Yes, she is my mother and yes, she names her houseplants. Her relationship with them is such that when she goes on holiday and I have to water them, she'll send me messages and ask about them, by name. I take 'Leonard' and she ushers me inside the house, embracing me in her usual, all-encompassing way.

'Something smells good?'

'Pork loin,' I say, taking her large fur-trimmed raincoat.

She stops to listen to the music. 'Are you also listening to disco? Are you ill?' she says, putting a hand to my forehead.

As we go into the kitchen, I hear that Stevie Wonder has turned into *You Make Me Feel* (*Mighty Real*) by Sylvester which is a brave jump for which I don't think my hips are quite ready. But I like that Mia thought it possible.

'It was some random playlist. Alexa, play Fleetwood Mac, *Rumours*.' And my mum smiles. This album, as majestic as it is, was the soundtrack to my childhood. It brings back memories of my mum dancing around our living room, telling me that she and Stevie Nicks were kindred spirits in their shared heartbreak.

'So, how have you been?' I ask her as she links her arm into mine and inspects what's cooking.

'I am good. I'm off to march later this afternoon.'

'What are you protesting today?'

'Fucking fracking.'

'I hope you wrote that on your placard,' I tell her as I busy myself over the stove. She opens up a cupboard and finds a wine glass, helping herself to the Pinot Grigio on the counter. It's a well-rehearsed Sunday lunch routine that we indulge in once a month, one that I won't mind saying I look forward to. Mum does what she does and starts sifting through random mail on my countertops.

'You are welcome to join us? We'll start at Pall Mall,' she says to me.

'I have marking to do. I'm sorry... Rain check?'

The fact is, I finished all my marking last night while I binge watched a new sci-fi space show on Prime, but I rarely commit to these rallies because I can't quite handle everyone's collective anger. Last time I went, an old lady screamed in my face and I believe that's how I got flu and had to take a week off work.

'Just be safe,' I tell her.

'I will, my lovely. I also need to introduce you to Mo.'

'Is Mo a new houseplant?' I ask tentatively.

'No, silly. Remember I went on that protest about the new high-speed train tracks and the badgers?' I nod. I remember it well. She bought a badger onesie for that rally. She was featured in the local newspaper and framed the article for her living room. 'He was there and we've struck up a friendship...'

I stop peeling veg to catch her eye. 'You have a boyfriend?'

'Possibly.' She pauses, looking unsure how much to share with me. She forgets I'm not a child anymore. I can partake in these grown-up conversations. 'He's got a ponytail.'

I don't know how to reply to that. A stubby one or is it free-flowing? With a bald patch or without? It's the difference between a rugged cowboy and a stage hypnotist. Mum stands there with her glass, awaiting my reaction. It's always been just her. My dad left when I was five, when I was too young to really remember him or want to try and track him down as an adult. Mum had dalliances with a few men but no one serious, no one who imprinted themselves into my consciousness but the news that someone is on the scene will always pique my interest. That I may one day have a stepdad. With a ponytail.

'Well, as long as you're happy,' I tell her.

'Happiness is a state of mind, it's not related to whether I validate my existence via another individual,' she tells me. I drop my green beans into a pan of hot water. That was always an important life lesson learned from my mother. She hated the idea of dependency, she had lived what she thought was the ideal and the norm – a husband and baby – but when that didn't work out for her, she was perfectly fine in her own company. I frown, thinking about this now. Is this why I'm a virgin – because I thought I was fine being self-sufficient? The oven timer gets my attention and I open the door carefully.

'For me happiness is one of your roast potatoes,' she tells me. I smile and take the pan out, scraping the outside of one of my potatoes for the full ASMR effect and hand it to her. 'If I achieve nothing more in life, I will always take credit for the fact I raised a man who learned how to roast a potato. Do I also spy a crumble?'

'Rhubarb, pear and ginger. At least if you get arrested at your rally, you'll be well sustained before I have to come and bail you out.'

She smiles and nibbles on her roast potato, swaying to *Dreams* by Fleetwood Mac. She always did this when I was growing up; she liked a twirl and always had a freedom in how she listened to music. I wonder why it didn't catch on. Maybe my mum knows?

'I have a question...'

'Shoot.'

'Do you ever remember me dancing? When I was little?'

She seems perplexed by the question before snapping her fingers to recollect a moment. 'I remember you dancing at your cousin Lorna's wedding,' she says. 'You were eight. You had a little waistcoat on, it was tartan and very sweet. Someone took a video of you dancing to ABBA.'

I'm delighted that's been immortalised somewhere, my only ever dance experience. 'But I'm not really a dancer, am I? In general. Is that weird?' I ask.

'You just weren't that sort of child. You were serious, you expressed yourself in different ways.'

'Like?'

'You read books, you liked running, you went through a phase of making your own badges...'

Nice. 'But never dancing?' I ask her, taking my pork out of its foil jacket and getting ready to carve it.

'Have you been watching all those dance shows on the television? Is this some quarter-life crisis where you think you might like to learn?' she asks me, confused. 'I think you'd be quite good at tap...'

'No,' I laugh. 'I was just thinking that maybe I don't dance enough. In life.'

'Didn't you go clubbing at university, attend graduation balls?'

'No, I'm a beer-cradling, wallflower sort.'

'What about when you hoover?' she asks me, getting plates out and topping up her wine.

'You dance when you hoover?' She gives me a look and I remember – of course she did. She used to wear earphones and dance like the spirit of Freddie Mercury had taken over her soul. It's a good memory. I listen to podcasts when I hoover. We are very, very different humans, bonded by a shared eye colour and a love of roast potatoes.

'Where has all this introspection come from, Ed? Did you want to have a disco break before lunch?' she says, her shoulders shrugging into action. She takes my hands and pulls me into the middle of the kitchen. Mum's dance style is contemporary dance twirling mode and I attempt to bob along. I can see she's clenching her mouth to stop herself laughing. I stop dancing.

'Are you pumping water?' she asks.

'I hate you.' I return to stirring my gravy.

This doesn't dissuade my mother who just dances on her own, in my kitchen, not really caring if her movements match the rhythm and beat at all. 'The world is full of different people, Ed. You dance when you're ready. Take your time,' she says, looking me in the eye.

'What do you mean?' I ask her apprehensively.

'If you haven't danced before then it's absolutely fine.'

I stop and stare at her. She knows I'm a virgin, doesn't she? My own mother. She keeps swaying and spinning to the mighty Fleetwood Mac. I return to stirring my gravy.

SEVEN

MIA

'AUNTY MIA!' A herd of very little people run in my direction, and I bundle them into my arms, kissing their foreheads, loving that noise of them being so excited to see me. I will admit, I like to be surprised in life, but nothing surprised me more than how much my heart would grow to love my nieces and nephews so very much.

'You're late!' my niece Bella tells me. Bella has the most perfect bob I've ever seen on a child. I love smoothing it down with my hands and squeezing her cheeks. I am late because that's generally how I roll for social occasions given that I am a teacher and my timekeeping is usually governed by a very loud school bell. However, this does not impress my sisters much. My dear older sisters who are always on time, who always look like they've not done their make-up on the Tube. I try to steady my breathing, so it looks like I haven't run here to this smart, North London brasserie for my sister's birthday lunch. Not even run from my own house. I've run from Beth's house where

Lucy and I fell asleep in the bathtub and atop the kitchen table respectively, after a night of dancing, drinking and snogging strangers called Howard. I may have slept. I can't remember.

'How mad are your mums? Like on a scale of one to ten?' I ask as I bend down pretending to still greet them, trying to avoid the side-eye from the other side of the restaurant.

'A strong seven,' Florence whispers to me, giggling.

'They've been calling you bad names,' adds her brother, Felix.

'Felix, they've been doing that for years. I'm used to it. I like the new haircut, kiddo,' I say, ruffling his blond curls.

Bella winds her body under my arm and I spin her, making her dress float up in a cascade of giggles. 'Again?' she asks me.

'Not now, Bells – we're eating... Mia...' Rachel says from the table. In my head, all I hear is Mum telling me off for having my elbows on the table. In certain lights, she even looks like her reincarnated, from the sensible knitwear to the crow's feet forming around her eyes. She glares at me with her angular mum bob, same chestnut colour as mine but sleek and straightened as opposed to my hair that looks like nesting material for a small pet.

'Sister, how goes it?' I say, going up to her and clawing an arm around her.

'You're half an hour late. We ordered without you. You know, the kids...' she says snootily, like I don't know that kids also, like us, eat.

'That's cool. I'll just share Bruce's lunch, won't I?' I say, putting an arm around my five-year-old nephew. 'Can I have one of your potatoes?' I joke. Bruce giggles.

'Did you get lost?' asks Alison, my other sister. Alison is less like Mum with her long blonde hair and sharp features but every sentence from her feels like it's steeped in residual anger. It's as if she's still angry with me for the time I stole her

favourite hoodie and left it on a bus, or the time I tried a complicated breakdancing move at her wedding, despite not knowing
how to breakdance, that left me with a bloody nose and a brides-
maid's dress she couldn't re-sell.

'The trains were messed up, that's all. Happy birthday by
the way,' I say, trying to defuse the tension by handing over my
gift to her. 'You're, what, thirty-five now?'

'Thirty-three!' she says, so loudly that an old lady on the
table next to us drops a fork. She fake smiles at me and takes the
gift bag, rifling through it, examining the contents and then
sliding it back in the bag. Charming. I spent a lot of time
running into that corner shop and picking out that wine. It's
Bulgaria's finest. I watch as she puts the bag on the floor and
then goes back to a conversation she was having with my
brother-in-law. I hear the words pension and investments and
feel my soul leave my body. I know where I belong today. I
belong at the kids' end of the table with the crayons because
they think that's the level of my IQ. I know I'm the youngest of
three but still. As much as I love this little lot dearly, they're not
good for achy hangovers. I sit down next to Florence and kiss
the top of her head.

'What are we doing?' I whisper to her.

'We're doing a food wordsearch,' she tells me, brandishing a
green crayon.

'You know when I was little, your granny used to draw
squares around the letters to make rude words.'

'How rude?'

I get an orange crayon and find P, O and O.

She giggles. 'Granny sounds fun.'

I look into little Florence's eyes, catching a glimpse perhaps
of my mum in there. 'She was... super fun.' And possibly the
glue that held us three sisters together, who connected us all.
Without her, I've always felt like the imposter.

'Who was having the chicken?' A waitress suddenly appears next to me, nestling plates across her arm, and little Felix puts his hand in the air. That Yorkshire pudding is as big as his face so he will definitely be sharing with aunty. The waitress clocks me.

'Oh, were you the latecomer? They ordered you some breaded mushrooms,' she says, putting a plate of deep-fried objects in front of me with a jar of mayonnaise. I've eaten worse but I'll definitely have to steal a five-year-old's roast potato now.

'Just the mushrooms?' I ask Alison.

'It's a Sunday lunch. Plus, we didn't know if you were going to show up and if you didn't, no one wanted to be lumbered with the nut wellington,' she says through gritted teeth.

I love how I've been a vegetarian since my late teens and still none of my sisters know how to deal with it. Rachel's the worst. At her wedding, all I got was soup and a bread roll. Bitch even made me wear mint. I looked like toothpaste.

'I did say I was coming. I texted,' I tell Alison.

'Yeah... but...'

'You're a liability,' Bella informs me.

'Bells! What did we say about repeating adult conversations?' her mother says in admonishing tones. I put my hand in my niece's to see her cheeks redden, her eyes glass over.

'What else did she say about me, Bella?' I ask her, picking at one of her carrots.

'You have zero responsibility, and you need to sort your life out,' Florence adds.

Yes, kids' end of the table assemble and unite. I glare towards the other end, where they all share a nice Merlot with their roast beef, having already grazed on olives and bread. Both my sisters married in their mid-twenties to men who I frequently mistake for each other given they are so bland. One is Gareth, one is Greg, and I buy both of them socks at

Christmas because neither of them have revealed anything to me by way of a personality. I see why they sit me at the kids' end of the table now. I am here to save their children in case they ever get caught in their fun vacuum.

'Well, it is true,' Rachel mutters out the side of her mouth. Alison titters in response.

'So, I'm late for your birthday and suddenly it's my whole life that's the problem?' I question.

'You're always late, for everything...'

'I see you once a month, Rach. How are you constantly aware of my timekeeping?'

'But look at you... What are you wearing, for a start?' Rachel asks me. 'You're in a gold pleated skirt, a cropped band T-shirt that I know you've had since university, and Converse. You look like a student.'

Yes, I went to a concert last night and woke up in a mate's house using an actual plate as a pillow, but I don't really see her point. I see her looking around this white linen-lined posh brasserie/restaurant, almost apologising to the other customers for me. *I'm so sorry she's lowering the tone, we had to invite her, she's "family."*

'Rach, I'm twenty-eight. It's gold, it's a party colour,' I say, posing to make the little ones giggle.

'I like it,' replies Florence and I give her a high-five.

'You should inject a bit of colour into your life. It's your birthday, Ali, and that dress looks like a granite driveway.'

'It's Ralph Lauren,' she says down her nose to me.

'I don't know what that means,' I retort.

'Rachel, she's doing it again...' she complains.

'Doing what?'

'Being a smart arse.'

The husbands sit there, tucking into their roasts, having been party to this drama for a number of years so they know

when to butt out. However, you see the fascination in the kids'
eyes, the want to know more, to see who will win this fight.
Rachel's lips pucker into a moody pout. Since our mum passed
six years ago, she's taken it upon herself to be a parent to me.
But maybe I didn't need one. My sisters married quickly after
her passing, almost as a response to not having a family
anymore, so they could build their own. I did the opposite. No
one should die at forty-nine. I saw it all so clearly. I wanted the
opposite to my sisters. I looked to live instead.

'Mummy, you said arse was swearing,' Bella says, looking
sternly at her mother.

I sit there smiling, biting into one of my mushrooms.

'I did but there are exceptions to that rule,' she says, sawing
away at her beef, looking up at Rachel and laughing while the
children sit there confused. I hope that beef gets stuck somewhere about her person.

'Better a smart arse than a frigid witch,' I mumble under my
breath.

'What was that?' Rachel asks me.

'Nothing, just a hot mushroom,' I say, puffing out my
cheeks. My fake blowing makes Bruce laugh and I like an audience so do it again. Again, a look. Just sit there and eat your food
and blend into this very bland, middle-class establishment. So I
am not allowed to gargle the gravy? Throw knives? Juggle the
children? OK then. I push my chair back and my sisters eye me,
looking panicked just in case I'm going to make a speech or sing.

'I'm going to have a wee,' I announce to the table, instantly
knowing I should have phrased that differently. 'Any little
people need a wee? We can all go together?' There are more
laughs and eye rolls as I leave the table. Do I need a wee? No,
but I need to take a breath. I grab my handbag and swerve my
way around other tables and waiters to the toilets. Inside, I go
into a cubicle, take a seat and put my head in my hands. I think
back to a night of dancing with two sisters who were the

complete opposite to the witches out there. Sisters who drank
and danced into the night and held each other's hair back as
they chundered into a skip but two people who obviously
worshipped each other. Maybe I go to these family events
thinking it might turn into something resembling that. A
moment where the sisters will finally accept me as one of them.
But the pile on always happens. Today they've gone early,
they've not even given me wine first. But I resolve to just grin
and bear it like normal. Be here for the nieces and nephews.
Get some colouring in, steal potatoes, ensure all those little
people get the bags of Haribo in my handbag over the course of
the meal so I can send them home completely sugared up and
wired.

Whilst I'm sitting here, I take my phone out of my bag. Is it
too soon to text the hot man I snogged outside the concert
venue? Possibly. There was definitely some charm about him,
potential, a very grabbable arse. But it's not too soon to stalk
him. I look up the contact on my phone. Howard Bean. Show
me your socials, young man. I log on to Instagram as a starter.
He likes the gym. And new trainers. And a sunset with a corny
philosophical quote about tomorrow being the start of the rest of
your life. Mini barf. And... Oh dear. It looks like he likes a girl
called Carrie. It takes all of three clicks to find out he lives with
Carrie, and they have a chihuahua together whom they refer to
as their fur baby but also goes by the name of Boujee. For the
love of crap. Seriously, Howard? I let you put your tongue in my
mouth. I sit there staring blankly at the back of the cubicle door.
I block his contact and let out a loud sigh of despair, one so loud
the person in the stall next door assumes me to be straining in
some distress. Bloody Howard. I open WhatsApp on my phone.

Eduardo, what are you up to today?

I wait for the three dots to appear, hoping they will. Bingo. I
smile.

I'm just finishing lunch with my mum. Why?

Can I come round?

I thought you were busy all weekend?

I was. I'm not now.

Are you hungry? I've made a very nice crumble. I think there's enough.

Yeah. See you in about an hour?

He replies with a thumbs up emoji. I put my phone back in my bag and leave the cubicle to look at myself in the mirror. All that running from the Tube did amazing things to my mascara. I look like a party badger. I will just eat my mushrooms then go.

As I leave the toilets, I think about how to leave. Should I fake illness? A Sunday teaching emergency? A house fire? I ponder this as I politely wait in the corridor for a group of people grappling to put their coats on, when suddenly, I catch sight of a box on a table in the corner. *Table 25, birthday cake, Alison.* I take a peek in the box. She's got some nerve criticising my gold skirt when there's gold sprinkles on this thing, her name ornately iced on in cursive font. I stare at the cake for a few seconds. I think about how she called me a smart arse. I then punch the cake. Whoops.

ED

'Hello.'

'Hi! Here, I brought you cake.' Mia stands there, handing me a napkin of quite decent chocolate cake to be fair, looking slightly forlorn for a Sunday afternoon. I can't quite read her mood or the outfit. All I know is that she's definitely not been to church.

'You have. Thank you. Where did you steal this from?'

She then does a very strange and unexpected move where she enters my flat and then backs me against my front door, her body pressed against mine and her breath warm against my chin. She smells like breaded mushrooms. Her lips search for mine and she kisses me softly.

This is new. I don't mind this. For a moment I kiss her back and then I push her away from me, gently. 'Is this how we're greeting each other now? We won't be able to do this on the bus. Or in the staffroom.' And then we both hear the flush of the toilet.

'WHO?' she whispers, her hands over her mouth.

I hear the door unlatching and footsteps until my mother reveals herself to us. Please don't be too much, please. Both of you.

'Hello! Who are you?' she asks curiously.

'Mum, this is Mia. My colleague...' I tell her.

'Mia! OH MY DAYS! Come here!' She reaches over and gives Mia a long, warm embrace as she widens her eyes at me over her shoulder. 'I've heard so much about you!'

'All good, I hope. Ed, you have a mum!' Mia tells me mockingly.

'I do. Biology dictates that I was born of a woman. I was not grown in a laboratory. Mia, this is my mum, Adele.'

'But people call me Addy.' Mum holds Mia's shoulders back and looks at her face intensely. 'Why have we not met before?' she asks her.

'I have no idea and I'm glad that's now changed,' Mia says and looks at both of us. 'You don't look anything alike,' she remarks.

Well, obviously not as Mum has her wild frizzy hair swept back in a hairband and is wearing sunflower dungarees and Doc Marten boots.

Mum rolls her eyes. 'No. Poor bastard is the mirror image of his father... But luckily, he didn't inherit anything else from the sod.'

I wouldn't know. I never knew him, but I stand there as my

Mum does the usual thing of disparaging his character to people she's just met.

'God, you're very pretty. You never told me she was pretty, Ed,' Mum adds.

'Yeah, Ed. Why didn't you tell your mother I was fit?' Mia demands, laughing to herself. 'Are you staying? We can have tea, you can tell me embarrassing life stories about Ed.'

'That is super sweet, but I have somewhere to be. But next time, I want this to happen. I never meet any of Eddie's friends. I was starting to think Nigel was the only person in his life.'

Mia giggles. There is a reason I've not introduced the two of them and that's mainly because I'm not sure I could handle sitting there while they dismantle me as a person. My mother also knows far too much. I don't need Mia learning that I slept with a teddy until I was thirteen. Rumours like that would travel with light warp speed through the staffroom.

'It's a date. It's lovely to meet you,' Mia says as Mum grabs her bag and comes to hug me. It's always a long hug with Mum, as if she's sending you off to spend time at sea.

'Eddie, your potatoes were par excellence. I adore you. I will call you in the week, my darling.'

'Love you, Mum. Take care,' I tell her.

Mia watches the interaction closely as I usher Mum out of the door, closing it softly behind her. I turn slowly, wondering if she's going to jump me again.

'ED!'

'Mia?'

'That's your mum?' she shrieks. 'She's brilliant!'

'Yes, you've seen her picture on my Facebook before. This is not a surprise.'

'She was just not what I expected. She had badges on her handbag about women's rights and fossil fuels.'

'Oh yeah, that's where she's going now. She likes a protest on a Sunday afternoon.' Mia looks completely perplexed. *She's*

confused? Imagine how I felt growing up. Mum was everything
– warm and open and I never felt anything but loved – but her
life was governed by a level of outspoken chaos. 'Thank God
she didn't catch us snogging. What was that, by the way?' I ask.

'I was being impulsive. I had a bad morning. I saw my
sisters.' She pouts, slouching her shoulders.

'The ones who treat you like an errant teen and have
matching Hondas?'

'You have been listening, the very ones,' she says, kicking off
her trainers in that way she does that is not good for her shoes. I
feel she may be here to mope but at least she brought cake.

'How was last night? Did you dance?' I say, following her
into my living room, examining her very gold outfit. She looks
festive, like a bauble, but her effortless cool allows her to carry
it off.

'I did. I also met a bloke but that won't be going any further.
I'm still allowed to talk to you about that stuff, yes?' she mutters
casually.

'I encourage it, to be fair. Why won't it be going any
further?'

'Met him at the Tube station, snogged him with a bit of light
frottage, stalked him on social media and turns out he's living
with a woman and a very tiny dog,' she tells me, making a
gesture with her hands that this dog is the size of her hand.

I put a hand in the air at the revelation. 'You just kissed me
at my door. Did you at least brush your teeth in between?'

'I borrowed mouthwash from Beth.'

I arch my eyebrows, wondering whether to believe her or
not. She heads over to the counter and starts picking at some
leftover cauliflower cheese. With her fingers.

'Well, with the kissing. Remember, I can't do spontaneous.'

'You're very sensible, aren't you?' Mia jests.

'Because I like you too much to ruin us.'

As I say those words, I realise I mean them and Mia stands

there quietly, taking them in. I am still holding cake. Let's shift the focus to the cake.

'So, tell me about this cake,' I say as I grab a fork from my kitchen drawer.

'It was from a birthday lunch. It's chocolate and salted caramel.'

'Why does it look like it fell on the floor?' I ask, putting the napkin down on my countertop. Mia has moved on to my potatoes and bites into one, her eyes closed in delight at the crunch.

'I punched the cake.'

'Is this a family tradition?' I ask, confused.

'No, I was angry. But no one saw me do it. I blamed it on the restaurant.'

'Smart, if maybe a little childish.'

'Yep,' she says sheepishly.

I tuck in, trying to read Mia's mood. I know she doesn't get on with the sisters but don't know whether to delve any further into that family drama. I can imagine living with her at some point in life would have been an adventure. 'It's good cake though, despite appearances. I like the sponge, good icing ratio... I think they've put orange through there, too. I...'

'Shall we have sex today?' Mia suddenly blurts out.

I cough, chocolatey crumbs spraying everywhere. She strikes me firmly on my back.

'Seriously? I thought we said next Wednesday? It's in our Google calendars,' I tell her. This was important so she wouldn't forget and diarising this as much as possible took any sort of romance out of the event, it made it organised and efficient even if she was intent on editing the event as much as possible to wind me up.

'I mean, I'm here. You're here. I shaved my legs last night to be able to wear this skirt, so it means I don't have to shave my legs again midweek. How does this fit in with your sheet changing schedules? I know this was an issue for you.'

I can't quite talk. Chocolate crumbs still line my mouth. If I wasn't leaning against this kitchen counter, my knees would possibly give way.

'I changed them yesterday. I'd need to shower first though.'

'Oh, me too. Together?'

My head may explode from the suggestion. 'Maybe not...' I've not bathed with a person either, ever. I can't have two firsts in a day. I'll overheat.

'Ed, your face is not reading enthusiasm to me. You're scrunched. If this is a bad idea, then tell me.'

Mia has that look on her face again that reads chilled. She's coming in here on a Sunday and just announcing that we should have some sex, like we should watch a film, have a cup of tea. I need to soak a pan over there. I need to put the pork away or the cat will get to it. My mum was barely in the building five minutes ago. There's a lot to compute.

'I've just had a big meal. I had six roast potatoes,' I tell her.

'Ed, we're not going swimming,' she laughs, her eyes shining at me.

I laugh back at her. Maybe we just need to get this over and done with.

'DO YOU HAVE A SPARE TOOTHBRUSH?' a voice shouts from the bathroom.

'No,' I shout back.

'That's cool. I'll just use my finger,' she replies.

Whilst I'm glad Mia is paying attention to her dental hygiene, I worry a little about this cavalier attitude to not having the right equipment for the job. Where else could she put that finger? I don't swear very often but holy shitting balls. I think I'm about to lose my virginity. I'm glad there's not a fan in the room. I'm also glad there's not been an ounce of spontaneity here. I got to clean my kitchen first, she helped and then I showered and arranged my things while she did the same and by 'things' I mean I put a condom on the night stand and broke the seal on the lube and spent a lot of time smelling myself. I also don't know how to appear when she comes out of the bathroom. Completely naked? Leg cocked up? Maybe I should wear a towel? My pants? Maybe I should be fully clothed. Dressing gown, let's go for a dressing gown.

The door opens. Shit. She's in a towel.

'How are your towels so soft?' she asks me, rubbing her hands over herself.

'Fabric conditioner,' I answer, confused. Is this foreplay?

'They're lovely,' she says, smiling. She's silent for a moment while she looks around the room.

'No Marvin Gaye?' she asks.

'I can ask Alexa if that's what you want.'

'Ed, no...' She laughs and it somehow relaxes me. It's a reassuring, familiar, almost satisfying sound, always infused with genuine happiness. I like hearing it especially in this very moment.

'I like the room, by the way. It's very clean. The Juliet balcony is a winner, very romantic.'

'Thank you,' I reply.

'I'm going to take off my towel in a moment. Are you going to freak out?'

'I can take my dressing gown off at the same time? After three?' I ask.

'Deal,' she answers. 'One – two – three.'

I can't quite breathe. I feel my hands over the sash of my dressing gown untie the loose knot and make a strange flashing movement as I open it and then drop the gown to the floor. Please find me normal looking. Am I supposed to be erect at this point? I don't even know.

'Hey.'

'Hey.'

'You're naked...'

'So are you...'

At first, I can't look at Mia. A mixture of nerves and shame and fear soar through my veins. But when I do look over at her, she's smiling, laughing quietly and somehow that smile is all I see. I mean, I see breasts, too. They're there, you know.

'Ed, that's quite a good penis,' she says.

I can't stop myself from glancing down. 'Quite?'

'Well, it's not micro, or like a baseball bat in between your legs.'

For some reason, I feel the need to return the compliment.

'You have a very neat...' I can't say the word, any word, so I gesture vaguely in her direction.

'Neat? Like cool or tidy?'

'Both?'

She grins and for a moment it's so intense I have to look away. 'Well, do you want to kiss or shall we just lie down?' I ask her. 'Over covers, under covers...?' I mimic the action of pulling a duvet over me.

'Let's go over and then go under if we get a bit chilly,' Mia suggests.

I nod but she moves towards me and suddenly I feel her hand on my arm. I flinch a little to feel her so close to me, properly naked.

'Ed, please relax. Trust me. I'm not going to hurt you. Just breathe...'

And with that, she holds me tightly. There are many things I feel in this moment. I feel safe. But I'm also conscious that Mia's nipples are pressed against me, my penis touching her thigh, her head nestled in my chest.

'I'm going to kiss you now,' I inform her.

I put a hand to her cheek to steady myself. I don't want to get this wrong. As soon as my lips meet hers, she kisses me back, her bottom lip pulling against mine. Crap, her hand is on my arse. She leans into me, and we fall onto the bed. She lies over me, her legs straddling my body. I am super, overly conscious that her vagina is directly in some sort of contact with my penis and I feel it harden under her body. I make a sound. It's supposed to signal pleasure, but it does resemble a dog crying.

'Are you OK?' she whispers. 'Your body feels like wire is running through it.'

'Hmmm...' I reply, unsure.

'Sex is about energy, pleasure, your body just giving into the sensation. Just take a deep breath for me...'

I do as I'm told. She's still looking at me. I have no idea what to say.

'Can I touch your breast?' I ask as it literally is dangling in front of me.

Mia bites her lip. 'You can, thank you for asking.'

I hold her breast. Then, without thinking, I kiss it and I see her close her eyes, murmuring in pleasure. Was that a good thing? I lick the nipple. I think she likes that. I won't lie. I quite like it too.

'I think... I think... Condom?' I ask.

She nods, smirking and dismounts me, lying beside me while I reach over to the nightstand and tear it open. Condom. I reckon I can put one of these on in fifteen seconds when I'm alone and want to have a posh wank, but it appears there is a difference when there's a naked woman in your bed, waiting for you. My hand is actually shaking, and it's not helped by seeing Mia lie there and touch herself whilst she waits for me. The condom slips out of the packet and I drop it on the bed but then as I pick it up and try and pull it over my cock, it slides over me. It's like wrestling with a jellyfish.

'You OK there, champ?' Mia asks, her fingers gliding over herself.

'Yep. Just...' I'm just glad my penis, with all my nerves, is still operating. The condom is on. Thank fuck. I sit there on my knees in the middle of my bed, Mia waiting. Crap. This is happening.

'So, do I need to do anything else here? Would you like me to touch you there or would you like oral or I can kiss you a bit more?' I ask, at some precipice of disbelief, like I'm about to reach the top of a mountain.

'Dude, let's pop your cherry,' she says, putting a thumbs up.

'Exactly the words I imagined would be said to me in this moment...'

And then that smile. 'Ed, you're thinking about this too much. What are you looking at?'

'I don't want to hurt you. Can I just examine the holes? Is that weird?'

She does a gesture prompting me to lie down and have a look, parting her legs gently. I lie looking up at it. It's a perfectly good vulva, just like in the textbooks and porn, except she has pubes.

'Do you want me to do the mouse thing, with the finger?'

'No.'

'OK.'

I crawl up to her at this point so I'm lying next to her, my eyes running up and down every inch of her naked body, not knowing where they should land. 'I feel like I should say something more significant at this point? This feels like a nice moment. Thank you.'

'It's alright. Ed. You're with me, you'll be fine.'

She turns to kiss me and I pull my body over hers as she feels down, her hand around my cock and guides it inside her. It's not an instant thing like you see in the films. It's a bit of wayward prodding and adjusting my hips and my breath getting deeper as I worry that maybe my penis isn't working or made for the job.

Oh.

Sex.

I'm having sex.

'Oh god, oh Jesus, oh God...'

I push into her, watching her head tilt back, her neck exposed. I inhale, the longest inhalation I've ever made. Oh god. I then ejaculate. Quite hard. Of course I do.

EIGHT

MIA

I'm not sure what I thought having sex with Ed was going to be like, I was curious, fascinated at the prospect, truth be told. I did have visions of it being fun. There was no way I wanted him to feel awkward, so the plan was to laugh through most of it, enjoy the moment, see my friend in a whole new light. I knew it was unlikely that it was going to end in orgasm.

Yes, it didn't last long. At all. But if I think back to my first, Toby – that was pretty similar. Knowing Ed, I should have guessed it would have been clinical. He looked at my vulva without touching it using the same concentration I reserve for Wordle, and he also was far too polite. Just grab that titty and make it your own, my friend. And, for a man of science, he did say God and Jesus quite a fair bit. I'm glad sex with me is a religious experience.

I also wanted him to enjoy it, to have a moment of happiness. Did he? I'm not quite sure. After he came, he seemed horrified it had happened that quickly, so jumped off and went to 'make tea' which actually is something men should do more.

When he came back, my knickers and T-shirt were back on. He also brought me crumble with custard, which I'd argue sometimes is better than an orgasm. He didn't talk much, I think he was in some state of shock so he just said thank you quite a fair bit. He showered. I napped and woke up to find Nigel staring straight at me. That cat knows what we did. I've scarred that cat for life.

'So, we were thinking as part of your review, we are going to sit in some lessons, ask the students and your peers for feedback. It's not a reflection on your work so far, but what we're doing with a number of staff members to raise standards across the board.'

I've taken in about half of what my headteacher, Alicia, has been saying, given I've been thinking about sex. With Ed. And the fact it's Tuesday and it's 2-4-1 at Domino's so pizza will be part of my future.

'That sounds fine. I've put Beth Callaghan as a referee. I have room for two more. Who else do you think could rate your performance?'

I pause for a moment, smirking. 'Ed Rogers in Science.'

She gets scribbling. I think of all the teachers I'm friends with who could do the same, except they'd be able to rate me more for my abilities to balance pint glasses on my forehead as opposed to my teaching. 'I'll think of the third.'

She scribbles in her notes, watching me with one eye as I bite my nails.

'You got me worried. I thought someone had complained about me,' I say, relieved.

'No. It's just that time of year. You're a valued member of the department. Miss Callaghan told me you also do some adult education classes, too?'

'Yes, some creative writing stuff in the community.'

'Well, we always value staff putting on extra-curricular clubs in that vein. Have you also had any plans to take on extra responsibility? You are very well-liked by the children,' Alicia mentions.

'That's kind of you to say, but we shall see...'

She studies my face for a moment for reasons I'm unsure. Alicia never married or had kids. There was a rumour she bonked Sean from Geography once, but she's given her life to this school, to these kids, to the point where you can't even see the person; she's married to this place, part of the brickwork. I love these kids and what I do, but I need to be able to leave here in the evening and not be Miss Johnson.

'Or maybe those drop-in counselling sessions happening at the moment, maybe I can put you on a few shifts after school to add to your portfolio. I think you'd be good at that.'

I nod, knowing I really don't have a choice, do I?

'And I will let you know how that review goes. Here are some forms I'd like you to fill out in preparation.' She hands over a file and my heart sinks down to the pit of my stomach.

'Wow.'

'A problem?' Alicia enquires.

'No, just paperwork. The bane of my life. That's a lot of reading.'

'Says the English teacher who deals in books.'

'Very true...' Except those books are written for me. 'Thank you, Alicia.'

I take the file and leave the office, seeing Alicia scanning my shoes as I do. They are Superga, Alicia. Kate Middleton wears these. I puff out my cheeks as the door closes, smiling at Alicia's forlorn and mainly silent secretary who separates herself from us mere faculty members by having her own personal biscuit jar.

'You OK?' a voice says from behind me, coming out of the photocopier room. It's the very sweet and shiny Miss Bell in yet another Alice band – she seems to have them in every colour. It's the end of a school day so this place almost echoes without the children, it's just the footsteps of frantic teachers getting as much done now so their work won't have to follow them home.

'Just paperwork and stuff. I see you've figured out the photocopier?' I say, glancing at the stacks of trigonometry worksheets in her arms.

'Yes. I have a card, all is good.'

'Excellent. Next I'll teach you how to get free cans out of the vending machine in the canteen.'

'Deal.' As we walk the stairs together to the staffroom, I notice this girl is very unlike me. It's the shiny patent loafers with a tartan skirt, a jumper in that sort of cashmere mix that I would buy, wear once and then it would sit in my washing basket because I'm terrified of spoiling it. It's very subtle accessories unlike my bright orange studs and matching Casio that I've had since I was a teen. What if she's a virgin, too? That could have been cute and Ed and her could have lost their cherries together. Instead of me sticking my ass (quite literally) in the way.

'So, what are you up to tonight?' I ask her.

'Oh, nothing much... I'm in a new flat so surrounded by mess and flatpack. I've got to sort out my life. You?'

'Oh, wine will feature highly. And a veggie supreme. I'll watch some shite on Netflix and then doom scroll through Twitter and then likely pass out,' I say, as she giggles. I miss out the bit about porn and a wank.

As we enter the staffroom, I see Ed standing over his desk, packing his bag. I've not seen him much since Sunday. Yesterday, he was good at avoiding me as he was on lunch patrol but today, I did spot him changing direction in a corridor to not have to bump into me. It was upsetting. It's not like I was going to announce to a sea of kids that I'd taken his virginity and part of this arrangement was that we weren't going to make this awkward. We were still us. He doesn't clock us as we walk in so my need for him to acknowledge me takes over.

'ED!' I shout loudly. He drops his lunchbox in fright to hear my voice then looks over at me sheepishly, smiling at Caitlin with reddened cheeks.

'Mia.' I can't quite read his look. I don't know if it's fear or shame, but it hurts that he would feel either. We walk over to his desk and I perch myself on the end.

'I had that meeting with Alicia,' I tell him, trying to break the ice.

He takes a deep breath and smiles. 'Did she fire you?' Business as usual.

'No. She was telling me about the new review process. I needed references so I put your name down. I hope that's OK?'

'I will tell her you're impossible, loud and disorganised...'

Caitlin watches the banter between us curiously.

'Perfect. You off now?' I ask him as he puts his coat on.

'I was. You?'

'I have to stay and make headway with some marking before I scoot, but you know what? I just found out something very interesting,' I tell him.

Ed ruffles his brow in response. Interesting can mean many things with me. I think it's interesting McDonald's stopped doing twister fries without personally writing me a letter to warn me of their intentions.

'Well, I was chatting to Caitlin here and she has just moved into a new flat and she has a lot of flatpack to build...'

I can feel this idea brewing in the same way I felt the photocopier idea simmering away, but I've done some work to try and mould Ed into a human sexual being and it's now par for the course that I should hand him over to someone who can move all of that forward.

'And I know someone who is excellent at flatpack. He actually enjoys it like people enjoy Scrabble.'

Ed closes his eyes at my subtlety again while Caitlin looks mortified.

'Oh, I wasn't on the blag for some help. I can get it done but...'

'I'm not even joking. When Beth in my department had a new baby and bought a house, Ed went round and offered to build the beds,' I tell her.

'I do enjoy flatpack. This is both sad and true,' Ed says, looking at the floor in despair as he holds up an Allen key that he keeps on his keyring, just in case there's a flatpack emergency. Caitlin spies it curiously.

'And we're a team in this staffroom, we help each other out,' I add.

'Well, if you're free and sure?' Caitlin says, turning to him. 'It's just some bookcases and drawers.'

Ed's face reads shock at this moment. This girl has agreed to have him in her flat. Will he know what to do with himself? 'I'm free... if you do need my help? If you'd rather not, then that's also fine. You don't have to listen to this one. I rarely do,' he discloses nervously.

'I could do with some help, but I don't have any food in. I don't know how I'd repay you.'

Ed starts to blush, heavily. Please, Ed.

'It's 2-4-1 at Domino's. He's a fan of the New Yorker.'

'Seriously? Me, too...' she mutters, surprised. 'Well, let me organise myself and you're welcome to come over and help a girl out. You sure you don't want to join, Mia?' she asks me.

'Oh, I'm shit at flatpack. I'd get in the way,' I say, knowing my place. Plus, a threesome is far too much of a jump for my novice friend here.

'OK then. I took the bus in.'

'I have my car,' Ed replies. 'I can drive us.'

Look at my wonderful plan falling into place.

'OK then, let me get my stuff. Give me ten?'

Ed smiles and nods as she heads over to the other side of the staffroom. I feel a sharp elbow to my ribs.

'How are you like this? You're embarrassing, like a match-making mother,' he whispers sternly.

'Ed, I just got you a date with a girl you like. The words you need are "thank you"...' I reply.

'It's not a date. It's flatpack assembly,' he argues.

'Well, I'm sorry I couldn't organise a more romantic soirée for you.'

He stops for a moment and his cheeks flush as if he's remembering that we had sex two days ago. Almost like the image of it popped into his head. I don't know how to respond, so clench my teeth and smile at him.

'Why are you smiling at me like that?' he asks.

'Because you're being weird. Please don't be weird. We said it wouldn't be weird,' I plead with him. 'Stop avoiding me around school.'

'I'm not avoiding you.'

'You are...'

'Do you think people know?' he whispers again, turning into me.

'That we've had sex or that you're not a virgin anymore?' His elbow goes back into my ribs. 'Ed, the only person who may know is Nigel.'

'The bloke who works in the canteen?'

'Your cat, and unless he's learnt how to speak or text then our secret is safe.'

I put my arms around him to hug him, to remove any sense of awkwardness and remind him nothing's changed. He's still my Ed and he's still my best mate. I'll never say that out loud though.

ED

I have been avoiding Mia like some weird teenage boy, mainly because Sunday left me mortified. Who comes after three

seconds of thrusting? Amateurs, that's who. She was kind, she
didn't shame me in the moment, but I did excuse myself to the
kitchen to rest my cheek on the cold countertop and take it all
in. I was no longer a virgin. The sheer relief of it was tremen-
dous, like a massive albatross was removed from around my
neck and I could throw it deep into the sea.

But I stood there for ages in shock. I've seen Mia naked.
She's seen me naked. Her nipple has been in my mouth. I
responded in the only way I could after that. I refused to talk
about it and brought her tea and crumble. She seemed remark-
ably happy about that. Now I wonder if anyone can really tell
I've had sex. Am I walking differently?

'This one comes in three boxes, I really hope they're the
right ones, I can't bear to go back to the shop,' Caitlin says,
carrying them into her living room.

And now, I'm here in Caitlin's living room. I'm not sure
what Mia's trying to achieve; it's not like I'm going to suddenly
not be a virgin and then get my rocks off with everyone I see.
Not when there's flatpack to build.

'Well, let's open them up and see,' I say, using my house key
to break the tape of the boxes. Is it true that I'm into this? Yes, it
is. I sometimes time myself building a Billy bookcase – which is
probably why I was a virgin into my twenties. I go through the
pieces in the box and count out all the screws and brackets.

'All accounted for,' I tell her as she also hands me a slice of a
pizza. On a plate. I already like her for this. Mia uses a piece of
kitchen towel, sometimes just her hands. I get distracted
wondering if she even owns plates, before refocusing. 'Thank you.'

'I'm sorry I don't have wine or a beer for you.'

'Diet Coke is fine, I'm a cheap date.' I said the word 'date.'
This is not a date. Yikes. I don't know how to tackle this, so I
bite into the steaming piece of pizza pretending it's not hot. I
look forward to the ulcers.

'So, are you local?' she asks me.

'About twenty minutes in the other direction.'

'Do you live alone? Married? Kids?' she asks me.

'Oh, none of those. I live with Nigel...'

'Oh, you're gay?'

'No, Nigel's my cat,' I say, laughing.

'OK then,' she replies.

Alone with a cat. I am really selling myself here. I put my pizza down and start lining up the parts of the bookcase in hand.

'I have three of these, so I am a dab hand at them.'

'That's good to know. I haven't known where to start here. I was in a house share before so have never had to fend for myself. Like, I can't get my head around lightbulbs,' she says, staring at the one above us.

'Well, it depends how bright you want the room and whether you want LEDs which are slightly cheaper to run...'

I can see I've bamboozled her.

'I can buy some for you. Or we can go to a shop and I can talk you through them?'

'That would be...'

'Illuminating?' I say.

She giggles. I made a joke that was mildly funny. Sometimes I wish I could record them for Mia. 'I had the same thing when I bought my own place. There's a lot to learn, I can help if you need tips.'

'That's very kind.'

She glances at me for a moment and I don't quite know where to look or be. Damn. Eat more pizza, Ed.

'Can I ask you a boring question?' she asks me.

'I encourage boring,' I say plainly.

'Who's your mortgage provider? I'm not sure my advisor got me the best deal.'

I stop for a moment and roll up my shirt sleeves. Now this I can do.

So it turns out I can build three Billy bookcases in an hour, whilst eating pizza and talking mortgage rates, and these are things that make us nerds feel like true superheroes. And now it's little things that I'm discovering that make me think Caitlin's the ideal woman for me. She has a little Ficus plant in a gold ceramic pot that she places carefully on the shelves of her new bookcase; she has a good thesaurus, likes reading historical biographies and she asked me to put a sheet down on the floor before we moved the bookcases because she didn't want to scratch the new laminate. These are all the things I look for. It was both a surprise and a shock therefore to be invited into her bedroom.

'Can you just jam it in?' she asks me.

'It would damage the hole, I might have to make it bigger...'

'How?'

'What tools do you have?'

Get your mind out of the gutter because if Mia was here that's where it would go. Caitlin hands me a power drill and I get to work, making that hole bigger so I can screw it down. Everything is innuendo now, I've been around Mia for far too long.

'That should work,' I say, placing my finger inside.

'You are good at this,' Caitlin mentions. 'Did you have a handy dad growing up?'

'Actually, no. It was just me and my mum. My dad left when I was five. You could argue I had to teach myself,' I tell her.

She hands over the rest of the screws a little sadly. 'God, I'm so sorry.'

'Don't be. I get by,' I say, trying to laugh off her sadness.

'People in far worse places than me. I had a good mum who did both jobs.'

'And how did you meet Mia?' she asks me. I feel myself blush at the mention of her name.

'Oh, we started at Griffin Road at the same time, we've been mates ever since.' Am I still her friend? It feels like we've levelled up somehow though I'm not sure I should be calling her my virginity taker.

'The P.E. guys say she's a bit unhinged...'

'Oh, she has her moments.'

'Tommy has some story about how she let the air out of his bike tyres. Is that true?'

It was the week after they slept together and he ghosted her so cruelly, she may have had some revenge. I told her how to do the tyres because her plan was to steal a knife from Food Tech and slash them.

'I have no idea. I wouldn't listen to everything Tommy tells you though.'

'No? He seems nice. He's a good laugh.'

'Appearances can be deceiving. Mia's one of the good ones, that's all I know.'

She nods at me, and I wonder whose words she's going to side with, the charismatic Tommy or the drawer-builder, Ed. I put my last screw into the drawer and then check the runners on it.

'Perfect. What's going in here?'

Caitlin empties a bag of knickers on to her bed. I stand there open-mouthed, not quite knowing where to look, willing myself not to stare at the sheer mint thongs, which would be both pervy and wrong.

'Well, I will leave you to that,' I say, putting both thumbs up like a complete idiot.

'You've been awesome tonight, thank you so much!' she says

sweetly and as I get up, she holds out a hand to help me steady myself.

'It's been kinda fun. You got anything else you want help with?' I say as I roll down my sleeves.

And then from out of nowhere, she's there, in front of me and she kisses me on the cheek. I can hardly breathe as she touches me. When I meant I could help her with something, I meant I could put up a shelf or bleed a radiator, but in this moment, I realise that I'm in this woman's bedroom. Is she hinting at something? I got pizza today. I got to be in her company and check out her books and paint selections, I don't need anything else. But this bedroom is small and we're standing here together in this enclosed space. Is she waiting for something? How am I meant to read this? I only had sex for the first time on Sunday. What is she hinting at? So, I do what any red-blooded man does and I stick out my hand.

'Well, you know where to find me. In the staffroom. Room 56, too. Thank you for the Diet Coke and stuff.'

She takes my hand and laughs. I then bend down and gather all the cardboard boxes and plastic packaging in front of me.

'Let me help you get these into recycling,' I say, almost running out of the door into the corridor of her flat. I need to get out of here immediately.

NINE

MIA

'DON'T DO IT, YOU SILLY BITCH! YOU DESERVE TO DIE!' I shriek at my computer screen, watching as a woman in a sexy thriller Netflix film goes back into a house where her ex-husband waits for her with a machete, just so she can save the dog. The dog will be fine. She will not, she doesn't even have shoes on, and that man is next level psycho. I stuff another piece of pizza into my mouth, languishing in a crop top and flannelette pyjama bottoms, wrapped around my pillow, my hair still in its towel turban from an hour ago. Is this film bad? Oh, it's awful, but this is what I do. I watch the unwatchable films to keep my opinions of art informed and well-rounded. And maybe after a day of trying to be intellectual and asking a thirteen-year-old to appreciate a Gothic short story from the turn of the century, I just need some predictable trash to get me through the day.

'MIA! Someone for you at the door...' a voice winds its way up the stairs. I'm going to have to get up and pause my film and for this I am very annoyed. I peel myself off the bed, shake out my hair and poke my head over the railings of the staircase to see the figure at the door.

'ED? What are you doing here?'

My housemate, Maxine, stands there like security. She's still in a power suit and has her serious no-shit commuter face on. I use all her conditioner but in return, when it's 2-4-1 Tuesdays at Domino's, I'm always generous with pizza and warm cookies which I hope compensates for the fact I'm a little allergic to housework.

'Thanks, Maxine. Did you get the Meateor pizza in the kitchen?'

She puts her thumb up and disappears into the living room. I skip down the stairs.

'What are you doing here? It's not even nine,' I tell him.

'You're wandering around in a bra. I can see your nipples,' he says, like this is a problem.

'It's a crop top, stop looking at my nipples then.'

'They're all I can see.'

As he stands there, I notice things about Ed that I've never noticed before and that could be because I've now seen him naked. He has a decent arse to start. It's grabbable, rounded. He has good forearms: not too hairy, not too pale, some definition there, probably from all that pre-sex wanking he had to do. He peers into my living room where the young professionals eat pizza and watch a high-end quiz show. I've sat in there with them before. It's not fun especially when you shout out the right answers and Brian (financial whizz kid; only wears white underwear) looks at you all snootily like that shouldn't be in your frame of knowledge. Piss off, Brian.

'Want to come upstairs?' He nods forlornly and I pat him on the head. 'Why are you here? How was flatpack making?' I enquire as we head up the stairs.

'We made the stuff. She's a fan of Margaret Atwood.'

'Aren't we all?'

I watch as he enters my room and does the same thing he always does which is to observe it like a health inspector looking for hazards. The pizza box on the bed, the dirty clothes piled on a chair, the assorted mugs gathering dust with half-drunk cups of tea. I kick a pair of knickers under the bed and pick up some other clothes, dumping them on the floor so he has a place to sit.

'Lovely,' he mutters.

I shake my head at him and crack one of my beers open on my bedside table, handing it to him.

'That's not good for the wood, you know,' he tells me, 'Not using a coaster.'

'My wood or your wood?' I question, going straight for the innuendo. 'I take it you're here to mope?' I say, reading the signs.

'Kinda. It was actually really lovely. We have a lot in common. She has a Ficus...'

'Is that contagious?'

'It's a plant.'

'And you love plants.'

'I do,' he says, taking a large swig of his beer. He stares into space and leans back into the chair, carefully taking off his shoes.

'So, what happened, you built her things and then left? How did you end it? Or did you do something embarrassing?'

'Define embarrassing?' he asks.

'Did you spill a drink so it looked like you wet yourself?' I ask, bouncing on to my bed and trying to find my previous comfortable position so I can counsel him properly.

'No.'

'Did you move the bookcase into place and realise you'd crushed her chihuahua?'

'No, she doesn't have a dog. This could go on a while,' he tells me, his face still looking like he's in pain. 'I shook her hand. I was in her bedroom, and she'd dumped all her underwear on the bed. I took that as a sign to leave so she could sort her stuff but then she kissed me to say thank you and I think there was a moment. Maybe? But I freaked out so offered her my hand to shake.'

'Well, that's good in a way. You didn't take advantage. It may appear gentlemanly.'

'But I was in her bedroom. I can't read these things. In the back of my mind, I thought what if she kissed me or initiated something and then I...'

'Shoot my load too quickly over her new flatpack drawers?'

'Nice,' he says, scowling at me. He leans forward to rest his elbows on his knees, his hands running through his hair.

I notice the forearms again, but I also laugh. I have to because this is how I will deal with all of this. It has to be funny. 'So you're telling me you completely overthought it all and left. Pretty much like Sunday...'

'I didn't leave on Sunday!' he retorts with indignation in his tones.

'You went to your kitchen. I don't know what you did but you left.'

'Mia, it was kinda embarrassing.'

'Dude, it was your first time. Chill.'

'I can't be that word. I don't even understand it. How?'

I want to tell Ed that I can get some weed and it would help, but he's always in this high state of motion and anxiety. He needs to eat pizza in bed and watch shite with me, that would be a good start. I beckon him over to the bed and he comes over and collapses in a heap. I wrap my arms around him.

'So what if I get to know her and then I have sex with her and it's over in seconds. There's no point...' he moans.

'Ed, every time you meet a new person, the sex isn't always on point. It's not like a film. You build that trust, you learn what that person likes and it gets better.'

'But I have zero skills, zero practice. I feel like a surgeon operating on a real-life patient when all I've done is practise my stitching on cushions.'

'You're telling me you shag cushions?' I ask.

'NO! It's an analogy, aren't you supposed to be an English teacher?'

'Aren't you supposed to be a Biology teacher?' I jest.

He sits up, takes a cushion and throws it at me, spying a box of potato wedges on my bedside table and stealing one for himself. I want to tell him there's dip for those, but I know that's not his style – no sauce. 'What's been your longest relationship?' he asks me.

I puff my cheeks out. 'Eighteen months maybe? I was fresh out of university. His name was Ben.'

'Did you have good sex with Ben?'

'Yes, when he wasn't having sex with other people...' Ed's eyes widen. 'It was good sex because I also loved him. There was a comfort and an intimacy there.'

I pause for a moment to think about Ben. A chance to reminisce about orgasms and spontaneous freeing sex but clouded by a moment when I found messages on his phone from lots of different women and I threw a cereal bowl at his head.

Ed curls into a ball on my bed and I pat him again like he's a large dog taking up space.

'That's the difference between you and me. All that breadth of experience, you know that sex gets better because you've acquired skills, you know what to expect... I have none of that,' he continues.

I think about the moment when he just lay there inspecting my vulva, taking it in like he had to memorise it for a school exam. He may be right. You can read as many books, watch as many sex scenes and download as much porn as your firewalls can handle but it's nothing compared to actually doing it.

'When I first had sex, I didn't know what semen was,' I admit to Ed.

Ed laughs hysterically. 'What did you think it was?'

'Well, I was sixteen. We were only told it looked like tadpoles. No one told me it looked like Spider-Man webbing. I freaked out and had to Google it.' I like hearing Ed laugh, he doesn't do this nearly enough. 'So let me be your sex Google. Do you have any questions from Sunday? Was it as you expected?' I ask him, intrigued.

Ed sits up and I see him visibly gulp. 'So you touched yourself while I was putting the condom on. Why?'

'Well, I didn't want to freak you out with foreplay... But generally, you don't want to put the turkey in before you've preheated the oven.'

'That's quite an analogy. So you preheated the oven yourself? Could I have offered you some lube?' he asks earnestly.

'Maybe...'

'So how do I preheat the oven? I'm thinking I should know how to do this, yes?'

'It's a good skill to have in your back pocket. If you can make a girl come first from foreplay then that's a big win, Eddie. Plus, if you're worried about busting your nuts too soon then it can add time to the sesh.'

He looks into space, that look of fear, confusion and pure shock on his face. I have no curriculum to my sex education but if I can send a man into the world who knows how to give head, properly, and not like a drunk lizard then maybe I'm doing a good thing.

'Ed, would you like me to teach you about foreplay?'

He nods.

ED

I don't know why I came to Mia's house, but it may have been the knowledge that she'd have alcohol and is good at dragging me out of my general feelings of despair. She'd make fun of me, make me watch crap telly and then tell me how it is, in her blunt inimitable style. *The reason you're fretting about sex is that you just don't know all of it. It's not just the willy going inside the vagina, there's a lot more to it. We've literally just skimmed the surface. So let me teach you.* Like a practical lab partner, I guess. Or maybe a Mr Miyagi-style sex guru. Knowing Mia, she'll get me to clean her house though, saying it's all endurance practice.

'Are we sure this is OK?' I ask her as I sit here in my pants on Mia's scruffy bed. I've been in Mia's room once before and it really is like walking into an art installation crossed with a haunted house ride at a funfair. You don't quite know what's going to spook you next, some old toast or a sex toy just lying out there for the world to see. Mia watches me as I try to get comfortable. It's not good form to ask her when she last changed her sheets, is it? I brush my hands over her tiger-print duvet. 'This is a nice print, where did you get these from?'

Mia stands there and takes off her crop top in front of me. Nipples again, staring at me. She pulls down her pyjama bottoms and reveals she's not wearing any knickers either. I take a deep breath that I may never exhale. She comes to sit down next to me.

'So, first things first... that is not foreplay, asking me about where I got my sheets. I got them from Habitat though...'

'Fancy.'

'Ed. Focus... So, foreplay can be verbal. You can talk to me about what you're going to do to me or talk about the effect I'm having on you...'

'You make me feel happy?' I tell her.

She wrinkles up her nose. 'Bit shit. I want to make you feel aroused, rock-hard, like I want you to feel feral with how much you want to nail me,' she roars, her fists clenched.

'Oh dear, really? Men have said that to you out loud?'

She grabs her phone from the bedside table and I watch as

she opens Tinder, scrolling through a line of started conversations.

'You speak to a lot of men,' I say, peering over her bare shoulder.

'Here – this is Scott, if that's really his name. He has a lovely turn of phrase.'

I hold her phone and feel my mouth go dry. 'He doesn't even know you and he wants to do these things to you. That's quite a thing... And it works?'

'It's more effective than the ones who ask me about my favourite colour.'

'Noted. Can you screen grab that for me and send it to me for future reference?' I ask her.

'One step ahead of you,' she says, pressing buttons and winking at me. She puts the phone down and turns to me. 'Right, next steps... So, when you're kissing and fooling about with a girl, that's when you need to do the work and find those places on her body that make her toes curl. Kiss me...'

'Now?'

'Well, yeah...'

She puckers her lips up and I smile as I move towards her, putting a hand to the back of her head. She's good at the kissing. I always thought she'd be more aggressive, that there would be more spit, but it's gentle, warm, and I lean my body into hers, pulling her in closer. She double taps my thigh and I lean away.

'Something I did?' I ask, mortified to have been tapped out.

'No, excellent technique but you're here to learn. Other places to kiss are the neck,' she says, running her fingers down her clavicle. 'And behind and around the ears. Be gentle there. I had one bloke who used to stick his tongue in there and it felt like he was jet washing my ear drums.'

I kiss around her neck gently, waiting for her body to respond. She does a little shimmy in reply and giggles. The sound makes me smile. It's a good sound. I'll keep going.

'That's the spot. Next up, work lower. Nipples. The nipples like to be kissed, sometimes sucked but not hard, not like you're suckling on them otherwise we'll definitely think you have mummy issues.'

I salute her. 'Can I play with them?' I ask, a little awkwardly.

'Yes.'

Naturally, not knowing that to do, I press her nipple in.

'Ding dong,' she laughs. 'It's not a doorbell. You can brush them, maybe massage the breast in general. When I'm more aroused, I may ask you to pinch them slightly, like one would with a nipple clamp.'

My face goes white at the mention of extra paraphernalia that I've only seen in porn.

'Ed. Calm down. Here, you liked licking them last time, give that a try...'

She pushes herself down the bed slightly and I take one in my mouth.

'Use your tongue to play with it... Like circle actions... Hmmm...'

'Is that OK?' I ask with my mouth full. She puts a hand in the air and I stop. Teaching moment.

'So, sex is also a way to bounce off each other's movements and sounds. If I'm moaning and arching my back and generally sound like I'm into it, then you just keep doing what you're doing.'

'And if you're saying nothing?'

'I'm bored, change it up. A good and considerate lover will tell you what works for them rather than just lie there and let you put in all that work for nothing. There is no point in doing that.'

I nod, mentally taking in all these notes.

'So, are we ready to go lower...?' Mia asks me. 'This is when it gets special.' I nod and she pushes herself down into the bed again, parting her legs for me. 'What I am about to show you is pretty important...'

She widens her legs, lifting her knees high and giving me the kind of view usually reserved for midwives. 'So you had a look the other day, I'm going to give you an assignment.'

'Spoken like a true teacher,' I say, trying to sound less nervous than I am. Please don't ask for anything impossible.

'Find my clitoris.'

I sit there, my mind like some mental flipbook of textbooks and scientific diagrams. I point to a general area above the urethra, gulping hard.

'Is that how you're going to get a lady aroused? You're going to point to her clit? Touch the clit.'

'You're bossy...' I gently touch her female parts, parting her vulva. This surprises me, how soft it is, I want to say like a new chamois or a baby kitten, but she won't like either comparison and I don't think that's the feral foreplay she was after.

'Bit higher, can you see my urethra...'

'Where the urine comes out?'

'Don't say urine again.'

'Noted.'

'Now feel for a raised area and press, really softly. Remember the mouse thing? Small circles...' I do as I'm told because I'm a little scared at this point but she inhales sharply and curls her back so her breasts are pushed forward. 'Yep, a-doodle-do. So...' she says, breathily. 'What you can also do is use the wetness from my vagina to wet your fingers and move it up to my clit and then that makes the movement a lot more fluid and... Ooooooh!' she moans.

'Shush...' I tell her. 'You have housemates downstairs. I don't want them to know you're giving me sex lessons.'

She giggles and pushes my hand away, shaking her body about as if she's trying to recalibrate itself. Her nipples are more pert, the pupils of her eyes dilated and she smiles, looking relaxed.

'So the other way to stimulate my clit is with this,' she says, sticking out her tongue at me. 'That's quite a step though. I find with oral you have to be in the moment. You don't have to do that if it's too much, we can work on fingers tonight...'

I shake my head at her. 'Nope, I want to learn it all, as quickly as possible,' I say, wobbling my jaw around in preparation. 'Like a student cramming it all in the night before an exam.'

She sniggers to herself. 'Well, be grateful I had a bath before you came...' She props herself on some pillows and parts her legs for me again. 'Right, so the best thing about head is the tease. Don't just dive in there like you're Tom Daley...'

'He's gay.'

'I know that, it was a diving analogy.'

'Gotcha,' I say, putting my thumb up at her.

'Kiss all around the area, my hip bones, my inner thigh, run a tongue along those parts, blow, lick... Build up the moment. Literally have it so I can feel your breath down there, on me,' she says, pointing to herself.

'Hmmm,' I say, remembering I shouldn't talk. Listen to her body. Let's do this then. I move my lips along her inner thigh. Ooh, that sounds like a happy sound. I'd do that again if I can remember what I just did. There are things I want to say but I need to focus and be in the moment. What I want to tell her is that her thighs are super soft, and I like the smell of her bath foam. It smells like vanilla.

'And then just lightly kiss or lick my vulva... softly...'

'Eyes open or closed?' I ask.

'Open for today so you know what you're doing but generally closed or it can be unnerving. You'll look like a crocodile in the undergrowth,' she says, laughing.

OK then. Time to give a woman head. Given I've just been

told the secret location of the clitoris, it feels like the right place to start there. I lick it gently, rotating my tongue around it.

'NOT SO HARD,' she says, creasing up.

'I'm sorry!' I say, her vulva still in my mouth, a hand in the air. I go more gently. So that bit is super sensitive. This is good knowledge to have. I hear her breathing getting heavier, a moan as she puts her arm behind her head.

'You can move your tongue around, explore the inside of my vulva, keep alternating the movements, find those special places.'

Despite the breathy tone of voice, she makes it sound so clinical, but it really is like figuring out a very cryptic puzzle. It's not a huge surface area but there are limitless combinations of things that could get her off.

'Down a little, flick your tongue in and out there... Just. Like. That.'

She puts her hand to the back of my hair, stroking gently. She tastes different. Sweet. And I suddenly understand what she means. To see her aroused is having an effect on me, everything is reciprocal and, like the high achiever that I am, I just want to do this right – get it right. She starts to grind into my face. OK, do I grind back? How am I breathing? Through my nose? Do I go back to the clit? I'll go back to the clit. As I do, she gasps out in delight. Small circles, like the mouse thing. This is very confusing to me. Do I use a finger, too? Just my face? Do I blow here? I've read it's dangerous to blow into a vagina. She might explode. Her moans get louder and louder. I'll keep going then.

'Just like that, just there... Hmmm...'

Maybe she's faking this to make me feel better. I'll feel cheated if this is the case as I'm working hard here, lips and tongue, and making a concerted effort to control my breathing too, like I'm diving for pearls. I might get lockjaw. Is that a thing? I think it's caused by tetanus. I teach modules on lockjaw. I wouldn't be able to talk. How would I explain this to the school? Oh, I got it giving cunnilingus to Mia Johnson in English. I concentrate on what I'm doing. She's getting really loud now.

'Fuck... right there, Ed... keep going... Oh my...'

She grabs at my head and thrusts herself into me, her body going into some strange spasm, her legs straightening. I glance up, her face is pointed to the ceiling.

'FUUUUUCK!' she shrieks. The housemates definitely heard that.

But then a leg retracts and she forgets I might be there, kicking me straight in the eye.

'OOOOOW!' I say, clutching at my eye and falling back off the bed on to the floor. I lie there and stare at the ceiling. Here lies Ed, who died from blindness and lockjaw giving a woman an orgasm. Any joy I should be feeling from that achievement is replaced with the worry that I may not have a retina anymore.

Mia cackles with laughter, kneeling up and peering at me over the side of the bed. 'Oh my God, Ed, I'm sorry... I didn't mean to...' She reaches out and helps me back up onto the bed.

'Did you...?'

'Come?' She nods, her cheeks glowing, not quite knowing where to look until there's a fierce knocking on her bedroom door.

'STOP IT WITH YOUR SEX NOISES, MIA! WE'RE TRYING TO WATCH *UNIVERSITY CHALLENGE!*'

And with that Mia collapses back onto the bed laughing.

'Was that foreplay then?' I ask her, still trying to work out if she's blinded me.

She looks at me for a moment and nods. 'Yes. Well done. Now's the time to shake a girl's hand,' she says, putting it out for me.

I laugh and shake that hand, firmly.

TEN

MIA

I normally tell my sisters this, but I can legitimately tell you that teething babies and tantrum-prone toddlers are nothing compared to teenagers. Teens are a whole new breed of human governed by hormones, peer-pressure and energy drinks. We want them to strive for independence but not go too far over the line. We want them to be empathetic, co-operative and work hard, even though their brains are stuck in some ape-like egocentric mist where all they're really programmed to feel is apathy and injustice. We want them to love us except they don't. All they love is Snapchat. Sometimes I think I should just teach via that and TikTok, using filters, making up dances. I would slay at making one up for *Lord of the Flies*. I could rap it.

'MIA! Thank God you're here!' a voice booms from across the room. It's Henry from Geography who still looks wildly lost in this school despite the fact he's been here for eight months. Looks like he got roped into this after-school counselling gig, too. 'There was a woman here before in dungarees, but she's gone and I thought I'd have to do this alone.'

'Well, I'm here,' I assure him. 'Did she brief you before she left? What do we do if we get visitors?' I ask, as I take a seat in this corner of the school we call The Hub – our centre for student pastoral care, the place where we throw a few beanbags and primary colours and send our angry disruptive kids so we can get on with our actual jobs.

Henry scampers over to a wall. 'Sort of. I was told this is the worry tree,' he informs me, pointing to a trunk made of craft paper covered in about twenty leaves. It's a bit barren considering it's spring.

'If the kids are worried about anything then we get them to write it down and put it on the tree so it's a problem shared and halved.'

And put on the wall for everyone to see. I am not too sure I understand how that works but smile nonetheless.

'And she told me to look after her pens, make sure the lids are on properly and no one steals them because she's labelled them with a UV marker,' he tells me.

'Then we will guard them with our lives,' I joke.

He nods like a puppy. 'Tea?'

'I always knew I liked you, Henry. Milk, one sugar.'

He heads to the kettle, smelling the milk as I wander around, blinded by the lime green walls of this place. *Life is like a camera, focus on what's important, develop from the negatives and if it all goes wrong then take another shot.* This quote is emblazoned on the walls in huge letters with Polaroid pictures of the staff. Smart. I'd argue I'm very much like a camera: it's easy to push my buttons, I can be extraordinarily complicated to figure out and I enjoy a tripod. Maybe I should put that on my bedroom wall. Or maybe on a mug.

'So, were you allocated your spot here or did you volunteer?' I ask Henry, as he wipes a teaspoon down on his shirt. I always like how Henry looks like he's been told to wear smart clothes and he's just gone into his dad's wardrobe.

'A bit of both. Someone went round the staffroom last week with a clipboard. I think I also donated ten pounds to someone's GoFundMe at the same time.'

I smile. 'Always dodge the clipboard. Though I think your money has helped someone's cat have a life-saving operation so feel good about that.' He nods, taking it all in. 'Can I give you some advice, Henry?' I tell him. I mean, we are here, it feels like the right place. He comes over with my cup of tea and pulls back a chair, leaning forward to listen. 'I like you. I think you're doing great for your first year, but you always look petrified, mate. You need to not look so scared. The kids will see that and they will punish you for it.'

'But what if I am scared?' he asks.

'Oh, you're allowed to feel it. When I started, I had a Year 10 class that made me want to shit myself, but you still have to go in, shoulders back and not let the fear show in your face.' I won't lie, this is excellent advice and I feel like that green frog creature thing from *Star Wars*. 'Give yourself a break, you're still so new.'

'A teaching virgin, some might say...' he jokes. Of course, this word means new things to me now, so I fake laugh. Unless he's a virgin too? What are the bloody odds? 'My girlfriend tells me I'm trying too hard. I just need to...'

Girlfriend, maybe not. 'Chill?'

'Maybe. Or write my worries down on a tree,' he tells me, gesturing towards it.

This makes me laugh and we both get up, cradling our mugs, to have a look at what the children of this school worry about.

My acne

Bullies who will never change

Pooing myself in an exam

Never getting over the end of Stranger Things

Maybe I should add mine. I'm worried I've started something very strange and untraditional with my colleague where I seem to be teaching him how to have sex. On one hand, I had a crazy orgasm the other night, the sort where you get stabbing pains in the back of your eyes and worry you're about to have an aneurysm. Ed was a diligent student who took instruction well. It was both a surprise and a shock that he had some skills. However, where is this going? I know I'm in the middle of a dating drought and my trust in men, in general, is completely shot, but I can't just keep having sex with Ed. Where does it stop? When I've taught him everything? Maybe I can set him an exam and mock up a certificate for him when I think he's actually ready to go out into the world? Congratulations, your cherry has been popped and you're now a Level 3 Sexual Being. It is a worry. A worry that won't fit on a leaf.

'Miss Johnson, are you doing The Hub today?' a voice suddenly asks.

'I am, Lola,' I say, watching my bus route mate hover by the door. 'Me and Mr Lay.'

Henry waves at her and Lola flicks her head up at him to acknowledge him there. 'Do you want some free squash?' he asks her. She nods and he scurries over to the counter, pouring her a glass then stepping back to let me take this one, as some other kids enter the room. No fear, Henry. Also, look after the pens.

'Did you want to talk about anything?' I ask Lola. 'Maybe you'd like to put a leaf on the worry tree,' I say, posing to frame it, a bit too much sarcasm in my voice.

'Nah, it's cool.'

She takes a flimsy plastic cup from my hands and scans the walls of this place. The problem is I teach about two hundred kids in a day so it's impossible for me to get to know any of them properly. Lola is talkative, smart, she never volunteers answers, but cruises along at her own speed.

'You dating anyone, Miss?' she asks, out of the blue.

'Unfortunately not.' I mean, I'm shagging Mr Rogers and orchestrating really good orgasms, but I'd hardly call that conventional dating.

'How old are you?'

'Twenty-eight. Are you dating anyone?'

'Yeah, do you know Ryan Longstaff? Skin fade, North Face Jacket, Adidas bag...'

'Hun, you've described nearly every boy in this school.' She laughs and it seems to have broken the ice. 'Come, take a beanbag, tell me of your boy troubles.'

She plonks herself down ungracefully and I smile because I need to tell her as a member of staff that her skirt is way too short. However, I think mine was about the same length when I was at school, so I don't want to be hypocritical. I take the beanbag next to her, hoping I'll be able to extricate myself from this later.

'It's just... There was this party at the weekend and I didn't go but people have been sending me Snaps of Ryan there and telling me he was getting with Isla Cummings.'

'That's a bit crap – Sorry. Bad teacher word.' She snickers in response but then she looks at me as if she's realising she may have an ally in me. 'Have you asked Ryan about this?'

'Yeah, he said it's people trying to stir up shit.'

'But the pics tell another story?'

'Exactly.'

'Do you like Ryan?'

'I love him, Miss. I love him so much,' she whines.

Don't laugh in the young woman's face, Mia. I remember that feeling of young love, of feeling consumed by it in some sort of *The Notebook*-esque way, envisaging a life and a future with a boy, signing your names together and thinking about what your babies would look like, what you'd call them. It's not love. It's raging hormones.

'Lola, if he loves you then he'd tell you the truth. Are you having sex?' She widens her eyes to look at me, wondering what she's supposed to say. 'Lola, I was sixteen once. It's cool.'

'Yeah, he was my first. That's got to mean something, right?'

I smile. Do you wanna hear a funny story, Lola? I was Mr Rogers' first. 'Lola. You are so young. Your first time will always mean something, but you'll leave this school, you might go to college or find a job and life will throw you in the path of lots of different relationships, lot of different versions of love...'

'Is that what you did?' she asks and I'm conscious there's a risk I may make myself sound like a bit of a ho now.

'I've tried on lots of different shoes.'

She scrunches her face up. 'Miss, you've lost me.'

'Analogies, remember them?' I smack my forehead with the palm of my hand. 'Did that lesson mean nothing?'

She rolls her eyes back like she's trying to find the information. 'Oh, so like the shoes are men.'

'Yeah, and sometimes shoes don't fit or you outgrow them or...'

'They rub in all the wrong places.'

I nod, slowly.

'So basically, I should dump him like the sad pair of fake Jordans he bought off some shit Instagram site that he really is,' she says, snapping her fingers.

I'm not quite sure how we've made that analogy fit but yes, if you have video evidence of cheating then Lola, you kick him to the kerb, or whatever the young folk say these days.

'You could focus on your schoolwork instead, think of the future. Exams next month...'

'And prom. I'll have to ask Deano now. I can't go alone. Thank you, Miss. You know, you're actually quite smart,' she says, getting up from her beanbag, revelling in this epiphany.

'It has been said. Sure you don't want to fill out a leaf? Remember if you're sexually active, use protection, too. Make good choices!'

She does a thumbs up and leaves the room. *Your first time will always mean something.* That came out of my mouth, didn't it? I should have let Ed have his LED tealights. I suddenly feel something quite unnerving, a sense of responsibility. I don't want to be like Ryan Longstaff. I don't want to hurt Ed or ruin this for him. Christ, if anyone has to make the good choices, it's me.

'Bonjour,' a voice says, as a head pops around the door. Speak of the devil.

'Ed.' Ed wears green today which has always been his colour as it brings out the accents of his eyes, eyes I've seen up close now so I know that for sure. Is it strange that this is my favourite shirt of his? Is that allowed? He does have clothes I don't like. He has that striped one that looks a bit like a pyjama top and the half-zip knitwear makes him look like a pro-golfer.

'Did you do something wrong? Is that why you're here? Did Alicia send you to The Hub?' he jokes.

'You're funny. Henry is also here. We're bonding.' Henry waves from across the room where he's playing a board game with some Year 8s. I really hope they're not conning him out of any money.

Ed leans against the door and I'm not sure if it's the light or the shirt but there is something different about him. It's become apparent in the last few days, I think he might be walking differently. It's now Friday, four days since my last 'tutorial' with him and he's not avoiding me at school anymore. Any initial anxiety seems to have dissipated since, well, he came face to face with my vagina. Maybe he's overcome his fears. It was like my version of flooding therapy. I think I'm just grateful I've not ruined anything here.

'So, are we still going to hang out this evening?' he asks. 'I have a meeting but definitely afterwards. We can go to mine?'

I smirk for a moment. I know he's trying to orchestrate this so he doesn't have to have sex lessons at mine. I know he has questions over the quality and cleanliness of my bed linen and towels.

'Actually, I'm taking us on a field trip tonight.'

He bites his lip. I guess in the context of what I'm educating him about, this could mean many things. Am I taking him to a sex club? A car park to go dogging? A sex shop?

He pauses, no longer leaning but upright with panic. 'Will I need anything for this field trip? Is it cashless? Will I need to get money?' he asks, a list of questions building in his head.

'Just you. See you in about an hour,' I tell him. 'You might need extra socks though.'

'Really?' he says.

'No, Ed.'

ED

Yes, Mia kicked me in the face after I made her orgasm but, I am happy to report, my eyes are still functioning. I'm not sure if it kickstarted a whole new light in which I see her these days. I think it might be gratitude. Not that I didn't feel that before, she offered me friendship, she was always kind to me, but now, it feels like I'm not just tucked under her wing, she's showing me all the ways in which I can fly. She would rightly give me a C for that analogy, but it wouldn't change the fact that I'm grateful to her. It feels like she's a crucial figure in my sexual development. And even though when we first had sex, shock and worry prevailed, I feel strangely comfortable with her now we've drawn up a firm agreement about our unique arrangement.

However, the words 'field trip' fill me with dread, because I know Mia, and she likes spontaneity, noise, and pushing people out of their comfort zones. Is she taking me to have sex in an actual field? That would be illegal and it's still spring so the nights do get cooler. I hope there's a blanket involved.

As she pulls up in front of the school in her tatty Fiat

Panda, she waves at me and I jump into the passenger side, watching as she moves a few crisp packets and her handbag into the footwell.

'Jump in, it's not far...'

'That's good,' I say, doing up my seatbelt, ponderous as to the noise coming out of her car radio. 'You are scaring me though. What are we doing? Is it outdoors? Are we going clubbing? You know I'm not really into that.'

Mia laughs, half singing along to the noise on the radio. 'You are hilarious. You're in old man chinos, we're definitely not going clubbing.' She places her hand in a packet of chocolate covered raisins and I watch as she scoops a handful of them up, some of them missing her mouth, rolling down to the seat and beyond. Is it bad that all I want to do now is run round this vehicle with my Dyson? She offers me a dig in her raisin stash and I politely decline.

'I'm good. Then where are we going? You know I also like some level of preparedness. You say I get anxious and it's usually because you're so leftfield.' I reach down for my phone and scroll through my apps. 'It says here that there's a seventy percent chance of rain in an hour. I don't have a coat. Are we outdoors?'

'No. But what if we were? You are always slightly preoccupied by what the weather's doing and I'll tell you now, that is not sexy.'

'It is practical. I don't want to sit around in wet pants.'

'Maybe I do...' Mia says, an eyebrow raised. I sit there not knowing whether to laugh, be scared or appalled. She teases me but I've never seen someone so unprepared for rain and the cold. I can't think of the number of times I've had to strip in the staffroom and give her my jumper.

'I'll have you know, I think Caitlin appreciates my practicality. I bought her some lightbulbs the other day which she thought were...'

'Shit?'

'It was a shared joke thing,' I try to explain.

I gave them to her in a gift bag which was probably going overboard but she giggled when she opened it. I guess it's a move in the right direction. First step, lightbulbs, second step, dishwasher salt. Maybe if I lavish her with practical household items then she'll fall in love with my sensible sincerity.

'Well, if you are going to get me gifts, please no lightbulbs. I accept wine and chocolates,' Mia tells me, scooting over a roundabout like she's competing in a Grand Prix in Monaco. I clench on to my seat. She slows her car down and pulls into a darkened car park. Crap, we're going dogging, aren't we? What on earth is she making me do? Then I see a scrappy sign over a building that seems to be connected to a church: SHEEN COMMUNITY CENTRE. Oh dear, are we here to pray? For me?

'Well, this is lovely. Am I allowed to ask what we're doing here?' I ask.

'We're here to learn. Are those shoes comfortable?' she asks me.

'Well, they don't rub or anything,' I answer.

She smiles broadly in return. A hand rapping at the window makes me jolt in my seat and Mia winds down the window. 'FRANK!' she squeals.

I don't even know dogging etiquette, but I am not comfortable with Frank watching. Also, why is he in a suit? Is it because we're London based? Does dogging get posh in inner cities?

He spies me in the passenger seat. 'Ooooh, you brought a friend? You never bring friends,' he enquires.

'Oh, this is Ed. Ed, this is Frank. It's his first time, so be gentle,' she says, slapping me on the knee. Please, no.

'A pleasure. I'll see you inside,' he says, winking, though I'm not entirely sure who he's winking at. Mia winds up her window and I go into panic mode.

'Mia... first time at what? Where have you brought me?'

She pulls a face trying to figure out my confusion and smiles. 'A tantric sex class.'

'MIA! That man must be seventy! What on earth?!' I shriek in high tones. 'In a church hall? That's got to be against their laws.'

Mia bites her lip. 'Yeah, we just line all the old men up on the floor, tell them to get their wrinkly wangers out and then we teach them how to hold that orgasm.'

'You are mocking me,' I say, crossing my arms.

She shakes her head, opening the car door, urging me to follow. I have no idea where she's leading me but there's a glow of lights coming from the church hall windows, a faint sound of music, and the smell of... chips? As she opens the doors, I shift her a look. Really?

'I know I said I didn't do clubbing, but this seems to be the other end of the spectrum, Mia?'

Inside the hall is what can only be described as a dance. For pensioners. There's a lone disco ball, lines of tables with teacups and bunting and a dancefloor where couples trip the light fantastic across the shiny parquet floors. I turn to Mia to chastise her again but instead she's waving at a few people in the room. She knows them? There was me thinking she spent her Fridays clubbing and sleeping with randoms when really she was here? Is this her way of telling me she has a fetish for older gentlemen?

She turns to me and links an arm through mine. 'You have two problems, Ed. One is that you don't really know how to talk to women. Two is that you need to cut loose, relax, feel comfortable in your own body.'

'So the answer to this is for me to chat up a granny and do a waltz?'

'So rude... I want you to converse, interact with these people, and I don't waltz, I salsa. We need you to find your groove, get your hips working,' she tells me, mimicking the motion.

'I don't know how to salsa.'

'Well, it was this or take you to a nightclub and make you grind against people.'

'I guess this is the better option then...'

'And they do a decent fish and chip supper, too,' she adds, walking me over to a table full of people.

An old lady in an emerald glittery number throws her arms around Mia then glances over at me, suspiciously. 'Frank told me you brought someone. How are you, gorgeous?'

'All good, nice to see you all. Love those sequins, Yolanda!' Mia says, standing back to admire her. 'Everyone, this is Ed. I work with him.'

'Are you courting?' a woman in a fur stole asks us.

'No, he just doesn't get out much so I'm trying to jazz up his social life.' Whilst this isn't a complete untruth, some of the old ladies stare at me with a look that can only be described as pity, like they might want to adopt me.

'Well, you've come to the right place,' Frank tells me. 'Can I get you a beer?'

I nod, conscious my hands are still in my pockets. 'Well, young man, I've been dying to get out there since I arrived. Do you dance?' Yolanda tells me, a hand to her hip.

'I-I... don't really dance. Maybe I'll just watch for now,' I mutter.

'Love, none of us can really dance, we just shuffle around. Come on... It'll make Esther over there in the feathers super jealous,' Yolanda jokes with me.

'Ed, when a beautiful lady asks you to dance, you do not refuse her invitation,' Mia says to me, putting her hands to the small of my back and giving me a gentle shove.

I look at Mia with a face of complete fear. She's throwing me into a sea of old people in fancy outfits with absolutely no life raft. Just my youth and work chinos. I hear a few older ladies at the table cheering me on.

I smile bravely at Yolanda. 'Well, I apologise in advance if I step on your feet and stuff...'

'Oh, I have calluses and bunions. I probably won't feel it anyway,' she jests. Sexy.

We walk onto the dancefloor and I glance back at Mia but she waves me away. I think I hate her for this. When we find an open space to dance, Yolanda places her crepe-like hand in mine, pulling me close in so our hips are touching and showing me where to put my hand to her back. I gulp hard and loudly. I've briefly seen those dancing shows on television. I won't be doing any of those moves but I think I can side-step my way through this, yes? I pray Yolanda doesn't want me to spin her. More importantly, I hope I don't have some strange reaction to the bodily contact and get a stiffy when I'm dancing with an old lady. This will give her the wrong idea and Mia will mock me for life.

'So, if you can count to four then we're on to a winner. Think of it like a box. Step back, let me follow... to the left... There you go... Have you never slow danced with a lady then?' she asks me. She wants me to talk through this, too?

'Umm, not really. Not proper dancing like this,' I admit.

'Well, I'm honoured to be your first.' I fake a smile and glance over to Mia who has both thumbs up in the air. Speaking of firsts.

'So, how do you know Mia?' I say, getting distracted and bumping into a couple and apologising profusely.

'She's a regular here. She teaches a group of us creative writing every fortnight, and she organises these evenings.' I stop for a moment to see Mia still stood in conversation, laughing and hugging everyone. 'Didn't you know this? And you two work together? At the school?' she asks.

'Yeah. And no, I didn't know this...'

'I knew her mother. She was the one who worked for the council and got this community centre started up, and Mia took it over when she moved back to London.'

I nod, still thinking too hard about trying to keep time but also thinking about how little Mia has told me about her life. I always knew she had sisters, but the way Yolanda speaks about her mum in the past tense makes me think she's not around anymore and I didn't know this. Of all the things she has shared with me, she never told me this. I didn't know about this secret community champion identity she had. Perhaps I assumed a lot of things about her.

'Ooooh, look at Esther. Bloody show-off.'

I turn to see a lady in the middle of the floor who is not taking prisoners. Christ, Esther, that's a lot of feathers. She seems to have come with a semi-professional partner who flings her about the dancefloor, kicking her legs high and wide. I hope she's wearing the right supportive underwear for that.

'She took up yoga a few years ago and thinks she's better than us. Look at that fake tan. She looks like a garden fence...'

I laugh at the competitiveness but quickly stop when I realise Yolanda may have her hand on my arse. Is she squeezing? I think she is.

'Yolanda,' I whisper in horror.

'That is a good bum... is she looking?' she asks.

I swallow hard, watching as Esther dances closer to us. 'Yes.'

'Oh, Yolanda – you found someone to dance with you? How lovely,' she says, a little spitefully. Lady, that tone is not going to win you any friends. Her partner looks me up and down.

'This is my new boyfriend, actually. Ed,' Yolanda says.

I have not been consulted about this but I'm not sure I have a choice. Esther is giving me the proper stink-eye, or maybe it's glaucoma. Yolanda pulls me in closer.

'Really? I guess the young lad must be quite desperate

then?' Esther murmurs. Yolanda grabs my hand and squeezes it tightly. I have to say something to confirm our relationship.

'That is really mean,' I reply, not hugely convincingly. 'Yolanda is a beautiful woman, and I am with her for many of her wonderful qualities,' I then improvise, Yolanda beaming at me for playing along.

'Like her dead husband's pension?' she retorts.

I recoil in shock, both at the spikiness and at being accused of being a gold digger.

'Well, at least I'm with the one man. You gave Frank crabs, you dirty whorebag!'

Bloody hell, I wasn't prepared for this, any of this, because suddenly, Esther launches herself at Yolanda, her hands stiff like claws and, like some bloody idiot, I stand there to defend this old lady who I've only just met. I hear fabric being ripped. Esther shrieking over the sound of the music. Esther's partner walking away like he doesn't want the drama. Or the blood. Is that my blood? Oh.

ELEVEN

MIA

'I WANT THAT WENCH BARRED!' Yolanda yells at me, as I try to fix her hair. Esther really went for her barnet and I need to place some of those curls back in place.

'Yolanda, it's not a pub. It's a tea dance. You're just as bad as each other. I didn't think I'd need to write a code of conduct for something like this,' I explain to her, pushing a small glass of wine in her direction to steady her nerves. 'Why on earth did you tell her Ed was your boyfriend? He could be your grandson. That's just filthy talk.'

Yolanda giggles then looks worried. 'Is he alright? First time here and he gets a left hook to the nose.'

'I'd have been better off taking him to a nightclub.' I look over to the kitchen hatch where Frank, previously a GP, is treating him with a fusty old first aid kit we found in the storeroom.

'You should go and check in on him. Make sure he's alright,' Yolanda says, downing her wine but also giving me some serious eyebrows.

'You can stop that. He's just a friend,' I say, my lips pursed.

'Mia, for all the years I have known you, you have never brought anyone here. That means something,' she says. 'He seems nice.'

'He is. Maybe too nice though, you know?'

'There is no such thing,' Yolanda mentions. 'I mean, I pressed myself up against him, too. He's got assets.'

'Yo, really?' I cackle. I mean, I know about the assets but if I'm going to bring that up now, this old lady will not be subtle.

'If I go check on him, will you promise to be good? Esther is over there eating her chips. Can you just leave her alone?' Yolanda shifts her eyes around like an angry toddler. 'Donna, can you keep her company?' I ask a lady at another table. Donna agrees but as soon as I leave, I see them huddle together for a bitching session. Maybe I should ban the wine.

As I head over to Ed, I think about what Yolanda just said. This has always been a safe space for me and not somewhere I would think to bring a boyfriend. Hey, let's go down to the church hall and you can meet all these people who smell like lavender and we can have a slow dance to Nat King Cole. Although I don't care too much for what other people think, even I know that's not a sexy look to impress a boyfriend. Maybe I trust Ed enough to let him see this part of me. As I approach him now, I'm not sure that trust will ever be returned though. I think he might have a tampon up his nose.

'All OK, here?' I ask him and Frank, assessing the damage. It's not just a tampon up the nose, it's a spoilt shirt and blotting up the rest of the blood with a giant roll of toilet paper.

'Well, I don't think anything's broken but there may be a bruise. Esther really landed one on you,' Frank tells him. Ed grimaces at him and shifts me a look.

'Frank, I can take over. Your dinner's ready when you are.'

'Mushy peas?' he asks.

'Always.'

He leaves, putting an arm to Ed's shoulder before he does. Ed refuses to look at me.

'Is that a tampon?' I ask him.

'It is. Frank used to be the qualified first aider for a rugby team and apparently this is the best way to deal with a nosebleed.'

I drag a chair next to him and start laughing, watching as the string hanging out of his nose vibrates in time as he joins in. Somehow, he's styling it out.

'I'm so sorry, Ed. I really am,' I say, through my laughter. 'I can replace the shirt.'

He shakes his head and wipes his nose with a handful of paper-like toilet tissue. 'How was your Friday, Ed? Oh, I got touched up by an old lady and then punched by another. I am not sure how this was supposed to help me,' he complains to me. 'How has this module taught me anything?'

'It should teach you to move quicker when an old lady's fist comes for you.'

'First you kick me in the eye and now this happens to my nose.'

'Love is a battlefield, my friend.'

I watch Yolanda and Donna conspire in whispers as Esther sits on the other side of the room with a wooden chip fork in hand, snarling. Never mind a code of conduct, I'll have to get security in hi-vis vests. I shake my head, smiling to myself, but notice Ed turned towards me, studying my face, trying to catch my eye.

'I'm sorry about your mum, by the way,' he says quietly. The words are so out of the blue that I don't quite know how to reply to them. I've never really spoken about my mum with anyone. It always feels too sad, too complicated.

'Yolanda?' I ask him, quietly, giving her some serious side-eye.

'You told me to converse with people!' he says, in his defence.

'To find out about her, not gossip about me,' I say, laughing but curious what else went down on that dance floor in the space of mere moments.

'I never knew you did any of this,' Ed tells me, turning to face me, his expression warm, proud even. I don't quite know how to look back at him.

'There's a lot you don't know about me.'

'Mia, you are the biggest over-sharer I know. You've told me stories. Like that time you had sex with that man and the dog ate the condom and needed surgery.'

'Because that's funny. That's a good staffroom story,' I tell him.

'But you do all of this yourself?' he asks me, looking around the room in wonder.

'Not exactly. I just book the hall and make the posters, get the caterers in. They do the bunting and choose the music. Apparently, they don't want to listen to Rihanna,' I say, joking.

'And you teach a writing class, too?' he asks me.

'You had a lot to chat about with Yolanda, eh?' I say, looking back at him. 'Yes, I teach a writing workshop, once a month.'

'That's really nice, Mia,' he tells me, no condescension in his tone at all, almost praising me. The compliment is warming.

'It was something my mum started, and I just took it over after she died. You're giving me Mother Teresa eyes here, but you should see some of the erotic stuff Donna writes, it'd send you blind...'

I know what I'm doing here. I'm making light of every question he asks me or it'll be far too sad. When I came back to London after university, I got an invitation from Yolanda to come to a farewell event in this very space. They were going to stop running the events and classes because of a lack of volunteers, zero funds – another part of my mother's legacy erased – and I couldn't bear to see that happen.

'You're a good person, Mia,' Ed says. My eyes meet his and I stop for a moment. It's a casual comment but one that really stakes at my heart. It's not something people say, or that I think about myself. Maybe it's pathetic to want or need that validation, but sometimes you need to be watered, to feel the sunshine of someone's words, to grow, to stand tall, to bloom. Coming from Ed, too, his words mean something. Do I thank him? Maybe not. So I just put a hand in his for a moment to let him know I heard him. Thank you for being here and seeing all of this. He squeezes it back. It's kinda cool.

The moment is suddenly interrupted by a change of tempo in the music. This is what happens when you put this lot in charge of their own playlists. They lure me into a false sense of security with all their war music and then suddenly, we're in the Buena Vista Social Club. The problem is they watch far too much Strictly. We almost got in trouble last month when Stanley dislocated a hip. I watch as Frank leads someone to the dancefloor.

'Wooo, FRANK!' I call out to the dancefloor as I watch his side-step. 'Look at him go,' I say, shaking my shoulders.

'That's how Frank probably got crabs,' Ed remarks.

'How do you...?' I enquire curiously.

'Don't ask. Is this salsa then?'

'A version of it,' I say, rising to my feet, dancing on the spot, uninhibited. For all that I can't do in my life, I can shimmy when the occasion calls for it. Ed watches, studying my feet. I take his hands and pull him up so he can join in.

'I can't shimmy. My tampon might fall out,' he says, matter-of-factly.

'That's not how tampons work,' I say, tugging his arms harder.

He stands there, almost in fight mode, waiting to defend

himself in case he gets injured again. I hold myself close to him. 'Salsa's a little more casual than the ballroom stuff. I'm going to get right up in your grill,' I say, my face close to his, widening my eyes. He smiles in response. 'And instead of following feet, you follow hips. Our bodies should just fit and flow together.'

'Like mating dolphins...'

'Not what I had in my head but let's go with that.'

'I saw it in a wildlife documentary once. The male–'

'Ed, not the time. What are your hips doing?' I ask him, watching as they go side to side and back and forth like he's dry humping my thigh. 'You're a science man. Think of a figure-of-eight motion,' I say, putting my hands to his hips.

'That's more of an infinity sign.'

'Exactly. Hips for life.'

He's learning for someone who hasn't done this before or even danced in his kitchen for that matter. It's like a scene out of *Dirty Dancing*, isn't it? Except I'm Swayze. Ed watches some people looking at him and I see that tension return to his body. I put a hand to his cheek to tell him where to look.

'Look at me,' I say, drawing him closer so my breath is warm on his cheek. He looks into my eyes and grinds a little more intently into me. He's getting there. I push him away and pretend to spin. Our arms get tangled, and I try to laugh it off. He pulls me in again, his fingers interlacing through mine.

'Good,' I say, looking him in the eye. 'Slow it down.'

Again, he does exactly what he's told and dare I say it, I think I may be a little aroused even with the tampon string hanging out of his nose. Is that allowed? It's nothing more than all the physical proximity and the bumping and grinding. It can't be anything else. But then I feel something else. I've never felt a cock do that before but that's an impressive skill. It's buzzing.

'Is that you?' I ask him.

He snaps out of the moment to realise what's happening.

'Oh yeah, sorry, my phone...' He takes it out of his pocket to read the message from the alert. 'Oh, it's from Caitlin,' he says, sounding mildly surprised.

'That's good?' I reply.

'She's asking if I'm free tonight to help her with something... if I can grab some food and go round?'

I try to hide the emotion in my eyes. I think I might be disappointed, but also can't help but feel excited to see his eyes shining, to see the happiness registering in his face. It's a good look on him.

'I'll have to go home first, change.'

'Take out your tampon,' I suggest.

'This is true.'

'You should go. It's Friday night, that's an invite. No school tomorrow.'

'I can get wine.'

'Exactly.'

'I mean, is it OK for me to leave? I know you invited me here, I don't want to bail, but do you need help with anything before I go?' he asks, looking around.

I shake my head. 'I have an army of help here, don't be stupid. GO! Jump in a cab and get yourself sorted. You better text me with details though,' I tell him, pushing him on the shoulder.

'Are you sure?' he asks, his eyes strangely intense.

'Surer than sure.' I give him a breezy grin.

He hugs me before he leaves and strides over to a few people to say his goodbyes before heading for the exit. Yolanda looks at me the whole time, staring at me pitifully, but not before making smoochy faces in my direction. I stick my middle finger up at her.

ED

It seems to be a week of firsts for me at the moment. First time having sex, first time giving someone an orgasm, first time dancing in public, first time being punched by an old lady and now the first time someone has ever asked me on a date. That text was not only unexpected but a complete relief. Turns out I didn't put Caitlin off with my lightbulb gift. She trusted me enough to invite me back into her home and choose a takeaway for the evening.

As I sit in the Uber to her house, I mentally make a checklist of all the things that will make tonight a success. I've had a quick shower, brushed my teeth, doubled-up on deodorant, changed my pants. I'm taking a taxi there just in case I get drunk and I don't want to drive, but I'm not going to initiate or have sex. She's a nice girl and I don't want any potential to be destroyed by doing this too early in our relationship. Give her time. I've also gone classy with the takeaway and opted for noodles and bento, which shows I'm sophisticated and also doesn't involve huge amounts of garlic, should we kiss.

I'm on my way. I'm nervous.

I look down at the text I sent Mia ten minutes ago, but the text remains unread. She's busy, dancing with old people, separating their fights. Maybe I shouldn't have walked out on the tea dance. Was that rude? She did tell me to go and it wasn't a date per se, unless she actually ordered fish and chips for me, in which case I should offer to pay for that. I want her to respond though. For some reason, her stabilising confidence would be nice right now.

'You off on a hot date, boss?' the Uber driver, Lazlo, asks me.

'Oh, I don't know. I think...'

'Nice work, what's her name?'

'Caitlin.'

'You been going out long?'

'Not really.' I don't think we're even going out at all.

'Well, you've bought food. That'll get you off on the right foot. She shit at cooking then?'

'I have no idea.'

He pulls a confused face in the rear-view mirror. Do you know where you are? Your own name? Do I need to drive you to a hospital? I know nothing. All I know is that I have clean pants on.

'Well, what could go wrong?' he exclaims.

Quite a lot if you're me. If Lazlo could be inside my armpits now, he'd know that I feel anything but confident about the situation. He pulls up outside her house.

'Well, have fun, boss.'

I smile. 'Thank you, Lazlo.'

As I get out of the car, the front door opens automatically and Caitlin stands in tracksuit bottoms and a T-shirt having obviously already done a bit of painting this evening. I'm glad I didn't opt for anything too formal. 'Oh my, you're here! I'm so glad,' she sighs as she walks up the path in her sliders and gives me a one-armed hug and a kiss to my cheek, taking the food from me. She smells like emulsion, her hair bundled on top of her head, slight paint speckles on one of her forearms.

'I am... Hi!' That is a suave opener, Ed Rogers. 'I bought bento. And wine.'

'Aren't you amazing? Come in... I'm so glad you were free.'

I don't know if being free on Friday signals that I'm not hugely interesting, but I won't overthink it. She just said I was amazing, and the compliment makes me blush slightly. We walk into her kitchen where she puts the bag on the side, gets out her bento and pops the lid, picking at an edamame bean. I guess we're not going to lay the table and have a meal together then.

'I'm starving. I came home from school and just got stuck into painting my bathroom,' she tells me, splitting her chopsticks and getting stuck into her crispy chicken. I approach the countertop tentatively to do the same, watching as she slumps on a kitchen chair.

'This is delish. Thank you so much. Are you OK? Your nose looks a bit sore. Did you get into a fight?'

I can't tell her the truth without looking like an idiot. 'I did. With a squash ball. It'll mend.'

I sit down next to her and she bends over for a moment to inspect it more clearly, putting a hand to my face. I can't quite catch my breath.

'You lemon,' she jokes. 'These are excellent noodles, by the way.'

'You're welcome. I didn't quite know what to get but then I thought, everyone loves noodles, right?'

'Very true.'

Everyone loves noodles? I'm so good with words. I crack open my bento box. 'So, you said you needed help with something?' I ask. 'Are you OK?'

'Oh yeah, well… I remember you said you were quite handy and I'm having trouble with my radiators. They come on when the hot water does and I don't want them to do that. I just can't seem to figure out the controls.'

In the back of mind, did I hope that she meant helping her with something was some sort of hidden euphemism? Maybe, but I don't want to overstep.

'Oh, well, when we're done here, show me where the controls are and I can sort that. It should be easy to reset.'

She breathes a sigh of relief. 'Thank you so much.' She stands up and opens the drawer, taking out a corkscrew and opening the wine.

'Do you know how much a plumber was going to charge me for coming round and doing that for me?' she moans.

'And I'm better than a plumber, I also bring dinner,' I tell her.

'Exactly.'

'I tell you, this new house thing is a nightmare. I keep bidding for pieces of furniture on Facebook marketplace, too, and nothing comes of it. It's so annoying...'

This is not something I know much about, but I make an effort to sound interested. 'What do you need?'

'Well, I need a coffee table. Something to bring the room together.' She shows me something on her phone. It's exactly the sort of industrial modernist piece I would choose, drawers for your remote controls so they'd never get lost, a shelf for assorted books and a tissue box.

'That is nice. You have excellent taste.'

'Why, thank you. So, after this and you sorting my heating, do you have more plans for this evening?'

I'm not quite sure how to respond to that. I thought we could chat over wine on your sofa, we could watch something on Netflix and see where the evening takes us? This is too open-ended.

'Well...'

'How are you with painting? I thought it'd be easy, but my finishing is awful. How's your finishing?'

I take a large mouthful of udon as she says that. I'm a bit quick off the mark, to be honest. I don't say that out loud.

There is one thing I know that will certainly need to happen after tonight. I will need new jeans. Even though I was able to strip down to a T-shirt to help her paint, there is splatter on these trousers that will never shift as I also used gloss to help with her skirting boards. The way I look now, it does appear that I'm a huge fan of bukkake and that's not a good look. I get up off the floor and straighten my back, hearing it click as I do so. I'll be able to tell Mia I had a lovely evening. It was that sort of fun courting ritual you see in films where we laughed at the forced proximity every time we met in the corners of the rooms, showing each other our glossy hands. She was also on all fours for most of the evening but it was so we could tackle her skirting. Even then, I wouldn't know how to manage that position as I've not covered that in my sex tutorials.

'What I don't understand, though, is why we are pushing so much funding towards the arts?' Caitlin adds.

Whilst both of us have been crawling along the floor, we've also had the time to converse like grown adults. This is what I always thought a relationship would be like (bar the painting). Chats in a grown up flat, over wine, about topics that are meaningful and make sense of the world.

'I guess it's to let the kids have a broader spectrum of thinking. It encourages better creativity, decision making, the ability to express themselves freely,' I add.

'True but I really think this is why we're missing out on people looking at STEM subjects as they get older,' she argues, also standing up. 'Ed, high-five me. I think we've done an excellent job tonight.'

I'm not a high-five person but I do what I'm told, giving a large sigh as her back is turned. The problem is, she is perfect for me in terms of compatibility. We are into the same things, she liked how I paired the wine to the noodles and when I looked in her loft to adjust her heating controls, all the boxes were labelled. Labelling keeps this world sane, I am sure of it.

'I've had a really fun night,' I tell her, hoping I don't sound too boring in that household chores bring me joy.

'You were excellent company, thank you for everything.'

There's a moment when we're standing there awkwardly looking around the room.

'We should soak your brushes,' I suggest. 'I hope you have turps.' She nods and smiles.

She's very pretty and perfect in so many ways, but I have no idea what I need to do here. Say, I've just learnt a simple box step in the waltz and how to salsa. Fancy a dance on your dust sheets? I've also learnt how to give orgasms recently, but I think that might be a step too far. I need to complain to my sex course provider again because none of what I've learnt helps here.

'Maybe a cup of tea?' she says, trying to break the ice. Or keep me here? I don't know.

I follow her to the kitchen and put her brushes in the sink, running the tap as she comes over to fill up the kettle. Interact. Do something. Anything, Ed. And as her arm is against mine, I lean over and kiss her. Is it a bit misaimed? Are my hands still in the sink? Is she holding the kettle? Yes. But I do it. She seems a little surprised but then puts the kettle down. My hands move to the back of her head. Her body presses against mine, the sweet taste of wine still in her mouth.

TWELVE

MIA

'Hi!'

'Hi!'

There is something different about Ed as he stands there at the front door of his flat. I look down to the floor. Usually, he has old man slippers on but today he's barefoot, his shirt is untucked, I don't think he's even combed his hair. It's an Ed I approve of, he looks lighter, more comfortable in his own skin.

'YOU HAD SEX WITH HER!' I shout, just as a neighbour is returning to their flat across the hallway. He grabs my arm and pulls me inside, putting a hand in the air to apologise to the elderly lady smirking.

'No, I didn't,' he replies, sternly.

'I brought you bagels,' I reply, handing him a paper bag. If this sounds kind then it's not, they're for me because I haven't had breakfast. 'Then why aren't you wearing slippers? You always wear slippers.'

'We kissed,' he tells me excitedly, walking through to the

kitchen, his voice almost fizzing with excitement. 'We actually kissed.'

There is a skip and hop to his step and I smile to see that one kiss can make him light up in such a way, how it relaxes his shoulders and makes his skin glow. As we walk into the kitchen, that same light floods the kitchen and I watch as he gets out his bread board to make me breakfast. I like how well trained he is.

'That was the huge emergency you texted me about at seven in the morning? Nice...'

'It's exciting!' he tells me. The last time I saw him this revved up was when we had coloured paper clips in the supply cupboard.

'So, a question... Why aren't you in her kitchen then, making *her* breakfast? What happened after the kiss?'

'She smiled and I didn't want to overstep so we had tea and then we kissed again when I left and then I went home,' he tells me, still floating around his kitchen to tell me the details.

'And had a wank?' I enquire.

'So romantic... I didn't want to rush it. It was such a nice evening, I helped her sort some things in her house. We have so much in common... she's so nice...'

He puts a hand to the kettle and stares at the kitchen wall. If it were me, I'd have nailed any potential love interest on the kitchen table but then he isn't me and I like the innocent joy in his face.

'Lordy, you've got the love bugs. Look at you,' I tease him.

He snaps out of his trance. 'I do not! What's the love bugs?'

'It's something my mum used to say when we'd meet a boy and come back all googly-eyed, not stop talking about them and start writing their names everywhere...'

'You've had them before then?'

'I got nits once from a fella with Jesus hair I shagged at a festival.'

Ed laughs and it's a relief and a joy to hear that sound, to hear it sound so authentic and genuine. He grabs a bread knife, throwing a bagel in the air and catching it before slicing it in half. Never mind the joy, it's the confidence that makes me smile.

'I don't really know what to do next, though? I didn't want to run straight into the sex thing. Should I take her out on a date?' he asks me.

'You're asking me?'

'Yeah. Because you know these things, right?' he tells me.

'Ed, I know sex. Ask me anything you want about that. But I've never had a cute relationship thing like what you're describing to me. Most of my relationships have been born from drunkenly meeting people in pubs.'

'Oh,' he says, looking slightly alarmed. It is true. I met one boyfriend on the night bus as I was trying to steal his chips. My relationship history isn't romantic meet-cutes in cafes, putting furniture together and feeding each other spaghetti. It's messy and raucous. I can't quite bear to see Ed's face though, like that was how he'd always imagined love to be. I can't shit on that, can I?

I go up to him and put a reassuring arm around his shoulder as he fills a cafetiere to make us coffee. 'Listen, I've watched enough romcoms though to tell you that a date probably comes next so she can get to know you and gauge your sincerity. Something in public that's fun and will require a slight level of proximity.'

'I was thinking cinema?' he suggests.

'Nope, sitting in the dark for two hours saying nothing?'

'Laser tag?'

'Are you twelve?' I jest. 'There's a cool pub I'll send you details for. You can hire pool tables, it's got good chicken wings, nice vibes. You can play pool, yes?'

'Pool is just angles and maths, isn't it?'

'Well, yeah. And go like this. Relaxed Ed. It's a good look.'

He looks down at himself. 'It's how I normally look, no?'

I bite my tongue, grabbing a bar stool at his kitchen island and putting my head down on folded arms. 'So, this was the big emergency? I could have helped you sort a date via WhatsApp and then I wouldn't have needed to get out of bed.'

He stands at the countertop and puts my bagel on a plate, spreading just the right amount of peanut butter on it and placing it in front of me. I shove it in my mouth, pointing at the toaster. It's sweet how he thinks just the one bagel is going to cut it.

'Mia, it's ten o'clock,' he points out to me.

'It's Saturday. Plus, you bailed on me last night, I am nursing that complete abandonment.'

Ed's eyes widen. 'But you told me to go!'

'I did. But it meant I had no one to stack the chairs at the end or help me put Frank in a taxi and he's deceptively heavy...'

Ed watches me leaning against his countertop. I can't quite make out what he thinks about all of that but I'm glad I made him go. I'm glad he was part of that space for a moment.

'Can you try to use the plate I've given you?' he asks me, watching crumbs fall to his countertop and pushing my plate a fraction towards me. He's never appreciated my casual eating style. He hands me the other bagel and watches me devour that one, too. I bloody love bagels.

'You're highly critical given I rushed round here in your hour of need. You didn't just bring me here for advice on dating venues, did you?' I say, eyeing up the coffee.

He shakes his head. 'I mean, the reason I'm also being polite with her is I also feel that I'm still, you know...'

'Virginy?' I ask, licking the peanut butter off my lips.

'Not the word I was looking for, but yes. There's still a lot to learn. If we end up in bed together, I don't want to...'

'Come as soon as she looks at your knob?'

He rolls his eyes. 'Such a way with words...'

'I only speak in truths, young Ed. So basically, you got me here for a sex lesson.'

He cringes at how I've defined the situation. 'I didn't know how to put that in a text. Do we need to keep diarising this?'

I laugh quietly. It will at least show this up for what it is, some efficient sex exercise, void of any romanticism whatsoever. 'Well, I wasn't planning on doing anything today. But next time text so I can prepare.' I think about how under my hoodie, I'm still wearing a crop top I wore to sleep. 'I'm down for this, you know I am but you're a teacher – you know how unprofessional it is to walk into a classroom without a plan, the right tools,' I explain, yawning.

'Noted. Tools. Actually, I'm glad you said that,' Ed mutters and he heads to his kitchen table where he picks up a cardboard box and a notebook. 'Can I ask you about some things?' I eye him curiously as he comes back to where I'm sitting, opens the box up on the counter and hands me a Rabbit – the sex toy as opposed to the animal. Is it a gift?

'So, after you showed me those sex toys the other day, I went back to that 'Love Shack' website and I bought this and, well, I've spent the last two days just looking at it. I may have to return it... if you can return it. I did check the terms and conditions and...'

I look deeper into the box as he studies the receipts paperwork and he's not just bought this. He's got three types of condoms, handcuffs and a small metal butt plug. I've created a monster.

'Ed,' I say thoughtfully, the Rabbit still in my hand.

'Mia.'

'Were you drunk?' I cackle.

'I panic bought it all.'

'Ed, people panic buy toilet paper, not sex toys... Do you even know what half of this does?' I ask.

'Kind of. I have questions about the butt plug? Whose butt does it go in?'

It's questions like this which do make me wonder how he's got this far in life. But I am here to educate, to turn this man into some sexual connoisseur. Maybe we're halfway there given he's managed to get these items out on the place he normally serves food.

'Well, it can go in either. Depending if that's what you're into?'

He nods and writes something down in a notebook.

'You're making notes?' *Goes in either bumhole.*

He ignores me. 'And do you take it in turns? Is that... hygienic?' he enquires.

'Well, even I would wash it between persons.' I study it. 'Metal is a strange choice. I'd have started with something rubber, a bit more pliable. Have you not experimented with these things? I know you've not had much experience but even if you're on your own, you've tried stuff out, right?'

He looks blankly at me. It's not a hard question, Ed.

'Well, no. I just have a wank. I've never explored beyond that. I have started watching more porn though, just to clarify matters. You know, as part of my education.'

He goes to his phone and starts scrolling through some pages, referencing the notebook in front of him. He must be the only person on the planet who watches porn with a notebook and a pen. He is keen, so keen to please and it's a little endearing.

'So, this video...' He shows me his phone and on screen is a lady with brown 80s bouffant hair and very shiny boobs being taken from behind and seeming very animated about the position she finds herself in. 'The shiny thing in her butt is... a butt plug?'

I nod, distracted by the sounds that the woman is making, which would surely upset the neighbours. He writes something down. I have students like this at school who write down everything you say. I wonder if he's going to whip out some highlighters soon. 'Not all girls are into that though. Permission first, always. And this sort of position can be good but get the good angles. Reach around, play with her clit, her boobs, a light tug of the hair... and don't go too shallow or...'

'It won't feel as good?' he enquires.

'Well, then you're just thrusting air up there, and the air has to come out somehow.'

Ed's eyes shift side to side as if he's trying to work out the physics of how that will work. Where does the air come out? Not out of her nostrils, that's for sure.

'That is a thing...?' he asks, looking concerned.

'Well, yeah – funnily enough, it's not featured a lot in those sex scenes you see on TV or in movies. There are... noises. I usually laugh it off, pretend you didn't hear it...'

Ed is still writing notes. I wonder what he's going to do with them. Is he making revision cards? Does he sit here at night, studying sex and all its different intricacies? I commend this commitment to wanting to get it right. Is it wrong to feel pride at this moment? Such a good student. If I had to write him a report, he'd be getting lovely comments about his work ethic from me at least.

'Right, next on my list...'

'There's a list?' I ask.

'G-spot... Where is it? Can you help me find it?'

I stop to look at him. 'Yes. But I'm going to need a shitload of coffee first. Service in this place sucks.'

He laughs and nods.

ED

So, this morning may not have been an actual emergency but the kiss last night with Caitlin was a big moment. It was perfect.

I can either capitalise on that or do what I always do and back away in fear and self-loathing. So I called Mia because she is the oracle in all of these matters and her tactics have worked well so far, but also because she was the first and only person I thought to tell this morning. I'm not sure why.

'So, the rabbit ears bit stimulates the clit while the main bit of the vibrator goes inside you...'

I like how both of us are lying on my bed in our underwear, our arms propping ourselves up, putting together sex toys like we're making very sexy Lego.

'Did you get batteries?' she asks me.

Oh no. I pull a face.

'Ed!' she says, shocked. 'You're normally so prepared. Take them out of that remote control,' she instructs me. I do as I'm told and she inserts them in the vibrator and it starts to buzz in her hand. Her eyes light up in a way I've not seen before.

'So this bit is the remote; you can control the strength and speed of the buzzing. The buzzing is what will help you because you hold this near her clit while you're inside her and her world will implode.'

'So don't put it in her?'

Mia bobs her head from side to side. 'You know, you have a decent wanger, Ed. Use the wanger first. Then use this to give her a more complete pleasure experience.'

I nod. 'Thank you for the compliment about my...'

'Wanger...?'

'Is that what we're calling it? I shouldn't call it that, right? When referring to it...?'

'No. Give it another name.'

'What? Like Charles?' I try to joke. She collapses on the bed in hysterics.

'It's your COCK. That's the only acceptable word when talking about it in the moment. Not pecker, willy, peeny, man-meat, definitely not a name... or we will laugh.' She smiles at me and sits back up. 'But yes, yours is fine. Decent girth and length, not too much foreskin.'

I will take that compliment. 'You also have a very lovely body, Mia,' I say, trying to return the compliment.

She pouts and shakes her head. 'Try that again but sexily.'

I take a pause to understand what she means. Like with a French accent and an eyebrow raised or an octave lower? I think back to lines of conversation she once showed me on Tinder.

'Your tits are outstanding...?' I say, a little hesitantly.

'Did you just give my tits an OFSTED report?'

I nod. She laughs and I bury my face in my bed. She pats me on the head.

'Don't be mean, I'm trying so hard,' I say in muffled tones.

'I'll give you some books to read, films to watch so you can learn some lines,' she reassures me. 'You're getting there. You had full conversations with Caitlin, you kissed her at the sink. It's progress. This is not the same Ed from three weeks ago.'

'Speaking of books, I have been doing some extra reading...'

I reach under the bed and both our heads peer over the edge as I reveal a selection of books I have curated recently on sex and sexual practice. I like how she lies so close to me, resting her head on my shoulder like we're just looking over takeaway menus. I open one of them up to a page that I have bookmarked.

'Ed, that is the Kama Sutra – ancient sex gurus used that. I know pretzels that don't bend like that.'

'But there's all this stuff about sustaining your orgasm, that's beneficial to me, right?' I add.

'Yeah, if you're tantric. You're too far down the line, Ed. This is stuff you do when you're in a relationship where you're thinking about ways to deepen your orgasm. This stuff requires trust and knowledge of someone,' she says, angling her head to one side to look over a diagram in more detail. 'We've literally done one position, on a bed and you lasted about twenty seconds, so you need to learn how to walk before you can run.'

Naturally, any man would feel a smidgeon of shame to hear themselves assessed in such a manner, but I am past this point with Mia now. She speaks the truth and I am here to learn and do better.

'So, I've been thinking about your little problem and, whilst I'm not a doctor, I think it was because it was your first time and you were excited and hypersensitive. So we need to build you up, and I think the best way to do that is when you think you're about to shoot your load, I want you to change position.'

I nod like I know what she's talking about, but in my head, I just have images of me throwing shapes in a game of musical statues.

'So, I need to teach you some positions. Lie down on your back,' she informs me, rolling over. I do as I'm told and she starts to straddle me so she's on top.

'I don't have a condom on,' I tell her, reaching down to remove my underwear.

'I can see that. Keep the pants on, this is purely instructional,' she says, sitting on my crotch. She bobs up and down for a moment. 'So this is me on top. This is nice for me because it's stimulating my clitoris. Nice view for you, too, I imagine. It gives me control, you can thrust back if you want and create a movement. I can also lean forward and then you have boobs in the face which, again, is a treat for you.'

She shows me all of this in a series of instructional moves that I've only ever seen when someone is trying to teach sport. She then swivels around so her bottom is facing me. I don't deny it's a lovely view and she has a very good bottom, but I do the good and decent thing by tucking her tag back into her spotted black knickers.

'This is reverse cowgirl,' I state confidently, despite this being my only knowledge on this matter.

'Very good. Now this, again, is a nice angle for me as I can play with myself while I do this, and you can see the mechanics of what's happening down there. And I can also...'

Mia pops herself on to all fours and then, well, there's no other way of saying this, but her butt is in my face.

'Sixty-nine you...'

I don't quite know to how to react to this, so I tap her on the back. She stops and looks over her shoulder.

'I have questions,' I say, putting my hand in the air.

'I can take a question.'

'So, in this case, the oral sex is reciprocal but what if...'

With her body swivelled around, I can see the confusion in her face.

'You smother me,' I ask. This is not a stupid question. 'I can get quite claustrophobic.'

She may not be facing me, but I can see her body shuddering with laughter. 'That would be quite a way to suffocate though. Muff asphyxiation. Breathe through your nose. Allow for a position where you both have some element of control. And whilst we're here, if you ever have your cock in her mouth, don't force it. Never push the back of a girl's head because that just tells us you're controlling and a bit of a dick.'

'Noted. I also need to ask about the etiquette here. Where do I ejaculate in those instances?'

She turns around to face me, slightly surprised. 'Look at you for asking. Well, just give her signals. Tell her what's about to happen and she'll do what's good for her. She may withdraw and finish you off by hand, she may swallow or spit.'

'Spit, where?' I ask, horrified.

'She won't be like a llama. Just maybe in a nearby receptacle. I once had a man whose sperm tasted like bad ham. I spat that out pretty quick.'

'Thank you for sharing.'

'My pleasure.' She sits back against the bed and beckons me over into a hug. I wrap my arms around her and rest my head on her chest. This has been an unexpected benefit of this arrangement. Mia has always been a hugger but after all our sessions she's keen to snuggle and draws me in to almost reassure me. I like the warmth of her skin, the curves of her body that accommodate mine, our legs tangling up as we hug.

I breathe in the smell of her. 'Are you using a new shower gel?' I ask her.

'Yes, raspberry and vanilla.'

'You smell like ice cream.'

'Thank you.'

'That's not sexy talk, is it?'

'Not really... The problem is, Ed, sex can't really be rehearsed in such a way. The best sex isn't really thought through like a dance routine or a script, it just happens. You're thinking about it too much.'

'I just want to be respectful, too. It's important to me that she can also feel safe with me.'

Mia squeezes me tight at this point and says nothing. This is probably because that's not very sexy at all either. I want you to feel safe? I sound like a bank. You can leave your money with me, I'll look after it. But Mia then straddles me again, pushing me back against the headboard, her body pressed against mine. She gyrates her hips over me.

'This is also good,' she says, looking me in the eye.

'That's quite intense. The eye contact, us all sandwiched together, the...' I want to say dry humping without making her sound like a dog.

'That's intimacy.' There is a pause as she exhales quietly, her face next to mine. She has very blue eyes, I've not seen them this close before.

'Did you know...?' I say, catching her gaze.

'What?' she says, breathily.

'If you have blue eyes, it means you have no pigment in the front layer of your iris.'

The intensity of her look shifts and she smiles and then kisses me gently on the lips and all at once, my wanger/cock/Charles reacts to this. She kisses harder and my hands move to the small of her back, reaching to the elastic of her crop top and pulling it up over her head.

'I... I...' I'm running through quite a lot of things in my head. Do I say something primal? When do I reach for the vibrator? A condom? Shall I offer to go down on her first? I know how to do that now. But she's caught up in the kissing and makes noises to tell me she approves so we'll do this for a moment. Oh wait, she's on her knees. Her nipple is in my face. And she's touching my penis. She has it in her hand and she's moving her hand up and down over it. I'm getting a hand job.

'We've not covered this,' I mumble.

'Ed, just go with it. Don't think about anything,' she whispers in my face.

'But... But...'

Clear my mind. Don't come too quickly. Don't come too quickly. You only changed the sheets yesterday. Should I count? That might help. One-Mississippi, Two-Mississippi. I think I've already lasted longer than our previous time at least. Think about something non-sexual. Houseplants. Fridges. Pens. Shit. She's getting a condom. Did she just use her teeth to open the pack? Is that allowed? She's putting the condom on me.

'Ed...'

'Yes,' I mutter, my eyes springing open.

'It's me. Relax. Just go with it. Just be here, now, in this moment and have sex with me...'

As soon as I hear her voice and look into her eyes, every part of me relaxes (not every part) and I exhale, my shoulders dipping, my back sinking into my pillow. Just have sex. Enjoy it, even. She slides herself onto me. I need to start counting again. That feeling. I can't quite describe it. The way it rises through my spine. I make a noise and she smiles. Is that a good sex noise?

I sound a bit like a baying cow. Oh dear. No. That feeling. Too soon, too...

'I NEED TO CHANGE POSITION!' I yell.

And with that Mia hops off me and curls up into a ball on the bed in fits of giggles. I look at her boobs jiggling about and laugh, too. What on earth are we doing? I have no idea but by gosh, I need work.

THIRTEEN

MIA

'YOU ARE HAVING SEX WITH ED?' Beth's voice shrieks.

'I don't think you said that loud enough for the kids in the back,' I reply, bending down slightly, hoping that might mask my embarrassment. I look over at a Year 7 child who cradles his lunchbox like a hot water bottle. He definitely heard that. I give him a look that says, tell anyone and you'll be on my radar for life. I am not sure why I relayed this fact to Beth but blame the end of a long school trip today where these twelve-year-old kids have been less enthused by Shakespeare performed live and outdoors and more with squirting fizzy drinks around and mooning people on the A316 as this coach crawls back to school. Please, let there be no more traffic or some of these kids will have to pee in their lunchboxes.

Beth sits there waiting for me to divulge more information, but the problem is I can't really say much more without revealing Ed's secrets. 'Well, yeah,' I say, sitting back into my seat. I always try to sit next to Beth on these trips as she brings Haribo. I steal one from the bag in her lap.

'That I did not see happening. Or maybe I did?'

'No, you did not,' I retort. 'In what world did you see Ed and I getting together?'

'It's a classic opposites attract, no? And I've always liked the friendship. It's very sincere,' she remarks.

'Well, don't buy a hat just yet. It really is just a casual thing to bide my time.'

'It fills a gap, shall we say?' Beth adds jokingly.

'Exactly. And, shall we say, he's not very experienced so I'm helping him find his feet because he really likes Caitlin, the new Maths girl.'

I go through my words in my head again. I did not out him as a virgin. I was very good there.

'So, you're giving him sex training?' Beth asks, confused.

'I wouldn't put it in those terms but, yes.'

'I have scenes from *Rocky* in my head here. Do you make him wear a sweat band and run up steps?'

'Yep... And we shag to the theme tune.'

Beth laughs so hard a Tangfastic goes flying across the seats. I'm not sure how to describe my arrangement with Ed anymore but I will admit that at the weekend, he said something about respecting me and making me feel safe and I've never been more aroused in my life. So I got a tad carried away, I allowed myself to derive some pleasure from the moment. That was until Ed barked at me like a football coach about needing to change positions. Then I stopped feeling the moment and I got a severe case of the giggles. Did it kill the moment? Maybe. But it showed us we needed to work on our transitions a bit more. It showed me that I will never be able to take sex with Ed seriously. He's Ed. Anyhow, after our giggles, he made me a sandwich. With his special pesto mayo. I also did my lesson planning there which was the best idea I've had in ages because Ed has excellent Wi-Fi and his crisp selection is unparalleled.

'It's just teaching him the importance of certain things,' I say, slinking into my seat so I'm out of earshot. 'Like it's not just a dick in a hole, it's paying attention to the whole area.'

Beth nods in agreement, pouting. 'Amen to that. Teach him the importance of nipple sensitivity, too.'

'Yep, I'm covering the whole shebang. When he's done with me, he'll be like Christian Grey – but a nice version without the red rooms and the trauma...'

Beth offers me another sweet and twists around to eyeball the kids who've started rapping some grime tune with questionable lyrics. 'But surely you should train men up for yourself? Not to pass them on to someone else?' she asks.

'Please. I will take great pleasure in passing him on. Ed irons his pants. I've never envisioned a man like that as part of my future.'

Beth smirks. 'Then who is part of your future?'

'Who knows? But he'll be more spontaneous, chill... He won't be obsessed with weather apps and office stationery.' Beth continues to smile broadly in her seat. 'Why are you smirking?'

'Nothing. This feels like a very charitable endeavour. I am impressed.'

I grin to acknowledge she's seen the good in what I'm doing. 'You know, I was thinking this the other day. I am telling him tricks and secrets that all men should know. Someone needs to write a book about these things. This shouldn't be my job.'

'But isn't that the job of time? The more people you date? The sum of our experiences?'

I can't say that for Ed, there's been no one to do that. I'm doing the job of at least four different past girlfriends at this point. 'Well, that depends on the quality of the girlfriend, no? I've dated men who've passed on nothing to me except a common cold.'

Beth giggles in her seat. She's been with the same man for a while now and has super cute little babies whose names all begin with J. She's constantly tired but there's a peace about her that makes me think that's what I want when I'm older. 'Just as long as you know what you're doing, Mia. I like both of you too much to have to pick a side if it all goes wrong.'

I know she's thinking of Julia and Graham (Biology and Physics) who were going out for three years and then broke up and used to have raging fights over their shared Dalmatian. We had to sit them on separate sides of the staffroom.

'It'll be fine,' I explain.

'So, when he moves on to Caitlin from Maths, what about you? Are you dating? Is there anyone on the horizon?'

I get my phone out to show her someone on Tinder.

'I chat to this fella occasionally. His name is Scott. He teaches in a private school in Surrey, so things in common, and he has abs. Look at the abs.'

Beth raises her eyebrows to look at him on my screen. Scott is a distraction, someone I've not met in the flesh, but praise be, the man knows how to sext and I've spent many an evening with my hand in my knickers having long-drawn-out conversations with him.

'He's a bit of a specimen,' she notes.

'He's got pants on in this pic, Beth. You should see the selfies where he's got his package out. He's certainly more my type. We shall see what happens...'

Beth continues to quietly laugh in her seat. I hear the Year 7s still singing in the back of the bus and pop my head into the aisle.

'YEAR 7, that is not appropriate for a school trip!' I yell. The lad with the lunchbox looks petrified.

'Then what is appropriate, Miss?' one lad asks me.

'Something where I'm not hearing women being referred to as "bitches".' The children giggle to hear the word come out of my mouth. 'Taylor Swift is acceptable,' I say, thinking how proud Ed would be to hear me recommend her.

The bus leans around the corner as we drive up to the

school and I see a crowd of parents waiting to pick up their darling little ones. This pain is finally over. We are hoping that the kids will at least have remembered something from today but most likely, it'll be the fact that Nathan with the giant puffer coat does farts that could kill small animals. As the coach stops, the children all stand up.

'PLEASE REMEMBER ALL YOUR BELONGINGS AND YOUR RUBBISH!' Beth shrieks. We watch them file off the bus to murmurs of, 'Bye, Miss... Thank you, Miss,' and Beth exhales, a sighed groan which tells me wine will be part of her Thursday evening.

'You teachers are bloody saints,' the bus driver tells us as we disembark. Beth stops to talk to him while I get off the bus and look into the early evening night air.

'Mia?' a voice calls out from behind me.

It's a strange thing. I know the voice, but I don't know why it's here. It doesn't belong here. I turn around.

'Rachel?'

She doesn't utter a word but stands there looking at me silently, the colour drained from her face, her eyes bloodshot and sore. I don't quite know what to do so I pull her into me and hug her tightly.

'I'm sorry about the coffee. It's all we have. Budget cuts,' I say, as I hand Rachel a mug, having found a sofa in a quiet room away from the hustle and bustle of the school closing down for the day. She does not look well, so given what happened to our mum, I can't help but jump to the conclusion that she must be ill. What other reason could she have to be here? She's never come to see me in my workplace before. Her hand shakes and I reach down to steady it.

'Where are the kids? Are they OK?'

'They're with Alison. I'm sorry to have to come in like this. I asked at reception, and they said you were on a school trip so I thought I'd wait around.' There's none of the usual arrogance in her tone and I don't know how to take that.

'It's fine. It's a surprise, that's all...'

'It's a big school, bigger than I thought it would be.'

'Rach... are you ill?' I ask her tentatively.

'Oh god, no. It's just...'

'Is it the kids? Are they OK?' I ask again, my mind shifting through all the possibilities. Please don't let it be the kids.

'It's just...' she says, her eyes welling up.

'Rach, you're scaring me.'

'Gareth is cheating on me,' she says, her tears starting to roll and her body caving in to have to say those words out loud. I grab her coffee before she spills it and pull her into me.

'Fuck.' I'm no animal but there are shades of relief there that no one is dying. Her body shudders as I hug her tight. 'How did you...?'

'It's a school mum. I came home to find them both at it in our bed. OUR BED. Her breasts on my pillow. A pillow that's been on my face. They've fallen in love. He's told me he wants a divorce,' she spills out, her face almost turning green like she may throw up. 'I haven't told anyone for the shame. I can't believe this is happening to me.'

'Not even Ali?' I ask her. 'But she has the kids?'

'They don't know. I can't bear to tell Alison. I told her I have stomach flu so they're staying the night with her.'

I hold her again, feeling her tears soak through my dress, and see how this news has broken her, completely. I'm not sure I'd focus so much on the pillows, but I can't tell her that now.

'Why can't you tell Ali?' I ask.

'Our husbands are friends. The shame that I've let my marriage crumble like this...'

I hold my hand up in the air. 'Hold up, you caught him in bed with another woman so how is this your fault?'

'People cheat for a reason. Maybe it was something I did that drove him away. Maybe I could have done more...'

As soon as the words leave her mouth, it unleashes an unhealthy amount of rage in me. 'Or maybe he's an absolute cock?'

'Mia, he's a good man, a great father. He's on the PTA!'

I narrow my eyes at her. 'And Harold Shipman was a doctor, I don't quite see your point?' She laughs under her breath and it's a relief to see her express that emotion. 'Rachel, take away all the positive facets of the man and there's no denying he's a shit husband for doing this. I will not have you blame yourself for this.'

'I just don't know what to do. He's still living with us. A letter came through the door the other day for him from a solicitor, so I think he's set the wheels in motion already. I keep thinking he's going to take the kids. I'm completely lost.'

It's still a marvel to me that she can be lost yet came and found me, but I keep my thoughts to myself.

'Then you need to do the same. My work colleague, Beth, had a sister who went through a nasty divorce. I can ask her for advice, see how they handled things – they had kids, too.'

'Really?' she asks me.

'Rachel, have we not met before? I won't have him steer this. They're your kids, my niece and nephew. If he's done this to my sister, then he will feel the full flames of the comeback. I've already plotted out half of it. I'm prepared to do unspeakable things.'

A look of terror overcomes her, which is strange as she should know I'm the vengeful sort.

'That sounds worse than what I mean. I was just going to poo in an envelope and send it to his work.'

This time she laughs through her tears and the sound is like music to me. I hold her again to let her know, despite any flaws in our relationship, that I am here. Always.

'So, why me? Why not a mate?' I ask her as she rests her head on my shoulder. For a moment, I think it's because I'm a screw up to her. My life is not perfect and it is chaotic so I can at least relate because I'm not on any sort of pedestal to judge.

'It's because out of all of us, you're most like Mum. And she's who I need right now,' she says, still in hold. My lip wobbles at this point, my eyes glazing over. I picture our mum in her absolute prime; a woman who fought to the bitter end, was loyal to her girls, had infinite amounts of kindness, who championed us like we were the only people in the world.

'Mum would do more than poo in an envelope,' I tell her. She laughs and I take my hands and wipe at her face. 'You have me in your corner. You need any help with the kids, you ask me, too.'

'But you live in a house share.'

'I have Netflix and running water, that's all you really need with kids.'

She stops for a moment. 'Can we go and get drunk? I think I need that...'

'Then you've definitely come to the right sister.' I pull her up from the sofa and open the door to the room, linking my arm into hers. 'Let me get some things from the staffroom and I'll meet you in reception.'

She nods. 'Thank you, Mimi.'

She's going for the heartstrings tonight, eh? That's what my mum used to call me. I leave her to head for the staffroom, taking large strides on the stairs, a strange anger pulsating through me thinking about Gareth. I hardly know him really but now I want to know his testicles intimately and crush them in my hand. I think about his poor kids. I need to up my aunt duties and ensure this doesn't hurt them. I push at the staffroom door a little too forcefully and slam right into the person standing there. Ed.

'Shit! I'm so sorry...' I say, hugging him. I'm not sure why I hug him, but I think it sublimates my rage at least. I step back when I see Caitlin standing there.

'I see the Year 7 theatre trip went well then,' he jokes, assuming my charging around to be associated with today's adventures beyond the school wall.

'Oh, you know...' My eyes shift between the two of them and I suddenly clock that tonight is date night. They're off for pool and chicken wings. I smile for a moment remembering when Ed asked me if it'd be bad form to sanitise his pool cue before use.

'I see you're off out. Have fun,' I say, trying not to give too much away.

'Do you want to join us?' Caitlin asks.

I look at the sheer panic in Ed's eyes. I mean, on the one hand, it's good he's kept this casual so it doesn't look too much like a date, but on the other hand, he does not need me cramping his style. Or maybe he does need me? Like some Jiminy Cricket style mentor to tell him what to do? How long will he need me there for, though? I'm not hanging around the bedroom telling him how to touch her boobs.

'Oh, it's cool. I have other plans,' I explain. I see her slip her fingers into his and grasp tightly. And I feel relief, because this is progressing into something sweet for my good friend. But there's also another feeling there that I can't quite describe.

ED

Balls, holes and angles. That's what Mia said pool was all about. I should be a pro at it because I have a maths brain, but it's also the perfect endeavour to show her some moves, lean over her and initiate some body contact. Mia even sent me some YouTube clips of romantic comedies where flirtations were started at a pool table, telling me to study the confidence and the swagger. I did. I watched those clips and took notes. I even practised standing in my kitchen with a mop beside the kitchen table, trying out my lines on Nigel.

However, like sex, it would seem dating and flirting are not things that can be rehearsed, especially when you're in a place that doesn't fit your vibe at all. I'm not even sure I have a vibe. All I know is that it's quiet, possibly does a good charcuterie board and doesn't blast alternative pop music at me like I'm in the middle of a festival field. For all my rehearsing, it might have also been a good idea to actually learn how to play pool because, like sex, it seems that I'm crap at that as well.

'I'm going to go for the red in the top corner,' Caitlin tells me, standing there with a hand on her hip, grinning at me. What also doesn't help is that Caitlin is quite a pool shark. I try not to feel totally useless standing here in a sea of turn-up jeans with my Korean-inspired chicken wings, washing them down with overpriced bottles of hipster microbrewery beer. Caitlin downs the shot and I clap.

'Seriously, are you some sort of professional pool player? I am very embarrassed,' I reply, over-chalking my cue, watching as she bends over the table with her short skirt and knee-high boots. I try to do the gentlemanly thing and not stare.

'Just a misspent youth with two older brothers. Your turn...'

I put the cue to my hand and pot the white ball. Skills, Mr Rogers.

'Oh dear, Ed,' she laughs. I can't quite tell if she's being cruel or trying to make me feel better, but I sigh and try to laugh with her. She retrieves the cue ball and makes some bizarre trick shot that means a big balding bloke on the neighbouring table claps. She curtsies.

I move to the table to take a shot and feel her arm touch mine. 'Your stance is a bit off. Try relaxing this arm a bit more, the movement should be in the elbow, not the hand.' She presses her body next to mine. She's basically stealing all the moves that I rehearsed with my cat. Try and breathe, Ed. I take aim, offer a silent prayer to the snooker gods, and pot a red.

'See...' she tells me, winking. 'Simple really.' She goes over to take a swig of her bottle of beer and smiles at me. Don't stare, Ed. 'So, it appears to me from your pool skills that this might not be a usual haunt for you then?' she asks me. I can't fake this, can I?

'It was Mia's suggestion. She's trying to rub off some of her cool on me.'

I think about those words as they come out of my mouth. Mia would laugh at that, a little too hard.

'Well, it is very cool,' she says, looking around the quirky signage and retro tables and chairs. This place is very Mia, mainly because they have six types of loaded fries. 'Speaking of Mia, you both seem a strange match,' she remarks. 'She seems very different to you. Am I allowed to say I don't think I like her?'

I can't help but frown as she says this. I don't deny Mia sometimes has unrelatable qualities about her, but it seems to be a bit of a snap judgement about someone Caitlin's only known for a month.

'She grows on you. Behind the noise is someone who's very kind.'

'Maybe,' she says, shaking her head from side to side, studying the pool ball configurations. 'Kind is a word I hear associated with you, to be fair. I've been asking round the staffroom about you, Mr Ed...'

I stand there with my cue, not knowing how to really hold it without looking like I'm going to dance around it, bristling slightly at 'Mr Ed' but trying to brush it off. 'All good, I hope?'

'I feel I need to sample the baking. The ladies in the office keep telling me you're a master baker.'

'I'm a master what now?' I reply, some old Britpop anthem drowning out the last bit of her sentence.

She laughs. 'Master baker.'

'Well, that can be arranged. What are you into?'

'Cake.'

'Any allergies, dislikes…?'

'That's very considerate – I'm not a huge fan of lemon.'

'Then I will avoid lemon,' I tell her. 'What else has been said about me then?'

'People have also been telling me how nice you are. Not a bad word from anyone, always helping people and super organised and polite.'

'Who are these people?' I stop for a moment to wonder with whom she's been talking. I hope this is not someone telling her I colour co-ordinate my Post-it notes because I'm not sure how sexy that is.

'I can't reveal my sources. But it ties in with what you've been doing for me and all the help you've given me around my new flat, so thank you.'

I smile. I mean, I've also helped her because I fancy her, but I can't say that out loud. I helped June in the office unblock a drain, but I didn't snog her afterwards. To that end, I'm not sure how to bring the kiss up. Does this mean she's just grateful for my help and doesn't want anything more? I want to respect the boundaries here. If she's not interested then I can back away, as heart-wrenching as that may be.

'It's my pleasure. It's been good to get to know you, too,' I add, not wanting to delve too deeply into what this all means.

'Likewise. I was unsure about this move to a new school, but I can see the silver lining now…'

She called me a silver lining, that's good. Tell her you like her. Go on, Ed. Tell her you'd love to get to know her more under a more formal guise of dating. But do people do that anymore? If I ask her if she wants to be my girlfriend, then I will sound like I'm seven years old in a school playground. I can almost hear Mia in my ear. Play it cool. Just let it happen. I watch as she pots three more balls. She's won every game since we started, not that I match her skills in any way, but I'd let her win if I could. Pool, Scrabble, Connect 4... I'd let her win everything.

'So, are you dating anyone at the moment?' she asks me. 'That was something no one in the staffroom seemed to know.'

I laugh. 'No. I am very single.' I shouldn't have said the very. It sounds a bit desperate but, in the back of mind, I realise it's not one hundred percent true; I have an unorthodox arrangement with Mia. She doesn't need to know about that.

'Well, at least I know now,' she says, strolling around the table.

I have no idea what this means so I take a large swig of beer. Just confirm what this is already.

'Oh, you'll never guess what. Remember my heating? It turns out the boiler is completely broken. Timer is shot. I've had a few plumbers give me quotes. Cheapest is £800...'

'Ouch...'

'Not a cost that anyone needs when they've just moved,' she moans. 'I guess I'll just have to get a short-term loan to suck up the costs.'

'Don't do that, the interest will be ridiculous,' I reply. I do some quick maths in my head and a very sensible part of my brain comes up with a solution. It's a grand gesture, one that would possibly overstep but it could help her. It may also read sincere, dependable – that can only be a good thing. I take a deep breath. 'I have some savings. I could loan you the money and you can just pay me back when you can,' I blurt out, waiting for her reaction.

'You'd do that?' she asks, slightly surprised.

Was that too big a gesture? Or too much money? 'Well, I know where you live,' I say, hoping that doesn't sound too aggressive. 'Not that I'd come and bang down your door and demand the money, but I know what it's like when you move into your own place. All those hidden costs are the killer.'

'You'd do that for me?' she asks, her attention taken away from the pool for a small moment.

'I'd do that for...' You. Tell her. 'Anyone who needed my help.'

She comes over and flings her arms around me. 'You're amazing.' And with that, she leans in and kisses me on the lips, a hand to my face. I can't feel my legs. Maybe this is the start of something great. I wrap my arms around her and let the moment take me. I am also very conscious I have some cue chalk in my hand that I might be squeezing into dust.

'Oi...' a voice suddenly booms from behind us. I turn. It's the large balding man from the table next to us. 'Get a room,' he says, laughing.

FOURTEEN

MIA

'Go left a bit... Down, just there... And right and ooooohhhhh... Yes, harder... Really go for it...'

'Is that too hard?'

'No, that's just right... Yes, yes, yes... Love it.... Right, you can stop now...' I wriggle my shoulders and pull my shirt back down over my back. 'You are good at that. I will have to employ your services more often.'

'You scratch my back and I'll scratch yours,' Ed jokes.

'That was quite funny.'

'I thought so.' Ed moves the laptop back onto his lap and I perch my head on his shoulder on this lazy Saturday morning. We haven't had sex again, Ed and I, not in the last week or so, since he started dating Miss Bell. Am I sad? A little. Because sex with him was different. I could be myself, tell him exactly what I wanted, laugh. But this hasn't stopped me from being his teacher and today, we are eating tortilla chips and salsa on his sofa and watching porn so I can walk him through some more of the basics.

'I feel I missed out not getting a blow job from you,' Ed says, as we watch a woman on her knees, really working on a gentleman's penis, mouth pumping hard like Pac Man.

'Well, you've obviously heard about my skill set,' I say, laughing.

'No, I just mean... So I know what to expect if she goes down there. Like this woman, she's using hands and also tickling the balls. Is that a thing?'

'Oh, it's not just the mouth. It's the hands, too. Us women are quite good at multi-tasking.'

'He's pushing her head. You said that wasn't the done thing...'

'Well done, Ed,' I say, patting him on the back, excited that he retained some of my more vital pieces of sex education.

'Can I also ask? He's quite clean shaven down there. Is that a thing? I thought only girls...'

'Well, I don't really like a big afro bush when I go down there so you can get your clippers and have a tidy. The worst thing is when you feel like you're having a floss.'

'The clippers I use on my head?' He looks appalled.

'These can be sanitised. Just have a light prune.'

He nods, eyes still fixated on the screen. I look at his trouser area – the porn doesn't seem to excite him in any way; he is here merely to be a student, which makes me giggle. He presses the pause button.

'This. This position. With her legs up by her ears like that... Do normal people do this?'

'Yes.'

'You're that bendy?'

'Not really bendy but I like how it feels, it means you can go deeper, so I attempt some version of that. I perhaps don't look so finessed and sculpted, shall we say.'

'Rubbish, you'd look great. You're much sexier than this woman,' he says nonchalantly.

I don't even try to respond to the compliment because he says it so calmly and sincerely. Do I reciprocate? I also find you mildly sexy these days? More than I used to? That doesn't sound right so I just stuff my mouth full of salsa instead. He goes to another clip that involves masks and chains and I see his eyes widen like saucers.

I reach over and click on something else instead. 'Definitely not for you.'

You can literally see his mind whirring, working overtime with questions. 'Can I just ask about the fetish thing? How will I know? How do people find out they're into things?'

'They experiment. Sometimes they find out by accident. I sometimes like a bit of role play.'

'Explain.'

'Halloween. I was once a cat, and I pulled a man at a party who was dressed as a full vampire. Teeth and accent and leather trousers and it was really hot...'

'I don't think vampires wear leather trousers.'

'Do you know any vampires?'

'No. Did you let him drink your blood?'

'Ed. No,' I say, laughing. 'It's role play, it's pretend. I just got on all fours and meowed a lot. I didn't crap in a litterbox, he didn't turn into a bat.'

This should be funny, but Ed just nods a lot, like I've opened a window into his brain that was very much closed and locked. He looks back to the screen where I've chosen a car sex video for him. I know exactly what he's thinking. That would not be good for the upholstery, be careful around that gearstick, have they put enough coins in the parking meter?

'So you really didn't have sex with Caitlin after your date?' I ask.

'No. We just had a lovely evening. We laughed, we went our separate ways, we met up for a Park Run on Saturday then had brunch and...' he sighs, '...it was perfect.'

'It's like something out of a sitcom. Did you wear matching Lycra?' I jest.

'No. But it feels like everything's moving in the right direction,' he says, watching the clip closely as the man in the video ejaculates over the woman's stomach. I hope they brought something to wipe her down with.

'And really nothing more than kissing?' I say, almost a little curious about how they couldn't have had sex.

'She slapped me on the bum after our run,' Ed says coolly.

'So cheeky body contact – that's good. I reckon next date could be the one. Cook for her. Intimate setting, bit of wine... BOOM!' I say, knocking my hands together in a strange explosive action.

'And not too soon?'

'No. Any longer and she may think you're friend-zoning her.'

'Noted. Thank you,' he says, resting his head on my shoulder.

'It's exciting. I'm the matchmaker who enabled all of this. Will you name your firstborn after me?'

'I will consider it.' And for a moment, I feel some strange emotion in the pit of my stomach again. It feels sad that maybe I will have to share Ed now and I won't be the only person he's ever been with. Do I tell him that? I don't think I should confuse him, so I feel some sense of relief when I hear the familiar ringtone of my phone going off in my bag. I reach around to find it, before examining the number that appears and answering.

'Rachel, all OK?'

Last week was the most time I've spent with Rachel since, well, since our mother passed away. After she came to school to tell me everything that was going wrong with her marriage, I took her to a Pitcher & Piano pub, I fed her hard liquor and I returned to her house where I held her hair back as she threw up. I gave her good advice (lawyer up; make the kids your priority) and less good advice (let's find you a revenge shag; let's have flaming shots) but I made her dance, sing, and shout into the night air as we were waiting for an Uber. I made her do all the things I do when I'm nursing a broken heart.

'Mia? Are you busy?' she whispers loudly on the phone.

'Yeah, all OK?'

'Can you come round? I've managed to get this appointment with a solicitor in the next hour, but I just need someone to sit with the kids. Could you come down?'

'Yeah, are you OK?'

I can hear a light rapping at a door. 'Yes, I just locked myself in the bathroom to take the call. I'M HAVING A WEE.'

'Where's Gareth?' I ask.

'Who bloody knows... Do you think you can make it?'

'Deffo, give me twenty.'

I hang up and Ed studies me curiously. 'All OK?' he asks.

'My sister is going through a messy separation thing, I need to get to her,' I explain, jumping up from the sofa, the overexcited moans of some girl on the screen in the background.

'Is she OK? I thought you didn't get on with your sisters,' he reminds me, watching my hurried reactions closely.

'I don't. But she's a mess. Imagine what a mess you have to be to come to me for help and advice,' I say, trying to downplay the moment. 'Sorry to leave you in the lurch.'

I say the lurch, but he has a wealth of information at his fingertips there. I should just leave him some bookmarks perhaps of what to avoid.

'Do you need any help?' he asks me, moving the laptop to one side and sitting up to see me gathering my belongings.

I look up at his face and there's kindness in his eyes, a look that defines him really. I shake my head. 'It's babysitting. You've spent the whole week with kids that aren't yours, I will respectfully spare you this.'

'I don't mind. I've not met your family. Could be interesting...' he says, looking more animated about the prospect than he should.

'OK then,' I say. 'Close that laptop though so Nigel doesn't go blind.'

'You're in a suit...' I tell Rachel as she opens the door to her four-bedroomed Surrey townhouse. I never quite understand Rachel's house. It's always very clean, like no one lives here. It's mostly jacquard cushions, ornamental birds and posh radiator covers which make me wonder where she dries her bras.

'Too much? It is a solicitor, I felt I needed to go formal,' she says, eyeing Ed standing behind me. I realise I haven't introduced him.

'Oh, this is Ed. He's a work colleague who's come to be nosy,' I say.

Ed shifts me a look. 'Hi, I can also be helpful. Nice to meet you. Rachel, is it?'

'Yes...' she says, taking his hand. 'Well, thank you for coming, too.'

'AUNTY MIA!' voices thunder from the top of the stairs and Florence and Felix run down and into my arms.

'So, kiddos, I'll only be about an hour at the dentist. Aunty Mia and Ed will make you lunch. Be good.'

'Why are you in a suit?' Felix asks.

'It's a posh dentist,' I reply unconvincingly.

Rachel leaves and the kids both stand there staring at Ed.

'Don't stare at Ed, you'll make him cry,' I tell them.

'Are you Mia's boyfriend?' Florence asks, her eyes wide open.

I laugh, a little too loudly. 'No, this is Ed, my friend. He works at my school. Ed, this is Florence and Felix, my niece and nephew.'

'It's good to meet you,' he replies, his hand outstretched for handshakes.

'Why are you here?' Felix asks, sidling up next to him, trying to sniff out sugar.

'Because he's very good at computer games. Be nice to him, please,' I tell them.

'Do you play Minecraft?' Felix asks.

'Yes, I do.' Even I glance at him in surprise at this point, but he seems to have instantly won these two over by saying that out loud.

'How about we have some lunch and then build something?' he says. 'You go set it up and Aunty Mia and I will come and find you.' They jump and cheer like he's just won them the World Cup and I won't lie, I'm slightly peeved at how quickly they've warmed to him. 'Kitchen?' he asks me.

I lead him through, the kids dispersing into another room, and I watch as he heads for the fridge, surveying the contents. He takes out some cheddar, ham, bread and butter.

'Your sister is a bit posh. She's not like you,' he chuckles.

'Rude. I am very posh actually.'

He spies some family photos on the windowsill, an old pic of my sisters and mum, and I try to dodge the inevitable questions by retrieving him a frying pan.

'Are you doing your special grilled cheese?' I ask.

He smiles. I remember when I had my heart broken once by a dick on a dating site and Ed made one of these for me. It's basically a fried cheese sandwich but it has special healing powers.

'So the kids don't know yet?' he asks me.

I shake my head. There wasn't a lot of time to brief Ed on the way here. I think I mostly exuded anger and venom towards her ex and the way Rachel had found out, so it's good that Ed is here to calm me down. He finds a chopping board and slices through the cheese.

'It's all very new. Didn't your dad leave you when you were quite young?' I ask him. 'You can tell me to piss off if you don't want to talk about it.'

'I didn't know him. He left when I was about five. I have hazy memories of a man in the house but not much else. Can I ask the same? Why is your dad not in that picture?' he asks, pointing to the one by the window.

'Heart attack. I was nine. Then I lost my mum to cancer when I was at university. I'm like one of those sad orphans in a Dickens novel.'

He smiles but I stand there for a moment and wonder why we've never shared this information before. I guess friendships can be at face value like this. Ed is someone I've seen nearly every day for years and our chat is mostly about work gossip, sandwiches and my poorly mapped out love life. Maybe something has changed between us, a new level of trust, a feeling like this is someone who's not just a work husband anymore. I go over and give him a hug and he puts his arms around me. I feel him squeeze me tightly.

'I am sorry about your mum. That can't have been easy,' he mumbles into my ear.

I'm not sure I want to let go. 'It wasn't but hell, it made me a survivor... You didn't have a dad, too. I'm sorry he left you. He's a twat for doing that. You're great.'

I feel his body shuddering under mine to hear my astute analysis of his situation.

'We're revealing far too much to each other these days,' he tells me.

'In more ways than one,' I retort.

He parts the hug and kisses me on the forehead. I close my eyes for a moment.

'Come on, let's feed these kids. Do you know if they have the mods for Minecraft?' he asks me.

I hand him a spatula, gazing at him in disbelief. 'I have no fucking clue, you absolute geek.'

ED

Mia has many faces, but she has one that reads absolute panic. If she's late for school, gets a text from a strange Tinder sort or realises she's drunk too much of an evening then her blue eyes get big like some strange animé creature and her smiley face drops to deadpan. It was the face she made when that call came in from her sister and it's what made me realise, in that moment, that she needed my help. Did I also want to meet her sister? Well, that too. Until then she only existed in caricature, like an evil Disney witch, as someone who Mia didn't really get on with, so it was intriguing that Mia was willing to drop everything to be by her side.

'So, if you go into creative, you can spawn loads of pigs.' I do as her nephew, Felix, tells me and fist-bump him for the know-how. Do I play Minecraft? I do. It's like virtual Lego with a vintage quality to the graphics. You can judge me but, until three weeks ago, I was a virgin of little social prowess and had a lot of time on my hands.

Mia watches me curiously as she bites into her fourth wedge of grilled cheese, using some sriracha from the fridge as a dipping sauce.

'Aunty Mia, your friend is very cool,' Florence says, snuggling into her.

'But is he as cool as me?' Mia asks.

The kids take their time to answer, and she hits Florence around the head with a cushion who giggles and throws it back at her. I smile to see how adored Mia is by these two. But to be fair, I see it all the time with the teens at school. Mia is a rock star amongst us teachers for the way she dresses and understands their lingo and pop culture references. I am obviously wasted there and should have gone into primary education where I could be cool for understanding Minecraft.

'Are you married, Ed?' Florence asks me, looking up at me through her brown curly hair.

'I am not.'

'But he has a girlfriend called Caitlin,' Mia explains to them.

I jolt to hear it explained so plainly to them. 'Well, she's not quite a girlfriend. I have a cat.'

Florence squeals at this point. 'I LOVE CATS! What's her name? What colour is she?'

'It's a boy cat and his name is Nigel. He's a tabby.'

'Can I meet Nigel one day?' she asks.

'It can be arranged.'

'Can I come to your house?'

Mia sits there laughing with her cheese and sriracha as I continue to be interrogated by an eight-year-old.

'I guess. Maybe with your Aunty Mia?'

'Yes, please.'

She hugs Mia and they nestle into the sofa, trading secrets of some sort and I suddenly feel a pang of something. I can't quite put my finger on it, but I think it might be sadness that this little girl's world is going to implode soon and Mia is putting all differences aside with her sister to be with her. She's a good aunt, a good sister. A good person. While I look over at them, we hear the key in the door and Felix drops the controllers to pop his head into the hall.

'DADDY!' he shouts, and Florence follows. Mia sits there and her expression changes. That's not a good face. Oh dear.

'You guys OK?' we hear echoing in the corridor.

'Yeah, Aunty Mia is here and she brought a friend. He's called Ed and he's really cool.'

Mia is halfway between a snarl and pure rage. I've only seen this face a few times – the last time was when the school canteen ran out of chips. I don't know what to do here. My first instinct is that when this man sees me for the first time, I shouldn't be knee deep in Minecraft. I put the controller down and go to sit down next to Mia.

'Breathe,' I say, putting a reassuring hand on her knee.

'I can't,' she says through gritted teeth.

We hear footsteps heading towards the TV room where we're sitting and a man in golf wear appears at the doorway, the kids attached to his hips. I stand up and try to smile.

'Hello, I am Ed. Nice to meet you.' I put my hand out and he shakes it reluctantly, eyeballing Mia.

'Gareth. Where's Rach?'

'She's at the dentist, Daddy. A posh dentist,' Felix adds.

Mia can't say a word, her jaw clenched, a puddle of sriracha on the plate in her hands. I've got that stuff in my eyes before, it stings. I hope she knows this.

'Can you guys go upstairs for a moment while I chat to Aunty Mia? Is that OK?'

'But Daddy, we were playing Minecraft with Ed,' Florence grumbles.

'Five minutes.'

The kids look at each other, not too naïve to see the air thick with tension, and head up the stairs looking back at me. I'm not used to confrontation, not at all, so I have no idea what to do here. Can I make you a grilled cheese, Gareth? You have good sourdough that has made my efforts sing this lunchtime. But instinct tells me I need to be here. To protect him from Mia at least.

'Look, I don't know what Rachel has told you but...'

Mia checks to see that the kids are out of earshot and stands up. 'But you fucked another woman in her bed. That is super classy, Gareth.'

Christ, even I felt that sucker punch of that comment and cringe slightly to see Gareth's face winded by that blow.

He pulls himself together and points a finger at Mia. 'You don't know our marriage, you can't come into my house and say things like that to me...'

'I'll say what I want. My sister has given you everything. She gave up her career to look after those kids, to look after this stupid house, and this is how you repay her... I thought you were a dickhead when she married you but thank you for confirming those suspicions.'

Rage and acid flows from her veins, her mouth, her eyes whereas I know my jaw is slack like I'm just witnessing a horrific car crash.

'That's it, just leave. Standing there eating my food and taking the piss... And take your boyfriend with you. Good luck with that, Ted.'

'It's Ed, actually,' I mutter, correcting him under my breath.

'No,' Mia says, standing there defiantly. I look over at her, still gripping on to her plate. Mia, I think, this is *his* house. We should do what he says otherwise I think that might be trespassing.

'Excuse me?' Gareth questions her.

'I'm not leaving until I've seen my sister and I know she's OK,' she replies. I like the tenacity, but I've already been punched by an old lady once this month and I don't need a repeat of that. 'Plus, I brought Ed here for a reason. He's not my boyfriend, he's a divorce solicitor. He's here to chat to her.'

If I was already confused about where this was going, then this doesn't help. I'm a Biology teacher. I'm not even dressed like a solicitor. I'm in a checked shirt. I gulp, standing up and attempting to smile to cover up this deceit. Gareth shifts his look to me.

'Yes. I used to go to university with Mia and she told me what was happening. I work in family law,' I say in serious tones that I may have heard once in a television ad advising people about getting a will. I wonder if there are other words I should say. *Objection! Sustained! You can't handle the truth!*

'She's moved fast then,' he says, looking at me.

'It's important she does so to protect her assets, the children. We've already received instructions about the house.'

'What about the house?' he says, his eyes wide.

I don't bloody know, it just sounded fancy. 'That's confidential,' I say, patting my pockets for some reason. As I do it, I watch Mia's rage melt away because there is entertainment in seeing this man get some small iota of comeuppance.

'She can't take this house,' he says. 'I paid for it.'

'And, by law, she is entitled to at least half of it.'

I mean, I assume that's the law, but this is a huge assumption I've made on my part from watching far too much *Law & Order* at university.

'That bitch deserves nothing.'

I pause at hearing that word being used to describe a woman, any woman. 'Rachel is also your children's mother so at a minimum, she deserves your respect. You can make this difficult or you can try to make this as painless as possible so you all can move on. I would urge you to think of your kids in all of this.'

Mia stops for a moment as I say this and looks at me intently. Mainly because for me, who hates confrontation, those words were quite mature and put-together. Gareth says nothing but looks me up and down. Please don't hit me.

'Well then, if you're here, I'm going out,' he tells me, reaching for his keys. 'Tell Rachel to text me when you're out of my house.' He eyeballs Mia before he leaves. 'Kids, I'm just going to the supermarket to pick up some things. Aunty Mia is still here.'

'And Ed?' Felix asks.

He turns to look at me. 'Yes, him too.' The children cheer.

I swallow hard at the venom in his eyes and watch as he

leaves. As the door shuts, I punch Mia in the arm. 'What the hell?'

Mia laughs and jigs on the spot, coming over to hug me. 'Yes, Ed! What a loser. Did you hear the words coming out of his mouth? He's lucky I didn't take his knob off with this plate.'

'Well done for not doing that much,' I mutter, still in shock.

'It took all of my self-restraint, I surprised even myself,' she says. 'And look at you! Well done, lawyer Eddie. That was masterful.'

'That's fraud. I think he saw right through it. I don't even know if that is the law,' I say, gurning.

'It's not fraud,' she says, smiling. 'That was role play 101.'

'It was?'

'Yep. Well played, young man.' Did she just wink as she said that? I really hope not.

FIFTEEN

MIA

'She then pulled at his balls until he begged for mercy... Who's the bitch now?' Donna reads out in her polite withered tones.

I stand there in the community hall space as those words just bounce off the walls, hopefully not into the church or the crucifix will fall off the wall. Frank, who mainly writes poetry about birds he's seen in his garden, shakes his head while Yolanda chuckles under her breath. Donna works in the charity shop at the weekends, she wears embroidered cardigans and pearls... what the actual hell?

'OK, Donna. I'm going to stop you there before Frank has a cardiac moment.' Frank's face is frozen in disgust. He literally just read out a first-person poem about being a robin. It even rhymed. His mind is too pure for Donna.

'I haven't got to the good bit yet,' she protests.

'There's more?'

'Well, it's a feminist piece about a woman who is fed up of the patriarchy. It's symbolic. You told us last time to think of the undercurrent, the hidden meanings of our work.'

'It's filth, that's what it is,' Frank mutters.

'Well, it's a darned sight more interesting than your shitty poems about birds.'

I close my eyes slowly. And there was me thinking educating teens was all the trouble I was going to face as a teacher. 'Donna and Frank, enough. This is a safe space for everyone to share their work openly and there is room for both. Even if it's not your cup of tea, I ask for respect. Please can you say sorry to each other...'

They exchange mumbled apologies from across the desk though I see Donna has her middle finger up subtly which I would call out if I didn't find it so funny.

'I like the premise, Donna, but the execution needs to be more subtle. There is no build up, no tension, you've gone straight for the jugular.'

She looks annoyed by the criticism. 'I'm getting people's attention from the off.'

'Or putting them off. The shock factor is off the scale. You need to draw them in first,' I explain.

I see her scribble down notes, not that she will pay attention to any of them. Every month, she comes to these creative writing lessons with pages of porn that make me worry for her husband, Terry, but also make me think I should be pointing her towards Wattpad to help top up her pension.

'What does teabagging mean?' Iva asks, reading through Donna's story in front of her. Iva is Czech and she comes to these lessons to try and improve her English. She writes short stories, murder mysteries that tell me who the killer is in the first paragraph. 'Is it to do with the drink? Is it like he's drowning in tea?' she asks, innocently, and I shove a cookie in my mouth.

'It's when a man dunks his balls in your mouth – the balls are the teabags,' Donna explains, very matter-of-factly.

The colour drains from Iva's face. Frank gets up and storms out of the room while Yolanda cackles with laughter.

I rub at my temples. 'Donna, I know Terry got a new hip last year, so no way does he have the balance to do that. Can you tell me where you learn these things?' I ask.

'I read. Reddit. I know things.'

Yolanda interjects, 'It's like you think we're old and we haven't been about. We all read that Fifty Shades stuff, we've lived, you know?'

'Not as much as Esther,' an older lady interrupts, also giggling.

'You lot are awful to Esther,' I say, trying to defend her. 'She went through hell when her husband passed so let the girl enjoy herself. Stop slut-shaming her.'

'Mia, you're allowed to enjoy sex, but you also have to understand it comes with feelings, manners, treating people with a bit of respect,' Yolanda comes back at me. She leans into the table, looking around for Frank. 'She slept with Frank. Broke his heart when she moved on to the next person and he takes tablets for palpitations.'

'Really? Oh man... Is he OK?'

'He stopped eating. I had to go round with ready meals,' Donna explains.

I stop for a moment to be put in my place. This I didn't know about any of them. I literally thought they did old people stuff like crochet, make jam and jump on the free bus to the shops.

The door opens and Frank tentatively returns to the room. 'Have we moved on yet?' he asks.

The room goes quiet and I nod, sifting through my notes. I like Frank. His wife died ten years ago, and he comes to the community centre for sanctuary, for friendship, and gives everyone good ex-GP advice. I'm not too ashamed to say that because my mum died so young, I do get paranoid about my breasts and my wonky nipples and on several occasions he's given me advice and reassurance.

'Actually, I was hoping to return to your poem, Frank. Is that OK?'

He nods, curiously, taking a seat.

'Robin, Lost. There's a lovely line here about how his wings feel clipped, he stands looking out into the snow, wondering how long the winter will last.' I smile as I repeat it. 'I like that sense of solitude you've created. It's subtle.'

He glares over at Donna whose face is completely deadpan.

'The robin does know there are other birds out there though, right? Just because the winter is here and he's out there in the cold, the summer will come, he will fly again.'

'Are you telling me to rewrite the ending?'

'Sad poems are good, ones that transform the emotion hit you more in the feels, you know?'

He smiles and I look over at Yolanda who winks at me.

'What is feels? Why am I hitting you there? Are they balls? Like the teabags?' Iva asks, and the whole room descends into laughter.

With the lesson ended and baby yoga about to start in fifteen minutes, Yolanda helps me stack the chairs in this huge hall space, defined by the shine and scratches on its parquet floor. I had my first snog in here and the last birthday party before my dad died. I remember every little detail. We hired a man to do the disco who had a playlist of five different songs, jam tarts and dayglo orange crisps, the boys all kicking the balloons around like footballs. To this day, it may have been the best party I've ever had.

'Yolanda, don't do the tables – you'll hurt your back,' I tell her, trying to snatch one of the trestles from her wrinkled hands.

'And you'll scuff your nails,' she informs me.

'True but I can fix nails.'

Yolanda writes me memoirs, anecdotes about family, almost

like she's journalling everything before her mind and memory give up on her. They are poignant tributes to her mother, recipes, stories of her background that are joyful and steeped in colour, set in lands far away.

'The girls and I were wondering about your friend and his nose. Is he OK? You know we still feel awful about that,' she enquires.

'Oh, Ed? Yeah, he's fine. Not broken. We told everyone he fought off some well-hard muggers to make him look manly and tough.'

She laughs. 'He seemed like a nice boy, you know? Does that have legs?'

I shake my head at her. 'You know, men and women are allowed to be friends. That's all he is.'

'Whatever, I saw the grinding salsa stuff in the corner,' she tells me, mimicking the moves.

'Stop that,' I say, pointing a finger at her. 'He's just... Ed.' I shrug my shoulders.

She does a strange dance with her eyebrows which tells me she doesn't believe me.

'Oh, shush. Plus, he kind of has a girlfriend. He's dating a teacher from our school so that puts the kibosh on that.'

Yolanda looks at me glumly, pouting. 'I bet she's not as great as you.'

'Well, few are,' I say, sticking my tongue out at her. 'But this is good for Ed. He's been a wallflower for so long, it's time that someone saw him for all his kindness and loyalty. He's such a good bloke. He can be so funny. He will be a great boyfriend and look after her and put her first and he deserves that, he deserves to be happy.'

Yolanda stops stacking chairs for a moment as I say this. 'And you don't deserve any of that?'

'Yolanda, I deserve Harry Styles, but he's just never available when I need him.'

She laughs and it rings around the walls of this place. 'What I'm saying is, you deserve to be happy, too, with someone like this Ed.'

'I am happy,' I argue.

'I hope so, lovely girl.' She comes over to give me a hug. 'That was all your mother ever wanted.'

A lump grows in my throat to hear the words. 'You're such a bitch for trying to make me cry,' I say, wiping my face with my sleeve.

'Your best bitch though, right?'

'Always.'

ED

Not that I've not planned this to the hilt, but tomorrow might be the day I have sex with Caitlin and the anticipation of the event has made me slightly nauseated. This isn't good. I can't be so nervous that I throw up. There's no coming back from that. What if the nerves affect my erection? What if I faint? I did that once at a school public speaking competition. It was a hot day and I fainted and someone had to get out some smelling salts, and slap me lightly.

The plan is Caitlin's going to come over here for a light dinner, nothing too carb heavy, a nice Chablis will be involved and then, hopefully, things will progress to a point where we will end up in the bedroom, which I've just cleaned vigorously, opening up the windows to let some of this fresher spring air into the flat. I've got new sheets waiting to go on, my pants have been freshly laundered, candles are waiting to be lit. However, Mia has told me things might also start in the living room, so I've also vacuumed the sofa and Febrezed the curtains. Why have I done that to my curtains? She won't notice my bloody curtains.

I lie down on my sofa and Nigel jumps straight on to my

stomach, as if trying to calm me down. I just want this to work, to feel less like some idiot who's never had love in his life, to feel like a fully functioning, normal adult. If this goes well then it could grow into a relationship. It could lead to sharing my life with someone who's cool, pretty and who shares my love of houseplants. We could grow a jungle here together, re-pot things, take selfies with them in the background. That's all I want.

It could be worse, I guess. I could still be a virgin and be going into this with zero experience, destined to fail. Thank God for Mia then, who at least taught me a handful of tricks to get me through. I retrieve my phone from my pocket.

Where are you? I text her.

I'm out.

I'm nervous.

Don't be.

Run me through it again.

After dinner, serve dessert and coffees on the sofa. Hand on knee, get a bit closer, snog and handsy and then let it go from there.

Do I give her oral on the sofa?

If it goes there. That's quite sexy. Just make sure she's comfortable.

Like get her a cushion?

I mean, that she's OK with what's happening. Listen to her body language and what she wants.

This is going to be awful.

It's going to be awful with that attitude. Can you fkn chill?

I don't know how to do that! How do you chill out?

With a drink and a wank, usually. I have to go.

I see Mia go offline and drop my phone to my side. I mean, I could do some lesson plans, go for a run and play a video game but Mia has a point. Alcohol will take the edge off. I walk to my fridge and crack open an Asahi, sipping furiously at the top of the bottle. Have a drink. And have a wank. That's also not an awful idea, to be fair. I've been reading up on this and it's also a sure-fire way to ensure I don't blow my tanks too soon. A strategic wank. Maybe that's a plan for 4 p.m. tomorrow before I peel the potatoes. Do I set a reminder on my phone?

I wander into the bedroom. Have a wank. I know how to do that. I've been doing that since I was sixteen. It'll be something to do. Shall I get in the shower? No need. Lube. I'll use some of that. I reach under my bed to the box of sex toys I panic bought to retrieve the lube, tossing that tube up in the air like a cricket ball. OK then, Ed. Time to relax. I lie down on the bed, adjusting my shoulders into the pillows, and pull my trousers and pants down slightly, squirting some lube into my hand and taking myself in my hand. Positive thinking, Ed. Think about Caitlin, here in your flat, in your bed. She's going to say nice things about your sea bass, and she will curl up on your sofa with a glass of wine in her hand and laugh at everything you say. *You are so funny and charming, Ed. I want you, Ed.* And she will get closer and kiss me and everything will just unfold like it does in a film. Her leading me to the bedroom, jumping into my arms with her legs wrapped around me. Her arms above her head, my body gliding over hers, her warm breath against my skin. *Yes, Ed.*

And a strange clanging sound? My eyes spring open for a moment, my cock in my hand. Was that my headboard against the wall? I hear the sound again. Clink, clink, clink. I sit up.

It's only then that I see it. It's the box of sex toys I opened to retrieve the lube, left open on the floor. Nigel is sitting there playing with the metal butt plug.

'Nigel. No! Drop!' I say, like he might be a dog who understands me. 'Bad cat!'

Nigel looks at me, unamused. I'm the bad cat? You're the

one masturbating in the afternoon, you dirty sod. Leave me to play. I like shiny things. He ignores me and continues to clink it against the wooden laminate with his paws.

'Nigel! Nigel!' At this point, I should get up. I should close the door and lock the cat in the kitchen, but given I have a raging erection, I decide to throw a pillow at him. This is not the right thing to do because I like my cat and don't want to be cruel, but it is also the wrong thing to do as the pillow hits the box of sex toys with some force. And I watch as a butt plug flies in a way that it shouldn't out of my balcony window that is slightly ajar, followed by a sound like it may be rolling.

'Shit, shit, shit!' I shriek as I scramble out of bed, trying to pull up my pants. I go on my hands and knees to the floor, prising the window open fully. Please. No. I search for it amongst my plant pots then peer over the side of the small balcony space to see where it's landed. I spot it glinting on the neighbour's balcony below. I jump back into the flat and put my hands on my knees to steady myself, wiping my sticky lube hands on my trousers.

'I hate you,' I tell Nigel as he stares at me from my dresser, and I frantically try to put the rest of the sex toys back in the box. I will have to seal this. What sort of wretched cat plays with a butt plug? How the hell do I explain this? I don't even know who lives in the flat below. Maybe it's someone who doesn't use their small balcony space? Maybe they'll just think it appeared. They won't think it belongs to me, it could have just fallen from a passing airplane. How the hell do I get it back? Do I tie a rope to Nigel and lower him down? Maybe I throw more stuff down there to move it. But then it will fall into the next neighbour's balcony. It will be a catalogue of disasters.

Have a wank, Mia said. It will chill you out, she said.

'Hello? Hello?' There's a voice coming from outside and I go over and stick my head over the balcony cautiously. Below, a man's head is in view. Not just a man. He's holding a baby. And a butt plug. I am going to hell but I'm also going to die from the shame.

'Did this fall from your flat?' he calls up.

'Yes... I am so sorry! I was cleaning and it must have dropped down. Did it hurt anyone? Break anything? I'm really very, very sorry!'

'Nope. All good. You coming down to get it?'

'Yep.'

I don't know why I say this. Yes, I will come and fetch my dropped butt plug and look you in the eye. It's not been used because I only panic bought it a fortnight ago, and I wasn't really sure whose butt it went in. I slip on some trainers, grab my keys and run down the staircase to the lower floor. I may have to move. I'd better find an estate agent. I knock tentatively on the door. When it opens, the man with the baby stands there, holding the butt plug in his hand.

'Christ, I am so sorry. I am so embarrassed,' I say, my mouth dry, cheeks ablaze. I await the judgement, the shame, the looks that will label me the building perv. That man on the third floor uses sex toys with such vigour that they fly out of the window.

'No harm done, mate. What is it? Like one of them wine stopper things?'

I pause for a moment.

'Yeah.'

'Well, I'm Nick. This is Mia.'

'Your baby is called Mia?'

'Yeah. Sorry, she's a loud little thing. There's a lot of crying.' I see the dishevelled look in his eyes, the fact he's still wearing pyjamas in the afternoon. I see mini Mia, unperturbed by the distress she causes this man, and smile.

'It's what babies do. I'm Ed. I'm really sorry about this, by the way,' I say, holding the butt plug up in the air. I need to stop doing that.

'Like I say, no harm done. You should pop down for a drink

sometime. We're big on wine in this house. You can meet my wife, bring your fancy wine stopper thing.'

I don't quite know how to reply to that, but I swear little baby Mia is laughing at us.

SIXTEEN

MIA

You deserve to be happy, too.

For the past day, Yolanda's words have rung in my ears. I do deserve love and I do deserve to be happy. It's not that I've stopped looking for these things, but it's made me think I've spent the last month seeking that out for Ed, to fix his virginity issues, and I've forgotten to seek these things out for myself. In a few weeks, Ed will no longer need me, and he and Caitlin will be revelling in the glow of a new relationship where I will likely no longer see him. I know how this works. But I won't deny it's been a tiny bit fun to be able to have proper orgasms with a willing participant. So maybe it's time to find those orgasms elsewhere, which is why I'm in a local pub waiting for Tinder Scott with the abs.

As I sit here, I check my make-up on my phone and see Ed is trying to message me. He does this now like an anxious child because his big sex date is coming up. I don't know how to tell him that you can't write a script for these things, you just need to let it happen.

This is going to be awful.

It's going to be awful with that attitude. Can you fkn chill?

I don't know how to do that! How do you chill out?

With a drink and a wank, usually.

'Mia?' I hear a voice from behind me.

I have to go.

I put my phone down and bite my lip, slowly turning around. Please don't be a catfish. Please don't be weird. Please don't be a dick.

'Scott?'

'Yep. How's it going? It's good to finally meet.'

'It is,' I say this slowly, not because he's taken my breath away. I mean, he looks like his pictures, nice T-shirt and jeans combo, I accept the trainers and the hair is styled well without being too sculpted. But dude, what's with the voice? That's some high pitch. Has he just had a hit of helium?

'Am I not what you were expecting?' he asks, registering my confusion.

'Oh no, I guess it's just strange to finally meet you in the flesh,' I reply, putting my hand over my mouth. There was me thinking it'd be bizarre meeting you after I'd told you in as many words about pretty sexually explicit things I'd be willing to engage in, but now I sit here wondering if your balls have dropped. It's a strange tone, like Chris Eubank crossed with a cartoon chipmunk. Is he putting it on? Is it supposed to be funny?

'Let me just get a drink. Are you good?'

'Yeah, all good,' I say, holding my bottle of cider in the air.

I watch as he goes to the bar. Damn you, Scott. There was something there that clicked so well via text. A brilliant line of conversation, sexually very in tune, a couple of cultural references in there that made me think we had things in common. But now I'm thinking of him talking dirty into my ear, the prolonged squeak he's going to make when he orgasms, and I bite my lip trying to keep in the giggles. Why does this happen to me like this? It's always something. Maybe I'm being too picky. He could have other assets. I've seen the assets for myself, and I could forgive a high-pitched voice if he's as good in person as he is on sext. I need to think about all the other qualities that make someone fanciable and future boyfriend material. He returns to the table with a pint and a packet of crisps. Salt and vinegar, that's a good start.

'So I'll start by saying, it's a bloody relief that you look like your pictures,' he says, taking a large sip of his pint.

'Have you been catfished before then?' I ask.

'Oh yeah. All the time, you?'

'I once chatted to someone who swore he was the drummer in Coldplay. Turns out he was a tree surgeon called Kevin.'

He laughs. Oh dear. It sounds like a car starting in the winter. Don't judge him, Mia.

'Well, I've had nothing that extreme but the number of women I've met who outright lie is ridiculous.'

This time it's time to focus on the words, less on the quality of his voice. 'They lie to you?'

'Oh, you know, they lie about how they look, their size. I've met some colossal women who've told me they're a size eight. You're what, a size ten?'

'Depends on the clothes shop,' I reply, biting my tongue to not say anything more.

'Well, I can see you work out.'

'I don't.'

I only go to spin classes for the beats and the free coconut water. He really said that about women, didn't he?

'Well, it must be all that sex you have then,' he comments. He winks and I feel a bit of my cider repeat up my nostrils. I've told this man too much already. Only two nights ago, I told him I wanted him to push me up against a wall and stick his assets in me. Now I've only been with him for two minutes and I want to push him off a wall. I reach over and help myself to a crisp and suddenly feel a short sharp slap to my fingers.

'Naughty,' he tells me, waving a finger at me.

I'm not averse to a slap in the right context but as soon as he does this, he turns his crisps around to face him.

'If you want your own then you'll have to buy them. I don't share food.'

What? He's generous too, eh? I can't quite seem to remove the shock from my face that he slapped me in an open place.

'Scott, how do you see this afternoon panning out?' I enquire.

He seems confused by the change of tack. 'Well, I thought we could chat, and you could see I'm not some serial killer and then come back to mine. We could make all your fantasies a reality.' He smirks.

I swallow hard to think about all the things I disclosed to him. Oh dear.

'So essentially, that would mean kissing, having sex and the exchange of bodily fluids. And you can't even share a crisp with me?'

'It's my thing.'

'Well, my things are generosity, kindness and an appreciation and respect for women. All women.'

There's an eye roll and I feel a sudden urge to slap him myself. I shaved my legs for this. I'm wearing a thong. You're not the only person feeling disappointment here. Was I supposed to just fall at his feet because of the abs, cheekbones and the bigger than average penis? It's going to take more than that, I'm afraid.

He drinks half his pint quietly and then pushes his chair away. 'Well, if you're one of those raging feminist types then that's not my bag, I'm afraid. A shame, you and me could have had fun.'

'It's you and I,' I say, like correcting his grammar is any sort of forceful parting shot. He grabs a coat from the back of his chair and yes, he takes his crisps with him like a sociopath. I wave but he doesn't respond, and I sit there nursing my bottle of cider, laughing to myself. I think back to a younger version of me who wouldn't have listened to the words. She'd have been swayed by the fitness and had a fling that went on for way longer than was necessary. So well done to me for showing some element of growth.

However, is it weird that at this precise moment I'm thinking about someone who would have shared his crisps with me? I think about texting him. I could go over and quiz him on sex stuff before the big day tomorrow, but that wouldn't be right. Maybe I should just jump on Tinder and start again. Or go home and watch porn. I look around the bar. I'm sure there was a time when you could pick up a person in an establishment such is this. One cheesy pick-up line and there was your meet-cute. But it's 5 p.m. It's a little early for that, maybe. I scan the bar. Too old, too denim, too tourist. However, my eyes then stop. Tommy from the P.E. department. Too much of a complete and utter dick. I hope he hasn't seen me, though this could be a really good opportunity to spill something on him or order him ten burgers with all the toppings that he has to pay for. I watch him chat to the barman for a moment, scowling from my seat until someone comes to join him. There's laughter, a hug, a hand to her waist and then a kiss. A long-drawn-out kiss.

As soon as I see who it is, I gasp loudly, the sadness overwhelming me.

Caitlin.

ED

It's midnight when I hear the knocking and for a moment, when my eyes spring open, I am slightly worried that Nigel has found that butt plug again and the noise is him throwing it around the room. However, I turn to see my clock, register the time and realise it's coming from my front door. At this time? Is the building on fire? Christ, I hope not.

I sit up, scrambling around to find a T-shirt, and head to the door. As I open it, Mia falls into my flat, clearly quite drunk and unable to stand. I catch her.

'Eddie,' she says, resting her head against my cheek.

'Mia? Wow, how drunk are you? How did you get here?'

'I ran!' she says, her body in a star shape and arms in a muscle man pose. 'We have to talk!' she exclaims, waving a finger in my face. 'Nice boxers.'

'Now? It's kinda late...'

'It's not. It's Saturday night. It's a time for dancing,' she says, breaking out some moves for me like she might be having some sort of fit.

I fold my arms, bemused. 'What did you want to talk about?'

'I went on a date with a man called Scott tonight. We met on Tinder.' She loud-whispers the Tinder bit.

I nod. 'I'm taking it that because you're not with Scott at this moment then it didn't go very well...'

Mia proceeds to charge through my flat, half dancing, half jogging. 'Where's Nigel?'

Most likely hiding given she's burst in here so loudly. 'How badly did it go with Scott?' I ask, assuming her highly inebriated state to have a reason.

She stops running away and turns towards me, frowning. 'He wouldn't share his crisps with me,' she slurs.

'Well then, that's a complete no-no,' I joke.

She stands there for a moment and looks at me, her face sad and dejected. This isn't the first time Mia has done this. We've had numerous drunken staff nights out that end in her chatting to me about her man woes. 'Please tell me you've not come here for crisps?'

She laughs in a drunken, overly loud way and pushes my shoulder. I try to shush her. 'Nooooo. I've had chips already but I couldn't finish them, so I very kindly gave them to someone at a bus stop.'

'Because you're all about the give...'

'You know me so well,' she says, tears in her eyes.

I urge her to sit down on my sofa to steady herself but as I put a hand to her back, she grabs me and hugs me tightly. 'We really do need to talk.'

'We need to sober you up.'

'I saw things tonight,' she says, like she's been haunted.

'I'm not surprised, it's the high street on a weekend. Everyone was probably drunk and misbehaving.'

'Oh, it was a complete state. I saw someone flash tit at the kebab shop. But that's not what I mean.'

I watch as her eyes roll about in her head. This might get quite painful, having to work out her half sentences like song lyrics. Why does she look so infinitely sad? Her eyes are just glazed over, looking at me like a cartoon deer.

'Mia, did someone hurt you? Were you out and drinking alone? That's never a great idea. You need to look out for yourself more.'

She pauses for a moment. 'Why do you say things like that? Why do you care?'

I can't quite read her tone. Is she accusing me of caring for my friend? My worry turns to confusion.

'Because I worry about you.'

'You shouldn't do that.'

'Well, sorry?'

I'm on some strange precipice, wondering if I need to leave her here in her drunken chaotic state so she can sleep this off or find out what's going on.

'Maybe you need to worry about you,' she mutters.

'What does that mean?' I ask.

'This Caitlin girl.' She rubs her forehead trying to find the words. 'Do we know enough about her? You've kinda jumped into that quite quickly. I think you need to give it time.'

I stop for a moment as the words come out of her mouth. 'This from someone who was just on a date with a man she met on Tinder...'

Mia eyeballs me, swaying slightly. 'That was a low blow.'

'You told me that she'd friend-zone me if I left it any longer. I don't get where this is coming from?'

'I just... I just...' She grabs my face with both hands and looks at me. Naturally, as someone who does not know how to read sexual cues in any way, I panic. Is she trying to have sex with me? Is that why she's here? I move her hands away.

'Did you come here for sex?' I ask.

'Noooo,' she says in horror, half-laughing. 'Ed!'

'You were looking at me weird...'

'There's two of you at the moment in my line of sight. I was trying to focus on you to tell you things.'

'That I shouldn't date Caitlin for some reason.'

'For good reason.'

'Because if I leave you then you won't have someone to furnish you with crisps anymore?'

'It's more than that...'

'Mia, you're not making any sense,' I explain in clipped tones, moving away to the kitchen to fetch her a glass of water. 'Drink this. You can sleep it off on the sofa.'

I stand there and she rises to her feet, tears falling from her face, a hand to her chest. The tears make me stop in my tracks.

'I don't want you to get hurt. You're a good man, Ed Rogers, and I... I... care about you. God, I don't know how to tell you this, I don't want to be the bad guy in this scenario.'

'Then let me be with Caitlin. Let me find out for myself

and be in a relationship. I've never done this before, and I need to just let it happen. You keep telling me that. That I need to learn. So let me do that. Don't come here in the middle of the night, telling me not to fall in love with someone.'

'You're in love with her?' Mia asks, eyes wide.

'I think I'm falling in love with her, yes.'

I've not said that out loud yet and it feels like a strange relief to be able to admit that, sex aside, I know I have the capacity to love someone and they could possibly love me back. But as I say it, Mia looks at a space behind me where a door opens and I turn to see Caitlin appearing, dressed in one of my T-shirts and just her knickers. I look back at Mia; she looks as though she's just seen a ghost.

'I'm sorry. Did we wake you?' I ask her, smiling at her dishevelled hair.

I watch as Mia and Caitlin engage in a moment of evil stares.

'Mia needed a place to crash,' I explain.

Caitlin nods. 'Sure...'

'Let me sort her out and I'll come back to bed. I'm so sorry.'

She nods, takes her leave and I watch as Mia stands there staring at the closed door.

'I'm sorry, I didn't realise you had company. I can go...' Mia mumbles, grabbing her bag and heading to the door, wiping the tears from her face.

'Mia, it's late. Let me at least make sure you're safe and get you an Uber,' I say, stepping towards her.

'I got this far on my own, I will be fine,' she says, and I'm taken aback by the curtness in her tone. As she gets to the front door, she turns to look back at me. 'So you slept with her?'

I nod, unable to contain my smile. 'I was so bloody anxious this morning, but I followed your advice. Don't try to plan or script it out, just invite her round for a drink. Let it happen... And it did...' I say, hoping my relief will erase any words said a few moments ago. 'And it was everything, it really was.'

Mia closes her eyes for a moment and shakes her head. 'It all went OK?'

'It did,' I say, confused.

'I have to go then,' she whispers.

'Mia?' I say, one last time trying to work out why she's here, why she's come here so late in the middle of the night, why she is so quietly devastated. 'I don't get why you're so sad.'

'I'm just drunk. I have to go. I love you, Eddie. Know that, always.'

SEVENTEEN

MIA

You have questions, I know. Why didn't I just tell him, there and then? I could have sat in the bar, like some French spy, and covertly taken pictures of Caitlin and Tommy and sent them to Ed. I could have burst into that flat and spoken the truth. *I saw that cow with Tommy. I saw him feel up her arse. I saw them kiss.* And when Caitlin appeared from Ed's bedroom, I could have rugby tackled her to the floor and pulled her hair and used my bad nails to do some real damage. But I didn't. I'm not good in emotionally complicated situations like that.

Instead, I saw Caitlin and Tommy in that bar. I saw them leave. I ordered a bottle of wine trying to work out what to do. I turned to a group in that bar celebrating their mate's 50th birthday to ask for advice. I got so drunk that I ran to Ed's flat. It's the longest I've ever run since school. I'm surprised my lungs didn't tell me to fuck off.

But when I got there, I lost my nerve, which I hope you know is unlike me. I tried to drip feed him what I knew. I tried to play it from a different angle. *It's too soon... do you really know her well enough?* Part of me heard him speak of his desire to work out all of this love stuff for himself, how I needed to take a step back. But there was a part of me that also got really emosh. I didn't want to hurt him. I never want to see him hurt. The final nail in that coffin was Caitlin appearing like some unholy apparition at the door. What an absolute bitch. How did she get here so fast? She was snogging Tommy only six hours ago.

But they slept together. And because that moment was everything to Ed, I couldn't tell him. I just couldn't. So I said nothing.

I've still said nothing. I jumped in a taxi to get home. I fell asleep on the back seat. I threw up in my kitchen sink and woke up in my housemate's bed. I didn't sleep with my housemate. I just got lost. In my own house. And since then, I've questioned everything a million times over. Why didn't I just go for her? I should've launched myself at Caitlin like some sort of demonic wildcat. But I didn't. I'm not sure why.

'Miss! Miss! I don't get this one – can I leave this question blank?'

I focus my attention back to my classroom where my first English class of the day are doing some sort of fun quiz activity that I downloaded off the internet to fill the time and to ensure I had a quiet half hour to let my head adjust to this Monday morning. I'd like to say they're all engaged in it but there's a row of them in the back with their phones out.

'Yep, just leave it blank. Lola, Brooke and Chrissie – I hope you're not using your phones to cheat?' I call out to the back of the room. I take the long walk down there to perch on the edge of their desks, a quick glance at their phones telling me that my fun crosswords are not on their minds.

'Are you shopping?' I ask them.

'Prom dresses, Miss. What do you think of this one?' Lola asks, holding up her phone to show me a red off-the shoulder number with an eye-watering price tag. 'Turns out Zara in 11P has exactly the same dress as me, no joke, so I have like two months to find a new one.'

She also has important life exams in the next months, so I'm glad this takes priority. I haven't really chatted to Lola much since she came to The Hub to tell me about her relationship problems but I'm glad she's still standing and there were no reports that came into me about any incidents of lunchtime fights.

'The red is a statement,' I say, looking over the dress again, thinking about how it's the same price as my monthly rent.

'I need to make a statement,' she tells me.

Naturally, I want to dig. You want to make that statement because someone stole your man or because you're still with that man and need to tell people to back off? Either way, I like the commitment, the chutzpah of this young soul.

'Then the red reads fire. Don't mess,' I say, winking. The bell goes. 'All, keep the quizzes. I hope they were useful. I will see you all tomorrow.'

I hear the usual scraping of chairs, the shuffle of feet, the moans and groans of having to take on another week as everyone starts to filter out of the room and I follow them out, mentally going through my day, thinking about my lunch later. Like the kids, I also have my priorities.

'Can we all keep on the left, please?'

I hear Caitlin's voice first, engaging in the impossible task of trying to do a bit of crowd control in these corridors but as soon as I see her, I stop for a moment to glare. I can't read that feeling coursing through my veins at the moment, but I know it's making me boil over like a bullock seeing red.

'OI!' I shout. The corridor stops moving. At least I know how to sort our crowd control problem. I swap over to Caitlin's side of the corridor as kids start to move, slowly taking in the drama.

'Miss Johnson? Is everything OK?' Caitlin asks, her face slightly panicked.

I pull her into an empty classroom. 'We need to talk,' I say, as I shut the door behind me. It's on. This is so very on.

'Is this about you bursting into Ed's flat on Saturday night?' she says, her eyebrows raised like butter wouldn't melt. I have an overwhelming urge to stick her Alice band where the sun doesn't shine.

'Kind of...'

'You were pretty drunk. What an evening though,' she mutters, her face filled with an innocence that makes me want to barf. I need to take that look away, don't I?

'I'm talking about you being at Pepe's Wine Bar on Saturday afternoon with your tongue down Tommy Wood's throat,' I say, any confusion about how I was going to deal with this situation suddenly gone.

Her smiley, innocent act flicks like a switch and she looks at me then laughs under her breath.

'You were there?' she asks. 'How embarrassing, were you following him? I knew you liked him but that's desperate.'

I furrow my brow at the insult. 'I was there on another date, actually. I'm asking because it was a bit of a shock to see you at Ed's the same evening. Who does that?'

'It's just casual with Tommy,' she says.

'But does Ed know? Ed really likes you.'

'Can I just ask, how is this your problem? Is that why you showed up drunk on Saturday? To tell him?'

'I'm mates with Ed... You can't be with him and be shagging Tommy on the side.'

'Excuse me?' she exclaims, her face etched in shock. 'I'll do what I want.'

'But it's Ed. Ed is a good bloke. Please don't do this to him...'

She frowns. 'I can't quite tell who you're jealous about me being with, Tommy or Ed.'

I stop for a moment as she says that, my rage at her callous nastiness making me shake my head. 'Decide who you want and just do right by Ed, that's all I ask,' I mutter slowly.

'Oooh, fit P.E. teacher or the geeky Biology doormat who does anything I ask? Tough one...'

And this is when I make quite a bad life decision. Because I could have launched myself at Caitlin in Ed's flat. I could have done it in that bar. I could have ended all of it there and then, but instead I decide to launch myself at her here and now, in this classroom. All I hear are chairs and tables clattering to the floor, and I'm aware of the faces of a row of schoolchildren peering through the door, and the frenzied scramble of hair and hands as I give her a sharp, pretty loud slap that echoes off the walls.

'FIGHT! FIGHT! FIGHT!' I hear in the corridors, people running, kids cheering. I hope they're cheering for me. Caitlin picks up a book and throws it at my head. I duck. You'll have to do better than that, bitch. I take on some strange fight stance like this is about to go down, street style. She reaches over and goes for my hair. I scream and lunge for the Alice band.

'MIA! Stop it!' I feel a pair of arms go around me, holding me back, and see Beth's face. 'What the hell is going on?' she screams. 'All of you, go to your classes, NOW!' she shrieks at the kids taking in the action.

'She attacked me!' Caitlin says, pretending to steady herself on a desk like she's some anaemic, weak wench. I realise the Alice band is in my hands, so I snap it. It might be my best life achievement. I shake Beth off and wait as other teachers start to file into the room including our head teacher, Alicia.

'What on earth is going on here?' she shouts.

Beth looks at me like she doesn't quite know how to help.

'Miss Johnson attacked me,' Caitlin says as a Maths colleague rushes to her aid, pulling her up a chair.

'You did what?' Alicia says, shock making her face curl up into a snarl.

I am speechless. Anything I want to say will make me sound like a child. She started it, she pulled my hair, she threw a book at my face. She's shagging Tommy from P.E. and Ed from Biology. She's a duplicitous, nasty cow. But I can't say half of that, not here, not now.

'I did,' I mutter. 'I apologise that the children saw that. That was poor judgment from me.'

Beth looks down to the floor, and I see a momentary smirk cross Caitlin's face as if she's wondering how she got away with that so easily. I stare at all the teachers glaring at me. This is nice Miss Bell from Maths. She brings her lunch in a floral lunch bag and wears proper shoes. What has come over you, Miss Johnson? We knew you were a loose cannon, but you've crossed a line.

'Beth,' Alicia says. 'Please can you ensure Mia's lessons are covered for the day. Mia, I'd like to see you in my office... now.'

ED

Hey, I'm free this evening? Want to come over for a takeaway? Wine?

And that was how it all started. A casual text at 6 p.m. on a Saturday. After I crawled back to my flat having retrieved my lost butt plug, I stood there and realised I needed to just jump the gun. What was Mia always telling me? I lack any form of spontaneity. I plan things to the letter and sex with Caitlin was something that just couldn't be planned. So I changed my sheets, I checked the expiry date on my sea bass and I sent that text. She'd just met a friend for lunch, so she was out and came over. Was it everything I'd planned and rehearsed? I wish I could remember. The night just comes to me in flashes of good, hazy memories. Good wine. Some soft jazz playing (not Taylor

Swift). Her head tilted back laughing on my sofa, her taking my hand and leading me to the bedroom, spooning her after the event, the streetlights bouncing off her skin, lying there full of relief and a glow that it had gone relatively well. That she was here, that this was the start of something possibly great. And yes, it did last longer than thirty seconds. I surprised myself. I think she had an orgasm. I certainly did.

'Hey...'

As I walk up to her now at the end of a school day, all I can feel is hope. These were the small things I fantasised about. Just having someone at the end of a day to go home with. Her face warms to see me and she reaches over to give me a kiss on the cheek.

'How was your day?' she asks, taking my hand in hers.

'OK, I think. You?'

'Eventful,' she says smiling, nodding. 'Can we go to yours? Maybe we can get some food in.'

As soon as she says this, I feel nothing but relief. It's been like this since Saturday. I was relieved she showed up, that she stayed overnight and let me make her coffee on Sunday morning, that she didn't blank or ghost me today, that she wants a repeat event at my flat tonight.

'Sure. Or I can cook?' I suggest. She smiles and we start walking towards my car.

'Have you seen Mia today?' she asks me.

'Why?'

She looks pensive for a moment.

I will admit to feeling some relief that Caitlin didn't leave my flat after Mia's impromptu gate-crash on Saturday. I'm not sure if this is her way of saying we need to discuss that.

'I haven't...'

'You've not seen her all day? Got any messages from her? Spoken to any of the staff?'

I shrug. 'It's been one of those days. I've been holed up with lab techs getting stuff ready for Year 9 dissections, going through exam prep...'

She stops for a moment as we reach my car. 'Then I'm actually not sure how to tell you this. Have you not heard the news?'

I hold my car keys in my hand, squeezing them tightly. I haven't heard from Mia since Saturday night and suddenly, terror lurches in my stomach. Did she not make it home? I usually text her or drop her a message to check in but I've been otherwise engaged. I feel terrible for not having made sure she got back safely.

'Is she OK? Don't tell me she's still hungover?' I say, trying to mask my worry with humour.

'She's been suspended,' she mutters.

'She's been what?' I say, in shock, taking out my phone. 'Why? I should call her and make sure she's alright.' I'm thrown into a blind panic. I can only imagine she was late this morning and didn't call it in. Or is this about something else? Something worse? 'She had a work review due. Maybe her in-class assessments didn't go well.'

I feel Caitlin's hands go into mine to calm me down, her fingers stopping me from dialling.

'Maybe give her a moment... Last thing I heard Beth took her home,' she tells me.

'I can't believe she wouldn't have called,' I say despondently, checking my messages and any trace of missed calls. I think of all the reasons why this would have happened. I helped Mia out with her paperwork for her assessments. That was all in line. Maybe Alicia had had enough of her flaunting her smart shoe policy. I always told her Alicia's warnings would have consequences. However, there is also an element of hurt that she didn't think to come and look for me or let me know if something that major had happened. The only thing I can think is that she was too ashamed.

'She loves teaching. This will really break her, you know?' I explain, thinking through the processes of why this would happen and what will happen next. Could she get fired? What about all these kids sitting exams? What about Mia's rent?

'You seem overly invested in Mia, you know?' she says, curtly, reading the panic in my face. I unlock the car and she gets inside. I'm not sure what she means but I get in, too, and watch as she puts her seatbelt on quietly. Maybe now is the time to clear that air.

'She is just a friend,' I try to explain to her.

'I have friends too but none that show up on my doorstep, drunk at midnight,' she says. Is she jealous?

'That's just Mia. It's what she does.'

'What did she say when she came round?' she asks.

I swallow hard, grateful Caitlin didn't hear any of our conversation that night. I've been trying to work out what Mia was trying to get at. Was this thing with Caitlin going too fast? Perhaps. She'd only been at the school for a mere couple of months and I'd only just started my foray into all things sex. But I think I was also right to tell Mia it was important that I started to take the lead with these things, to act from my gut, to chuck any plans in the bin.

'She was just on the scrounge for food.' I feel my eye twitch as I say that. The car suddenly goes very quiet. Something is wrong here. Do I put the radio on? Maybe she's heard that Mia gave me sex lessons. I knew that might come out in the wash. Oh God, please don't let it be that.

'Well, you know... I can see you were being a good friend to her but sometimes I think she takes advantage of you.'

'I don't think she does,' I say, trying to defend Mia. If only she knew the ways she's helped me in the last month.

'You're just so different, too. You're so good at what you do. They don't suspend people for no good reason. Sometimes you don't need people's bad energy in your life like that... I'm not sure she's good for you. I certainly don't understand her.'

I keep my eye on the road, thinking through her words. I've never questioned my friendship with Mia. It's always worked, there's never been that imbalance where I feel I don't want her there. She's quietly featured like some piece of quirky furniture that just belongs in the room.

'I just think if we're going out then I don't like the idea of her being in our orbit,' Caitlin continues.

There is a lot to dissect there. We are going out? Is that an official thing? Did she really just say that? I think she did, but it seems to be contingent on Mia being in my life. To hear her say that out loud feels unnatural, and there's a barbed tone to her voice that I've not heard before.

'Are you asking me to choose?' I ask her, tentatively.

She shrugs nonchalantly and I keep both hands on the steering wheel trying to figure out what she means. I'm a rookie in all of this – not just the sex, but relationships and women. My history of misunderstanding them and their intention is the stuff of legend. What I say now is crucial, isn't it? I don't want to give up on Mia, but I feel all that hope in my chest for what this could be with Caitlin and I want to keep it there. I want this to work out. Obviously, I say none of this out loud though. I don't know how.

'So, I can make a green curry, if you like?' I suggest, hoping talk of Thai food may help.

'Sounds gorgeous,' she says, putting a hand to mine on the gearstick. I turn to glance at her as my car pulls up to a traffic light.

'Weren't you wearing a hairband this morning?' I ask her.

'Oh yeah, it snapped. Silly thing,' she replies.

I smile.

EIGHTEEN

MIA

'Hi, you don't know me. Are you Rachel?' Beth asks at my sister's front door, while I half hide behind her borg coat.

'Yes, I am. Mia?' she says as I obviously haven't hidden myself very well. Beth turns to look at me, shrugging her shoulders, as if asking how we should tell my sister I've just been suspended from my job. Beth did offer to bring me back to hers, but I didn't want to burden her, and I thought Rachel would have more expensive alcohol hiding away for me to drink anyway. I step ahead of my dear work colleague.

'I've been suspended from my job.' Rachel grits her teeth in horror. 'I hit someone.'

'You hit a child? For God's sake, Mia!'

She ushers us both into the house, looking around in a panic in case her posh neighbours heard that.

'I hit a teacher.'

As she shuts the door behind us Rachel looks at Beth, her head cocked to one side.

'No, I'd never hit Beth. Beth is awesome. And why would she be here if I'd hit her?'

'Well, you better come through and explain yourself then. Beth, it's lovely to meet you.'

'Where are the kids?' I say, arching my head around the doorframes, hoping they're there to act as a distraction.

'They're with Gareth.' I glance at Beth who widens her eyes as she realises that Rachel is that sister. The one she put in touch with a lawyer. It's been an eventful fortnight. Rachel and Gareth told the kids, they've orchestrated their separation, he's renting a flat nearby. It's been dramatic, new and all her emotion can be read in the lines on her forehead. 'Tea?'

'Wine...?' I suggest.

'Is it too early for wine?' she says.

'No such thing. It's happy hour somewhere in the world,' I say. And Rachel does a very strange thing. She laughs. At a joke I made. She rarely does this – she finds me as funny as toothache most of the time – so it's nice to be able to make her do that. 'What were you going to do without the kids tonight then?' I ask her, looking her up and down.

'Eat posh crisps and start a box set. Shouldn't I be asking the questions though? You hit someone? Are the police involved? Is the person alive?'

I give Rachel a series of looks as she leads us to the kitchen and grabs a good bottle of Rioja.

'If she wasn't alive then I would be on the run. Have you got an attic I can hide in?' I ask. It seems Rachel does humour but not sarcasm. 'And no police, it was just a slap.'

Even though I felt immense pleasure in the moment at giving Caitlin what for, the regret slowly veils my being now. It was not a clever move. I've let her win and at the expense now of my job. And despite everything, I cared about all those kids in my classes and my work. This was a stupid time to be suspended, just before their exams. 'I'm such an idiot,' I say, taking a seat and resting my face on Rachel's cool granite kitchen counter.

'Not your wisest move,' Beth informs me, a hand to my back.

'Make sure you take care of my kids, Beth. I'll write you notes of where my exam classes are at and what needs to be done. I'm sorry – you don't need that extra work... I can't believe I messed up like that. I don't even know how to fix this.'

Beth starts to pat my head, knowing none of this is an easy fix.

'Did she deserve it?' Rachel asks, taking a sip of her wine.

Again, a surprise here from the eldest sister who I expected would be a bit more judgemental about my being jobless and wanting to drink before seven in the evening.

'She's dating Ed...'

'The boy with the nice chinos that you brought here...?'

'Yes.'

'We like Ed... yes?'

'Ed is a friend, and we all love Ed. Anyway, it turns out Caitlin, the girl I slapped, is also sleeping with Tommy from P.E. on the side and when I confronted her about it, she said some pretty nasty things about Ed. And it riled me.'

Rachel nods, taking in my account as she pours out a healthy measure of wine into her very shiny wine glasses.

'Riled you? You're very eloquent this afternoon,' Beth says, slipping off her coat and taking a seat at the breakfast bar in the kitchen. 'More like she pounced on that bitch. It was like something out of a girl gang prison show.'

'That I did,' I say proudly.

Rachel laughs. Perhaps a more barbed response now given that my pouncing may have cost me my job, my career, my livelihood. 'Well, that's our Mia for you... She likes the chaos.'

'What? I do not!' I protest, my hands in the air.

'You do! Mia loves a scrap, a chance to have a difference of opinion,' she explains to Beth. 'We always thought it was because you liked the chaos, the conflict, the challenge. She buzzes off it. You weren't built like me, shall we say?' she adds.

'What? Boring and mundane?' I jest.

'Such a little cow, too,' she says, shaking her head.

Beth puts a hand in the air. 'I am one of five sisters, you don't have to tell me how little sisters work,' she says, taking a large swig of wine. 'I just have many questions. Why have we still not told Ed about Caitlin? I feel we need to tell him... No?'

'About the fight or Caitlin?'

'Well, all of it? You went to Ed's flat that night, you didn't tell him then and you still haven't told him now.'

I look down at my wine and swirl it around in my glass. 'How do I tell him something like that? He likes her so much. It would break his heart.'

Rachel furrows her brow trying to fill in the gaps of what she's been told. 'Hold up. So you saw Caitlin with another bloke. You went round to tell Ed but...'

'Caitlin was already there...'

'So you bottled it?' Beth asks.

'Or,' Rachel adds, 'seeing her there with him made you a little sad. Am I allowed to use the word jealous?'

Beth looks surprised as the words come out of Rachel's mouth, suggesting she was thinking that much too. Normally, I would protest such words. Jealous? I don't get jealous. How absolutely ridiculous. But instead, I sit there quietly and sip my wine.

'PLUS, MIA'S BEEN SLEEPING WITH ED!' Beth blurts out.

I glare at her while Rachel struggles to keep on her stool. 'Aha! I knew it! I knew when he came round that there was something going on. The plot thickens then. You have a crush on him.'

'Don't use the word, "crush" – it's very teenager,' I say.

'Then a case of the love bugs?' she jests, sounding all at once like my mum.

'Shush. Yes, we had a friends with benefits thing going which was fun and maybe I'm a little sad that it is coming to an end...'

'She was sex-training him,' Beth explains.

Rachel raises her eyebrows at me. 'He just hadn't had that much sex before and had questions, so I ran him through some stuff.'

'For the love of Christ, was this a paid arrangement?' Rachel asks.

'Of course it wasn't!' I shriek.

From Rachel's expression, it seems she still doesn't quite understand what she's been told and what happened there, but hell, neither did I. It was a drunken admission of virginity on my bathroom floor that led to sex that led me to seeing Ed in a whole different light. In a light which makes me think I care about him in more ways now. Like I want to lie next to him for a bit longer, have him scratch my back forever and eat lunch with him every day. I realise I am very quiet as I go through these realisations in my own head.

'So, through these sex lessons, you think you may have fallen for him?' Beth asks. 'You told me he irons his own pants, and you didn't see that as part of your future.'

'Well, maybe I need someone to iron my pants for me...'

'I knew it.' Beth beams. 'It's a staff wedding. We can hire out the gym for your reception.'

'Yeah, never happening,' I joke.

'I still think he needs to know though. About Caitlin. Even if it's an anonymous letter or something?' Beth adds.

I shrug my shoulders sadly.

'Or at least tell him how you feel. She's been on the scene for a month. You and Ed have history, proper friendship there. Maybe he'll realise what he's wanted the whole time has been there, right in front of him,' Beth explains, trying to squeeze some romanticism out of the situation. The same Beth who teaches *Romeo & Juliet* as a love story whereas I teach it as a tragic tale of the futility of grudges and crap parenting.

I shake my head, laughing, watching Rachel as she studies my face, taking long sips of her wine.

'But Mia, why wouldn't you?' she asks.

'Because for the past five years, Ed and I have made a joke over how terrible we would be as a couple. We are polar opposites. I dance in public, he does not. He organises his mugs by colour, any mugs I've ever owned, I've stolen. I go out, he stays in. I am late for everything, he is half an hour early. It's a recipe for...'

'Chaos,' Rachel says, smirking.

'I just don't think he feels the same way,' I say glumly, resting my chin in my hands. 'This whole time, it's been about how much he likes Caitlin.'

'Who's a queen bitch! So take her down and then move into that space,' Beth says.

'And what if he doesn't want that? Then I'll have lost one of my very best mates. I don't want that to happen,' I say.

We all sip our wine together, mulling over that fact. I can see it now. I could run to Ed's house through warm early summer showers. It would be the perfect time to make a romcom admission of love. To say, Ed, you bloody idiot. I think I've fallen for you. Don't ask me how or when but for some inexplicable reason, I'd like us to be together. I'll fight Caitlin now over you. I'd snap all her Alice bands. Be with me. Let's take the bus into work forever. Let's fall in love.

But I can see him standing there, looking embarrassed and pitying me. Or maybe he'd laugh. He'd say, I don't think it would work, Mia. We're just too different. You haven't even watched half the *Star Wars* films and you eat like a small wild pony. I don't think there's anything there. I don't feel the same way.

And that would break me.

ED

Hi, leave Me A Message. Geddit? Mia. Message. You know the drill.

'Mia? It's me. I'm sitting in a supermarket car park calling you because I've left you a few WhatsApp messages and you've obviously seen them because of the blue ticks, and you are refusing to message me back. I believe the young people call that being a ghost and I find it incredibly rude. Especially as it means I'm being forced into actually leaving you a voice message and it's likely you will not listen to this too. I'm thinking back to all those times I've called you from Starbucks asking you what you want and you never reply and then you show up asking me why I didn't buy you a drink. Hold up, excuse that noise. It's someone just pushing the trolleys back.

'Are you OK? What happened? Was it the review paperwork? If it was then I can go through it again and check everything was filled out properly. I hope you didn't submit that draft copy where you said that modern languages could suck it because you were jealous of their school trips budget and you said you knew for a fact that half of them used it as a chance for an orgy and to get absolutely blotto on cheap continental wine.

'Was it anything else at school? Anything to do with a kid? A parent? Exams? I've been racking my brains trying to figure it out and everyone I've asked either doesn't know or they're being very vague. I just don't know what it could be because despite everything, I know you, you're a really good teacher and it's stupid that they would do this so close to exam season. It just makes no sense at all. You know you can chat to me if it's anything like that and I will try to help you. Please tell me and just let me know you are all right. Hold up. Did you try to smoke on school grounds again? Did you say something to Alicia? Did Mr Bush catch you calling him 'fire crotch?' It's either that or the shoe thing or maybe you racked up too many late marks. I keep telling you that the 7.42 a.m. bus is cutting it way too fine especially when there's traffic on the high street.

'Anyway, I'm in a car park because I'm on my way to pick up some stuff for dinner. I'm going to Caitlin's and I've offered to cook for her. I was going to do a green curry but then I thought spicy and if there's the remote possibility that we might have sex then I probably don't want a sensitive digestion being a potential issue. So I may do lamb chops with herby gremolata, maybe fish. I think I cooked that for you once when we first met but then you were vegetarian, so you basically had to eat the gremolata like cereal. Umm... Things are going well with Caitlin. I think. I need to run some things by you with the sex side but that can wait. She's into me doing things with her feet and, well, you know how I am with hygiene. I can't ask her to wash them first, can I? I mean, fungal nail infections are a thing so putting a foot near a moist area like a mouth is not good. Sorry, I said the word moist.

'Caitlin also said some things recently. About you. She's not quite sure about our friendship. I've tried to explain things to her. I thought it'd be good if we went out for dinner together so she could get to know you. That would be good. I really like her. I really want this to work out.

'I'm going to go and buy some lamb now. Mia, if you are listening to this in five months, then forget everything I've just said. I really hope you're OK. Just send me an emoji or something to let me know you're fine and that we're good. I have to go as the people next to me are loading their shopping into their car and they think I'm weird. Bye. It's Ed, by the way. Bye.'

NINETEEN

MIA

'That's the price per glass.'

'Per glass? Are you having a laugh?' I ask, scanning through my purse looking at my last bank note. 'Do you take cards?'

'We do actually,' the lady behind the counter tells me. Of course they do. This isn't some crappy summer school fair in a field with a Mr Whippy and a burnt sausage in a bun. This is Rachel's kids' private school summer bazaar. A bizarre bazaar where I can buy soy candle melts, partake in a Reiki workshop and have just paid eight pounds for a glass of Pimm's.

'There are carbonated beverages if you prefer?' the lady tells me. The lady is wearing an Alice band and for reasons only I know, this means I dislike her instantly. I look over the carbonated beverages. Not a Diet Coke in sight. It's all dandelion and burdock. I don't like this one's look. She thinks I don't belong. I want to say it's because she thinks I'm not posh enough for this event, but it could be because I do carry a Powerpuff Girls wallet. I can sense you judging me, too, but I like the size of it and the number of truly useful zipped compartments.

'I'll take the Pimm's,' I reply. It better not be a cheaper supermarket alternative. 'Don't be stingy with the fruit, that's my five-a-day,' I joke. She doesn't laugh.

'Excellent choice,' she replies in snooty tones, questioning the morals of someone who'd not want to hand over their money willingly for the sake of children's education.

'Oh, there's a £1.50 card fee, too.'

Do not throw anything at this woman. Be good, Mia. I promised my sister I would not embarrass her. Even though I might not have a job now, and that might be the last of my money, I tap my card on the machine. Bankrupted by a summer cocktail.

'Thank you.' *Would you like to leave a tip?* the machine asks me. Yeah, don't trust people wearing Alice bands. That's an excellent tip.

'All OK here?' Rachel joins me at the counter, looking hassled. 'I can't do this... I don't think I can do this...' she blurts out. 'It's just the small talk and the chit-chat and pretending everything is OK when it's not. I should have just thrown a sickie or not come.'

'Do I need to slap you?' I tell her. She stares at me and fake laughs, linking her arm through mine. 'I'm here. It's fine. You're here for your kids. Flo is doing that dance thing on the stage in a bit and you're here to support because at the end of the day, you are her mum and you're a really good mum.'

I've had to feed Rachel these small positive affirmations recently to pep her up, reminders of who she is and how she's not allowed to let her small-dick-energy husband win. It's not a lie either. For all their failings as sisters, my nieces and nephews are proof that my sisters excel as mothers. They threw all their love and being into motherhood. It's very reminiscent of how our own mum did things. I grab at Rachel's hand to steady her. Since I went to Rachel's, I never quite left. I hung around on the pretence that I could keep her company and spend time with my nephew and niece, but in essence, it was because I felt a bit lost. My confused feelings for Ed aside, I feel petrified without my work, directionless. Going home to my house would have made me feel worse, more alone, so I stayed with Rachel for the distraction, and we have essentially mothered each other through these awkward times. And none of these times is more awkward than today where I'm here to be some sort of social bodyguard.

'We can leave as soon as Flo does her thing. Look, run me through the dynamics again because it's a lot of women today with pastel nails, Gucci belts and matching midi dresses.'

Hoping this might distract her, we turn our backs to the bar casually, and look over to the event in full swing.

'What's wrong with a midi dress?' Rachel asks me, as she lifts the floral skirt of her own to the air.

'It's mum uniform.'

'It's comfortable and appropriate,' she says, looking down at my denim cut-offs. I'm not apologising for these. There's a stage, I'm bringing a cool festival vibe that's very much missing here.

'Well, tell me about the ladies with the matching Chanel straw handbags,' I say, subtly trying to point them out. 'I don't care for their body language,' I tell Rachel.

'They're Penny and Jenny.'

'You're shitting me, they actually rhyme?' I exclaim a little too loudly.

'I'm not sure how much I trust Jenny. She lives for the gossip and the passive-aggressive Facebook posts.'

'Oooh, I like me one of them.'

'Penny once drove into a lamp post at school because I suspect she day drinks.'

'These are all excellent factoids, Rachel.'

'Melanie does a lot of charity work with hedgehogs, Nancy has a company selling overpriced sweet cones, Paulina has run six marathons, Vivien does pole dancing.'

'Vivien sounds like friend material,' I say.

Rachel laughs. She still remains clamped to me, arms linked in a way we've not done since we were kids. I can't quite tell if this makes me happy or sad, that it's taken some majorly horrible life event to bring us closer, but there is something that flows heavy through me, some need to defend her and ensure she can undergo no more harm.

'They all knew... I think that's the problem. It feels so hard to rebuild that trust knowing that they all knew,' Rachel says, fiddling with her necklace.

I look over at all these mums gathered in their mini cliques and sense some sadness that Rachel doesn't know how to stride over to them anymore and just chat, ask about the weather and the price of Pimm's.

'How do you know they knew?' I ask.

'One actually told me at the school play. She said no one knew how to say anything.'

'Yikes.'

'So, for six whole months, I was at that school gate chatting to them about homework and school discos when really all they were thinking was, hey, your husband is fucking George T's mum.'

'Why do you call him George T?'

'Because there are three Georges.'

'And George T's mum is not here?'

'Jane? No. Jane is not here... yet,' Rachel says, eyeing the crowd closely. Jane. George T's mum was the woman that Rachel caught in her bed that fateful morning. Rachel had been set to go for a haircut but instead came home as she thought she'd left the iron plugged in. Instead, she found her husband. Plugged into Jane. On their bed.

'So, what do all these women know then?' I ask, putting my hand into some complimentary wasabi peas on the counter.

'Well, it depends who you talk to. They know of the affair

and they know that Gareth and I are divorcing. People put different spins on it. I've heard all sorts of rumours... I heard someone say that we slept in separate bedrooms and that I withheld sex from him.'

'Did you?'

'I did not. We did it at least once a week. I used to have lingerie.'

'Those are decent averages, sis. Well done. Did you let him do you up the–'

'MIA!' Rachel shrieks, and her cheeks flush. 'Yes.'

I choke on a wasabi pea that I suddenly realise are not free but belong to a person next to us. I push the bowl away as Rachel steadies me.

'Drink some Pimm's, you buffoon,' she says to me in amusement, patting my back. As she does so, children start to filter onto the stage and a teacher picks up a microphone as we all recoil from the feedback. Parents wander to picnic blankets and camping chairs and I notice one family have brought a basket of goods that includes smoked salmon and crostini. I wonder if they'd like to adopt me.

'Well, hello everyone, and thank you for supporting the Kingsley House Summer Bazaar today. Have we all petted the llamas? I have, aren't they lovely?'

There are llamas. To ride? For free, I hope.

'So we are going to kick off today's talent show event with a lovely musical piece from Tabitha and Prudence in Renoir Class. Please can we give them a round of applause?'

I process everything that was wrong with that sentence and watch as two girls approach the stage with matching pigtails and the nemeses of musical instruments, the recorder. I am sure I've seen a horror film that started like this. They start playing and I laugh as subtly as I can through my nose at the quality of the sound.

'Don't you dare,' Rachel tells me, gripping my arm tightly in restraint.

'There are birds in a bush over there that are covering their young in fear...'

It's Rachel's turn to snigger and a woman looks over at us. I watch as a grandmother actively turns off her hearing aid. Is that the end? Please let it be the end. One of them has gone a strange raspberry colour from blowing way too hard. Take a breath, kiddo. The end. Out of sheer relief, I clap a little too loudly and wolf whistle, which results in an elbow to my ribs.

'Is it all fucking recorders?' I ask Rachel. This was not signalled to me. I was told there'd be alcohol, cheese and a raffle. In the sunshine. The sound from those pipes could make those llamas go feral.

'Why do you have to say "fucking recorders"?' Rachel mumbles.

'That was not an answer...'

But before she can either confirm or deny, her attention is drawn to a marquee across the way selling patisserie. I've been in that tent. I refused to pay £5 for a Portuguese custard tart when I can buy two whole boxes of them in the supermarket for that price. However, by the tent stand Gareth and a woman, chatting merrily to another couple, having the temerity to laugh but also wear matching blue striped outfits, just in case anyone was mistakenly thinking they weren't a couple. I hand Rachel my overpriced drink.

'Just take a big sip of that...'

She does as she's told but I see her hand shake, her breath stuttering, and a tear roll down her cheek ever so slowly.

'Shit,' I say, taking off my sunglasses and handing them to her. 'Wear these. It'll be OK... Breathe...'

'Are they actually matching?' she asks me.

'Yes. But they look like twats. Don't even look at them. Look at this little boy doing his tap dancing. Look at him, like a little Fred Astaire,' I say, trying to divert her attention.

'He's not. He's kind of awful... This is awful...'

'Oi! Not here. I am here. Focus on me. Focus on that woman over there selling coasters with watercolour birds on them. We can go over and ask her if she does any with tits on them. We can give them to Ali for Christmas...'

Rachel turns away to scoop up tears with the edge of her dress sleeve and my heart breaks for her. This is some sort of public shaming for her and for the many times I've tried to persuade her to be strong and put on a front, I've maybe asked too much of her.

'I don't know what you want me to do? I really want to punch him. Please let me do that?' I ask her.

'You've just slapped your colleague and now you're going to punch another person at another school.'

'I'd do it for you...'

'Permission to do it in a less public place. Wearing a bala-clava so you won't get in trouble.'

'Consider it a deal,' I say, fist-bumping her. 'Where is Jane's husband, by the way?'

'I don't know. We sometimes see him at school things, serious balding man, always in a suit.'

I scan over all the parents. Never mind the tap dancing, I can see what Rachel is really sad about and that's the whispers, the people looking over at them and then at Rachel, seeing if this is affecting her in any way.

'I don't think I can do this, Mia. I'm going to go outside for a bit. Can you take a video of Flo? Please?'

'Do you want me to come with you?' I ask her, mortified to see her so broken.

'To watch me cry in my car? Just give me a moment. Be here for Flo.'

She hands me her drink and slinks away and I stand there, torn about where I need to be. The tap dancing lad is done and bows a handful of times more than is really necessary, and I see Flo in the wings, ready to ballet for the masses. I watch as Gareth leaves Jane's side for a bit and heads to the front of the stage to watch his daughter. As he does, Jenny congregates by her side. I shouldn't do this, should I? But chaos. I like the chaos. And no one knowing who I am today may very well work in my favour.

I sidle up next to Jane and get my phone out as I stand there, filming quietly. I sense her looking me up and down. Florence comes out and scans the crowd and sees me, waving.

'Excuse me, do you know Florence?' Jane asks me.

'Yes. My name is Clementine Le Saucisse. I'm from the Royal Ballet.' I straighten my spine and turn my feet into a first position to cement this claim. 'Florence's dance school sent me.'

'Oh, really? Are you here just to see Florence? My daughter is dancing soon... Cassie?' Jenny asks me.

'Oh, we're not here to see your daughter. Without sounding harsh, arms like spaghetti and a certain lack of grace in her movement...'

'Really?' Jenny asks, looking over at Florence. Ballet is not her thing maybe, but I like how she dances through the facial expressions.

'Yes.'

'Does Florence's father know you're here?' Jane asks me, gesturing towards Gareth stood nearer the stage.

'Her mother knows. Rachel, I believe? Really lovely lady. Is that the father?' I state, faking disbelief.

Jane starts to blush, and that frisson of discomfort just pushes me on, a little further.

'It is,' Jenny states. Jenny loves her gossip. I hope you do some good work for me here, Jenny.

'Oh, it's just I met someone else the other day at their house. I must be confused,' I say.

'Another man?' Jane asks me.

'Oh, yeah... Definitely not that man. He was taller, broader, he looked like he worked out, incredibly charming,' I say, laughing.

'Who was this man?' Jane asks, confused.

'Well, not him,' I say, pointing towards Gareth. 'He definitely didn't have that greying, retired football pundit look about him.' Jenny looks down at the floor trying to hold in her giggles. 'Strange, from the way he was with Rachel I assumed they were married... Plus, that man knew how to wear denim! I saw the outline of things that would have taken your eye out,' I say with a grin.

Both women stand there, mouths open.

'Oh, you must excuse me. This is a children's event. Sometimes I forget where I am.' Florence comes to the end of her dance routine and I wave at her, just in time to see Rachel reappear, clapping and cheering too. I notice I'm still recording.

'There's Rachel. I must go over and say hello. Oh, you match the man in the front,' I tell Jane. 'That's... bold. Lovely to meet you both. Enjoy. There are llamas...' I turn to hide the glee on my face and stride over to find my sister. She sees me coming and even with the sunnies on, I can sense the distress in her face.

'Were you just talking to Jane?' she hisses when I reach her.

'Yes.'

'Mia, what did you say?'

'It's all good. I may have to leave though. Finish up here, I'll wait in the pub down the road.'

'What the hell did you do?' she asks me.

'Chaos,' I say, calmly. But Rachel is no longer looking at me. She's looking at a man stood by a llama enclosure. Balding. Very serious man. In a suit. Unlocking a gate. Now that is chaos.

'Rachel, is that possibly Jane's...?'

She nods. 'I'll get the kids. We can leave together.'

ED

'Mum?'

'Yes?' she replies, sitting back in her faded yellow striped garden chair, closing her eyes to feel the sunshine on her face.

'You cut the crusts off my sandwiches,' I notice, laughing, looking down at the lunch she's prepared on her rusting garden table. She doesn't open her eyes but puts her sandalled feet up on a chair. I also like how she's gone to the trouble of getting my favourite bacon crisps, poured me a giant pint glass of Fanta and got in some little mini cheeses and Kit Kats, all served on a novelty plate, with a spaceship on. The same set-up she used to get out when I'd have my mates round to play Mario Kart.

'That's how you like it.'

'When I was eight. I am twenty-eight now. I eat my crusts now.'

'Force of habit, shoot me,' she says, looking completely unbothered. 'Isn't it lovely when the sun actually makes an appearance in this country? Close your eyes, Ed... Take it all in...'

I pretend to play along, half of my sandwich in my mouth, but I know what she means. London's two-week summer is here, you must absorb it all while the moment lasts. I open one eye and watch her bask, hair bundled atop her head in a loose bandana. She reaches out for her glass of lemonade and takes a long sip. It always feels like my mum has never changed, just like her home. You see it in the velveteen sofa in the front room with its worn cushions, a yellow ukulele that hangs on the wall, Mum's pine dining table that also acts as a craft station/mail room and her overgrown garden, filled with stone statues of woodland creatures in interesting poses and a boggy pond to the rear. I first got drunk in this garden. I was with two A-Level friends and the drinking was purely out of curiosity, thinking we needed to get that much done before we went off to university. We threw up in the pond. My mum lost frogs. I never confessed it may have been my doing.

'I like having you here, in my garden. It reminds me of when you were little and you had your sandpit,' she tells me, her face still turned to the sun.

'Which I can't believe you still have,' I remark, looking at the faded blue plastic shell-shaped structure propped up against the fence.

'It's a part of your childhood,' she tells me. 'Like that teddy you slept with until you were in your teens. I've kept him, too. What was his name again?'

'Beary White,' I remind her.

She laughs. That was a good name though, for a bear. I stuff the last crustless quarter of sandwich in my mouth and stand up, rolling up my sleeves.

'Well, when you're done taking in your vitamin D, give me a hand with this trellis,' I say, reaching for a hammer. She stretches and I put out a hand to pull her out of her chair. I'd like to say I'm here in my childhood garden to just eat retro snacks and take in the sun, but the reality is, in a few weeks' time, exams will have finished and the final year kids will be attending their prom for which I've volunteered to make frames for their group photos. Given Mum is keen on making a placard, I knew she would have the tools, paints and garden space for me to get this done.

'I'm glad you asked me to help you with this. We haven't done anything like this for a while,' she tells me, putting an arm around me.

'You come round to mine. I make you lunch. I come on your protests sometimes.'

'Not because you believe in the cause. You worry I'm going to get myself arrested. This is nice, it feels collaborative. Like when we used to build forts together,' she remembers animatedly.

'Mum, I need to remind you again that I'm twenty-eight...'

'They were good forts.'

'You had skills with gaffer tape,' I tell her. That she did, she was that sort of mother. A life held together with gaffer tape and love. She lifts the trellis up and I start hammering the small tacks into the edges. I notice a terracotta plant pot by the fence and realise that there are stubs of what look like old spliffs sitting there. I say nothing.

'So how are things with you anyway?' she asks me. 'How's the love life?'

She always asks me this, though in recent years she's started to say it in resigned tones like nothing may ever happen in that respect. Maybe today is the day to surprise her.

'So something has happened there. Developments, shall we say...'

'Developments?' Mum asks me, alarmed by my seriousness.

'No. I'm dating someone.'

Mum stops for a moment, downs tools and yes, that's a tear in her eye. I knew the reaction would be over the top but didn't expect crying.

'Please tell me that's allergies. Why are you crying?' I ask, bemused.

'I am allowed to be happy. I've waited for this day for a long time. I'm thrilled.' She comes over and swings her arms around my neck and kisses my forehead. I'm conscious that the splodges of paint will smudge all over my shirt. 'You should be more thrilled, though. It feels like you've just told me bad news. I'm not reading your brow here.'

'It's just very new and I want it to go well.'

'You're procrastinating then...'

'Maybe...'

'Is it too soon for a lunch?' she asks me.

'We're having lunch now.' If you can call it that.

'No. Can I have lunch with her? I'd love to have lunch with her.'

'Then no.'

'I'm not embarrassing though. I'm a bit loud and tactile but I'd be nice to her. She's already met me.'

'No, she hasn't,' I say, confused.

'She has. When she came to your flat and I had lunch and was just leaving...'

'I'm not dating Mia!' I shriek.

Mum looks into the air for a moment trying to figure everything out. 'Then who are you dating?'

'Her name is Caitlin. She's a Maths teacher at my school.'

'Caitlin? But you always talk about Mia,' she tells me.

'What?'

'You do. It's always an anecdote about Mia. Oh, she did the funniest thing the other day... She helped me do this... She's vegetarian, you know...' she says, mimicking a voice that I think might be mine.

'I do not,' I reply indignantly.

'Eddie, I know more about Mia than I do most people. I figured it was just a matter of time before you worked out you might like her.'

I pick up a nail and bang it into the wood with perhaps a little too much gusto. Maybe it's at the mention of that name because the problem is I haven't heard or seen from Mia in almost a week. This happens. Usually over the summer when she goes off to a Spanish island to kill her liver and dance on beaches in the middle of the night, but never during the school term when something as important as a suspension has happened. She hasn't returned my messages, emails or voice notes. I am also at a tricky impasse where I know Caitlin isn't keen on her so I'm doing all my messaging in secret, which doesn't sit well with me.

'Something I said?' Mum asks, as I continue to hammer nails into the wood.

'I'm not dating Mia. If anything, Mia seems to be avoiding me at the moment.'

'Why? Is it because you're dating Caitlin?' she asks, sensing the hurt in my voice.

'No. Well, I don't think so. She also got suspended from school and she's been laying low since.'

Mum pulls a face. 'Suspended?'

'Yeah. Caitlin heard it was because of some GDPR issue where she gave someone's address out to a parent. Just a simple mistake. I've tried to get in touch to see how she is. Went round to hers but she wasn't in. Or not answering the door. It's just frustrating,' I remark, because it is hugely frustrating to worry about her when she doesn't even want to acknowledge me.

'Or maybe she doesn't like the Caitlin thing and she's ignoring you,' Mum comments.

I think for a second at how she turned up at my flat that night, drunk, warning me off her. Is there something here that I'm missing?

'She's just Mia. I guess she needs some time alone to understand her mistake. I bloody hope she hasn't used it as a chance to go on holiday. I just thought she'd...'

'Need you...?' she tells me, putting a hand to mine, reminding me not to take my feelings out on the trellis.

Mum has a point. I've never quite understood my friendship with Mia but for all our differences, I always thought that in a difficult moment like this, she would know that I am here for her. She can come to me, and I will listen and help or bake her something vegetarian with lots of cheese. I hold her in that much esteem, I'd even use feta. In return, even though it's only been a week, I'll admit to missing her. I want to chat to her about Caitlin, I want to tell her that I managed to get one of my Year 8 classes to actually shut up and do some work the other day, I still look out for her clambering on the bus, chatting to the bus driver while she digs around for her Oyster card that I've always told her she should keep in the same pocket in her bag.

Mum watches me thinking these things through quietly, helping me stand the trellis upright on her lawn. 'So, tell me about this Caitlin then?' she asks, sipping noisily on her glass of lemonade, out of the same chipped glassware she's had since I lived in this house.

'She's about five foot seven, blonde, slim.'

'Am I a policewoman asking for a witness statement? I'll need more than that.'

I smile. 'She teaches Maths, we're into the same things – noodles, books, houseplants...'

'Is she funny?'

'Is that important?'

'Well, life is a strange old beast. It's nice to have someone to share some lightness with.'

'She reads Atwood.'

'Known for her laugh-out-loud humour...'

I pull a face at her. 'She's just nice. I really like her. It feels like a grown-up relationship, something that could really go somewhere...'

Mum smiles at this at least, to hear me in a happy place, with someone who has potential.

'Well, happiness is good. When the time is right then I really look forward to meeting her,' she says, patting me on the head again. 'Are we painting this then?' Mum asks, looking at me curiously.

'Yeah. I was thinking white. And don't laugh but Mia put me in touch with some ladies at her community centre who'll do some flowers for it.'

'I'm not laughing. This will look lovely. I have some fairy lights you can use too. I hope these kids understand how much effort you're putting into this. I don't remember you having a prom?' Mum asks.

'Oh, it's an American tradition we seem to have inherited. I had an end-of-year dance in the school gym where I spent most of my time sat on a bench drinking Coke.'

I don't really remember the event well as one that marked the end of my education. The popular kids who understood the music just spent their time dancing whilst the rest of us lined the perimeter of the room wishing for the time to pass quicker, less hopeful about pulling, more petrified.

'I remember that! You wore the same suit you wore to your grandad's funeral.'

'I was a style icon even back then.'

'Did you smooch anyone to the slow dance at the end?'

'Smooch?'

'You know what I mean!' she jests.

'There was a girl called Monica who was in my Higher Maths class and she attached herself to my face.' I'm not even joking, there was a moment where the suction and the spit made me think we'd managed to surgically graft ourselves together.

'Delightful,' she says, laughing under her breath. She uses an old butter knife to open a tin of paint and runs her fingers across the bristles of one of her paintbrushes. 'You know, you never spoke to me about all of that – girls etc. And I am sorry there wasn't a man about either to chat to you about relationships when you were growing up. I always thought I failed you in that respect.'

I shift Mum a strange look, shaking my head. 'Failed? Never. I just kept a lot of that to myself.'

'Maybe if you'd had a dad, you could have shared it with him?'

'Or not. I had you. It was enough,' I tell her plainly because it is true.

I look over and Mum wipes more tears from her cheek. I'd hug her if I wasn't holding a hammer, but I think it's true. Nothing she ever did or didn't do got me to where I am now. She did everything right. I think I was just slow off the blocks, smiling to think about something someone once told me.

'Well, what about you? You spoke of your Mo friend the other week at lunch. Is that still going?' I ask.

'Mo only washes every other week to save water. So, no.'

I laugh.

'I'm fine as I am, Eddie. I've never gone without love. I've only ever wished that for you. I'm glad you've found Caitlin. I'm sorry I made those assumptions about Mia. I hope you work that out. I liked her, she was...'

'Scatty, mad as a hatter, loud, verging on ridiculous...?'

'I thought she was good for you, Eddie. That was all.'

TWENTY

MIA

'MISS! WHY ARE YOU HIDING BEHIND THAT TREE?'

I stand perfectly still behind that tree in my sunnies and raincoat, like a statue, hoping that wasn't directed at me. Bloody hell, way to make me sound like a complete perv.

'MISS JOHNSON!'

They've used my name now, so I have to appear, don't I? I look around hoping there are no members of staff about this place. I am not entirely sure about the terms and conditions of my suspension, but I haven't been back at school since I was told to leave and I am still waiting for the outcome pending Alicia's investigations. However, I awoke today knowing I had to at least show my face out of support to catch my Year 11 kids as they come out of the gym, fresh from their English Literature exam.

'Yes, it is I,' I say, waving my arm and taking off my sunglasses sheepishly. The kids all crowd around, some of the girls hugging me and I watch them all as they hold their see-through pencil cases under their arms, relief etched onto their faces to have finished another of these wretched exams.

'Why are you here?' they all ask me.

'Just to check in. How are you guys doing? How did it go? Did Miss Callaghan send you all my messages?'

'Yeah, we got them... And the revision booklets,' says Bianca Titi (fake tan addict; gets her homework off Wikipedia).

'I'm so sorry – look, I bought you all sweets too,' I say, opening up my tote bag and letting them have a rummage. 'What came up with *Macbeth*? Was it the witches?'

'Yeah.'

I do a strange high-five to myself move that makes the kids laugh. 'What did I tell you? These things go in circles. They haven't done the witches in ages. Did you get your quotes in? Did you all use the word prophesy?'

'Yeah, we did,' Haydn Pinto (buzz cut; surprisingly good speller) says. 'And we spoke about the weather and pathetic jealousy–'

'It's pathetic fallacy, you muppet,' Bianca interjects.

He'll have lost a few marks for that but I'm not sure I care. They made it through and no one is crying or appears pissed off or looks like they may hate me so we're all good. Let's hope for some passes so they can get through the next stages of their lives. I always try to play it cool throughout the year, but the fact is I do care about these kids and what they end up doing. Half of them won't end up studying this subject of mine but at least some of them will keep reading and know how to write a banging formal letter of complaint to someone when they get older.

'And English Language in a few days. Are we set? Does anyone have any questions?' I ask.

'I have a question,' Jerome Dixon (hard-man act; doesn't mind Shakespeare) pipes up. 'Is it true what they said about why you're not teaching at the minute? What's the tea?'

I pause. 'Yes, I had to have emergency surgery. It was my appendix. It was very painful.'

They all stand there staring at me.

'We heard you lamped Miss Bell from Maths,' Jerome continues.

I stand there attempting to still look like the figure of authority that I'm meant to be and figures of authority don't hit other human beings. I shouldn't have lied as I still own an appendix and I don't know how to blag that anymore.

'We had an altercation,' I explain.

'Well, good,' Jerome tells everyone in his thick London tones. 'Because she's a cow.'

'Jerome. Enough of that. Whatever happened, I was in the wrong and the school thought it good that I have a break for a bit.' That said, I like you a bit more though, Jerome.

'But we miss you, Miss,' I hear someone say and the murmurs of agreement make my heart swell for a moment. I think they might miss my constant supply of sweets, but I don't say that out loud. I always have a bag of something in my desk, a trick taught to me by the brilliant Miss Beth Callaghan.

'Well, strangely, I miss you all too. Are you OK? All your other exams are going well?' I ask them. They see the concern in my face and note its sincerity.

'Biology tomorrow. Mr Rogers says he's going to make us all breakfast beforehand. Actual bacon.' I pause for a moment to hear Ed's name, smiling to know he'd do that. He'll use nice butter on the bread, too, because he's scared of the chemical make-up of margarine.

'Well, don't forget me and my Haribo. I hid behind a tree too,' I joke for the laughs. 'I am glad Mr Rogers is looking after you. Keep going, you're all amazing...'

'Thanks, Miss. At least you care enough to be here,' Jerome Dixon adds.

'We all care, Jerome,' I tell him.

'That witch Miss Bell don't,' he says, his eyebrows furrowed.

'You really don't like her, eh? Did she give you a detention or something?' I enquire curiously. All of them are strangely silent with me as I say that out loud.

'Sometimes you just know when a teacher comes in and all they're thinking about is how much they don't want to be there,' Olivia Seaman pipes in. My ears start to prick up as Olivia says that because Jerome has a mouth on him. I once confiscated icing sugar off him that he was trying to pass off as cocaine. Olivia listens though, she keeps a neat pencil case and some-times seems scared of her own shadow. For her to even speak up now is unlike her.

'What do you mean? You're all OK for Maths though, right? For your exams?' I ask, worried for them. Maths is a core subject, they all need to pass that.

'We've literally had to teach ourselves. She's just different to you,' Olivia adds, smiling.

'I've heard sus things about her, too,' adds Jerome. 'I know someone from her last school and apparently she was sleeping with the deputy head. He was married with three kids, and it all went to shit. His wife came into a school assembly and there were absolute scenes, I tell you. She was in her dressing gown. You can see the videos on TikTok. That was why they moved her on,' he announces to the small crowd of teens around us.

As it's Jerome, there may be some elements of exaggeration in this tale, but the story still raises my hackles, especially as I know she's also been with bloody Tommy from P.E.

'Jerome,' I say, trying to calm down his hearsay.

'It's true, Miss. And apparently, she conned him out of a load of money, too. He had to re-mortgage his house.'

'I've seen that video,' Olivia tells us. 'That was Miss Bell? Really?'

A selection of the kids gather round, like bees around the

gossip pot, nodding and adding their input. *She's a right moody one, she once gave me a detention for breathing.* No one seems to be a fan of Miss Bell, which secretly makes me very happy but does make me worry slightly for the one person I know who likes her very much. There's a panic that sits in my bones to think that if any of this is true then she will definitely take advantage of Ed. She already is taking advantage of Ed. And I feel pangs of guilt that despite everything, I've not handled this well at all. I should tell Ed. I can't have her stamp all over Ed's good heart for a minute longer.

'Prove it.' I shouldn't have said that. That was not a professional move, but I guess neither is waiting by a tree in my sunnies, stuffing kids full of sugar.

'We've just been in an exam, Miss. We don't have our phones.'

I dig around in my tote for my phone and open up TikTok, hoping they don't see that my algorithms mainly bring up videos of people making their cats dance and make-up tutorials. I let Olivia put words into the search bar and lo and behold, a video comes up of a lady in a dressing gown giving someone on stage merry hell. On the one hand, I wish there was such drama at our school assemblies, but I can tell from the blazers that it's definitely St Quentin's on the other side of town.

'See, that woman sat there, that's Miss Bell,' Jerome tells me.

'That could be anyone, someone needs a better camera on their iPhone,' I say, squinting.

'She's wearing an Alice band,' Olivia tells me.

'Lots of people are wearing those these days,' I lie, still squinting. If she is being shamed in front of the whole school, then she's unfeasibly calm about it all. Maybe she's a sociopath. Maybe my poor Ed is with a sociopath. I think about the money element. Ed has savings and a nice flat. If she takes that then all he will have left is Nigel and his *Star Wars* memorabilia.

'So did you really lamp her?' Jerome asks, his eyes lit up at the thought, mimicking a boxer's right hook.

'Altercation, Jerome...'

'That means you hit her, you are the GOAT, Miss,' he says, grabbing my hand and trying to get me to engage in some sort of gangsta handshake.

I don't deny it this time. I feel someone pat me on the back to congratulate me.

'Is it true she's also shagging Mr Wood from P.E.?' a voice interjects.

As soon as I hear this, my heart fractures a little. I'm not the only person who knows. I doubt Beth would have spread it around the staffroom like tattle, but I can only think Caitlin's not been subtle with how she's flaunted herself around this school. If the kids know then Ed will find out soon enough in the most hurtful of ways. At least it won't be via TikTok though, as he has no idea what that is.

'I wouldn't know. Look, you lot do me a favour and get home, get on your Biology revision and do Mr Rogers proud tomorrow. If you have questions for next week's exams, then tell Miss Callaghan and she'll drop me an email. Yeah?'

'Sure. Are you all right, Miss?' Olivia asks me, noticing my expression has changed.

'Yeah.'

I've done this all wrong, but I can't tell these kids, can I? I should have told Ed from the moment I found out, but I failed him. I should have put any of my own feelings aside and at least been a good friend. I should tell him now.

ED

If there's one thing about me, it's that I take on other people's stress and this happens the most during exam period. I can put on half a stone because I worry about those kids. I worry about their revision notes, whether they will study the right topics, whether they've had breakfast or enough sleep. Tomorrow, I'll stand outside that exam room with pens, in a phenomenon known as pen panic, where I bulk buy black biros and just give them out like sweets. Take extras, kids. You may have forgotten to cram the parts of a respiratory system but at least you will have ink.

'Hey,' I say, as my neighbour opens his front door.

'Hi. You're the man from the flat upstairs. Sorry, I've forgotten your name. I forget my own most days.'

'Ed. You are Nick and Mia,' I say, pointing at the baby who at least finds my face mildly amusing. 'So, I went a bit mental with my baking and I just wanted to drop this round. They're apple and cinnamon crumble muffins, no nuts.' I hand over the cardboard box in my hands where I've carefully listed out the ingredients. He looks at me strangely. Neighbours don't do this anymore, do they? The only thing we should be sharing is each other's Wi-Fi and knowledge of bin days. I hope he doesn't think I'm weird. 'I just... I can hear Mia has been up a lot and I saw your wife the other day by the mailboxes and it looked like she was asleep standing up, so I thought...'

I'm not hugely prepared for this man's reaction as he stands there and starts crying. Baby Mia looks up at him.

'I'm sorry,' he says, wiping his eyes on his sleeve. 'I'm so tired and this is really fucking nice. Is this your job? Do you own a bakery?'

'No, I teach, but it's GCSE exam day tomorrow so I made the kids breakfast. And this year, I went overboard.'

I think about why that happened. I usually bake extras for Mia who has five muffins on the bus before we've even got through the school gates. Maybe mini Mia can enjoy them instead. I know nothing about babies, but I am sure she will enjoy the cake.

'Well, I am happy to have reaped the benefits. This is pretty awesome of you. Thank you,' he says, wiping tears from his face. 'I can't believe I cried in front of you.'

Well, I dropped a butt plug on your balcony so maybe we're even.

'Look, if you ever need a hand with anything then let me know. I haven't been around a lot of babies, but I can bake, pick up milk. I always have coffee...' I tell him, gulping loudly. I'm not quite sure why but maybe because a move like this is very unlike me. It's me being vaguely sociable. Again, I hope he doesn't think I'm weird – I'm just not used to this.

'That's kind, mate. Thank you,' he says, noticing the other boxes in a shopping bag. 'You delivering to the whole building?'

'Oh, I'm like the muffin man tonight. One box for my girl-friend and the other for...' I look at baby Mia and smile. 'A friend...'

'Lucky them. Thanks again, Ed. Say thank you, Mia,' he says, taking her hand and waving it for her. I wave back, turning to the stairs and making my way down to the lobby.

Tonight, I will be the Just Eats Muffin Man, driving around and delivering baked goods so that Nigel and I didn't eat all the extras through sheer stress eating. This will also take my mind off exams tomorrow, hoping that all the kids have remembered to go through genetics. They always forget genes.

As I get in my car, I think about what I just told Nick too. I'm going to see my girlfriend. That phrase doesn't sound awful. I have a girlfriend. The muffins will be a surprise today as she went home after school with bad period cramps and said she just wanted to get into her bed. Even that felt like a turning point in our short relationship; it felt like something she divulged to me that was personal, that allowed her to be vulnerable in front of me. Periods. I don't have them obviously, but I had a mother who had them. Maybe I should buy her some painkillers, too. Or a hot water bottle. She will have one of those. The muffins will be enough. I hope.

I also hope they will be enough for Mia, too. I heard rumours she popped into school today to see her GCSE kids and was looking for me. We must have missed each other but it's a start, right? She was looking for me so maybe she's not angry with me. Maybe she was just giving Caitlin and I a moment to settle into our relationship. I will heal any rift with muffins. She loves these muffins. I'll head to hers and hope she's there.

I have so much to tell her. I think this Caitlin thing is working. She's stayed at mine a few times, we've been to the cinema together, I've bought her a spider plant, she's talked about doing something together over the summer. Maybe a short holiday to the Greek Islands? I will have to buy shorts. Mia will have to help me choose them because she makes fun of my shorts. We have sex. I think the sex is going OK but still, there are things to run through. Like where does one put one's hands when receiving oral sex? Mia told me not on her head. On my hips does not feel right, neither does behind my head. Not that I'll practise these things with Mia, we can't do that now, but I have cake, so hopefully she will give me tips at least.

The radio on my car suddenly cuts out and a phone call comes through. As soon as the name pops up on my car display, I smile broadly with relief, almost desperation to talk to her and hear her voice. I answer the call and try to keep my cool. 'You're not dead then.'

'I am. This is me speaking to you from the great beyond.'

'I told you my phone reception is better than yours.' There's a silence, during which I hope she's contemplating her contract with Virgin mobile. 'Are you OK, Mia? I was worried.'

There's a pause. 'I'm fine. I'm sorry I never replied to your messages.'

'Suspended?'

'It's a long story...'

'I have time. I heard you were at school today?'

'I was chatting to my kids post exam. I looked for you but...'

'I left early.'

'And you're not at your place now?'

'No, I'm just delivering muffins to Caitlin. She's not feeling too well tonight.'

There's another pause, one that I don't want to question.

'Well, that explains why I'm sat outside your flat and no one's answering the door.'

I grin. It makes me happy that she's come to visit, to kick off her shoes at my front door and eat all my food, like the universe is as it should be. I glance at the clock in my car.

'I can be there in twenty minutes? Can you stay put? I made you muffins too. I was going to find you and drop them to you tonight.'

'Are they the apple ones with the crunchy streusel topping?'

'Obviously.'

'Then I will go around the corner to buy some wine and meet you back at yours.'

'Excellent stuff. Mia,' I say, turning into Caitlin's road. 'Is it bad to say that I've missed your face?'

As soon as the words come out of my mouth, I realise it's a show of emotion that she will rib me for and that's not what we do. Maybe the problem with Mia and I is that I never tell her enough how much her friendship means to me and how important she is in my life. Maybe I need to say it aloud more. If not out loud, maybe write it down on a postcard or have it written on a mug she can use around the staffroom.

'I've missed you too,' she replies. 'You plank...' And there's the ribbing. 'I'll see you in a bit.'

She hangs up just as I pull into Caitlin's road, and for some reason, I feel relief. Relief that I still have a Mia and that I've not scared her away. I'll have to smooth this over with Caitlin who I know isn't fond of her but in time, they might learn to like each other. We'll all be teaching together still so it makes sense.

I find a parking space and grab one of the boxes from my passenger seat.

Buy white. That pairs well with baked goods, I text Mia.

Posh wanker, she replies back.

I laugh and ring the doorbell of Caitlin's flat, looking down at my phone.

'Food's here!' I hear a voice say from behind the door. But I stand there for a moment trying to register who that voice belongs to. That was a male voice.

'Grab the door, babe...'

I don't know what to do. I feel the urge to run, to hurdle over this privet hedge next to me, to escape. The door opens. Tommy? From P.E.? The P.E. teacher? He doesn't have a shirt on. His eyes widen as he sees me and we stand there staring at each other for a moment.

'Steady Eddie, what are you doing here?' he asks me.

'I made muffins,' I reply blankly.

And then from the kitchen, Caitlin appears, in a dressing gown, her bra visible, clutching a half-filled wine glass. 'Bring it upstairs, we can eat it in bed!' she shouts but then she looks up and sees me. Like I say, I've never had a period myself but she's looking surprisingly well for someone headed to bed with excruciating cramps. Seeing topless Tommy was enough but this just cements the horror.

'Ed? What are you doing here?'

'I made muffins...' I say, wishing I had better words at this precise moment. I think Tommy laughs under his breath. There's no way I'm handing them over now though. I stand there weighed down by shame, by embarrassment that I thought this was anything more than it was. I want to say it's like my heart breaking, but it feels far more mortifying than that. It feels like any shred of hope I had in my heart being plucked out like feathers. I was going to buy new shorts for you. I might cry but God, that would be the worst thing I could do in front of

Tommy and his abs, so I turn, my hands having crushed the cardboard box in my hands.

'Ed!' I hear Caitlin call after me.

I keep walking, bumping into an Uber Eats driver as I go. I am not a horrible person, but I hope they both eat that takeaway and it gives them severe gastric distress.

'It's not what you think,' I hear her voice echoing through the early evening air. I then walk past her bin to see the lid half open, a dead, shrivelled spider plant poking out the gap.

No, Caitlin. It's even worse.

TWENTY-ONE

MIA

'I don't quite know how to tell you this, but it turns out Caitlin is some two-bit ho bitch and you are better off without her. I'm not even joking. Get out now, while you can. I can help you find someone else. We can jump on Tinder and find you a nice girl who's into cats and plants. Or hey, crazy idea but what about li'l ol' me? We could give us a go. I know it seems like a wild idea because you're chalk and I'm cheese. Not even a mature cheddar, like some crazy continental cheese that you need to store in a separate box in the fridge, but I care about you, Ed. The last month has told me that above all things, I care about you, and I am curious to see where that goes. What do you think?'

I think you're talking to yourself in your car, Mia, and a moment ago, there was a man putting the rubbish out with a very cute baby who saw you and may call the police.

Even though Ed told me to get some white wine, I still got something with a screw top, and it turns out that was a genius move as I can now undo that lid and take a swig for Dutch courage. You can do this, Mia. You can't be weak now and back out of telling Ed because you're scared of hurting him. Being with Caitlin for the long-term is what will hurt him more.

After I chatted with my GCSE kids, I went back and studied that TikTok clip in more detail. I looked at different versions of it, I scrolled through the comments. Was it her? Has she just left a trail of destruction in her wake? I wasn't allowed to say it before, but I am glad I marked that girl's card. I should have slapped her harder. Maybe that should be the priority. I need to get him away from her and then let the dust settle and tell Ed about my hugely confusing feelings for him further down the line, so the two things don't get mixed up. That would work better, I feel.

A car pulls up into his block of flats. Shit, is this him? No, it's an old lady in a taxi. I take another swig of wine and get out of the car. I'll go and wait by his flat, sit outside his door like the stray cat that I am.

'Mia?'

I turn as soon as I hear his voice, my heart fluttering a little to see him. He's looking dishevelled, which is unusual for him and it's suddenly wildly attractive to me. I really do like him, don't I? I can't quite read his expression though. Also, if those muffins are for me then they're very squished.

'Hello, stranger.'

His expression reads blank, sad. 'You've already opened that wine, haven't you?'

'I got thirsty.'

He grabs the bottle off me, unscrews the lid and then takes a huge swig. Ed is drinking in public; this is major and that is more than a swig. He chokes a little, removes the bottle from his mouth and then stares into space. Knowing Ed, this may mean he's already drunk.

'Caitlin is sleeping with Tommy from school.'

As soon as the words leave his mouth, a weight feels like it's lifted from my shoulders, but I realise I need to act shocked, like I didn't know this already.

'What the actual...?' I say, opening my mouth. I should have taught Drama. 'How did you find out?'

Please don't be via the kids, via TikTok.

He passes me the bottle and shrouds his face with his hand. 'I went round there with muffins because she told me she had period cramps and Tommy was there without a shirt, she was in a dressing gown. They were going to eat a takeaway in bed.'

'Oh, Ed...' I say, my eyes glassing over to hear his disappointment, to see the devastation in his face of having found them out like that. This is awful. 'I'm sorry.' I wrap my arms around him, and I feel his body shudder. Please don't cry, Ed. Please don't be sad. 'Let's get you in and we can finish off this wine. I've got you,' I tell him, using the sleeve of my coat to wipe his face.

He nods, walking towards his building. 'This is a bit embarrassing. You never saw this...'

'Did you cry in front of them, when you saw them?'

'No. I also didn't let them have any muffins,' he says.

'Strong response,' I say.

'I should have punched him, right?' he asks me.

'No, that's what I would have done. You're not me.'

We climb the stairs, and he opens the door to his flat, the sadness in his eyes unbearable to see. He walks in, kicking off his shoes like a tired child and I watch carefully. That's usually my move. I follow him quietly. When I get to the kitchen, I pause at the sight that greets me. Boxes of muffins lined up on the table, stacks of bread rolls, bottles of smoothies and juice. I walk over to the table where he's written tags for the bottles.

Aerobic respiration = glucose + oxygen -> carbon dioxide + energy + water

Good luck, from Mr Rogers

All of them have different equations, all handwritten with

bubble writing. This beats me by a tree with a handbag of Haribo all day long.

'Ed, you did all this?'

He shrugs, standing there silently.

'Are you OK?'

He shakes his head.

'Oh, Ed...' I go over to him and embrace him again.

'I should have listened to you. You said I was diving in too fast. Maybe I scared her off. Maybe this was something I did,' he says, his head on my shoulder.

My body freezes for a moment to hear him turn this on himself. 'No, I won't hear you say that.'

'He's better looking than me, he's more experienced,' he moans.

I push him away. 'But he's also a dick. You know he's a dick. You've seen what he's like. There is really no comparison here.'

'Maybe it was a sex thing.'

'Then what you're saying is I'm a shit teacher and I find that very insulting.'

That didn't raise the smile that I hoped it would and I feel overwhelmed by a mixture of panic and sadness. I grab his face with both hands and make him look at me.

'You did nothing wrong except be you. You were kind to her, so kind, so for her to do this says more about her.'

He forces a smile and takes another swig of wine. I need to tell him, don't I? This is all her. She possibly did this at her last school too. This is his first proper semblance of a relationship and I can't let this harm him.

'Maybe it is just me. A virgin at twenty-eight... there's a reason I've been single for so long. I'm just not an attractive prospect. You tried your best, Mia, but maybe I'm just completely destined to be alone forever.'

'You have me...' I say, my throat closing as I admit that much.

He puts his hands to his face and I peel them back. He looks down. I could just tell him everything. Now. But let's not forget, I am also me and have no clue what to say. Or do. So I put a finger under his chin so he's looking at me. I kiss him. As my lips meet his, he at first doesn't react. I want to say something, anything, everything but instead I let the pheromones take over and then he kisses me back. And it's an Ed I've been hoping would make an appearance. It's spontaneous Ed, not asking me where he'd like to put his hands, but lifting me up on to one of his breakfast bar stools and letting me wrap my legs around him. His kissing gets more urgent, and he moves down to my neck as I arch my head back, my body curling into his. His hand moves up my skirt and I feel his fingers stroke the inside of my thighs.

'I'm sorry... I'm so sorry...' he whispers. 'Is this too much?'

I shake my head. Hello, are you Ed? Ed, who didn't know how to do this a month ago. He pushes my knickers aside and slips his fingers inside me and I gasp loudly.

'I don't know what I'm doing...' he says, his voice breathy and nervous.

'On the contrary,' I say, staring into his eyes.

'I don't want to have sex with you like this,' he admits.

As soon as the words leave his mouth, I stop for a moment and he moves his hand away. 'Like what?' I ask, confused by what he means.

'Like some sort of revenge for Caitlin. Out of anger. That doesn't feel right. It's not fair on you.'

He backs away. I'm not quite sure how to tell him that those two minutes of hot fondling were actually OK with me. We can keep doing that if it helps with the heartbreak.

'And I don't need you having sex with me because you feel sorry for me,' he admits, grabbing the wine and taking a long swig again.

'I never did it because I felt sorry for you...'

'Well, that's what you were doing now. Trying to convince me that I'm not some bloody sad loser...'

'You're not a loser.'

A tear rolls down his cheek.

'I gave her money.'

I close my eyes for a moment. 'How much?'

'About a grand. I'm never seeing that again, am I? God, I'm an idiot.'

He stands there, the pain visible through his whole body. I don't want him to think about any of that hurt or run through all those realisations of how his brief dalliance with Caitlin came to this. Seriously, just shag me. I don't care. Because I don't want him to think about all the food he cooked for her, the DIY service he provided and now the money he gave her. To have been taken for a mug like that will make him feel about an inch tall. I want to take that hurt away. I want him to shag me because I do care, I do care about him.

'I should have said something sooner,' I whisper out of the corner of my mouth.

It's Ed's turn to stand still for a moment. Shit. I said that out loud, didn't I? 'What did you just say?' I try to run through how I can spin the words that came out of my mouth, but I can't lie anymore. 'Sooner... What should you have said?'

'That night I came round. I knew then that she was bad news...' My voice trails off.

'Mia, that was nearly two weeks ago,' he mumbles.

'That Saturday night when I came round drunk, I'd seen her out with Tommy and I was trying to tell you and then she was here and I didn't know what to do so I confronted her at school and...'

'But... But... You didn't think to tell me after that? You ignored all my messages. You knew for all that time and didn't think to...'

'I was going to tell you today. I found out other stuff. She did this at her last school, she also conned people out of money,' I blurt out, panicked, trying to cover my tracks.

'But you didn't tell me before. You are my best friend, Mia. I thought... You let me find out like that? Tonight? That was a better option?'

My bottom lip starts to wobble and the air sticks in my throat. I am his best friend. 'Ed, I am so sorry. I messed up. I just didn't want to see you hurt.'

'Just shamed and embarrassed instead,' he says, anger in his voice, and a pained expression like I've totally betrayed him. I reach out to touch him, but he shakes me off, taking another swig of wine.

'I am not the bad guy here. You're angry but don't take this out on me,' I warn him. But the problem is, I am here. In this room. Not Caitlin, not Tommy, the emotions are swirling around, and I am in the firing line.

'But you're Mia...'

'What does that even mean?'

'I trusted you with all of this. From the start. I let you into this secret that I hung on to for so long. So to get this far and for you to let me down like this... It's almost worse than what Caitlin has done.'

I stand there for a moment to let that sink in, to let the barb of his words penetrate before I start to cry, properly. Because for all the things I adore about this man, I never knew he could be cruel like this. Not to me, at least. 'I've let you down? Me? I have to go,' I say, grabbing my things.

'Good,' he mumbles through gritted teeth.

'You can seriously fuck off,' I tell him, seething.

'No, you can!' he yells. 'I'm glad they suspended you.'

I swivel on the spot. 'Really? You're happy my career is on the line? You shit. You know what?' Tell him. Tell him that despite it all, you might be in love with him. That you hate that you've hurt him. That you want to be with him, despite everything. I glare at him. 'I hope you and your stupid cat are happy together because you don't deserve me. I'm done here!' I yell.

Nigel looks over at me from the windowsill. Seriously, Mia? How have I got dragged into this? And with that I leave. The anger makes me want to scream. I stamp my feet, slamming his door and kicking it as I go. Do I grab a box of muffins with me as I leave? Well, yeah, I do that too.

ED

'Oh my god, Mr Rogers – this slaps! It's better than McDonald's, man!' one of the boys says as he sits down at his desk, puffer coat still on in May, three muffins in his hand.

'You're very welcome. Please use the napkins otherwise I'll get into trouble with the cleaning people.'

'It even says good luck on the napkins!' a girl hollers.

Well, if I'm going to theme things I go all out. I sit there at my desk, slightly spaced out, bereft, lost. Like I've just woken up from a coma. I didn't sleep last night. Seeing Tommy at Caitlin's was like a punch to the guts but knowing that Mia knew all the time and didn't tell me was the knockout shot that left me seeing stars. If I didn't feel like the butt of the joke before, being a twenty-eight-year-old virgin, I certainly feel that now. I hear a group of kids laughing at the back of the classroom and paranoia shoots through me, wondering if everyone knows what a complete loser I am.

Last night, I just sat on my sofa, staring at a television show about wedding dresses because I didn't even have the energy to change the channel. Four hours of wedding dress shows. Sweetheart necklines are everyone's friend, did you know that? And at 5 a.m., I got up and grilled a fair bit of bacon for these kids. I did the work of a small army of caterers, hoping it would take my mind off things. It didn't. But look at all these kids now.

Even if they don't ace this paper then I at least did something else right.

'Mr Rogers, this is bussin'...' a boy tells me from the back of the room. I hope that's good. The boy is Jerome Dixon and I'll be frank, even at sixteen, this kid is cooler than me, to the point where I'm a little intimidated by him.

'Thank you, Jerome,' I tell him, watching him read the tags on the bottles.

'Independent variable, that's when...' he says, covering his eyes, '...*you* make the change to explore its effects.' He snaps his fingers in the air to get the answer right.

I am pleasantly surprised and give him a round of applause. That's two marks right there.

'Sir, you going to prom this year?' he asks me with a mouthful of bacon.

'I am. I'm chaperoning.'

'Have you been on the prom website page and put down two songs you want played?' asks a girl. This girl is called Olivia Seaman and I suspect she's part of the prom committee who for the past two weeks, when they should have been revising, have been trying to wrangle the budget so they can get a foam machine.

'I haven't.'

'What songs would you choose, Sir?' asks Jerome.

'Well, that is an impossible question,' I say, thinking back to my Spotify most played lists and a certain person who pored over the songs and laughed. Think cool, Ed. 'Maybe something by The Weeknd.'

Did I say his name right? Is he The Weeknd? Mr Weeknd? Or just Weeknd. I see Jerome nodding. I may be cool, just a little bit cool.

'I'll make sure we get that on,' Olivia adds, writing something down in a notebook. I better go and research those songs again. They are strange beasts, my Year 11 kids: all on the verge of something great when they walk out of this school in a month's time, flirting with adulthood, pretending they don't care. I don't suppose I am their favourite teacher or that any of them will remember me in a few years' time but I'm glad they don't hate me. My class of 2019 – they didn't care much for biology. One of them actually drew a picture of me in their books and told me Biology 'sucked serious balls.' I'm glad I've progressed past that year.

'But first, exams,' I say, mainly focusing my attention on the kid at the back with a Biology revision guide out, filled with Post-it notes, looking like they may vomit. 'Any questions before you go in?'

'Reproduction, Sir,' Jerome says.

'Plant or animal?'

'Animal. So, you're telling us the wee isn't stored in the balls then?' he jokes, pointing at me, grinning.

I am silent for a moment. Until Jerome starts laughing, along with some of the boys on his table. The class join in. I think this is a joke, not at my expense per se, but a class joke. I want to laugh, but seriously, if anyone puts that down as an answer then I'm leaving this profession. 'You're funny, Jerome. What is stored in the testes?'

'Hormones and jizz, innit?'

'Thereabouts.' I smile. 'Any other questions?'

'Mr Rogers, do you have a moment?' The voice comes from the corridor and I turn to see it's Tommy from the P.E. department. Shit. I don't know what the protocol is here. In some show of macho masculinity, I think this is where we should wrestle, no? I should charge at him, but I also need to set an example in front of these kids, headed into their exams. Can I missile something at him? A muffin? A conical flask? Orange juice?

'Is it important?' I ask him in dry tones.

'Yeah, it is.'

I look over at the kids who are all viewing this exchange, eyes fixed on the both of us, nibbling on their bacon. 'I'll be outside if anyone needs me,' I tell them even though they're mostly sixteen and don't need my help. 'Please be sensible with the ketchup.'

I get up and head out, watching Tommy from behind, my shoulders dropping to have his physical being flaunted in front of me like this. It's all Nike Tech fleece, and shapely calves and thighs. I really hope you've not dragged me out of my classroom to laugh at me. He turns to face me in the corridor.

'Look, I thought it was important we had a chat after yesterday,' he tells me, putting his hands out like he's explaining some sort of sports move to me.

'Yesterday, what happened yesterday?' I ask him plainly.

'Yeah. That's funny.'

'Well, please do clarify what it was.'

'We've only hooked up a couple of times. It's not serious. I didn't know you two were a thing as well.'

'Well, we're not now...'

'You dumped her?' he asks me.

'I haven't put it in a formal letter, but she was lying to me and shagging you at the same time so yeah, those are not great foundations.'

'We weren't shagging-shagging...' Tommy explains, looking around for kids with open ears. 'I think I quite like her...'

'So, it's like how it was with Mia, I guess?'

'Look, I don't know what Mia told you but that was a one-time thing.'

I shrug. 'Not really. You flirted with her via text for weeks, got her hopes up and then as soon as you got what you wanted, you cut her loose again.' I was there through all of it and as much as I am angry at Mia right now, maybe someone does need to hold up a mirror to Tommy's treatment of women. My tone is steely, cold and really not very like me at all, but I don't care. Go on, tough old P.E. wanker, take a punch, because you humiliated me enough last night, you can't do much worse.

'You'll probably do the same with Caitlin. You forget I was there when you and Steve started that bet about how many of the faculty members you could get through in a year. You up to double figures yet?'

His stance suddenly changes from someone who's trying to be my mate to classic bully, as if he's thinking I'm head-to-toe Nike and you're in GAP chinos, you loser. I'm not sure what he wanted this conversation to be about. Did he want to compare notes? Is that what lads do? I don't know what feels worse: the idea that Caitlin strung us both along or that I finally have something in common with this man.

'Who are you, again? Oh yeah, Mr Science Nerd? The fact is you couldn't compete,' he says, spitting out his words.

'I didn't realise it was a competition.'

'Girls don't want blokes like you at the end of the day, simple fact. You're boring.'

'I see that now. They want bell-ends like you.'

'Who are you calling a bell-end?' he asks, puffing his chest out.

I look around that empty corridor. 'I believe it's you.'

He laughs and pushes my shoulder and I glare back at him even though I still don't know what I'm doing. I've never welcomed a fight in my entire life, I'm usually watching the fights or hiding in the shadows taking a side. He bench presses things and planks. I'd have to go street and just try to aim for the soft bits.

'If Caitlin thinks the better option is some cretin like you who takes every opportunity to disrespect women and treat them badly, then I obviously misjudged her. You are welcome to each other.'

Or I can just stun him with complicated insults. I see him scan through the words I just said.

'Look, mate,' he grunts at me.

'I'm not your mate.'

'Well, obviously. Do you want to take this outside?' he says, palms up, gesturing at one of the fire doors.

I laugh under my breath for a moment. This, again, is not the best thing to do because I see every sinew in his face stiffen ready to take me on. I'm only laughing as outside are the school tennis courts. Are we going to grapple on the tarmac? That could be the crowning glory of these last twenty-four hours, to get a wedgie from this P.E. shithead in full view of the science block.

'What are you, twelve? Do you want my lunch money too?' I tell him.

'You think you're smarter than me?' he says, standing a bit closer to me. I notice kids by the door of the classroom peer around.

'Remind me why you're here again? To rub it in my face?'

It's his turn to laugh now. 'Look, I was trying to just clear the air given we work in the same place.'

'You mean you're here to mark out your territory, I get it.' He should literally just slap out his cock and pee in a circle on the floor. 'She's yours. Not mine.' It still stings to say that out loud, to admit to myself that she probably never liked me that much.

He pouts. 'Best man won, Steady Eddie.'

I have no idea what to say to this man anymore. I should warn him not to lend her money. Maybe he should do what I did last night and delve into her past life in her old school where she broke a few other hearts, destroyed a few more lives. But perhaps the best thing I can do now is let him find that out for himself. Hopefully, once she's cleaned him out of his life savings.

'Yeah,' I say, resigned to the fact that I have lost. He laughs quietly at me. I've lost all sense of hope that love is something for me. It's better to be alone than to feel as crappy as this, to be standing here next to this man being insulted, bullied, belittled – in a school no less. 'Their Biology exam starts in half an hour. I think we're done here.' I turn away from him and take a big breath before returning to the classroom, taking a seat by my desk and picking up a muffin. You are alone, Ed, but you make good muffins at least. The classroom is unfeasibly quiet for Year 11 and I glance up to see all the kids are looking at me.

'You all right, Mr Rogers?' Olivia asks.

'Yeah,' I say, through a mouthful of crumbs. Not really. They all stare back at me. I hope those aren't looks of pity or I really will cry. 'Right, someone have another muffin before I eat them all. Anyone else have any Biology questions?'

TWENTY-TWO

MIA

The problem with partial unemployment and bunking in with my sister is that she's not letting me do all those things that I would do normally if I was in my house share. If I was on my own, I'd lay in until midday-ish, I'd binge watch *Ted Lasso*, wank in between and medicate my confusion and possible heartbreak with Deliveroo and not even good Deliveroo, like veggie burgers from the chicken shop with limp chips and bad coleslaw that's swimming in pale, watery mayonnaise.

Instead, Rachel gives me routine: she gets her kids to wake me up and she makes me sit at a table and eat breakfast with her, foodstuffs I rarely consume at breakfast like overnight oats and blueberries. Rachel has time to grate apple. She gives me lists of things to do like dust her bookshelves and buy milk. But buy the right milk. The shit hits the fan if you bring the wrong milk into her house. If it sounds awful then it is, but it isn't, because overnight oats have kept me regular at least, the kids distract me and I'm using Rachel's caviar moisturiser which is doing wonders for my complexion. In return, I look after my sister, I limit her alcohol consumption, I recommend books to her. I'm the better option than Alison who has told Rachel that she's 'not tried hard enough to make her marriage work for the sake of her children.' That phone conversation ended in screams and a mug breaking but hey, at least I am Rachel's favourite sister now.

'How is this place still standing?' Rachel asks me.

'Possibly asbestos.'

Today is my day to lead the routine and I've brought Rachel to the community centre to join in one of the classes. The one thing about Rachel is that she needs to leave her house and remember who she is. She gave up a career to become obsessed by milk and she needs to slowly come out into the world, meet people, remember the smart, snappy girl she once was who has a degree in French. Because if I had a degree in French then I would be finding myself a Frenchman, the sort who would wear a scarf all year round, with good hair, who spoke with his hands and who'd make wild passionate love to me like in an illicit film from the seventies.

'The curtains are still the same. You haven't changed the curtains?'

Rachel doesn't look at the community centre with the same romanticism as me. To me, it is a place where we had every birthday party from the age of five to ten, the place Mum took under her wing and infused with so much love and energy. I have happy memories of her running story time sessions for little people who'd sit on her lap and make her drawings. Rachel sees the heavy seventies curtains and the cold toilets with the scarily noisy cisterns.

'Why would I change the orange curtains? That's a vintage look now.'

She gives me a look, knowing my interior design is based

around things I've found in skips and sprayed with Dettol. 'So what course are we doing today?' she asks me, still not wholly convinced this is for her.

'I went for fun. And what is more fun than... a ukulele?' I say, using jazz hands to illustrate the levels of fun that we will be having.

She's frowning. 'Come again?'

'It was that or felt making.'

'What the hell will I do with a ukulele?'

'Learn a skill and a jaunty tune. If you ever go to Hawaii, you can be at one with the locals.'

'This is ridiculous,' she tells me, stopping in her tracks in the car park.

'This is fun. You need to remember how to have fun. You'll love the teacher, too. Her name is Donna.'

Yes, Donna with the sidebar in pretty graphic porn also likes a mini guitar. Who knew? Rachel's face speaks otherwise, the crestfallen look of a kid who's received clothes for Christmas. I link an arm into hers and do a little happy jig to get her in the mood. Surprisingly, this does little to boost her enthusiasm, especially when she walks into the room and sees that the average age of the room is around sixty.

'I think I prefer it when you get me paralytically drunk,' she says. 'Or when you bring me to summer bazaars and you tell everyone I'm dating a man with a giant penis. That was fun.'

'True, but we also need to diversify and I've paid for a block of five of these things so you're locked in with me here,' I say with my thumbs up.

'Great.'

'We can learn a duet. We can perform it at Christmas like we used to do when we were little. I can make tickets.'

This at least makes Rachel laugh and she finds a blue plastic chair and takes off her coat.

'Donna!' I shout from the back of the room. 'This is my sister. Hook her up.'

Donna gives me a thumbs up. 'The one with the shithead husband?'

Rachel swivels her head around to me.

'The very one.'

Rachel glares at me, going to retrieve her instrument as I laugh and take a seat.

'Shithead husbands. I know all about them,' a voice says to me. 'I had one many moons ago.'

The lady next to me wears a floral headscarf and denim jumpsuit. 'Well, I'm glad you got rid. I hope he has since lived a life of misery and inconvenience,' I reply.

'Like a lifetime of incredibly itchy crabs and never being able to find a parking space,' she suggests.

I laugh. However, as she turns to me, I recognise this woman's face. Have I taught you before? Is it from the tea dances? Hold up, I do know you. 'You're Ed's mum?' I tell her.

Her mouth drops open. 'I thought I knew you! Mia. We met that one time,' she says, her eyes beaming. 'Adele. Fancy seeing you here. I didn't know you played the ukulele?' she says, excitedly.

'Oh, I'm here with my sister,' I say, pointing. 'We are trying new things. I teach Donna creative writing, so I thought we'd try this.'

She looks over at Rachel who waves back even though she has no idea who she is.

'That's great. We love Donna, she makes the ukulele inter-esting, shall we say.' I can imagine. She gets out a bright yellow ukulele from its case but watches me curiously and then looks at her watch. 'I'm guessing you're still on suspension then? It'll be why you're not at school?'

I smile as she says this, for one moment thinking I've been caught out as a teenager. 'Yeah. How did you know?'

'Ed. Are you OK?' she asks me. 'That can't be easy.'

I look into her eyes and for one moment, I see Ed. It's an enquiring and kind look, like a hug with the eyes and for one moment, my heart skips to remember him as my friend. As someone who I miss so very much.

'Kind of.'

'Can I ask why you were suspended? Ed alluded to something to do with admin. You can tell me to mind my own business if you don't want to talk about it?' she says, leaning forward, putting a hand to my knee.

'It was a bad behaviour thing.'

'Oh. Well, you know what they say about well-behaved women, they rarely make history.'

'True.' I laugh as she says that but suddenly, I also think about what she may know or not know about Ed. Do I give out details? I slapped down the bitch who broke your son's heart. That should give me plenty of good points in your book. However, by that same measure I also messed up plenty with him. I guess if she knew the half of it then she wouldn't be so civil with me. 'Have you seen Ed recently? Is he OK?' I ask her.

'Oh, you know what it's like around this time. Exams, prom... He's got sports day today. I won't see much of him until the summer holidays start.'

She doesn't know. I don't know whether to tell her because I don't want Ed to have no one in this process and have to go through this on his own. However, I get the feeling that if I spill here and now then Ed will never forgive me.

She processes what I've just asked her, frowning. 'You haven't seen Ed? I thought you two were friends. Is he spending all his time with Caitlin these days?' she enquires.

She really doesn't know. I can't tell her.

'Is she nice, this Caitlin girl? I can't wait to meet her.' Bite your tongue, Mia Johnson. 'He's just been on his own for so long. He deserves a bit of happiness.'

I feel the emotion swell in me as she says that because she's right but he's not quite there. I don't think he's very happy at all. I say nothing, I just smile. I'm here to learn a jaunty tune, is all.

'Hi! I'm Rachel,' my sister says, intervening, holding on to two ukuleles. 'I got you a black one to match the colour of your heart,' she tells me, still seemingly unimpressed that she's here. Either that or Donna read her some of her porn.

'Lovely to meet you. I'm Adele.'

'Adele is Ed's mum,' I inform her.

Rachel runs through a gamut of facial expressions at this point. Ed? Chinos Ed? Who you think you're in love with? Is this coincidence? Or is this a set-up? But the look she finally lands on in three short seconds is one of condolence. 'I'm sorry to hear what happened there.' I glare over at Rachel, shaking my head subtly. 'He seems like a nice guy.'

Ed's mum looks back at me, intensely worried. 'What? Is Ed alright? Don't frighten me, Mia!'

I close my eyes. 'The thing with Caitlin ended. They're not together.'

Her shoulders slump to hear it and I feel the weight of her disappointment.

'Oh, don't worry, Mia gave her a good slapping,' Rachel adds.

Ed's mum looks back at me again. 'Really?'

'What was that about well-behaved women?' I try to joke. 'But she wasn't as nice as Ed thought she was. I'm sorry you have to hear that from us.'

'Oh, Eddie. Is he OK? I never like to bother him about his love life, but I do worry. There's a twenty-four-carat heart in there. He's a good person.'

My face freezes to hear her say this as I know exactly what she means. I feel awful that it's taken me this long to realise that much. Adele looks into space for a moment to register how she will deal with the information just given to her.

'Do you want to know something funny? When Ed told me he was going out with someone, I immediately thought it was you.'

Rachel looks down to the floor grinning when she says that.

'He always talks about you. I thought he had a little crush and one day he'd realise how much he really cared about you, but hey... Maybe it's just meant to be someone else. Not this awful Caitlin girl, at least.' I silently blush as she says it. 'Thank you for always being there for Ed, for sticking up for my boy. Thank you for everything you've taught him.'

Christ, does she know about that? I bloody well hope not. Rachel knows though and when I glance at her, her nostrils are flared large like black holes which could suck the air out of this place. Don't you dare.

'Do you want to go for some tea after this? I think we should chat,' I say to Adele.

'I'd love that,' she says nodding, tuning up her ukulele. 'You can tell me everything.'

'I'll try.'

There's a sudden clap from the front of the room and Donna hits a high Mariah Carey style note to get our attention. 'So, everyone, welcome. I'm Donna. If you are new today, we're going to go slowly especially for that new mingebag at the back.'

I poke my tongue out at Donna and stick a middle finger up at her. Rachel looks over at me and laughs.

'Just pick up your ukuleles and hold them against your tits. Not you, John, you don't have tits,' she continues. 'And altogether, we will start with a G-string. Come on, John, show us your G-string.'

Rachel continues to laugh. Told you it would be fun. But that's quite tame for Donna, you wait till she talks about strumming.

ED

There's one day of the year in this school where if I were in charge, I'd throw it in the bin and maybe set it on fire. I'd ban it for eternity and I think at least eighty percent of the kids would be on board with that and they'd cheer for me and hold parades in my honour. That day is sports day and I hate it with a passion. Where is Maths day? Biology day? English day which could be a day of Scrabble or reading books aloud? You see, sport is a very divisive topic for me. I run to keep fit because, as a biologist, I understand the benefits of increased lung capacity, fitness and exercise. However, I also know from experience that it was the kids who were good at sport that ruled the roost. They were kings who could do no wrong because the school relied on their sporting achievements to build their name and brand. Kids who were good at Maths raised the grade averages, but they were not the rockstar football kids who could win you trophies. So, yes, I have resentment towards the sporty kids because it turns out you can leave school and come back and it's still the sporty ones who get all the accolades. Case in point, as I stand here watching Tommy chatting to Caitlin by the long jump pit, flirting in front of all and sundry. Christ, he may as well be dry humping her leg.

'I need you in your colour houses, please! Mr Sachs, can you tell us why you're wearing tracksuit bottoms and not the school P.E. shorts today?'

'Because this day is a pile of wank,' young Mr Sachs replies. I look down to the floor as Mr Sachs is led away from the sports day activities for the morning.

'God, I hate this,' says Henry from Geography. This is Henry's first sports day and he has a face on him like he's been chosen to be a tribute in the Hunger Games. He doesn't run, he claims his body doesn't even know how. His sport is played on a

PS4. I know this because I play FIFA with him and he's a known and awful cheat. Alicia likes to drag us all out for sports day, thinking this will give us a sense of community but all the adults who aren't inclined when it comes to sport become hugely resentful about it. 'I'm literally wearing pyjama shorts because I own zero sports clothing.'

'You own tracksuit bottoms,' I tell him, on the assumption that most men do.

'Ed, I'm not like young Mr Sachs out there. My trackies are not used for sport. They're my stretchy pants that I use when I've eaten too much.' I laugh under my breath as he smooths down the T-shirt over his gut and picks off what might be an old cornflake.

'Can I hide here?' asks Beth, as she comes over. I can tell Beth is also not that way inclined as she is in Converse. 'I hate this so much. Also, half these kids aren't wearing sunscreen, they're going to fry. Look at that blond kid there, he looks like a plum already. We're going to get a letter from his parents, for sure.'

'Are we sure he's not having some sort of episode?' Henry asks, a little too calmly given that the three of us have a duty of care.

'Who knows?' replies Beth. She sees me looking over at Tommy and Caitlin again and bites her lip. She's friends with Mia so I suppose she knows more about that whole situation than most. 'Oh Christ, look at Ted,' Beth exclaims, trying to distract me. Ted is from Music and refuses to retire, the sort of person who has stories about this school when they first got computers and still has a flip phone. Ted is wearing a floppy hat, sandals with socks and we've got him up a ladder with a big stick sorting out the pole vault. I hope we know where the defibrillator is.

'That's one metre, two,' Henry tells me, and I write the

number on my clipboard. We are in charge of the shot put today. I have no idea what we're doing but Henry is just pulling a tape measure around and all the kids are telling us this strange cannonball we're getting them to toss about is too heavy.

'Are you sure?' the kid asks, obviously hopeful that he had more upper arm strength than he really did.

'Yeah,' I confirm.

'But in the Olympics, they throw them, like, miles,' the kid continues to argue with me.

'Yeah, and they're also Russian, eat five chickens a day and take a lot of steroids. You'll make up for it in the running, I'm sure,' I say, trying to find some sort of school spirit in me.

'AND NEXT WE HAVE THE TEACHERS' RUNNING RACE. 400M ON THE TRACK. PLEASE, IF YOU'VE SIGNED UP FOR THIS THEN CAN YOU MAKE YOUR WAY TO THE START LINE!' an excitable voice echoes through the tannoy. Did I sign up? I did because someone from the office went round with a clipboard and I was guilted into it, but this was before Caitlin, before falling out with Mia. Mia always tells me to dodge the clipboard. I never listen.

'You'll have to take over shot put duties, this is me,' I say to Beth, unenthusiastically.

'Really? That's exciting,' she tells me.

'It really isn't. Half of these kids have their phones on them despite the fact they shouldn't so it's likely they will take pictures and videos of my running face.'

'Can I cheer for you?' she asks. 'Henry! Ed is running!'

Henry salutes me. 'Taking one for the team, Sir.'

Or not. I stroll over to the start line which feels more like a firing line. It's a bizarre selection of staff members, all regretting their life decisions, all wearing sports socks they've stolen from family members, one in cycling shorts that perhaps reveal too much. Ted from Music should really not be here. I see someone lunging. Shit. That's Tommy, isn't it? Caitlin comes over to give him a water bottle and they both look at me.

'Ed,' Caitlin says to acknowledge me. We've never really finished our relationship. She didn't even try to text to explain, and I didn't chase. Naturally, seeing her every day here is awful, so I spend a lot of time avoiding her, leaving school at lunch and eating my sandwiches in the leisure centre car park down the road. I put a hand up to say hello then turn away. The humiliation continues.

'And we have a really varied selection of staff today in this race. Please can we ask you all to step up to the line...'

'GO, MR ROGERS!' I hear a voice scream from the crowd. I think that was Beth. I hope she's monitoring the shot put properly because those things can cause a lot of damage. But then another voice, a boy, screams the same. 'YOU GOT THIS, MR ROGERS!' Who was that? I can't quite tell if they were genuine or mocking the voice from before.

'Ready to lose again then, Steady Eddie?' says a voice next to me.

Really? I mean, I probably will. He's a P.E. man, an ex-footballer, he has the calves for running. Mia told me my Asics are the sort of trainers old people wear on cruises. I don't reply but still hear the murmur of cheers in the crowd. ROGERS, ROGERS! chants a group of girls.

'AND I WANT YOU TO TAKE YOUR MARKS, GET SET AND...'

'ROGERS, ROGERS!'

Who is that?

'GO!' But as the voice on the tannoy says go, I feel an elbow to my ribs, a push. He did what now? I stumble and lose my footing, watching as he runs ahead of the field. I hear booing. Just run, Ed. You know how to do that. You do this every other day. You can't do anything else in this moment. Just run.

ROGERS, ROGERS!

I'm not hearing that, am I? It makes me pump my arms a bit more until I'm caught up with Tommy on the third curve of the athletics track. There are kids running alongside us. YOU CAN DO THIS, MR ROGERS! I glance to my side. Do I teach you? I don't even know you. By the final straight, the air burns in my lungs. I'm more of a jogger so this is hard work. The lactic acid builds in my muscles, just this straight and then we're done. I'm keeping up with Tommy. This is strange. Could I actually beat him?

YOU CAN FUCKING DO IT, MR ROGERS.

That was definitely a child, and that child is going to get into trouble. I run. Possibly the fastest I've ever run in my life, flashbacks to a time when I ran down a hill when I was nine years old and ran into a tree and lost a tooth. Run, Ed. Just run it all out, all that emotion, all those feelings, the strange events of the last month. Just run. I make the last push, through a tape measure at the end and collapse to the floor. My lungs hurt. It all hurts. But the noise, the cheering is like a wave. Who are they cheering for?

'ROGERS, ROGERS, ROGERS.'

I see the shadow of Alicia appear in the light, standing over me. 'Well, someone has a fan club.' I look down at my shirt where, in the melee, someone's put a gold #1 sticker on my chest. I can't quite breathe, let alone talk but I don't quite understand what happened there. Who was cheering? And for a brief second, I think and hope it could be one person. Mia. She was the sort of person who would cheer (and blaspheme) like that openly and I used to hate it, I thought it loud and brash, but maybe I didn't see how much it kept me going. It wasn't her, though, this time. I sit up and watch Tommy on the floor across the way, cradling his muscled calves, telling someone next to him that he's pulled something. That's why he lost. I might smile. Laugh even. I need some water though.

Before I die. Someone appears beside me and offers me a hand.

'Mr Rogers, my G...' I look up into the light, my sweat blinding me a little.

'Jerome? What's going on?'

'You beat Mr Wood. At his own subject. You are the man,' another lad says, patting me on the back as I rise to my feet. I'm sweating a fair bit though. I do wish I'd worn a more effective deodorant.

'You were all cheering. Why?' I ask them, bending down to put my hands on my knees.

'Because we like you. We heard what Mr Wood said to you outside our classroom that day, before our exam. That's not right.' I turn and Olivia stands there, explaining it all to me. 'No other teacher made us breakfast either. No one cares. I mean, maybe Miss Johnson does. She brought us sweets.'

'Mr Wood is a massive dickhead,' a lad says, and they all laugh. I pull a face to sort of indicate that I agree. That's not professional. I try to change that, hoping I just look out of breath and distressed instead.

'Miss Johnson cares. More than you know,' I tell them.

'Well, yeah. She's amazing. We properly stan her. We can't tell you how much we loved her after we heard she slapped Miss Bell,' Olivia explains to me.

'She did what?' I stop for a moment. She slapped who? 'She slapped Miss Bell?' I ask, making the motion with my hands in case this is them speaking in Gen Z slang again.

'Yeah. Some kids from Year 8 saw it,' Olivia continues. 'Didn't you know about that? She got suspended. Don't you teachers talk to each other...?'

'She slapped Miss Bell because she was angry with her for being a sket with Mr Wood behind your back. She was your mate and she legit put her job on the line. For you,' Jerome tells me.

'How do you all...?' I gasp.

'We're not stupid, Sir. It's not some equation in an exam. We pieced it together ourselves. How did you not work that out?' Jerome continues. I should be angry at him questioning me like this, but I stand there looking into space, wondering, thinking about how I only ever saw Mia keeping secrets from me, not really anything else in between.

I see Beth's face appear amongst all the kids, shocked. 'I thought you knew too.'

'I didn't. I heard she got suspended because of a data protection issue,' I say.

'Who told you that?' Beth asks me.

'Caitlin...' We both look over to see her nursing Tommy and his fake injury. It's just lies on lies with that one. How has she managed to dupe me so many times? 'So she found out about Caitlin and Tommy... and slapped her?' I repeat to Beth, leading her away from the kids.

'Yeah. She did more than that. They had a proper full-on fight,' Beth explains.

'You didn't say anything?' I ask Beth.

'I assumed you knew the real reason why. I did wonder why you pushed her away so hard, though.'

'I didn't know,' I admit. I take a deep cleansing breath and hold my hands to my face.

'She's Mia. She cares about you so much,' she says. 'I don't want to stir anything up but maybe think about why she did what she did?'

'Because she's prone to flying off the handle?'

'Or...?' Beth pauses, trying to draw the answer out of me.

'I'm not an English teacher, I don't know how to read between the lines,' I tell her, confused.

'Let me spell it out for you. I think she might really care about you, Ed. Maybe. Possibly...' Beth hints, her face rising to a blush to say it out loud.

But as soon as the words leave her mouth, it is some sort of lightbulb moment. Despite the fact I am a big sweating and dripping mess and my legs could very possibly give way, I feel strangely empty because in this win, this small moment of victory in my life, something clicks into place and I really wish Mia was here, right now, next to me. The both of us, together.

TWENTY-THREE

MIA

'Does yours have a beard?' I ask Florence.

'Yes.'

'Is it Lucas?'

Florence throws herself onto the bed to feel the bitter taste of defeat. 'You're too good at this game. Are you cheating?'

'Are you accusing me of cheating?' I say, insulted, a hand to my chest.

'You've won five times in a row,' she moans. 'A nice auntie would let me win and buy me sweets.'

'Allowing you to win teaches you nothing, but we can do the sweet thing, any time.' I smile. She comes over to hug me and I squeeze her so tight. It's not been an easy month for these little ones, and I wish I could squeeze all that hurt out for her, but at least these kids know I'm here. They will never beat me at *Guess Who?* but I will always be there for them.

'When are you going home, Aunty Mia?' Florence asks me, staring at my bags in the hallway.

'Tonight, I've got to go home. I left a ton of food in the fridge and it's starting to grow beards of mould, so my housemates are complaining.'

Florence giggles. 'Can we come to your house some time?'

'Maybe.'

'You also said we could go to Ed's house and meet his cat? Can we do that?'

'Again, maybe,' I say with a hint of sadness. I've not spoken to Ed for an age, both of us a little too angry and stubborn to make the first move but with school and exam periods in the way, it's also not been a priority. I'll have to apologise to that cat, too, for saying he had a stupid name. Nigel deserved better than to be dragged into our argument.

'Did Aunty Mia not let you win at *Guess Who?* again?' Rachel says from the door.

'Yeah,' Florence says, gathering the game boards. 'So I'm going to go and beat Felix instead,' she tells me, sticking her tongue out.

I laugh as she leaves us, Rachel coming in with a cup of tea and sitting down next to me.

'No biscuits?' I ask her.

'How do you eat so much and just stay so thin, I hate you for that,' she tells me.

'That'll be a no then,' I say, taking a sip of tea. Rachel makes excellent tea, but she's taken it upon herself to limit my sugar intake which is one reason why I'll be glad to move on.

She sips her tea quietly and looks at me. 'So... I'm going to say this out loud now before you go and before I don't get the chance... but you will be missed round here,' she says, not quite looking me in the eye. I'd reply with my biting wit if her words didn't strike a chord somewhere, deep in the heart of me.

'Thank you for putting me up. I appreciate it. I'm sorry for all the times I didn't buy the milk with the red lid,' I say diplomatically. 'And I don't want to take credit for anything, but I feel you're in a better place compared to that day you showed up at my school.'

She purses her lips, trying to hold in a smile. 'I am. And I don't mind you taking some of the credit for that. I hope that investigation works out with the slap and stuff.'

I shrug my shoulders. I've filled in countless written testimonials, appeared in front of a hearing board and got my union involved but I'm still waiting to hear whether I can go back to school, so for now I remain in limbo, drifting back to my house so I can be an adult in my own space, hopefully not drifting towards a life of day-wanking and Deliveroo.

'I bought you a gift,' Rachel tells me, putting both hands to her knees.

'You never buy me gifts...'

'I buy you shit at Christmas.'

'You buy me gift cards.'

'And you give me dusty wine that you've either just taken out of a cupboard or bought from corner shops.'

We both look at each other, guilty as charged, and laugh. She goes over to a sideboard and obtains a large coffin shaped box wrapped in brown paper with a bow and I smile.

'That's a big gift. Is it a Mr Frosty?'

'No, it's not a fucking Mr Frosty.'

I slide my fingers under the paper and rip it off to reveal a ukulele, a red one. Not even one of those cheap ones with the plastic strings that they sell in toy shops, it's a proper ukulele.

'It's a good brand. I'm not duetting at Christmas with you playing those crusty ones Donna keeps.'

I run my fingers over the strings and smile broadly. 'You got one for yourself too!' I squeal.

'Yes, mine is green. I look forward to still seeing you once a week at the community centre,' she tells me. I smile because she had fun, and she wants to continue having the fun. With me.

Despite the very sad circumstances that led to this point, it feels nice to have her by my side, as a sister.

'You know, we could get Alison involved and we could be a trio,' I suggest.

'In time. For now, well done for smashing her birthday cake,' she tells me, matter-of-factly.

I raise my eyebrows, trying to look innocent. 'That wasn't me. It was a disgruntled member of staff...'

'More a disgruntled sister,' she laughs, her arms reaching out to hug me. I take that hug and rest my head on her shoulder. 'Mia May Johnson. The littlest sister, her heart full of chaos, the one I thought I didn't need.'

'I'm glad you found the space,' I joke.

The doorbell suddenly rings, and I hear the sound of little footsteps scamper to the hallway to go and answer it. 'Were you expecting anyone?' I ask Rachel and she shakes her head. I arch my head over the sofa and smile at the people standing there.

'Beth?' I say, rising to my feet.

'Thank God you're in. Come, boys, in you go,' she says, carrying a few bags with her, sippy cups and snacks. 'Boys, this is Aunty Mia and Florence and Rachel – these are my boys, Joe and Jude.'

They all amble into the house and I smile to see Beth in mum mode to these two chocolate-haired cuties in matching hoodies and Converse.

'I'm so sorry for invading your house on a Saturday like this. We're off to the park, but I had to swing by first...'

'No apology needed,' Rachel says, 'Come on through, boys, and we can get you some juice. You two go through to the living room. I also have biscuits.'

I pull a face knowing I didn't get those biscuits but follow Beth through as she straightens herself out and re-ties her mum bun. 'We came on the bus which always feels like a good idea until they keep pressing the bell and decide to take off their shoes,' she tells me, an early summer sheen of sweat covering her face.

'Drink?' I ask her.

'In a minute. I come with news.' I try to read her facial expressions as she wipes her face down with one of her son's muslin blankets. 'It's good news. Very good news. Basically, you're off the hook, you're coming back on Monday. Alicia went to St Quentin's to see why Caitlin was passed on to us and it was as we thought, a complete shitshow. Actually, one of the teachers there wanted to pass on their congratulations for you slapping her. You can also be thankful for a Year 8 child who saw that whole fight and told us about it.' She pulls out some papers from her rucksack, 'And I quote, "You were acting in self-defence cos Miss Bell went for your hair too and threw a dictionary at you."'

'Seriously?' I gasp, exhaling deeply.

'Seriously. You're in the clear. Please come back. My department doesn't work without you. I have a sub who just keeps showing YouTube in her lessons.'

'That's not what we're supposed to do?' I reply. I go over and throw my arms around her neck out of sheer relief. 'I will see you on Monday. Thank you for everything you did to make this happen. Seriously, thank you so much.' There may be a tear in my eye to think that this short debacle is over but that I can also go back to something that I've grown to love.

'One more thing,' she mentions, sitting down and flicking through the paperwork in her lap. 'Your review came back and it's all perfect, a few things to run through when you get back but nothing I'm hugely worried about.'

I sit down next to her, puffing my cheeks out that the good news just keeps coming.

She pauses on one piece of paper. 'And you're not supposed to see this, but I thought maybe you should. It's a peer review. I mean, I'm pretty pissed off because it beats mine hands down but I thought you should read it. Please read it,' she says, handing the piece of paper over as I eye her curiously.

I first met Mia Johnson when we joined Griffin Road at the same time. From the outset, it struck me that this was someone deeply embedded in getting to know people, not just her students. She's an incredible ally and counsellor to all members of staff and encourages a wonderful sense of inclusion in all she does. She gets to know people, almost intimately. But when she does, she makes them better versions of themselves, she pushes them out of their comfort zones, she floods them with kindness and unwavering support until they have no choice but to go with the flow, to swim, to not be scared of the water anymore. Ask any student or teacher and they will tell you she's acutely funny, sociable, helpful and an amazing champion of community both in and out of school. She is not only the best of teachers, she's the best of people. My only wish for her? I wish she just knew that about herself. I wish she knew that I'm the teacher and person that I am because she's been by my side the whole time; in that way, she's the best educator I could ever wish for.

Edward Rogers

(Science – Biology)

I look up and Beth is crying. I realise I am too at Ed's perfect words and we sit there together, sobbing, my heart aching, wondering why he couldn't have just said this to my face, though, you know?

'Shit, did you get fired?' Rachel says from the doorway, a bunch of kids by her side.

I shake my head as she tries to work out what's happening and I clutch the piece of paper to my chest.

'Look,' Beth says, wiping the tears from her eyes. 'I haven't got involved up to this point but please, go to him. Tell him how you feel. I beg you. I want this to have a happy ending. You don't write like that about someone you don't love. And we should know, we teach English Literature.' She smiles broadly.

'Are you sure he wrote this?' I ask her.

'Every word. Go to him,' she pleads.

I nod, standing up. 'I guess he'll be at home, I could go over now.'

Beth shakes her head. 'He's at prom.'

'Prom? That's today?'

'It is.'

I look down at what I'm wearing, denim cut offs and a T-shirt. 'I can't go to prom like this!'

'You could borrow one of my dresses?' Rachel says, standing there grinning.

'I can do your hair with clips,' Florence adds.

I sit there looking down at the words. Oh, Ed. The very wonderful Mr Rogers. I'm going to have to shave my legs again because I'm coming to find you. It looks like I'm going to prom.

ED

Did you know Priya Vijay spent £800 on her prom dress? I know because she's told everyone as she got out of her limo and walked up to Richmond House Hotel where prom is taking place. I suspect she's been drinking.

'It's red, Mr Rogers, and it cost £800!' she tells me excitedly.

'You look amazing!' I tell her in return. 'Have fun!' I keep telling them to have fun. What I really want to tell them is to approach tonight with a sensible head. If your parents have spent this much on your outfits then try to keep them clean so they can attempt to re-sell them, don't drink so much that you have zero memory of the night, don't live the evening on your phones.

I scan the lines of kids waiting to get into this grand place, limos and sports cars lining the gravel drive and one horse and carriage that has held everything up as the horse decided to take a dump halfway down the drive. I used to have my reservations about this end-of-year ritual, but I quite like how our proms, at least, have become a celebration of every type of kid in our year; no one turns up alone, they find their tribes, they dance and laugh, moan about the buffet and every moment seems to be a mass celebration of their five years in our school.

'That's some serious drip, Mr Rogers,' a voice says from behind a pair of sunglasses and a burgundy red tuxedo.

'I almost didn't recognise you, Jerome.'

In a move where for a moment I think he's going to punch me, Jerome goes to fist bump me and I manage to meet his fist with mine. Look at me, I'm dripping, apparently. Which hopefully means I am slightly cooler than I was three minutes ago. I stand there like some sort of teacher-bouncer in my Marks & Spencer suit. Yes, the same suit I wore for my graduation five years ago and that I also wore to a cousin's wedding and have worn to four proms already. I may not be stylish but, by God, I am thrifty.

'Oh, to be young again and not have to wear a bra,' Alicia says to me as she, too, watches everyone file past us. I'm slightly perturbed to hear Alicia talk about her boobs, but I smile all the same. I love how she's come in her everyday work suit but with a fancy necklace to tell us she can also get dressed up when needs be. 'By the way, lovely work on the photo backdrop, Mr Rogers.'

We glance over to see my handiwork propped up by the hotel entrance, transported here in the school minibus, strewn in some fairy lights my mum found in her loft. I like how the girls have already used it for their numerous group photos and selfies. I like how the boys have no idea why it's here.

'It was my pleasure,' I reply.

'Now, can you help me work out that smell? Is that weed?'

'Oh no, I think it's just a heady mix of Dior Sauvage, Lynx Africa, vape and fake tan,' I joke.

She laughs but in an instant switches to her serious headteacher face. 'Well, remember to look out for alcohol, Mr Rogers. I don't want a repeat of last year.'

I nod. Last year, someone spiked the chocolate fountain with rum and a lad called Billy Bonewell fell face first into it, spoiling one girl's white dress and resulting in a £300 cleaning charge. I remember that moment clearly as Mia thought the chocolate was poo and was convinced a child had defecated themselves. Oh, how we laughed. I sigh to think about how we've both used prom in that way, seeing it as an end of year jolly for ourselves. Where we would stand and laugh at some of the girls' ridiculous dresses, Mia would partake in photos and dancing with some of the students, and then stuff her clutch full of sausage rolls for the car ride home.

'I can't believe he's done that. I hate him, I hate him, I hate him!' I hear as a girl runs past me, once perfect make-up streaming down her face. Oh dear. Unfortunately, at these events, there's always one, but given it's the first hour of this evening I need to check she's OK. I head outside to see her standing by some box trees, sobbing, not a friend in sight.

'Hi, all OK?' I ask her, passing her a tissue from a stash in my pocket. It's Lola from one of my classes.

'Do I look a state, Mr Rogers?'

I can't tell a sixteen-year-old she looks like a very pretty goth, can I? I don't think that was the look she was going for.

'You may just need to tidy up the eyes.' I gesture in a mascara applying motion. 'Who do you hate?' I ask her.

'RYAN LONGSTAFF!' She caterwauls that name through the night air like a banshee hell-bent on revenge.

'Did he hurt you?' I ask.

'He turned up to prom with Isla. I'm going to kill him! KILL HIM!'

I shudder a bit at the volume, but I can understand the emotion, having had my heart trampled on recently. 'Or not.

You've just done your exams. You don't want to go to prison,' I reply, calmly. 'Look, Lola...'

'Yeah.'

'Please don't let him spoil your night. Don't make it about him. That means he's won.'

She looks at me for a moment. 'He's just a shit fake pair of Jordans.'

She's lost me with that analogy, but I nod and smile.

'How do I look?'

I get out my phone to show her her face.

'FUCK! Can you stand there for a moment while I sort my eyes?' I nod as she gets out tissues, eyeliner and seems to solve everything in one fell swoop. Like a lot of the girls here, the dress is not quite there. The sort that might disintegrate in the rain which isn't good news for her as my weather apps tell me there's a seventy-eight percent chance of rain at eleven o'clock. I hope she has a coat. But hey, maybe now isn't the moment for practical. 'Is that better?' she asks me.

She still looks like spiders are attacking her eyes, but I nod and give a thumbs up. 'Try to have fun tonight,' I tell her.

'Oh, I'm just going to dance it out,' she says, looking down at my footwear, possibly judging me for it. 'Miss Johnson was right about you, you're a good sort, Mr Rogers,' she tells me, grabbing me in a hug, before scuttling away in what looks like very unsupportive high heels.

I stand there for a moment and close my eyes to take that in. She always bigged me up, didn't she?

'You are a good sort. I was right.'

As soon as I hear the voice, something just feels brighter, more right with the world. I look out into the darkness of the hotel grounds and Mia emerges from behind a hedge in a strappy black cocktail dress and blue earrings. But it's the smile I really notice, the one that's always made me smile back. I take in a sharp breath. I then scan down to her feet.

'Alicia better not see those trainers.'

'You know I can't walk in heels,' she says, grinning. 'Stellar advice there for young Lola, by the way.'

I shrug my shoulders. 'Just me bonding with the youth, you know,' I say, throwing up what I think might be a gang sign but probably isn't. I study her face for a moment and realise how much I've missed it, how much I've grown to love her blue eyes, the way she wrinkles her nose at me, the way she bites on her scrappily painted thumbnail when she's concentrating.

'You're here,' I tell her, still winning with my smooth talk.

'I'm not suspended anymore. I'm officially a teacher again.'

I beam. 'That's good news. I was thinking before how this prom felt wrong without you going through the buffet and stuffing food in your clutch.'

She laughs, exposing her neck, and her mouth wide open. I've missed that big loud laugh, too.

'I just thought it doesn't work without you here. Any of it really. Like you weren't at sports day...'

'Well, I might take a leave of absence every year if it gets me out of sports day. I heard you won a very important race.'

'I got a sticker, too.'

'Fancy.'

She walks up closer to me, and I can't tell what urge is stronger, the one to wrap my arms around her or to try and kiss her. I put my hands in my pockets to stop them reaching out for her.

'I'm sorry, Ed. I'm sorry I never told you about Caitlin when I found out,' she tells me quietly.

'And I'm sorry. I pushed you away when I probably needed you most. I know now what you did and why you did it and–'

'I snapped her Alice band,' she interrupts me. I didn't know this detail, but this fills me with a strange sense of satisfaction.

'You did that for me...'

'For you...'

'I... I...' I don't know what to say next. Please don't leave me. Please stick around? I missed you?

But instead, she puts a finger to my mouth to tell me to shush, looking me in the eye. 'I read your peer review.'

'You weren't supposed to see that.'

'But I did. Did you mean it?'

I nod my head, unfeasibly emotional for some reason as I watch her eyes tear up. 'You are the bestest teacher, ever.'

'That's not a word.' she replies.

'Yes, it is.'

'I wrote you a peer review, too.'

'You did? Did my department ask you for it?' I ask worriedly.

She laughs. 'I did it, just for fun.'

'You did extra work, that's very unlike you. What does it say?'

She shrugs and pulls out what is clearly a receipt from her clutch. 'Best person I know. Great in bed. Makes excellent sandwiches. I think I've fallen in love with him.'

I stop. 'Mia?'

She doesn't reply but stands there letting those words hang in the air, waiting for a response.

'Mia, I wrote at least one hundred and fifty words in my testimonial. That's just lazy!' I say, laughing.

She shakes her head and smiles. 'What do you say? You and me? I think it could work, you know?' I sense the nerves in her voice, the emotion in laying herself bare and it's a Mia I don't know at all.

I step towards her and take her hand. 'I think it could be a thing...'

'A thing?' she asks, trying to hold in her smile.

'I'm not allowed to call it a thing, am I?'

She shakes her head.

'I think it could be everything, is that better?'

And with that, I grab her without any sense of awkwardness, without overthinking anything, without any hesitation, and I kiss her. And I smile as our lips meet because she taught me how to do that, to let go, to let things unfold without a script. And it is everything to hold her in my arms, to feel her kiss me in return. It makes me so incredibly happy to be in this moment, realising that the person I love has been next to me this whole time, stealing my crisps.

'G'WAN, MR ROGERS!'

We part to see bunches of faces in the windows of this hotel, cheering. I wave at them, and Mia looks around incredulous, pointing at them. They all appear from the doors leading out to the patio.

'Miss Johnson, are you back?' one girl says, coming outside to throw her arms around her.

'I'm back,' she tells her.

'You're coming to dance, yeah? Both of you?' a boy asks, pointing his fingers to the sky, his sunglasses possibly hiding that he's stoned to the hilt. I hear the mixed beats of something from inside that room and widen my eyes. A hand slips into mine and I grip it tightly as the group of kids usher us inside.

'Don't look so scared,' she says, a broad grin on her face.

'I don't get all this Stormy type music,' I explain.

'Stormzy,' she corrects me, laughing. 'Ed, don't worry. You're with me. You'll be fine.'

Has she said those words to me before? I think she has. And with that, she takes both of my hands as we jump with the crowd of kids, lights bouncing off Mia's face, limbs flailing everywhere, my pulse beating in time with something inside me. I look up to the ceiling and close my eyes. I've never done this before. Ever. And for once, I don't think I care. I have Mia now. I'll be fine.

EPILOGUE

MIA

'I got you something,' Ed says, handing over a perfectly wrapped box with a ribbon. It's very Ed. I don't wrap gifts like this. I feel the gift is enough, I have made that effort so how it is presented is somewhat irrelevant. Is this food? I hope it's food. He does this a lot, the little gifts. He leaves them at my desk or on my pillow. Sometimes they're books, comedy coasters, chocolate bars, occasionally they're lone condoms with a Post-it Note and his attempt at drawing a cock and balls. I open the box and inside is a teeny tiny yellow rake sat there in the tissue paper.

'I am not sure what this is, Ed,' I say, perplexed, wondering why and how this might be used for sex. I don't think I want to rake my vagina.

'It's a back scratcher. Look, it has a telescopic handle so you can get those itches right at the centre of your back,' he tells me excitedly.

'But I like it when you scratch my back,' I complain.

'But you have a very itchy back. It's like every night. You really need to moisturise more.'

'That's like buying me a vibrator and telling me to sex myself because you're too tired to do it yourself.'

He frowns. 'Oh, I like the sex bit. I'll keep doing that bit. I'm just trying to streamline my duties.'

I laugh loudly and reach over and kiss him. I don't have to pull my shirt down because my breasts are out, my whole naked body is out in Ed's bed on a Sunday afternoon and it's not a lesson in sex. It's just two people, hanging out, who had some pretty awesome sex an hour ago but who are taking a break with cake and some *Star Wars*. Do I want to watch this? Maybe not but I like seeing how excited it makes Ed to see these strange people and toad creatures, wrapped in hessian, touring through space with their laser beam weapon things.

'This is still very confusing to me, there's so much to watch. Who is this Mandalorian fella? Why can't we see his face? Is it actually Luke Skywalker...?'

'It isn't.'

'Then how does Yoda get so old?'

'That's not Yoda.'

'Looks just like him.'

'It's Grogu.'

I pretend to be interested. It's a lot to take in and I should be good with something that has lots of characters. I teach *A Midsummer Night's Dream* every year. Ed cheers in bed as the Mandalorian wins some sort of gun fight. I don't say it out loud, but the Mandalorian is fit even though I haven't seen his face yet.

'How do you still get crumbs in your hair when you eat?' he says, glancing over at me.

'I just do. It's a skill.'

He bends down and licks some crumbs off my collarbone, and I giggle. His lips hover there by my neck and he kisses me slowly, his body shifting over to my side of the bed until he's on top of me. I think this *Star Wars* thing might have given him the horn, but I won't argue with how he gets his kicks.

'Can I ask you a question?' he says, the energy between us shifting as his lips move down to my breasts and my stomach. 'It's just there is something I think I want to do. Don't judge me.'

'Go on...' I say curiously.

'If I got a Mandalorian costume, could we...?'

'...I was just thinking he was fit!' I say excitedly, sitting up. 'You could guide me through sex and say *this is the way* in a different voice.'

'Not in my actual voice?' he says. 'I'd have to do voices?'

I laugh to see his distress and both of my hands reach to his face, kissing him to take it all away, trying to reclaim that moment, that energy where we can lie here and have lazy Sunday sex for the rest of the day.

'Hold up. You don't want me to dress as Yoda, do you?' I ask.

He laughs.

ED

No. I don't want Mia to dress up, but this is why I love having sex with her. It's not just sex. It's laughing so hard my laptop falls off the bed, it's seeing her smile at me and feeling completely at ease. And it's not the sex I've seen in porn all these years. In all that porn, I never saw anyone get cramp, I never heard the friction of two bodies rubbing together making armpit fart noises, I didn't see anyone fall off the bed or have to reach for a towel because sex is actually really quite a messy endeavour. I never saw the high-fives at the end. And I like being able to lie on top of Mia and not care about anything except pleasure, not having to pretend to be anyone else. I mean, I want to try the Mandalorian thing, but I'd still be me under there.

'You haven't answered my Yoda question,' she says, in between kissing me.

'His name is Grogu. And have we not met? The body paint would rub on the sheets. I just want you. As you are...'

'Really?' she says, as I take one of her nipples in my mouth. I stop and look up at her, her crumb-lined hair all ruffled against my pillow, big eyes smiling down at me. Yeah, just like this. I take a wisp of hair and tuck it behind her ear. 'I mean, we could give you a headdress, maybe Ahsoka Tano?'

'The lady with tentacles on her head?' Mia says, in hysterics.

To hear that sound makes me kiss her again and I feel myself get hard, and like some well-rehearsed routine she guides me inside her, both our faces reacting to the moment, her exhaling softly. I lower my body over hers. It might not be very interesting, but I still think this is my favourite way to have sex, so we can chat and I can look at my favourite person at the same time. She sits up slightly so our bodies are closer, at angles that I know will work for her. I slip my fingers over her to touch her at the same time and she bites her lip to let me know she's having fun. I like that she still likes having sex with me because I bloody love it. She puts a hand to my hair and pulls it gently.

'Ed...?' she says in breathy tones.

'Mia...?'

'Keep going but throw something at that bloody cat. I can't do this when he's looking at me...'

I thrust but turn my head to see Nigel sat by the wardrobe, judging. 'Nigel, please can you fuck off?' I cry.

Naturally, this does not move the cat who still sits there. You absolute perv of a cat.

'Ed, you swore... You never swear!' Mia says, looking at me laughing. 'I'm the swearer in this partnership.'

'Well, I'm joining your club. Did you like the swearing?' I say, an eyebrow cocked high.

'Say something again.'

'I like fucking you?'

'Oooh, I felt that,' she says, smirking at me, grinding her hips into me.

The cat, however, is less impressed. I throw a blanket in his general direction, and he watches it land and then sits on top of it.

'Excuse me,' I say, as I dismount and chase him quite unsexily out of the room, holding on to my erection with my hand and closing the door. Mia sits there on the bed, laughing as I hobble around. It's still a shock to see her there. Mainly because it's Mia but because she's a naked woman in my bed and I will never tire of seeing her there, seeing the soft curves of her belly, the outline from her hips down to her thighs, the way the light casts patterns on her skin. And I watch her while contemplating my life from seven years ago. Thinking how I used to lie there of a Sunday afternoon with *Star Wars*, with cake and my own dick in my hand. This is a nice addition to proceedings, the perfect addition. She could try to keep the crumbs off the bed, but I love that she's here. I love her. She pats the bed, encouraging me to return.

'Where you at, Ed Rogers?' she says, lying down and stretching out. 'Come back here and swear at me some more.'

'Yes, Mrs Rogers,' I say, saluting my wife.

'What's with the face?'

'Nothing. I was just thinking... I was reading a book and saw this position I want to try. Can I teach it to you?'

We both pause and then burst into laughter.

'Sure thing.'

A LETTER FROM THE AUTHOR

Dear lovely reader,

Hello, there! You're bloody marvellous! Thank you from the bottom of my heart for reading *Sex Ed*. If we've met before then hello again but if you're new – welcome, take a seat... it's a pleasure to meet you. I'm Kristen.

I hope you enjoyed reading Mia and Ed's story. If romcoms laden with innuendo are your thing then stick with me. You can keep up to date with all my latest releases and bonus content by signing up at the following link. Your email address will never be shared and you can unsubscribe at any time.

www.stormpublishing.co/kristen-bailey

And if you enjoyed *Sex Ed* then I would be overjoyed if you could leave me a review on either Amazon or GoodReads to let people know. It's a brilliant way to reach out to new readers. And don't just stop there, share the love on social media, gift the book to your mates, drop WhatsApp notes to everyone you know.

I can't tell you what a joy it was to write this book. Was it educational? I hope so. In many different ways. I thought I did the research with my last book but it turns out, you can be forty-two and still learn new things about sex. Like, butt plugs. There are lots of different types and colours. I also had to look up a lot of that factual biology stuff about testes. Who knew? I hope Mia and Ed have helped you learn something new and informative for your own reference but I hope they've also made you look at love and friendship in a different way. Always marry your best mate, I did. It's a marvellous thing.

If you are a long-time reader, you'll know sex seems to be a theme I write about a lot. Why? Who knows. I know I wasn't taught a lot of what I really needed to know about sex at school. A lot of my sex education came from real-life experience and well, as Mia would say, trying on a healthy number of shoes. However, I hope I'm at a place in my life where I can say real sex – sex between two people who love and trust each other – can be a really positive (and funny) endeavour. I will always keep writing about sex in this way because I think it's important to make sure people have honest conversations about their pleasure, their bodies and their sexuality without shame, guilt or negativity. I also hope you can relate on some level. I mean, I hope you've never had your wanger stuck in a fan but I hope your sex life is fun. And by fun, I hope sex makes you smile, that you have glowing orgasms and that you occasionally fall off the bed because you're having such a good time. Because if you've never fallen off the bed then you're doing it all wrong.

I will leave it here. For anyone who's possibly a fan, you get top marks for spotting all the previous book references and I hope you liked seeing Beth and Lucy again. I love those girls so much. Did you also spot all the slightly rude surnames in this book? That took me forever to research so please go back and appreciate my very juvenile efforts. Thank you to all who suggested a name on social media especially the person who gave me a list of words (e.g. Pinto) that mean very different things in other languages.

I'd be thrilled to hear from any of my readers, whether it be with reviews, questions or just to say hello. If you like retweets from Fesshole, then follow me on Twitter. Have a gander at Instagram, my Facebook author page and website too for updates, ramblings and to learn more about me. Like, share and follow away – it'd be much appreciated.

With much love and gratitude,

Kristen
xx

www.kristenbaileywrites.com

facebook.com/kristenbaileywrites

twitter.com/mrsbaileywrites

instagram.com/kristenbaileywrites

ACKNOWLEDGMENTS

Me.

I'm acknowledging me first because girl, you wrote this when the chips weren't even down. They were scattered all over the floor and they'd turned off all the lights. Still, you kept going, even through the house plague of Christmas 2022. Even when you didn't quite know where and how this was going to be published. Every punch, every turn, you find the energy to sit up straight and continue to tell the world your silly stories. It's time to say out loud that you've done good here. Well done. Just go easy on yourself once in a while. And brush your hair.

Storm Publishing. You're not what your name suggests. You're actually really bright, calm and positive, and you offered me a new home when I was a bit lost. You're like a super sunny day, really. Vicky Blunden and Oliver Rhodes, thank you for all your support, encouragement and advice, and all the lovely people behind the scenes. Publishing this book with you has been like the warmest of hugs and I will forever be grateful.

Thank you to the husband. Thank you for telling me I'm not funny because that spurs me on to be even funnier. Thank you for looking after me with cups of tea, premium hugs and growing to respect the fact that I am not a morning person.

Oi, kids! There's a reason I can write about Snaps, Minecraft, proms and GCSEs so well and that's because of you. You think I'm not listening in the car, but I hear it all. I watch your TikToks even though I don't understand them. I like wearing your trainers and when you tell me my cooking hits different. I like how we've upgraded from Peppa Pig to Pink Pantheress. I like how you're all still my favourite humans, how you're growing into mini adults and challenge me, inspire me and make me laugh the loudest.

My eldest did his GCSEs last summer and there was something that made me look at teachers in a whole different light. When I was at school, I never saw it myself but by God, teachers – you do a bloody awesome job. I know this because I certainly didn't teach my kid half of what he knows. And I've had years of my children moving through schools and watched teachers who've not just imparted knowledge, they've got to know my kids, they've prepared them for life and inspired them massively. You are all excellent people. Except P.E. teachers, I still have my reservations there.

Here's some people you should all know about. Over the last few months, they've propped me up and kept me sane and helped with my research (about school stuff, obviously). Thanks, guys. I appreciate and love you all: Bronagh McDermott, Danielle Owen-Jones, Graham Price, Adam Bogdan, Mitch Siddons, Elizabeth Neep, Jo Lovett-Turner, Sara Hafeez & Michael Kiwanuka. I don't know you personally, Michael, but your voice gives me life and seriously, I think we'd be excellent mates – you know? I'll also thank Pedro Pascal in case he sees this.

And finally, I have the best readers, I really do. They laugh at all my jokes, keep reading my books and then tell their mates all about me. I don't deserve you. Thank you for sticking with me and for all your reviews, blogs, posts and kind messages. You're the reason I keep doing this. That and I don't know how to do anything else.

Printed in Great Britain
by Amazon

30316147R00189